# MORE PRAISE FOR *Across a Star-Swept Sea:*

"A charming bit of light adventure."
—*Publishers Weekly*

"A good bet for readers looking for strong female protagonists,
characters of color, or just an enjoyable romantic adventure
with a science-fiction spin."
—*Kirkus Reviews*

"Peterfreund's novel is riveting and intense. Readers
will love this page-turning story and its dramatic climax."
—*Romantic Times*

"Engrossing and fast paced."
—ALA *Booklist*

"Complex in both plotting and themes, this science-fiction
revision of *The Scarlet Pimpernel* offers political intrigue,
narrow escapes, and forbidden romance."
—*BCCB*

"A well-paced story led by a strong and likable heroine."
—*SLJ*

"Delicious romance, class warfare, and genetic
engineering—Diana Peterfreund will ensnare you
with this sci-fi twist to a classic story."
—Cinda Williams Chima, bestselling author of
the Heir Chronicles and Seven Realms series

# across a
# star-swept
# sea

*Also by Diana Peterfreund:*
FOR DARKNESS SHOWS THE STARS
RAMPANT
ASCENDANT

# across a
# star-swept
# sea

## DIANA PETERFREUND

BALZER + BRAY
*An Imprint of HarperCollinsPublishers*

Balzer + Bray is an imprint of HarperCollins Publishers.

Across a Star-Swept Sea
Copyright © 2013 by Diana Peterfreund

Library of Congress Cataloging-in-Publication Data
Peterfreund, Diana.
  Across a star-swept sea / Diana Peterfreund. — First edition.
    pages cm
  Summary: Sixteen-year-old Persis Blake struggles to balance her life as a socialite
and a secret spy in a future where Regs, or regular people, have power over the
Reduced—those genetically engineered or drugged into physical and mental
impairments.
  ISBN 978-0-06-200617-2
  [1. Social classes—Fiction. 2. Spies—Fiction. 3. Government, Resistance to—Fiction.
4. Science fiction.]  I. Title.
PZ7.P441545Acr 2013                                              2013003082
[Fic]—dc23                                                              CIP
                                                                        AC

Typography by Carla Weise
14  15  16  17  18    CG/RRDH    10  9  8  7  6  5  4  3  2  1
❖
First paperback edition, 2014

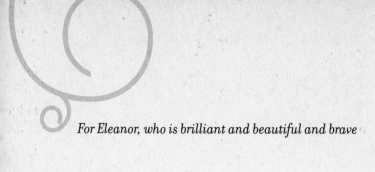

*For Eleanor, who is brilliant and beautiful and brave*

*The history of the human race pivots on two points: the development of agriculture, which created civilization, and the Reduction, which destroyed it.*

*Before the Reduction, the few impoverished or dissenting peoples who didn't genetically engineer their offspring had been the object of scorn and pity. But a generation later, when these "perfect" children could only produce mentally and physically impaired Reduced babies, it proved what a colossal mistake had been made. The bulk of humanity affected by this tragedy—the Lost—did not accept defeat lightly. Instead, they turned on those who'd escaped unscathed, making them the targets of envy, hatred . . . and, with the Wars of the Lost, utter annihilation.*

*After the wars were over, the survivors looked with horror and dismay upon what they had wrought. There was hardly any place left on Earth to make a life, and few untainted by Reduction left to live one.*

*In desperation, two poor servants defied their Lost masters. Out of the wars' most terrible weapon, they terraformed a new home, an oasis in the wreckage of the world: New Pacifica. There, they declared, they'd rule forever over those responsible for the Earth's destruction.*

*It didn't work out that way.*

—"HUMAN RIGHTS IN ALBION:
A TERM PAPER BY LADY PERSIS BLAKE"*

---

* Note: Though Lady Blake received an A– on this essay, her instructor saw fit to send a flutternote to her father, Lord Torin Blake, regarding the propriety of a young lady using such incendiary language. Lord Blake responded: "Actually, that sounds about right to me."

# One

IF THE WILD POPPY dared return to Galatea, Citizen Cutler was ready. He'd stationed armed guards at the entrance to the estate and placed an additional ten soldiers around the perimeter of the taro fields. Though no Reduced could even attempt escape, Cutler knew the real danger came from outside. The flowery Albian spy had "liberated" at least a dozen enemies of the revolution in the last few months, but it wouldn't happen on Cutler's watch.

During the better part of the morning, a sea breeze had moved across the sunken fields, stirring the taro leaves and making the water shiver and ripple like the skin of a snake. The Reduced prisoners moved slowly and methodically through their plots, following an ancient and, frankly, unnecessary tradition of cutting each root by hand and replanting the stalk to be ready for the next harvest.

The former lord of the estate—his name was Lacan, though Cutler doubted the man remembered it after being Reduced—sloshed and stumbled through the field, hacking away at the taro stalks with a knife entirely too dull for the purpose. His gray hair was matted to his neck with sweat and mud, and his once-haughty mouth hung slack and stupid. As Cutler watched, the man's grip slipped, and the blade sank deep into his thumb.

Lacan wailed, and the guards began to hoot and holler. Cutler didn't budge from his position, leaning against one of the unused harvesting machines. Let his soldiers have their entertainment. It was boring enough out here on the rural east coast.

"Shouldn't we help?" asked his newest recruit, a girl who hardly looked old enough for basic training. Her name was Trina Delmar, she'd arrived this morning, and she never shut up. "Looks like he cut himself pretty bad."

Cutler shrugged and spat into the swamp. Silly girl. It was always the girls who got weepy over watching the prisoners. "That's the former master of this plantation. Do you think his kind ever cared for the thumbs of your ancestors, back when they kept Galatea in their grip?"

"Grip's not so good anymore!" cracked another guard.

"Don't feel bad for these aristos, Citizen Delmar," Cutler went on. "Had they ever cared about us, the cure for Reduction would have been discovered long before it was."

That's why it took a reg to make the Helo Cure, two generations back. For hundreds of years before the cure, most people who weren't aristos were born Reduced, sickly and simpleminded. They said only one in twenty had been a natural-born reg, with a regular brain and intellect. The Helo Cure stopped Reduction in a single generation—after the cure, every baby born was regular.

And now, thanks to this new Reduction drug of the revolutionaries, the aristos would have their turns wallowing in the muck. Out in the field, the old lord was wailing and clutching his wounded hand to his chest. Cutler gave him a week—two at most. Reduction wasn't designed to be a death sentence, but sharp knives and idiots rarely mixed.

"But Lord Lacan actually fought to distribute the cure to the Reduced," Trina said, "back when he was young. I've seen a picture of him with Persistence Helo—"

Cutler glowered down at her. "You don't know what you're talking about, Citizen. If he's here, it means he's an enemy of the revolution. An enemy of regulars like us."

But Trina was still casting pitiful glances at Lacan. The recruit had been an annoyance ever since she'd shown up, questioning the pill dosage and schedule, as if it mattered that Cutler handed out the pink Reduction pills slightly more often than required. Once they were Reduced, it wasn't like a few extra pinks could make them stupider. Plus, Cutler liked to watch the aristos writhe a little. Not much else to do all the way out here.

Now that idiot recruit was in the field. She was approaching Lacan, who'd returned to ineffectually swiping at the taro stalks with his uninjured hand. That was the Reduced for you. They'd work until they collapsed.

"Back to your post, Delmar!" Cutler cried. He wasn't about to be shown up by some freshly cooled recruit.

The recruit ignored him and smeared some ointment on Lacan's injured thumb before wrapping it in a bandage.

"Did I tell you to administer aid to this Reduced slime?" Cutler said, churning into the field and slamming the butt of his gun into Lacan's side. The old man fell into the taro, and Trina winced. "You'd better watch it, Delmar. I'd hate to give a bad report to Citizen Aldred."

Trina didn't even look up. Good. Maybe he'd scared her back into line.

"You're not here to help them. You're here to keep them away from the Wild Poppy. Every time we lose a prisoner to Albion, it undermines the revolution."

"What undermines the revolution," she snapped back, "is—" but she ducked her head and went silent when she saw the dark look on his face.

Just then, a skimmer zipped down the path between the fields, dust clouding up from its lifters. There was an empty caged platform behind the cab. "Officer!" called the driver, a young man wearing a military uniform.

Cutler waded back to the edge of the field and squinted up into the cab. Trina trailed after, to his further irritation.

"Transfer request," the driver said, holding out his left hand. His oblet sparked to life in his palm, revealing a hologram of Citizen Aldred's face.

"All Reduced on outer plantations are to be transferred back to Halahou city prison," came Aldred's voice from the image.

"I've heard nothing of this." Cutler pulled out his own oblet, and its black surface glinted in the sun like the obsidian pebble it was named for. No new messages from Halahou. No new messages at all.

The boy shrugged. His military cap shaded his eyes. "Figures. I get bad reception out here in the middle of nowhere, too."

Cutler snorted in agreement. "So what's the problem?"

"I think—" The boy jiggled his oblet, as the message fizzed in and out. "It's the Wild Poppy," he explained as they waited for it to reload. "Citizen Aldred said even the increased guard isn't sufficient to keep the spy from stealing our prisoners."

"I've taken care of that." And if Aldred would leave the comfort of Halahou occasionally and come see what his lieutenants were doing out here in the country, maybe he'd know it. But Cutler would never say that aloud. Citizen Aldred had liberated them all—first from their uncaring, foolish queen and now from the aristos who had followed her lead.

"Here it is," said the driver, as the image of Aldred began speaking again.

"All Reduced prisoners to be fitted with nanotech collars to prevent removal from Galatea by foreign forces."

The boy leaned out of the cab and dropped his voice. "I heard the collars will choke 'em to death if the Poppy takes them off Galatea." The boy smirked, and Cutler grinned. This was the type of recruit he needed around here. Tough-minded and right thinking.

Nanotech collars. Now that would be a sight to see. If only Cutler could get rid of all his idiots so easily. Then again, maybe he could. "Delmar, you help this boy load up the prisoners and accompany him back to the capital."

"That's not necessary—" the boy began.

"Oh, but it is," said Cutler. "I haven't kept these prisoners under control all this time just to have the Wild Poppy break my streak on their last trip across the island. Her recruit form says she's good with a gun." He nodded at Trina, who was already gathering the aristos. "And it'll do her good to see how the revolution *wants* these prisoners handled." It would also get the aggravating recruit out of his hair.

The boy scowled, but Cutler shrugged it off. Trina Delmar could be *his* problem now.

IF ASKED, PERSIS BLAKE would have agreed with the odious Citizen Cutler on precisely one point: the young recruit was indeed her problem. But it wasn't an insurmountable one. After all, Persis had just single-handedly scooped up the Lacan family right from under the nose of ten soldiers and their officer. Persis could handle one more revolutionary, even if this Citizen Delmar was sitting in her skimmer.

And though the increased guard presence was a nuisance, Persis couldn't help but feel a jolt of pride that, after six months of missions, the revolution was finally recognizing that the Wild Poppy was a real threat. Now, she just had to figure out how to get out of this predicament without ruining it all.

*Think, Persis, think.* Her long hair itched, shoved up under her Galatean military cap, but she ignored it, focusing instead on the girl sitting quietly by her side as Persis maneuvered the skimmer down the raised path that crisscrossed the swampy taro fields. Citizen Delmar looked too young to be a soldier; but then again, at sixteen, Persis was far too young to be her country's most infamous spy, so she knew well how deceiving looks could be.

And whoever Trina Delmar was, she'd gotten on that officer's nerves, which alone was worthy of more investigation. Persis had easily pegged the officer as the sort of petty, sadistic man who wouldn't even bother to double-check his orders as long as Persis promised to inflict yet more cruelty on the prisoners. Her new palmport app was working wonders—with it, she could remix syllables from any of Aldred's propaganda speeches to create whatever message she desired on her dummy oblet.

"I didn't realize we recruited so young," Persis said as they crossed the old wooden bridge that separated the Lacan estate from the main road. She'd left the jammers she'd used to block incoming messages to the officer's oblet on, just in case someone on the plantation figured out the truth and tried to message Trina. "How old are you?"

"Eighteen," the girl said so quickly Persis knew it must be a lie. "And you're one to talk. Your voice hasn't even changed yet."

Perhaps this was a bad topic. She adopted a slightly gruffer grumble. "So you're good with a gun?" Best to know, especially since Persis's one weapon was concealed beneath the gloves of her disguise, and the supplements she'd taken were only good for a single shot.

"Very," said the soldier, and her tone was more matter-of-fact than defensive this time, so it was probably true.

"Well, that's a relief," Persis said, though she was thinking the opposite. "We wouldn't want to be caught by the Poppy without any defenses."

The skimmer picked up speed as it left the sunken maze of taro fields and hovered along the road bordering the northern coast. To the right sat cliffs and, far below, the black sand beaches that formed the boundary of Galatea. Beyond lay the glittering sea separating them from Persis's home of Albion. The two islands were shaped like crescents about to kiss, but this far east, the distant shore was a bit too far to make out with the naked eye.

The guard was not enjoying the view. Instead, she cast a quick look back at the pathetic lot of prisoners huddled on the bed near the intake fans. "Careful with your speed. Those prisoners have had a tough enough day already."

Persis raised her eyebrows. Sympathy from a revolutionary guard? Well, that was unexpected. She decided to press. "There was a Reduced—a true Reduced—living near me when I was very young. Probably the last one left alive. But he wasn't like . . . this. Mute, yes, stupid, yes. But not these clumsy, broken people."

There were those throughout history, and especially before the wars, who had believed in gods, immortal beings meting out punishments and rewards to humans based on some rarefied score sheet. Some believed that Reduction was retribution by these gods for humankind's attempt to perfect themselves. Of course, that was silly.

Humans had been attempting to perfect themselves since the dawn of time. They created tools because they had no fangs or claws. They created clothes since they had no fur or scales. They invented eyeglasses to see and vehicles to travel faster; they protected their bodies from diseases and performed surgery to cut out things that could hurt them. They'd genetically engineered themselves before and after Reduction. It hadn't been a punishment—it had been an unfortunate genetic mistake.

It shouldn't be a punishment now, either. And Persis wouldn't rest until she'd stopped it.

"They say it's exactly what real Reduction was like." Trina was parroting the party line.

Persis pressed harder. "Who says?"

"Everyone!" Trina snapped. "The . . . medics who made it. And Citizen Aldred, of course. You're going to get charged with insubordination if you keep talking like that."

Persis rounded a curve and began to climb the bluff to the promontory where Andrine lay in wait. This Trina was a mystery Persis didn't have the leisure to unravel. As she straightened the steering wheel, she began to loosen the fastening of the glove covering the palmport on her left hand.

"Oh, I can do better than that. Want to hear?" Persis asked.

"No," the girl lied, even as she leaned forward.

"I think Reducing aristos is cruel and unusual punishment," she stated, yanking the glove off as she drove. "I think that instead of changing things for the regs in Galatea, the revolution's just punishing aristos."

The girl's mouth was open in shock, which was convenient for Persis's purposes. She'd need a direct hit for the knockout drug to work. She lifted her hand and summoned her focus. . . .

"I think it might be, too," the girl said, and Persis stopped.

She lowered her hand back to the steering wheel. "You do?" Maybe she had this girl all wrong. A Galatean soldier could be a true help to the League of the Wild Poppy—particularly if she was good with a gun. That was one area where Persis's expertise was lacking. After all, they didn't teach combat at cotillion.

The girl nodded. "But I'm not stupid enough to say it. You're as bad as my brother. I swear, everyone around here is asking for trouble. Now, you keep your eyes on the road and I'll keep a lookout for the Wild Poppy."

Persis sighed. At the top of the bluff, a large, bare rock jutted out from the cliff, the remnant of some old explosion from the island's fiery birth. Persis clenched her jaw, readying the command to her palmport even as she steered the skimmer to a steady stop.

"What are you doing?" Trina spluttered, straightening. In the caged bed, the Reduced prisoners were watching them with wary eyes.

Persis opened her hand, but the moment Trina caught sight of the golden disk set in her palm, she lunged at Persis and they both careened out of the cab.

"Who are you?" she screamed as they landed in the dust. Even as she fell, Persis withdrew the mental command to her palmport, halting the app. She couldn't afford to use it unless she had a clear shot.

Trina was reaching for her gun, and Persis kicked and slapped, trying desperately to dislodge the soldier's grip.

The pistol thumped against the ground and slid beneath the skimmer's lifts.

"Stop!" Trina cried.

"You stop!" Persis shouted back, struggling to fight the girl as they each lunged toward the gun. Where was Andrine? She could certainly use backup right now. The Reduced watched silently from the cage. She wished any of them still had a mind.

At the same moment, both their hands closed tight around the gun barrel and they wrestled in the grass. Trina raked her nails across Persis's face and knocked off her cap, then reeled back in surprise as hair the color of frangipani came tumbling down on them both. Persis used the opportunity to wrench the gun from the recruit's grip.

"You're a girl?" Trina spluttered.

Persis stood, gun trained on Trina. She sighed and swept her yellow and white ropes of hair out of her face with her free hand. "This surprises you? *You're* a girl."

The girl's face was filled with disgust. Persis shook her head and shrugged. It was disappointing, really. They were *almost* in agreement.

Trina, her face contorted with rage, kicked out and swept Persis's feet out from under her. Persis felt the girl's fingers on her gun, and everything was a cloud of dust and hands and white and yellow hair.

Out of nowhere, she heard a chittering, and a red streak darted between them, sinking sharp little teeth into Trina's shoulder.

Trina screamed and again pulled away, and Persis

scrambled to her feet. "Slipstream, heel."

The sea mink let go of Trina, trotted obediently to Persis's side, and wiped his whiskers with his flippery paw. His long, sleek body was damp from his latest swim, and the soldier's blood hardly showed against his deep red fur.

Still holding the gun on the girl, Persis caught sight of Andrine racing up, her ocean-blue hair trailing out behind her. "So good of you to show up," Persis said to her friend.

"Sorry for the delay." Andrine unlocked the cage and began unloading the prisoners. "You didn't mention you were bringing an enemy combatant."

"Last-minute addition," Persis replied lightly. Trina was still crouched on the ground, holding her bleeding neck with both hands.

"I know who you are," she said with a sob. "You're the Wild Poppy."

"What a brilliant deduction," Andrine said as she helped the last of the victims off the truck. "Exactly how long did that take to put together?"

Persis gave her friend a quick look. Now, now, there was no need to be smug. They were pointing a *gun* at the poor girl.

"And you're finished," the soldier spat angrily. "You have no idea who you're dealing with. You have no—"

Now Andrine chuckled. "Awfully high-and-mighty for a girl who was almost a snack for a sea mink, isn't she?"

The soldier's eyes were wide and wild. "I'm going to tell Citizen Aldred everything."

"Oh, really?" Persis said, tilting the barrel of the gun

toward the girl's face. "How do you plan to do that from beyond the grave?"

At once she felt a hand on her elbow. At first, Persis thought it was Andrine's, though she knew her friend had more faith than that. Persis wasn't actually going to *shoot* the soldier. After all, she still had her palmport dose—she could just knock her out. She risked a glance out of the corner of her eye.

Lord Lacan stood there, silent, an expression nearing clarity in his somber old eyes.

Persis lowered her arm. "It appears you have made a powerful friend, little Galatean." She sighed. "But what to do with you? You have no idea what it is you're fighting for."

"Of course I do," said Trina. "My country."

Persis stared at her for a moment, then laughed. "I was going to say you were very foolish, seeing how outnumbered you are. But in fact, you're terminally brave. And that should never be snuffed. Besides, I like your style. That move with your foot there almost had me. Very well, then. I will let the Lord Lacan decide what will happen to you."

Trina looked baffled. "But he's Reduced. He can't even help himself."

"Don't worry, little soldier," Persis said as something began to spin out of the golden disk set in the center of her palm. The girl's mouth had opened again, which was remarkably convenient. "We take care of that part, too."

A moment later, Trina Delmar collapsed on the ground.

Another mission accomplished.

# Two

THE ROYAL COURT OF Albion was often likened to a riotous garden, but it buzzed with more than bees and was filled with colors never found in nature. Bougainvillea hedges encircled the public court and hibiscus topiaries lined the aisles, but no flowers could compete with the whirlwind of gowns, cloaks, leis, and most of all, the towering hairstyles of the island's most fashionable aristocrats. Their chatter drowned out the sounds of the sea beyond, the constant hum of flutternotes zipping to and fro among the courtiers, and even the delicate tinkle of the famous Albian water organ.

One particularly crowded corner was currently occupied by Lady Persis Blake and her retinue of admirers. This evening she wore a simple, bright yellow sarong fastened about her neck with a length of crocheted gold links, and a matching gold wristlock—the leather fingerless glove that covered the palmport on her left hand. The elegant fall of her gown could only be achieved using the finest of Galatean silk, a difficult product to come by since the revolution began, but you could count on Persis Blake to have the inside scoop on where to get the best fabrics. Its hue matched exactly the yellow tones in her hair, which had been twisted, braided, and otherwise arranged so that its upswept yellow-and-white strands resembled the frangipani flower on the Blake family crest. Her beauty stood out, even among the kaleidoscope throng of the court.

In the six months since Princess Isla had ascended the throne as regent and brought along her old school chum as her chief lady-in-waiting, Persis had become one of the court's most glittering and popular members. Hardly anyone remembered a time when a party or a boating trip or luau was complete without the addition of Albion's loveliest, silliest socialite.

Even better, almost no one at court had been at school with Persis before she'd dropped out—no one who could paint a very different picture of the girl who was gaining quite the reputation for being nothing more than stylish, sweet, and above all stupid.

Along with her gown and her jewelry, today Persis wore a look of sheer boredom as the conversation took a turn in the direction of the revolution. The casual observer would guess it was because such an ornamental creature would find politics a tedious topic.

The truth was, no one here had a clue what Galatea was really like these days.

"The southerners' civil war will spread to our shores," said one young courtier with obvious aspirations to the Royal Council. "And when it does, we must quell any reg uprising before we find ourselves in the same predicament as the Galateans."

"Surely not," Persis said. "It's hard enough finding silk merchants in Galatea who remain open these days. I'll simply die if the Albian shops close down, too."

"How like a woman." The courtier chuckled indulgently. "Lady Blake, if there's a revolution against the aristos in Albion, what you wear is going to be the last of your concerns."

"Never!" Persis replied. "I have a reputation to uphold. We mustn't let a silly thing like war make us forget our duties."

There was another ripple of laughter among the young men sitting near her.

"I'm serious!" she added, forming her mouth into a pink pout. "Even with my responsibility to Princess Isla and her royal wardrobe, my dear papa hardly ever lets me sail down to visit the shops in Halahou anymore. He says he fears for my safety, but you'd think he'd spare just a smidge of concern for my clothes as well. If any of you fine gentlemen know the identity of the Wild Poppy, won't you please ask him to rescue us some dressmakers on his next trip to Galatea? It's getting old that all he's been rescuing lately are other aristos. Honestly, they aren't useful for anything but competition."

"If I knew the identity of the Poppy," said one of the courtiers, "I'd be the most popular man on both islands. In Albion all the ladies would adore me"—several ladies tittered as proof—"and in Galatea, I'd be Citizen Aldred's very best friend. The Poppy is Galatea's most wanted."

"Then my proposal would solve everyone's problems," Persis argued. "Citizen Aldred probably wouldn't mind so much the loss of a tailor or two, and I would get that meticulous Galatean attention to sartorial detail that I've been missing. Everyone wins!"

"Except the aristos," mumbled another of the courtiers, but no one listened to him. After all, talk of prisoners was deemed ever so dull by the Albian courtiers, and thinking about Galatean aristos they knew who might even now be imprisoned did terrible things to one's mood.

Just once, Persis wished she could steer the conversation in this direction instead of away from it. Would things change if more aristos started questioning the Council's hands-off position regarding the war? Would it be worth it to try, even if it endangered her carefully wrought disguise?

She looked up to see Tero Finch gesturing to her from the edge of the circle. As a freshly cooled member of the Royal College of Gengineers, Tero's clothes weren't quite as stylish as the aristos surrounding him, but his height, broad shoulders, and perfectly dyed metallic bronze hair still had several of the young ladies turning his way. "Persis," he called, "the princess can see us now."

With a trilling laugh that grated even on her own ears, Persis sprang to her feet. "I must leave you, lovelies. Please make sure to have some good gossip when I return."

She met Tero, and together they ascended the wide marble steps to the terrace.

"Where's my sister?" Tero asked under his breath. "You didn't get Andrine arrested, did you?"

"Probably in Scintillans Village by now, safe and sound and doing her homework," Persis reassured him as they entered the throne room of the princess regent of Albion. Tero was convinced Persis and Andrine were risking their lives with every trip to Galatea. That he was right hadn't dissuaded them yet.

The sunset filtered through bamboo blinds drawn over the colonnade that formed the outer wall of the room. Vases three meters high were stuffed with drooping palm fronds strung with orchid leis, and the scent of the royal flower hung heavily in the room. Princess Isla sat in the middle of the floor, heedless of the giant white cushions strewn nearby. Her wide-legged white pants were gathered in bunches in her lap, and her white cape lay forgotten on one of the chaises behind her. For a moment, Persis could imagine they were children again, playing with puzzles or building pillow volcanoes on the floor.

Isla held her left hand out to the toddler who sat before her, a bright-eyed boy who squealed with delight at the tiny golden threads leaping around on Isla's fingertips.

"It works!" Tero cried, dropping to his knees at the princess's side.

"Another new app?" Persis asked as she gathered the trailing ends of her yellow sarong and sat down, too. Tero seemed to spend half his time at his new job in the Royal College of Gengineers developing palmport apps for Isla.

And the other half secretly working for the League of the Wild Poppy.

So now it was jumping threads. The week before it had been an app that would allow Isla to control the playlist on the water organ in the courtyard. And before that, Tero had cooked up some code that combined optic identification with a visual skin, which if you ran the app made Councilman Shift look like an armadingo. Anything to make Isla laugh, or even forget for a moment that she wasn't just their schoolmate anymore. She wasn't just Persis's best friend. One little accident, and she'd found herself an orphan, a mother, and a ruler of a country on the brink of war.

"What kind of supplements does it take to run it?" Persis asked, as if none of that mattered, and they could talk as they used to.

"Intense ones," Isla said with a sigh, "but it's a real flare with the king." She shrugged, and the figures crumbled into shimmering dust around the gold disk inset in the center of her palm. The baby squawked in protest, but Isla grabbed him and turned him upside down until he started laughing again.

"The King of Albion," Tero added with mock haughtiness, "has exquisite taste for a child who only recently began walking." He smiled at Isla and bowed his head. "I'm glad you liked it, your Highness."

*Your Highness.* When had Tero gotten so formal? There'd been no bows ten years ago when he was crashing their slumber parties and chucking cuttle jellies at their heads.

But a lot had changed since then.

Isla watched Tero leave, then patted the king on his diapered bottom. "All right, Albie. Go play while your sister talks to Auntie Persis."

The infant King of Albion obeyed, toddling into the waiting arms of his nurse.

"Princess," said Persis gaily, keeping careful watch of

the toddler and his keeper, "I've just come back from Galatea and I've brought you some . . . lovely silks."

"More of the usual?" asked Isla, lying back against the cushions and flicking a few locks of her silver hair behind her shoulders. Unlike Persis's hair, Isla's color was natural. Everyone knew the hair of Albian royals went white in their teens—it was such a genetic signature of the dynasty that even if Isla still had the dark Polynesian hair of their youth, she would have had the color removed. It was hard enough gaining recognition as the island's rightful ruler.

Persis giggled. Loudly. "Are you telling me you're bored by my efforts to bring you the best Galatea has to offer?"

"Not at all," Isla replied, darting another glance at the king's nursemaid, "but I find myself more curious about another Albian smuggling Galatean goods to my shore. I've heard rumors the Wild Poppy has just concluded another raid today."

"I've heard so, too," replied Persis, taking care that her tone was every bit as gossipy. "Apparently, he rescued Lord Lacan and all his family."

"Even the children?"

Persis nodded.

Isla could not contain her smile. She immediately sobered, however. "But that's only six. I heard the Poppy made off with ten refugees."

"Goodness, Princess!" Persis exclaimed. "You can't expect *me* to know anything about that!"

"Persis . . ." Isla could look very royal indeed, when she chose.

"A few regs who ran afoul of revolutionary principles . . ." Persis confessed, "most likely."

"*Most likely*," Isla repeated, pursing her lips, "knowing what a soft sell the Wild Poppy is. I wonder whatever *he* thinks I'll do with all the reg refugees he crowds onto my shores."

Persis gave her friend a hopeful smile. "*He* probably thinks you'll do right by them, given what a benevolent despot you are." She'd been teasing Isla with the title for years, ever since they'd learned it in ancient history classes. But school was out now, for both of them. Isla was the de facto ruler of the island, and Persis—well, Persis had other activities to keep her occupied.

"And give my Council members yet another reason to suspect I know his identity?" Isla asked. Albie's nurse-maids were maintaining a respectful distance, but you never could tell.

"Surely they don't think that?" said Persis, looking skeptical. "I thought everyone in Albion knows you care for nothing but competing with me for being the prettiest dressed woman on the island. You're regent in name only, and you intend to let the Council decide the direction of the country until the king comes of age."

Isla stared at Persis, a warning blazing in her dark eyes. Persis stared at Isla, a twinkle in her amber ones.

"Fine," said the princess at last, giving her friend an indulgent smile.

Inwardly, Persis breathed a sigh of relief. Isla might be the most regular-friendly ruler Albion had ever known, but she felt no particular obligation to the regs from Galatea, especially since it had been their revolution that had torn the country asunder.

Yet Persis couldn't help but pity the poor regs she'd rescued while on the Lacan mission. They'd been trying to lead simple lives, untouched by the perverted aims of the revolution, and had been Reduced merely for standing in support of the innocent Lacans.

This war was a travesty. If only she could save them all.

If only Albion would. But Persis knew Isla's hands were tied. And while her friend focused on the needs of her nation, Persis did what she could to provide the assistance both girls wished the country would.

"What do you think the Council *would* say to the Wild Poppy, if it had the chance?" she asked the princess.

"'Stop bringing us poor people?'" Isla suggested.

Persis snorted with derision. "Even the Galatean aristos are poor when they get here. They've been stripped of their estates and all their worldly possessions."

"Not to mention their brains."

Persis rolled her eyes. "Thankfully, that wears off." Detoxing from the Reduction drug wasn't a pleasant process, but it was better than the alternative.

And until the Galateans stopped punishing their regs along with their aristos, the Wild Poppy would be an equal-opportunity rescuer. Persis was a Blake, and an aristo, too, but her mother was a reg. And, more important, suffering was suffering. No one should have their mental capabilities stolen from them. Ever.

The nursemaids herded King Albie off for his nap. Isla watched them until they'd left the room. "With any luck, this revolution will wear off, too, and the Galateans flooding our shores will regain their fortunes and find a way to pay us back for our kindness." Isla shook her head. "I was not supposed to rule, let alone to do so in such interesting times."

Persis placed her hand on her friend's shoulder. There were whispers in court that Isla's father might have prevented the revolution. He could have counseled Queen Gala at the start of the strife. There were still claims that the revolutionaries had played a part in the boating accident that had claimed the lives of old King Albie, his wife, and his eldest son a little more than six months ago.

Persis didn't believe that, but she *could* put stock in the theories that Citizen Aldred and his army acted when they did six months back because they knew that Albion, still reeling from the loss of its king and grown heir, could hardly step in to help when the Galateans deposed, and then Reduced, their own queen.

Queen Gala had been the first victim of this monstrous new "Reduction drug" the revolutionaries were calling pinks. Two weeks into her sentence, she'd been found dead in her prison cell. Another accident, the revolutionaries had claimed.

Then they'd fed the queen's corpse to her own guard beasts, the pod of mini-orcas she'd kept in her private cove near Halahou. After that night, Persis had been sure her own country would speak up against the revolution's tactics, sure that Isla's righteous fury over the death of her neighboring monarch would translate into action against her killers. But six months later, the Albian Royal Council was still dithering and, worse, preventing the princess regent from doing anything at all.

Some said they wished to avoid war at all costs. Others feared the revolution might spread to their shores. But the loudest voices of all were the ones that were using the strife as an opportunity to advance their own causes—especially the cause of making the princess look weak.

Now Isla stood and shook out her pants, which fell in creamy wrinkles to her feet. The white was strategic, too. Against the lush colors of the courtyard and the garish dress of the other courtiers, Isla stood out. Cool. Unapproachable. Unmistakable. Persis grabbed Isla's cape off the floor, but her friend made a face as she took it. "I hate this thing."

"Trappings of power," Persis said, helping her friend with the clasp. And Isla could use all the trappings she could muster, too. The Albian laws against female inheritance not only kept Isla from becoming the true queen but also made even her temporary regency suspect in the eyes of most of her people.

When the king was still alive, the Albian Royal Council had been held up as a model government compared to the Galatean queen's absolute power. In Albion, the monarch was subject to checks and balances by the Council. But now Persis and Isla saw the truth they hadn't learned in school—the Council could also hamstring the ruler and blame lack of action on her.

Their only recourse was the Wild Poppy—and they could never let anyone know.

"Ah, well. Kings of old wore feathered cloaks and giant metal crowns every day. It's a wonder they could walk." Isla sighed. "Fifteen years before my brother can take over."

"And how many before you do?" said Persis, then immediately regretted it. Isla got enough doubt from the Council and the populace. She didn't need it from her best friend.

Isla's face turned grim. "Galatea is Reducing its citizens at the rate of dozens per day. The country is being torn apart by a war. With that on the horizon, how do you think it would be viewed if I condemned the Council for their inaction?"

"I understand that, but—"

"But what, Persis?" Isla's commanding voice was tinged with an edge of frustration. "I don't want a war in Albion. If that means playing nice with the Council until the dust settles from my father's death, so be it."

The Council argued that intervening in Galatea might cause a commoner uprising on their shores. But Albian aristos were none too happy to see the court do nothing while Galatean aristos were tortured and Reduced. Isla knew it. The dangers of an aristocratic coup would hurt *her*, not Council members. And Persis was sure the Council leaders—mostly aristos—knew *that*.

"And if the Council *leads* us into civil war?"

"Then I'll count on the Wild Poppy to save us." And with that, Isla brushed aside the bamboo blinds and the two girls exited into the courtyard. Even the silly girl Persis pretended to be could read her friend's intent. The conversation was over. And perhaps that was for the best.

It wasn't as if they could change anything. All Isla had was Persis, and all Persis had was the Poppy.

Outside in the courtyard, water trickled melodically through an artificial creek and down a series of musical locks. The water organ had been designed during the reign of Isla's grandfather by a natural-born reg and was one of the prides of the Albian royal family. Their early support of natural-born regs as well as quick adoption of the Helo Cure were two facts the Council liked spread far and wide in order to keep the population in support of the monarchy. The state-run sanitarium for those with Dementia of Acquired Regularity—or Darkening, as most laymen called it—should have been a third, but no one liked being reminded of the shadow that lay over the cure.

Not even the Darkened.

All around the courtyard, hibiscus bloomed and palm fronds waved above the heads of the courtiers, who wandered in groups, gossiping about the Wild Poppy's latest exploits or which aristo had been found with another's wife. Here and there you heard the buzz of flutternotes winging from person to person, carrying messages or promises or even just sensations. It was a waste of energy, but all the rage nonetheless. Persis was partly responsible for that. She supposed it couldn't be helped.

All anyone wanted to talk about was the Wild Poppy. Every aristo in Albion who wasn't claiming to be his secret lover had broadcasted a desire to become so, should the Poppy be interested. Sometimes, Persis had the wicked temptation to play a trick or two. What would they do if they did get a wild poppy—shaped flutter, telling them to, say, meet him at dawn in the gazebo on the north promontory, wearing nothing but a lei of poppies and a smile? But she wouldn't risk it. She had real work to do.

Which reminded her. The situation with the young soldier earlier today had been far too close for comfort. Her hand drifted up to touch the towering pile of yellow and white braids, curls, and twists that was the envy of every girl at court. Persis loved her hair. She loved the way it framed her face when she studied her reflection, the way it set off the deep golden tone of her skin. She loved how each twist and knot reminded her of the hours her mother had spent with her on the stone lanai of Scintillans, teaching her how to braid.

Her mother had once been the reigning beauty of Albion, and her thick, full hair was one genetic legacy in which Persis could take pride. But if she had to sacrifice it for the Wild Poppy, for the mission, she would. After all, the days of braiding her hair with her mother on the lanai were long gone.

A flutternote buzzed about her face, shaped like a flying fish. Andrine. Persis stripped off the wristlock protecting her palmport. The flower sank seamlessly into the disk in her hand, and the message whispered across her consciousness.

*Cargo safely transported to clinic. All still unconscious.*

She closed her eyes briefly, focusing to compose her reply. She coded its shape as a poppy, rather than her default, the Blake family's frangipani.

*Keep the soldier asleep until further notice.*

"Persis?" Isla asked, eyeing the spun-sugar flutter-note assembling itself on Persis's palmport. "Is everything all right?"

And indeed, it was rare for Persis to conduct the Wild Poppy's business in public.

As the flutternote was whisked away on a breeze from the sea, Persis forced a smile. "Nothing I can't handle."

The soldier Persis had captured during the Lacan raid had been an unexpected complication. Until now, Persis hadn't taken anyone from Galatea except revolutionary prisoners, and she wasn't quite prepared to deal with a prisoner of her own.

"I've been considering some improvements to my . . . workout clothing," she said meaningfully. "Conventional methods aren't quite sufficient for our needs lately. I'm thinking of trying something a bit more . . . radical for my workout tomorrow."

Isla regarded her for a long moment. "Genetemps are dangerous."

"So is getting caught by the Galateans."

The princess shook her head. "I don't like it, Persis."

"You don't have to. Genetemps can be found fairly easily on the street in Galatea these days."

"As the horror stories that make their way across the strait prove daily," Isla replied. "How many deaths has back-alley gengineering caused since the revolutionaries stopped policing it?"

"Not as many as the revolutionaries' own drugs." Persis refastened the wristlock over her palm. Besides, the risk posed by a genetemp was less dangerous than wrestling a gun off a Galatean soldier, as she'd had to do earlier today. And if Tero had enough free time to be making palmport apps for the amusement of Isla and Albie, he could whip up a few genetemps for her.

"What if you get sick?" Isla asked. "How ever will I explain it to your parents?"

Persis bit her lip. How would Isla react if Persis revealed that a genetemps accident might be the least of the Blake family health concerns? "You'll tell them it was in the line of duty. That should be sufficient for Torin Blake." And her mother, if it happened to be a day she remembered she had a daughter.

"And to the court? To the Council?"

"Easy." She shrugged, pushing thoughts of her mother from her mind. "Everyone knows Persis Blake is foolish enough to try anything."

# Three

As the sun peeked its head over the lip of the sea, lighting the shore with a rosy golden glow, the Ford children stopped writhing and fell into an odd, restless sleep. Sharie hoped this was normal. Her contact hadn't told her exactly what to expect from the pinks—just that the children would be easier to transport to revolutionary officials if they were already Reduced.

She didn't like the look of them, lying there on pallets with pink foam drying around their mouths. She didn't like the fact that her contact was supposed to have been here well before sunrise. If the Fords noticed the children were missing—if they found her with them like this . . .

Finally, she couldn't stand the sight of their pathetic little figures anymore, and she escaped to the beach. Soon enough, the shadow of a skimmer loomed long across the sand in front of her. She hadn't expected it from the direction of the beach but instead from the road. It didn't matter. The pickup was here at last. The driver was . . . not exactly the police escort she'd expected. Then again, maybe the revolution preferred to do such dirty work through unofficial channels. The woman was a crone, hunched and craggy, with ropes of gray hair and deep-set eyes surrounded by masses of wrinkled, peeling skin. She was swathed in a heavy, hooded robe, and as she moved to lower the skimmer's brakes to the sand, Sharie could see that her hands were encased in long linen gloves.

"You're late," said Sharie, wondering if the old woman would even be able to help her move the bodies.

The woman rolled her ancient shoulders. "Money doesn't have an expiration date. But the revolutionary army's offer does."

Sharie quickly ushered the lady into the house before she could change her mind. The three children were still unconscious but sleeping fitfully. Pink stains crackled along their cheeks and throats and lay in spongy mats in their hair.

"You gave them pinks," the woman stated flatly.

"Yes," said Sharie. "As instructed."

But the woman made no response other than, "Where's the fourth?"

"Couldn't get to her. She's the heir, so she gets her own wing." Sharie rolled her eyes. "You know aristos. Even under siege, they have to keep up appearances."

The old woman snorted, a phlegmy, disgusting sound, and reached for the leather purse hanging at her side. "So, the agreement was a hundred each, right?"

"Three hundred," Sharie corrected. She hadn't braved

smuggling the children out of the Ford estate's blockade for pocket change! "Three hundred each."

The crone paused, thinking. "Well, without the heir, I won't get full price for the lot. The plan's to trade these children for Lady Ford and her husband. It's them Citizen Aldred wants—they're leading the royalist resistance. But without the heir, Lady Ford might just decide her other children are spares, necessary sacrifices, just like all those guards who've been dying to keep the blockade strong against the revolutionary forces."

"They won't," Sharie insisted. She could see the deal crumbling before her eyes. "They might be aristos, but the Fords love all their children. Believe me, I was their nanny for five years."

"Five years," said the crone. "You took care of these brats, and now you're Reducing them?" She whistled through her teeth. "What are you gonna do with the money? Buy a nice new life in Halahou where you never have to take care of some aristo's spoiled spawn again?"

Of course. Sharie had no experience other than child care, and with the aristos dropping like flies, there was no one left to hire her anymore. Might as well get as much as she could while the getting was still good. The Ford children were doomed anyway. The blockade would fall, and when it did, the whole family would be Reduced—them and anyone caught helping them. Sharie could see the writing on the wall, and she had no intention of being there when it crumbled.

The crone was making some mental calculations as

she looked at the sleeping children. "A hundred and fifty each. That's my final offer, and you'd better take it. Time's running short."

"Fine."

The woman handed over the money in the leather purse. The coins clinked against one another, surprisingly heavy. Sharie had never held so much money in all her life—or much metal money at all. The Fords had paid in royal credits, all nice and aboveboard. But with everything still in flux with the government, it was best to carry cash. Especially if you weren't exactly working aboveboard.

She slung the purse around her shoulder, then, one by one, helped the old woman carry the children into the back of the skimmer's cab. As she settled the youngest, Mardette, the girl's eyes fluttered open.

"Guuuuuh," she mumbled.

Sharie swallowed. Mardette had a beautiful singing voice. She wondered if Reduced even knew how to carry a tune.

They'd be captured anyway. They'd be Reduced anyway. There was nothing Sharie could do to stop it. If she tried to help them, she'd wind up punished, just like all the other regs on the Ford estate. Sharie squeezed the purse hard, reassured by the weight of the money inside. And in addition to her wealth, she'd helped the revolution. They owed her now.

"By the way," said the crone as she climbed back behind the driver's seat of the skimmer, "what's your plan if Ford's people come looking for you?"

Sharie shook her head. "If they could escape the

revolutionaries' blockade, don't you think they would?" She needn't worry about the Fords, anyway. The revolution would protect her. Sharie had picked the winning side.

"Hmm," said the crone, and took off.

As soon as she was gone, Sharie ran back into the house. The pallets on the floor still held the pink-stained imprints of the bodies of the Ford children, and Sharie averted her eyes. At least she had the money. She thrust her hand into the purse, reveling in the cool feel of the coins. This money would be more than enough to start her life in Halahou. She opened the purse, the better to see her reward. There they were, forty-five silver pieces. Money for nothing, except saving herself from the wrath of the revolutionaries. Light from the rising sun filtered in through the cottage windows and glittered on the surface of the coins.

Which began to change.

Before Sharie's eyes, the engraving on each coin began to melt and swirl on the surface. Sharie blinked hard, but the optical illusion continued. She grabbed one of the coins and brought it close to her eyes. The face of old Queen Gala blurred, the lines becoming sharp and jagged, until they re-formed themselves into the shape of some sort of sharp-leaved flower.

She shook her head in shock and dismay. Nanotech wasn't used on coins. Had she been tricked, given counterfeit money by that old crone? She flipped over the coin to see what it showed on the back.

*My eternal thanks, the Wild Poppy*

The coin thudded to the counter. Sharie staggered backward. *No.*

There was a pounding on the door outside. "Sharie Bane? We've come for the children."

Sharie clutched her hands to her chest, feeling the trap close tight. How could she have been so foolish? With trembling fingers, she opened the door. On the threshold stood two revolutionary guards and a third figure—a young woman in a pair of smart black pants and a matching military jacket with an insignia that marked her as a captain. Sharie's gaze dropped to the name embroidered on the woman's coat.

*Aldred.*

Vania Aldred, the young captain in charge of the Ford siege. Citizen Aldred's own daughter. Sharie's throat went dry.

"You *are* Sharie Bane?" the captain asked, cocking her eyebrow until it disappeared under her dark bangs. Her black hair was unfashionably long, and straighter than water flowing from a tap.

Sharie considered feigning ignorance. "I—"

The woman brushed past her, scanned the room. "Where are the Ford children? Have you failed to deliver on your promise to the revolution?"

"No . . . I . . ." Sharie's gaze shot to the coins on the counter. The young woman—hardly more than a child herself—looked that way, too. She picked up one of the coins, then hissed and let it thud back to the counter.

"You idiot. What did he look like?"

"An—an old woman." Sharie swallowed, stepping back. "Please, how could I have known? I didn't . . ."

The captain gave a little jerk of her head. "No, you didn't do anything you *should* have." She turned, marched toward the guards at the door, and whispered a few orders. The guards started forward.

"Please . . ." Sharie begged.

"Useless idiots like you," Captain Aldred said, "don't deserve your brains."

JUSTEN HELO STROLLED DOWN the dock, hands in his pockets as if to protect the oblets he'd hidden there. He doubted anyone could actually see the pebble-sized computers, but he still felt better with his fists around them. So far, his escape had been uneventful. The staff at the records hall had barely noted his visit, and guards near the palace gate had merely inclined their heads in his direction as he passed. Now he was one narrow strait from safety.

Was he really going through with this?

Did he have a choice? As soon as the officials at the Lacan estate began to notice what he'd done, arrest would be right around the corner. He'd no longer be able to put his uncle off, no longer be able to prevent his research from becoming a mockery of everything he'd spent his life working toward.

Up ahead, a beautiful yacht tugged impatiently at its mooring ropes. It was Albian by the look of the rigging. Better and better. Travel between the nations had slowed since the revolution, but Justen had hoped there'd be someone at the port of Halahou who might give him passage. He strolled by the ship twice, hoping to catch a glimpse of the skipper, but saw no one on deck. On his third pass up the quay, one of the guards looked at him for a little too long, his eyes lighting with what might be recognition.

This had been a mistake—the latest of many. He should have known his uncle would guess his plans. There was a reason Damos Aldred had been the first to challenge Galatea's ruling elite in the centuries since the island had been created.

"You there," said a guard, and Justen tensed. But the man, clad in his revolutionary uniform, was not pointing in his direction but rather at someone behind him. Justen turned to see a figure staggering down the dock. Tall and elderly, the woman was an aristo by the look of her outfit, a cascade of silken ruffles in rust and midnight blue from her collarbone to her ankles. Her hair was arrayed in an elaborate tangle of curls and braids the color of storm clouds. Justen was surprised. He'd doubted there was an aristo on all Albion with natural-colored hair. And this aristo was most certainly Albian. A Galatean noble who'd somehow avoided the revolution this long would not come out dressed in such finery. That was just asking for trouble.

"You there," the guard repeated. "Identify yourself."

The aristo, whoever she was, paid no heed. She was focused on the yacht, as if she could maneuver herself aboard by sheer force of will.

An intoxicated Albian aristo entertaining herself with cheap thrills in the slums of the dock district. Contempt flashed through Justen and with it, regret. For all its claims, the revolution hadn't done much to help the poorest regs. What was the point of punishing aristos for their behavior if the victims weren't protected?

"Stop at once," the guard cried.

The woman did stop now, and Justen noticed for the first time how iridescent the ruffles of her gown were as they shimmied and shivered in the sunlight. A split second later, he realized why. The aristo was shaking—shuddering so hard it was a wonder her teeth didn't shatter in her mouth.

Genetemps sickness. That's what it looked like, at least, and the most likely culprit if she'd been partying in the slums. With the instinct born of years of medic training, Justen reached out to her, and she collapsed against him. He clutched her head as she twitched and trembled in his arms. Greasy gray paste smeared onto his fingers from her braids. She slumped in his arms as boots pounded the planks behind them.

There was about to be trouble here. Trouble and attention, neither of which he could afford.

As the first of the guards reached them, the woman was yanked out of his hands. "Who do you think you are?" the guard shouted as she dangled like a limp eel in his meaty grip. "Aristo scum, you answer to us."

Justen began to back up. Thankfully, they didn't seem half as interested in him. On the yacht, he saw a flash of turquoise as an occupant peered over the rails at the commotion. The woman in the guard's grip looked up at the boat and shook her head once. But even that effort seemed to be too much for her, and her eyes rolled back in her head.

Another guard snorted. "This one looks like she just got her first pink. If we wait 'til it takes effect, we can have some real fun."

At this, Justen stiffened, and a chill shuddered through his veins. *Her first pink.* So this was what it had come to on the streets of Galatea? Making jokes about the Reduction drug? He really *had* been sheltered. And if he didn't get off this island, it would get much worse. For everyone.

Caution fled, and he opened his mouth, speaking in a voice more accustomed to addressing lab techs than dock security. "Gentlemen, can't you see? This woman is an Albian, even if she's an aristo, too."

"And who do you think *you* are?" the first guard asked, looking down his nose at Justen.

Justen straightened, though it still didn't make him as tall as the soldier. "An interested bystander, sir, and a friend of the revolution. You know Citizen Aldred has granted immunity to visiting Albians. We certainly wouldn't want to anger their princess over this silly aristo, and neither would those in the palace. Am I right?"

"That's your opinion, young man."

"Correct, it is." He was ready to unleash his secret weapon, when the aristo proceeded to vomit all over the pavement.

The guard grimaced. "Let Albion have her, then." He let go and the woman collapsed on the dock, senseless. When the guard kicked her, she barely even grunted.

Justen's mouth opened, but he said nothing. As long as they left, and left her alone, a kick would not hurt her worse than the genetemps sickness already had. He reached down and pulled her up again. The shaking had only worsened.

"My boat," she croaked.

"Yes," Justen replied curtly. Messing around with temporary genetics was foolish at best and deadly at worst. Since the revolution, the market for unlicensed genetemping had flourished in the Halahou's sketchier neighborhoods, offering everything from glow-in-the-dark skin and feathers to snake eyes and sex changes. It was all the rage among the teen regs—even Remy had expressed interest in giving it a whirl, until Justen had explained exactly what could happen to her if things went wrong.

Genetemps were also wildly popular with bored Albian aristos looking for a little adventure on holidays down south. Justen didn't bother to hate them. The hell that was genetemps sickness was punishment enough. This one, though, was old enough to know better. She looked like she was as old as the Helo Cure.

He dragged the old woman back to her ship, where the turquoise-haired Albian he'd spotted earlier met him at the ramp. She was a few years younger than Justen, with full, rosy cheeks and a keenly intelligent glint in her deep brown eyes. "Thank you, Citizen," the girl said, grabbing the older woman out of his grasp. "I appreciate your assistance with my grandmother. She's . . . quite frail . . ."

"She's got genetemps sickness," he snapped at the girl. "I'm not an idiot. The code's breaking down badly and her cells are going into shock. Do you have a medical kit on board?"

Turquoise cast her grandmother a fretful look and said nothing.

"Listen," Justen hissed. "She needs medical care or she'll go coma. I'm a medic. I can treat her here, or we can take her to the hospital in Halahou. Your choice."

Turquoise went for the kit. Justen arranged the old woman's body on a cushioned bench. He brushed her hair from her face, and gray grease smeared on his fingers. The color was fake, he realized, noting how the gray flaked off her braids.

The woman's eyes fluttered open. He'd expected the watery, sunken look of age, but they were a clear, golden brown. And her wrinkles appeared fewer and far shallower than they had on the docks.

"An aging genetemps?" he asked, as if he were back in the clinic surrounded by other medics. "There's a new one."

"It didn't work right," the woman said, the croak subsiding to leave the voice of a girl. "It was supposed to make me look thirty, not ninety."

"Ah." Justen nodded. This aristo was no one's grandmother. She must have been trying to get into an establishment with age restrictions. Though it didn't explain the gray hair. He'd never understand the motives behind what passed for Albian fashion. The crazy hair colors, the ridiculous ruffles . . .

The turquoise-haired girl reappeared with a medical kit. "You're awake," she said with a sigh of relief.

The aristo held out her hand to her companion. "Andrine, is everything ready?"

Turquoise—Andrine—nodded.

"Good," croaked the other one. "Ready the *Daydream* for departure as soon as my Galatean savior is done here."

Justen saw his opening. "Actually, as I was telling your friend, you're in dire need of medical attention. I'd like to offer my services to you during the crossing. I'm trained as a medic."

"That won't be necessary."

"I disagree." He hesitated. "I am in search of passage to Albion anyway. If you won't accept my care, I would be happy to pay you for the trip. But either way, as a medic I'm ethically required to offer my assistance."

The woman regarded him for a long moment. He wondered how old she was really. If she'd taken aging gene-temps, she might be even younger than he was. "How nice it is to see that all Galateans have not abandoned their morals. Fine, you can come with us. You must tell us, though, to whom I am in debt."

He glanced behind him, to the docks. None of the guards lingered. Besides, as long as he was leaving, it didn't matter. "My name is Justen Helo."

Andrine stepped back. The aristo's eyes widened. It figured. Even Albian party girls knew what that name meant.

"Citizen Helo," she said softly, "it's an honor."

"Justen," he ground out. If he never heard the title "Citizen" again, it would be too soon. And who was this aristo kidding? An honor? There was vomit drying on her collar.

She inclined her head. "Lady Persis Blake, at your service."

# Four

WARM SILK CRADLED HER cheek, and sunlight dappled coral along the insides of her eyelids. Slowly, Persis emerged from sleep. Her limbs felt like washed-up seaweed, and her body ached as if she'd swum for miles. The soft sway of the hammock was her only comfort. She tried to open her eyes, and a dagger of pain sliced through her temples.

Memory flooded into the wound. The mission. The genetemps. The young Galatean on the docks. The one who'd said his name was—

Heedless of the pain, Persis forced her eyes open. *Justen Helo.* She'd been too out of it on the boat to question the Galatean's claim. She'd been too out of it, even, to figure out a way to avoid giving him passage after he'd helped her.

Andrine should have known better than to let some stranger on the boat, even if his name was Helo. Persis must have been very sick, indeed, for her friend to have taken the risk. At least Andrine had brought her back home to Scintillans. But what had become of Justen Helo?

There was a soft chirp and the sound of claws against the polished bamboo floorboards. A tug on the silk of the hammock near her legs and then she felt the familiar weight and warmth of Slipstream wriggling up her body and curling into her arms. His whiskers tickled against her skin as he snuffled his otter-like face into the crook of her elbow. He blinked at her, his enormous, round eyes filled with concern.

"It's all right, Slippy. I'm home," she whispered.

"And awake," said a voice beyond the folds of her hammock. Persis clutched Slipstream tightly. "That was sooner than I expected. You must have a great constitution."

With effort, Persis sat up. The sea mink snuggled against her, his velvet fur sun-warmed and dry, which meant he hadn't gone fishing yet this morning. Justen Helo stood by the steps leading to the garden, little more than a dark blotch against the sunlight. Her privacy screen hadn't been drawn, which left the panoramic views of the Scintillans cliffs beyond the edge of the garden open wide before her. Though she'd woken to the sight nearly every morning of her life, Persis now blanched. She didn't need a Galatean revolutionary—she didn't need *Justen Helo*—to see how opulent her bedroom was.

"How long was I out?" she asked, hating the way her voice crackled over the words. Persis tried to recall anything specific about him, but the only thing that came to mind was a vague memory of a story from childhood about his parents dying in some sort of reg riot, leaving Justen and his sister orphans.

He'd clearly grown up since then.

"All day and night," he said, his tone still formal, medical.

Which meant that he'd already been here in Scintillans for a day? How did she hope to explain that to her parents? Her father had forbidden visitors, lest anyone see her mother during one of her spells. Even Andrine knew not to come up anymore, though she didn't know the reason. What had her friend been thinking, to dump Justen here?

Probably that no one in New Pacifica would deny a Helo hospitality.

"Are you in pain?" he asked, his tone somehow containing both concern and command. Maybe Andrine hadn't had a choice about leaving him here. Justen had insisted on caring for her on the boat. Maybe the medic—a *Helo* medic! The mind boggled—felt his duties were ongoing.

"Not as much as I probably should be," she replied. "I'd been led to believe that genetemps sickness was more severe." Tero had given her an earful about it before he'd handed over the drugs he'd concocted.

He should have spent a bit less time lecturing and a bit more coding.

"It usually is," Justen said, drawing nearer. He was slim of build, this Galatean, with natural dark hair cut close to his head in proper revolutionary fashion. High, sharp cheekbones like spear points gave his face a severe, serious air—or maybe that was the glare he was shooting her from beneath his pointed black eyebrows. He'd be handsome—if he ever cracked a smile. His eyes were very dark and very keen, and he wore an expression that reminded Persis more than a little of the images she'd seen of his famous grandmother. He placed the back of his hand against her forehead. It was cool and dry. No wristlock. No palmport. His nails were short and neat but unpolished. "But I'm pretty good at what I do. I caught you early."

Persis swallowed with a dry mouth. *Caught?*

"Next time you go to Galatea to party, Lady Blake, I suggest you stick to safer intoxicants than genetemps. And not just because of the risk of sickness. If the genetemps isn't properly formatted for breakdown, you might get stuck with the code for life."

She nodded, then gingerly maneuvered her legs over the side of the hammock. *To party.* She was safe, then. And grateful she'd had the wherewithal, even in the grips of genetemps sickness, to craft a believable excuse for her condition. If Justen thought she'd accidentally overaged herself, he'd be unlikely to connect her to the crone who'd just liberated his nation of an entire family of besieged children.

Though he was also certain to find her beneath his contempt.

Tero Finch was a dead man. She couldn't wait to get her hands on the young gengineer, provided, of course, that there was anything left once his sister, Andrine, had her shot. She was surprised she couldn't feel the tremors from whatever eruption must be going on at the Finch house down in the village. Bad coding? She had half a mind to send a strongly worded flutter to his old gengineering instructors. And she was done letting him fiddle with Slipstream's code whenever he wanted. Her pet was a sea mink, not a guinea pig.

As she put weight on her aching legs, Justen turned his head to the side in an expression Persis recognized from her mother's nurses. It was the gesture of a medic seeking to allow his patient some privacy. Justen Helo, the medic. A *Helo*. Standing in her *bedroom*.

Persis tugged at the thin fall of seafoam silk until it covered her upper thighs and stood. Slipstream slid from her lap and landed, light as a cat, on the floor. Her hair had been washed clean of the paint she'd used in her old-woman disguise, but she had yet to see if the genetemps had left any permanent damage to her face.

Wouldn't that be a fun bit of news for the Albian court! Lady Persis Blake, disfigured on an ill-advised pleasure trip to Galatea. She really would kill Tero if that was the case.

And more than seeing her reflection, Persis needed to find out what had happened to the Wild Poppy's cargo. As soon as she reached her bathroom she engaged the privacy screen, closed her eyes against the pain still thrumming across her skull, and summoned her focus for a flutter.

The next thing she knew she was sprawled out on the smooth onyx floor, her cells screaming for mercy.

Above her, Justen's voice sounded foggy, distant: "—idiot aristo." She felt a pinprick against her arm, and the pain subsided. Persis blinked until her vision cleared.

"Hey," he said. "Listen." He waved her own left hand before her eyes. It was floppy, loose on her wrist, the bright golden disk of the palmport blurring against her skin. "You cannot use this thing until you fully recover. You hear me?"

Persis cringed. She'd ignored Isla's warning, but the princess had been right. Genetemps was a bad idea. Forget what the drug might have done to her face. It apparently made her stupid, too. She knew the energy requirements of a palmport, and had been well aware that she didn't possess them at the moment. She pasted her best "Persis Flake" face on and giggled. "I have to use my *hand*, silly."

He dropped her hand like it was a piece of rotting fish and stalked out of the bathroom, grumbling something under his breath that sounded to Persis like "useless."

Good. Useless was the impression she needed to make. Clearly, she was off to a good start convincing Justen Helo.

Shoving herself to her feet once more, she reengaged the screen and pulled the lever on her bath. A rush of hot mineral water flowed into the high-backed basin, and Persis tugged off her shift and slipped into the slightly sulfur-scented water. She didn't even bother with perfumes. The obsidian wall above the bath was polished to a high sheen, and she checked out her reflection. Bloodshot, baggy eyes, but that was probably the sickness, not any lingering effects of the genetemps itself.

"By the way," came Justen's voice from the other side, "your friend gave me a message for you. The one with the blue hair?" His tone dripped with disdain. "She said she took your packages straight to your tailor."

More good news. Persis slumped in her bath, allowing a small smirk at the thought of the league's medic, Noemi, being called a tailor. Noemi would hate that. But she would know what to do for the children. Persis leaned her head back as the heat soaked into her aching muscles. "Thank you."

*Thank you, Justen Helo.* Persis covered her face with her hands and groaned. Her whole life, she'd imagined what it would be like to meet a member of that famous family, perhaps when she went with Isla to one of Queen Gala's parties. But it had never happened. Instead, this was what happened: Justen Helo had saved her life, and she'd thrown up on his shoes. So much for the elegant, charming Lady Persis Blake.

There was silence for several minutes on the other side of the screen, long enough for Persis to contemplate falling asleep again. But Justen couldn't leave well enough alone. "Lady Blake? Do you plan to be very long in there?"

"Am I keeping you from an appointment, Citizen Helo?" She knew the Scintillans servants would have seen to all Justen's needs, not only because he was Persis's guest but because of his famous name. Regs would do anything for a descendant of the Helos. Justen was no doubt considered a model citizen back home.

And *that's* why letting him wander around out there unattended might not be the best idea. With a groan, Persis pulled herself up to a sitting position in the warm, soothing water. She'd soak her bones later. For now, she needed to deal with the Galatean revolutionary standing in her bedroom.

She dialed in the instructions to her bath, which promptly responded with a flow of frangipani-scented water. Rinsed and perfumed, she emerged, dried off, and garbed herself in an ocean blue kimono that covered her from neck to foot. Properly armed, she exited the bathroom only to be greeted by an empty space. She looked around in confusion, and spotted Justen outside in the garden, near a table set with breakfast for two. He was kneeling on the vibrant, manicured lawn, while Slipstream balanced on his hind legs, his long neck stretched up as he begged for the bit of manguava cake Justen dangled over the sea mink's glossy black nose.

"He'll balance treats on his nose if you want," she said from the steps, squinting as the full sunlight hit her face.

Justen tried it and sat back on his heels, impressed. "Very well-trained pet you have."

"That's what my father paid the gengineers for." Persis turned her attention to the sea mink. "Slippy, end!" Slipstream flipped the cake off his snout and caught it in midair as Persis stepped off the stairs and onto the soft, loamy earth of the lawn. "Ever seen a sea mink before?"

"We don't use gengineering for personal pets in Galatea," Justen said, rising to his feet, "just for stock animals, guard beasts, stuff like that."

Stuff like mini-orcas to feed your enemies to. But she wouldn't dwell on that now. Not when Justen had been so kind as to save her life. Not when she was in the midst of showing him what a shallow socialite she was.

"Slipstream is an excellent guard beast," she replied as the animal scurried to her side. "I've never had my yacht stolen even once." A servant had set out a breakfast she wasn't quite prepared to tackle until the tsunami in her gut died down. Instead, she poured herself a cup of jasmine tea and sank into the cushioned chair. "So, Citizen Helo, have you been enjoying my estate?"

"Justen is fine, Lady Blake."

She smiled at him over the cup. "So is Persis. After all, we're good friends now that you've spent the night at my place."

His gaze flickered away from her then, and Persis's smile grew wider. She'd have answers from him yet. He might be handsome and famous and smart, but she was Persis Blake.

"So, what brings you to Albion . . . Justen?"

"Just a vacation." He shrugged, but he still wasn't quite meeting her eyes. "You visited my country for fun."

"I can't imagine your wanting to leave Galatea when things are going so well for you back home." Persis crossed her legs, allowing the silk of her robe to part past her knees as Justen did his best to ignore the sight and busy himself with the teapot. The Galatean was hiding something.

Justen poured himself his own cup of tea, then took a long draft. After a moment, he looked at Persis again. "No, not really. No true patriot of my homeland would relish the violence happening now. I am a regular, I am a Helo, but I do not condone what is being done to Galatean aristos."

His words hit hard. Persis swallowed and fought the urge to pull her robe closed. Maybe he wasn't hiding so much as seriously disturbed by the horrors in Galatea. "I'm happy to hear that," she managed.

"I wouldn't feel comfortable accepting the hospitality of any aristo without explaining my objections to my government's tactics."

Persis longed to ask him why, then, if he was a Helo, he didn't use his influence to stop them? Why was he not fighting to help his countrymen, the way his grandmother had when she'd invented the cure? *Persis* was fighting. What was wrong with the rest of the world?

But that wasn't the sort of thing Persis Blake asked anyone anymore. Not the Persis Blake who'd spent the better part of the year convincing everyone that she was empty-headed and ornamental and absolutely indispensable to the glittering court of Princess Isla. Those sorts of questions were reserved solely for the Wild Poppy these days, and the Wild Poppy was out of commission—at least until Persis recovered from Tero's mistake.

"What is it you wish to do while you're here?" she asked instead. "I must say, you've fallen into excellent hands—though you might not think so after yesterday. I'm rather popular at court. I'm sure I could get you an invite to a party there." In truth, the entire court—aristo and reg—would salivate for a glimpse at a Helo. Bringing him would only cement her ranking at court.

But somehow, Persis had trouble imagining Justen would enjoy it.

"I'd like that, thank you," he surprised her by saying. "Do you know the Princess Isla at all?"

What did he think "popular at court" meant? "I'm her chief lady-in-waiting."

Justen looked nonplussed. "Like a maid?"

Persis smiled indulgently. "It's how royals say 'She's one of my best friends.'"

Justen blinked. "Really? Oh . . . good. Because I've come to Albion to meet her."

Was that disappointment he was not quite able to hide? Why would he be disappointed to have fallen in with such a well-connected aristo? And what did he want with Isla? Persis narrowed her eyes. This required further observation.

As did Justen Helo.

By the time the aristo had done her hair, her clothes, and her makeup, Justen had gone through the entire catalog of her gengineered rodent's parlor tricks and wandered around the grounds of her sprawling estate twice. No one could deny the place was as beautiful as the girl who lived here. Perched on a high cliff at the southernmost edge of Albion's western peninsula, the house seemed like a cliff flower itself, blossoming in shades of brown and black from the earth. Most of its rooms lay open to the sea air, covered only by vast, petal-shaped roofs that swept overhead, supported by thin, translucent columns of onyx or crystal. Justen could see slits in the external walls, hinting at screens that could be drawn to protect the interior during the rainy season.

The water surrounded them on three sides, vast and glittering beneath the sun-drenched sky. From up here, you could barely hear the surf, and the sharp, living smell of the water faded into a simple salty freshness. Justen paused at the western cliff edge and stared at the endless ocean. Once, long ago, before the Reduction and the wars that had broken the very heart of the world, there'd been other lands, other people. People who lived and breathed democracies, people who'd accomplished their goals without spilling a single drop of blood. The Galateans had failed at this. *Justen* had failed.

All he'd ever wanted was to help people, like his grandmother had done. And now, when things had gone so wrong he had no choice but to escape, the only place left to go was Albion. The only mercy he could hope to get was from another monarch.

That was, if Persis Blake ever finished getting ready.

Everywhere he went, he felt the eyes of the estate servants on him. He grew tired of their obsequious attempts to bring him things—snacks, perfumes, changes of clothes in monstrously garish colors. Most of all, he hated the way every last one of them called him Citizen Helo. They probably meant it as a mark of respect, or even support for the Galatean revolution, but if anything, that made him feel worse.

"Citizen Helo, I just wanted to take a moment to thank you—to thank your family—for their gift to the world."

"Citizen Helo, both my parents were born of the cure. Bless you and yours."

"I hate to bother you, Citizen Helo, but I'll never forgive myself if I don't say it. It is such an honor to be in the presence of someone descended from Persistence Helo. Everyone here at Scintillans is overwhelmed. Is there anything I can get you?"

This last one planted a notion in his head, and he stopped the servant, a blue-haired butler. "Pardon me, but the lady of the house . . ."

"Lady Heloise Blake? She and Lord Blake are away at the moment." The servant eyed him. "Oh, you mean Persis."

But Justen already had the information he needed. He

snapped his jaw shut. *Heloise. Persis.* He should have seen it before. Those names were no accident. And yet, why would aristos bear them?

"Citizen?" the servant prompted.

Justen shook his head. "I was just wondering how long she'd be."

The older man laughed. "Yes, she does like her clothes, our girl. These days, it's all she seems to care about."

*Our girl.* Now, Justen examined the estate with new eyes. He'd been too concerned for his patient's welfare when he'd arrived yesterday afternoon, and last night and this morning he'd been busy trying to make a plan for the future, but now he finally began to take in the details of this aristo estate. The little fishing village nestled at the base of the cliffs was filled with neat, tidy houses, not ramshackle cabins like one often saw on the plantations in Galatea. Happy, plump children ran about the lawns of the estate itself. The servants practically whistled while they worked. Were things so very different in Albion?

He knew that the Reduction's end had been handled differently in the two nations of New Pacifica. In Albion, mandatory education for regs and fair wage laws had been passed. There'd been reg representatives on the Royal Council for more than a generation. But that couldn't have made a true difference, could it? As Uncle Damos said, they still had a king calling the shots. One only had to look at the way they treated the women of Albion, the way aristos like Persis led such decadent, useless lives, to see how rotten the system must be.

But then again, those names . . . something was strange about Scintillans.

"Are you ready to go?" came a voice at his back. He turned to find Persis in a sari the color of sunset. Jewels sparkled along the hem and neckline. Her hair was piled on top of her head again, in a fashion he was sure was exceedingly intricate but looked to him like nothing more than an osprey nest. On top of it all perched a ridiculous fascinator shaped like a bird of paradise and made entirely from real feathers. Her skin was clear and golden, glowing with a vitality one would never have guessed possible for a girl so recently recovered from genetemps sickness. Her light-colored eyes were winged with kohl, and her wide cheekbones and full lips were the same sparkly rose color. Perhaps her complexion was being helped along by a good deal of Albian cosmetics, then.

The sea mink, its glossy red coat set off by a jeweled coral collar, frolicked at her feet.

The aristo frowned at him, as her gaze traveled down his body and over his simple black shirt and pants. "Oh, you didn't change, I see."

"Where did you get your name?" he blurted.

Her eyes snapped back to his face. "Where do you think?"

"From my grandmother."

"Well," she said, with a tilt of her head that sent the feathers shaking. "I see you have at least some of her smarts."

"Your mother—"

"Is a reg, yes," she said, her tone clipped. Was she . . . embarrassed by that fact? Justen couldn't tell. He had never known a half aristo before. Not a legitimate one, anyway. Not one who was friends with royalty.

Persis tapped at her gloved left hand, then seemed to remember she was still recovering. "Well, let's go. The royal court of Albion awaits."

And now Justen realized he had no idea what to expect.

# Five

JUSTEN HAD TAKEN TWO sea voyages with Persis Blake so far but had yet to see her touch the controls. On the way back from Galatea, she'd been unconscious, and now she left the yacht on autopilot while she downed palmport supplements and stationed herself at the cabin's wall port to exchange what were apparently rather urgent messages with her tailor.

The autopilot's docking mechanism was somewhat shaky. Justen went below to call to Persis, who rolled her eyes in frustration at the interruption. "The *Daydream* won't sink," she said with a wave of her hand. The image of a keyboard hovered before her, its letters flashing. "Now leave me alone. I'm a bit rusty at this wall port business. I can't believe it actually makes you *type*. With your *fingers*. Like some kind of *primitive*."

The yacht commenced banging its sides into a slip.

What kind of girl, Justen wondered, possessed such a gorgeous vessel as this and treated it with all the care of an old shoe? The same kind whose papa had purchased her a personalized pet, Justen supposed. If she did end up sinking her yacht, Justen had no doubt her aristocratic father would just buy her another, and another, and another still.

If Persis weren't the quickest way to gain access to Princess Isla, he would have found a way to ditch her by now. But he didn't have a better plan for getting into court, and he had to admit that before the docking procedure, the trip around the point of Scintillans and up the west coast of Albion had been picturesque—all blue, sunlit sea and wind that smelled of salt and fire. Justen had remained on deck, enjoying the view of the cliffs receding into the smooth slopes that characterized the outer shores of Albion, watching the sea mink frolic in the wake, and wondering if maybe, all things considered, he hadn't been spending a bit too much time in his lab.

At first glance, Justen decided the royal court wasn't so very different from the stories they told about it in Galatea. The water organ was gorgeous if ostentatious, the outrageous clothes nearly blinded him, and the appallingly decadent fluternotes whizzing every which way were apt to give him a headache if he remained in their midst for too long. He'd learned about their operation during his medic training and had always been relieved that the craze hadn't caught on in Galatea. Parasitic biotechnology that drained the body's own nutrients to operate? It was foolish and unnecessary. Why couldn't the Albian aristos use oblets, like everyone else? He fingered his own precious oblets, still hidden away in his pockets. Their smooth edges clinked against each other, solid and reassuring. He may have left his homeland

and his sister, but at least these would be safe . . . and out of his uncle's hands.

Thankfully, he saw no fellow Galateans in the crowd of the courtyard. Though anyone in the Albion court would probably be an enemy of the revolution, he didn't need a report of his whereabouts to reach Uncle Damos so soon. Even more thankfully, his host ushered him quickly through the throng and into a small, white, orchid-draped antechamber to await an audience with the princess regent. Persis had walked into the palace with her sea mink like she owned the place, and had to brush off several court-iers along the way. And she'd managed to bring him to the princess straight off, too. Persis must have been telling the truth, then, that they were friends.

And, yet, she was the daughter of an aristo married to a reg. Would wonders never cease?

The princess, too, looked just like the images he'd seen of her. She was a few years younger than he was—about Persis's age, with silvery hair and an all-white gown that seemed almost practical after the rainbow of colors and iridescence he'd passed through outside, even if it was covered in waves of floating feathers and crystals that tinkled as she moved.

One of the standard complaints about the old Queen Gala had been that she'd acted like an Albian woman rather than a Galatean one. Shallow, silly, and more interested in parties than politics, in clothes than in culture. Justen could only hope that Isla defied expectations. Her friendship with Persis boded ill. He'd heard the princess didn't wield much in the way of true power in Albion. And with an airhead like Persis as her lady-in-waiting, perhaps there was good reason for that.

Then again, beggars couldn't be choosers.

"Greetings, Galatean," said Princess Isla, spreading her arms in a gesture of welcome. "My friend Persis tells me I'm about to be bowled over by you. But given the number of Galateans that wash up on my shores these days, I wonder what she finds so impressive *this* time."

Persis looked at the princess and scowled. Isla smiled serenely. The aristo favored her princess with the ghost of a curtsy. She was holding yet another half-empty bottle of supplement drink. Justen imagined her tongue must be just about curdled from the sugar overload by now. She obviously couldn't wait to get back to her palmport. Why anyone would subject their body to that kind of punishment when an oblet could run off its geothermal battery for weeks at a time was beyond him.

"You two go ahead and have your little chat. I think I'm recovered enough to boot this up again, right?" Persis waved her left hand at Justen.

He gave a noncommittal shrug. She'd probably be fine, given her supplements, but he couldn't imagine she had any messages left to send after the flurry on the *Daydream*.

Palmport advocates said it was as close to telepathy as the human race had ever come, but Justen didn't think it was worth the cost. Besides, you still needed oblets for data storage and any large information transfers. Palmports were only as good as the memories of the people using them, their data little more than digestible, untraceable nano-sugars. And given the type of people who ran them—people like Persis—they were useless for anything more than silly games and gossip.

Persis seemed satisfied anyway. She plopped onto a nearby cushion and ripped off her wristlock. He swallowed his scowl. What he had to say was not fodder for Albian gossips.

And what, exactly, would that be? Certainly not the whole truth. Princess Isla was an aristo. If she knew about his involvement in the revolution, she'd put him in prison and then he'd never be able to right the wrongs he'd caused. Better to start with part of the story.

"Your Highness," Justen said, finding those words every bit as difficult to speak as "Citizen" had been to hear. He guessed not all his revolutionary principles had been extinguished, despite what he'd learned. He gave her a short, stiff bow, then straightened and looked her right in the eyes. She was a royal. Not a god. "My name is Justen Helo—"

Her eyebrows rose and when she smiled this time, she looked less like a monarch and more like a teen getting a birthday present. Even from royalty, then.

"I'm the grandson of Darwin and Persistence Helo. And I'm here to ask you for asylum."

At this, Isla blinked in surprise, but Persis just looked bored. Justen wondered if she even knew what "asylum" was.

"And," he added, "I need it to remain a secret."

"Why?" asked Isla. "I assure you I would have no compunction celebrating far and wide that a Helo would prefer living in Albion to braving the revolution."

She was sensible at least, even if she had silly taste in friends. Maybe she just kept Persis around for fashion advice, though Justen wondered how advisable even *that* was. "I'd prefer my countrymen think I was just visiting your island," he said, "at least until I can contrive to get my little sister out of Citizen Aldred's house." Even if his uncle guessed the truth, a public lie might be enough to protect Remy.

Persis lifted her head, her eyes keenly trained on his face. "Wait, that . . . revolution guy in Galatea has your sister imprisoned? Now *that's* interesting!"

The princess batted her hand at her friend, and Persis sighed and returned her attention to the diagnostics hovering above her palmport disk. Justen bit back his frustration. Isla didn't seem to mind the girl's presence, and as a foreign reg, what right did he have to ask for an aristo's removal? Besides, it was Persis who'd brought him here. He'd just have to bear it.

"Not imprisoned," Justen corrected. Brainwashed maybe. Just as he'd been until recently. "Citizen Aldred is her guardian." He'd been Justen's guardian, too, and probably still thought of himself as such, though Justen was eighteen now.

It was amazing, all the thoughts that oozed out as soon as a single crack appeared in the surface of your beliefs. How long had Uncle Damos been planning the revolution? Had he known ten years ago, when he first agreed to take custody of the orphaned Helo children, how much goodwill he'd earn from the regs of Galatea?

He couldn't have guessed that it was Justen who would hand him the weapon he needed to overthrow the government. Even Justen hadn't known that when he'd done it.

"Guardian," Isla said now. "Not that far from 'guard.'"

Justen nodded in relief. So she *did* understand. "Right now, that's the measure of it. We're valuable to the revolution as symbols of the cure."

"You'd be valuable to us as the same," said Isla. "I take it you don't wish to trade one gilded cage for another?"

"I'm not a symbol," said Justen sourly. "And I'm certainly not a symbol of this revolution."

"I like you better already," Isla said. The bamboo blinds separating the antechamber from the court rustled. "Persis, darling, go see who it is bothering us."

There was a man there, stuffed into yet another garish outfit and looking annoyed. "Who is that Galatean?" he hissed at Persis. "What is the princess doing with him?"

Persis pressed her hand to her chest. "Why, Councilman, a lady never tells."

"Then what are *you* doing in there?"

"Wouldn't you like to know!" And she shut the blinds again. "That won't hold him for long."

"Of course," said Isla. "Councilman Shift can't stand the possibility that something, somewhere, is happening without his permission." She sighed. "So far, this conversation has annoyed the chair of the Council and done damage to my reputation. I hope it's worth it, Citizen." She turned back to Justen, her skirts swirling around her, and fixed him with a queenly look.

He shocked himself by feeling the urge to step back, or bow, or sink to his knees. How did they do that, these aristos? He knew they weren't born with such superiority, no matter what aristos claimed. Rather, both aristos and the people from the lower class had been indoctrinated since birth in their roles as master and underling. He thought he'd been taught to resist it, that the revolution had leeched it out of him, but the instinct obviously ran deep.

"Tell me, sir, if you please, what excuse you plan to use to your countrymen and your sister as to why you remain in Albion at my court. Surely you cannot prefer our aristocratic ways to the revolutionary ideals of Galatea?"

"I—hadn't thought that through, yet." He'd been too focused on getting out of Galatea before his grandmother's work could do any more damage. Before *he* could. Escape was the priority. Excuses—and apologies—could come later.

Isla clucked her tongue and turned to her friend. "Persis, dear, wherever do you pick up these people?"

Persis was studying Justen with an appraising eye, as if he were a bolt of silk or a particularly fine hat. "This one picked me up, actually. As in, off the ground. He rescued me from the docks in Galatea."

"*Rescued?*"

"Yes," Persis admitted sheepishly. "I was suffering from genetemps sickness."

Isla frowned. "I *told* you that would happen." She stamped her foot. Royally, Justen noted. The way these two talked—they *were* real friends. A clearly clever princess and the half-aristo idiot socialite whose idea of a good time was to troll the slums of Halahou for genetemps and cheap silks.

Justen might be out of his depth here in Albion.

The princess returned her attention to him. "Why are you fleeing your country if you're in such good graces with Citizen Aldred? You're in no danger there."

"But I am," he said. As soon as reports came back from the Lacan estate, Uncle Damos's suspicions would be verified. And, of course, Justen would be the prime suspect. "I no longer agree with the actions of my countrymen. I cannot support the revolution now that they've turned to"—he took a deep breath—"petty revenge and violence against innocents. Social justice is worth fighting for. A reign of terror is not."

"So," Isla said, "if you don't act like the good little revolutionary, Aldred will make an example out of you?"

"Exactly." Of course she knew how it worked. She was probably well versed in such methods of despotic rule. He'd been taught about its dangers by Uncle Damos himself, long before the revolution. How had it come to this—Justen Helo standing in the Albian throne room and casting his lot with a monarch?

"But you're a Helo," said Isla. "Aldred is not so foolish to do anything publicly."

"Perhaps not," he admitted, "but I've seen him in private."

Persis's mouth made a little round O. "You mean you think he would give you or your sister that Reduction drug I keep hearing about?"

Justen was hoping not, though it would be a fitting

punishment for Justen's disobedience, and Aldred knew it. There was nothing his uncle liked more than poetic justice. That's why he'd pounced on the pinks.

Justen couldn't decide if he was angrier with Remy or himself. A few days before he left, he'd confessed everything to her—all his doubts about the revolution, even how he'd sabotaged an entire batch of pinks ready for shipment to a prisoner estate out east. He expected shock but also support. Instead, his fourteen-year-old sister started brainstorming ideas on how to backtrack from the mess he'd made, as if he could. He'd already been barred from the labs. Uncle Damos suspected . . . something.

Remy didn't get it. He wouldn't take his actions back, even if it were possible. They'd exchanged some harsh words. She called him an idiot. He called her a child. And then she'd run off somewhere, likely to sulk, and wouldn't answer his messages. He waited as long as he could, but figured Remy would be safe if he left. After all, *she* was still a model revolutionary citizen.

Isla began another circuit. "I can't retrieve your sister for you."

"Ooh," said Persis, popping up from her focus on her palmport. "You know who might be great at that? The Wild Poppy."

Justen snorted. "Right. Does he take requests?"

Isla paused. "What makes you think I have any control over what the Wild Poppy does or doesn't do?" Another turn, another flick of her cape. "Me? Control one of my own subjects? Hilarious, *right, Persis?*"

"Yes, Princess," said Persis obediently, and returned to her device.

"And pointless at any rate," Justen said. "Unc—Citizen Aldred is a dangerous man, Your Highness. I don't think anyone in Galatea truly understands what he's capable of."

Isla whirled around and faced him. "I believe, Citizen Helo, that I can name several Galatean aristos who do."

With a flare of embarrassment, Justen looked away from Isla and from Persis, whose attention was on him again. Was she entertained by watching him implode in front of her princess? Her expression, however, was one of kindly warning, and Justen remembered that though she was an aristocrat, she was of lower status than her royal friend. She had more experience than Justen did dealing with her. And how had Persis been treating the princess? Always carefully and with deference.

He supposed he could learn something from her after all.

"What I meant," he said, more quietly this time, "is that the royal palace in Halahou isn't some work camp at an old estate."

"It's a good thing the Wild Poppy can't hear you speak that way," Isla said to Justen. "Judging from the spy's behavior thus far, he'd see it as a challenge."

"Ooh," Persis cooed, grinning. "Do you really think he would?"

"*Shut up, Persis.*" Isla turned back to Justen and continued, her tone clipped. "And I don't think it's a good idea to empty your nation of all its revolutionaries, thank you. We have enough problems here as it is." She resumed pacing.

"You want to remain here. You need a reason that will not arouse suspicion back in Galatea." She glared at him. "What is it you do when you're not being a spokesperson for a bloody revolution?"

"I'm a medic," he said. "A scientist, like everyone else in my family." Except his sister, who claimed she wanted to go into the military like Uncle Damos and their foster sister, Vania. Little wonder Remy had toed the party line when Justen had told her how twisted their revolution had become and the steps he'd taken to stop it.

"Humph." More pacing. "And how long since you finished your training?"

"Technically . . . I haven't. I just turned eighteen, and I've been a little distracted recently." Uncle Damos had pulled some strings to get him installed at a lab despite his lack of a degree. The Helo name had probably helped as well. And of course, it had helped Justen feel quite beholden to his guardian. He'd been played like a fiddle.

"Don't feel bad," Persis piped in. "I dropped out of school, too."

"I didn't *drop out*. I took a leave of absence to concentrate on my research."

"Oh, that's a good one. I should try that excuse on my father. 'I'm taking a leave of absence to concentrate on my shopping.'"

Justen didn't dignify that with a response. He'd been trying to save lives, not expand his wardrobe. Then again, Persis's pursuit of silks had probably harmed far fewer people than his own research. "The point is—"

"The point is," Isla said, cutting him off, "we have scientists. *Grown* scientists. All you offer is the Helo name."

He clenched his fists at his side. Who was this child princess to say who was grown? He must be allowed to continue his research. If not, then everything—his defection, losing Remy, and the suffering of who knew how many Galatean aristos—would all be for nothing.

"And every moment we remain here, the gossip about our imaginary romance grows stronger. . . ." Isla crossed to the blinds, peering through at the crowd and shaking her head. "Rumors are everything in this court. Sometimes I think they matter more than the truth. . . ." She gave a little hop, and the crystals on her gown chimed. "That's it!"

"What's it?" asked Persis.

"A rumor. A romance." She pointed at Justen. "He's here because he's in love."

"With you?" Persis looked skeptical.

The princess turned to her friend. "No. With *you*."

At once, Persis and Justen shook their heads.

"I'm sure we can come up with a better plan than that," Persis said quickly. Justen wasn't so sure Persis was capable, but he was willing to let her try.

"No," said Isla. "This is it. Don't you see it's perfect? It solves all our problems at once." She began to tick them off on her bejeweled fingers. "It's a valid reason for Justen to remain in Albion. And Persis is my best friend. If I approve of your relationship, it will reflect well on the monarchy and give me some leeway to condemn the revolutionary activities. The regs love the Helo family. They won't be inclined to revolt if they know the toast of the Albian aristocracy is close with one."

"You want me to *date* him?" Persis asked with gritted teeth.

"Yes!" Isla beamed. "It's a romantic tale. He saved you on the docks of Galatea. We'll be . . . vague about the reason. And brought you back, nursed you to health, blah, blah. Love at first sight. People will eat it up, Persis. You know better than anyone how much people adore a good aristo/reg love story."

A pout crossed the aristo's face. Isla was no doubt talking about Persis's parents. But Justen was beginning to see the plan's merits, as long as none of his friends back home got wind of what a shallow flake Persis was. They'd never believe he'd fall for an aristo like her, reg mother or no.

"We'll parade you around a bit, make sure everyone thinks you're madly in love, stage a few cozy moments, and everyone's happy."

"We don't have to . . . get married or anything?" Justen asked, suddenly concerned as to what the princess meant by "cozy moments."

Isla waved her hand dismissively. "No, we shouldn't have to take it as far as that."

"Shouldn't *have to*?" Justen pressed.

"I find this . . . inconvenient," Persis said at last.

"Why?" Justen turned to her. "Will my presence cramp your social schedule?"

Persis glared at him, her amber eyes as fiery as her gown. "Why yes, if you must know. Look at the way you dress, for one." She pleaded with Isla. "Do you honestly think people are going to accept someone like me with someone like him?"

Justen rolled his eyes.

Isla was no more patient. "He's a *Helo*, Persis. Believing you'd want one on your arm is not going to be much of a challenge. As a trophy, if nothing else."

Persis's pout deepened as she seemed to realize the princess was right. "I'm really busy right now," she tried.

"I'm asking you." Isla drew herself up to her full height and stared her friend down. "*I'm* asking *you*. There's no one I trust more with our precious Galatean."

Something passed between the two women. Something Justen couldn't hope to understand. But whatever it was, Persis relented.

She shook her head in defeat, then transformed before his eyes into the sparkling socialite and threw him a coy, seductive smile. "All right then, lover boy," she cooed. "I guess it's time to make our debut."

# Six

WHEN THEY EMERGED FROM Isla's private chambers, it seemed as if every eye in Albion was upon them. Persis had to give her new sweetheart credit, as he looped his arm in hers and marched bravely down the stairs of the terrace and into the fray. Slippy skittered beside them, chittering as he avoided people's heels and stopped to lap from the water organ and groom his whiskers with the edge of his foreflippers.

"Aren't you afraid he'll get trampled?"

"Oh, Slippy can take care of himself," Persis replied. Much better than the average sea mink, too, thanks to Tero's gengineering efforts. She watched him slink up to one courtier's golden lion tamarrel. The tiny orange creature was attached to its mistress by a long, glittering chain, and there were jewels glinting in its full mane and bushy, squirrel-like tail. In its tiny paws it held a slice of star papaya, and it bared its monkey teeth at Slippy as the sea mink approached. Slippy lunged.

"Oh, no you don't," Justen chided, smoothly scooping

up Slipstream around his long midsection before the animals could tussle. He smiled and bowed his head as he presented Slipstream to Persis. "Your beast, my lady."

She cuddled the sea mink to her chest and eyed Justen carefully. He could be dangerous when he turned on the charm, this handsome young revolutionary, this medic with a famous name and a desire to escape Galatea so strong he'd leave his sister and cleave to an aristo he clearly despised. Maybe he, too, was a spy.

The next half hour was filled with the bustle of small talk, while Persis introduced her "dear friend, Justen Helo" to the Albian courtiers, who were naturally delighted to make his acquaintance. By unspoken agreement, Persis and Justen kept their conversation easy and flirtatious, befitting a couple that had met only the previous day. As news of the Galatean newcomer spread throughout the court, whispers reached Persis's ears.

"Look at him. Besotted!" Justen was apparently an excellent actor in his own right.

"And why shouldn't he be? She has her mother's face." Well, yes, but that face seemed to have left him unimpressed.

"Leave it to Persis Blake to bring home a Helo." In truth, he was just the latest in a long line of Galateans she'd brought over. Not as rich as some, not as grateful as others.

"Her father married the most beautiful reg of his generation. Why shouldn't Persis catch the most famous of hers?"

She pursed her lips as the chatter spread. Isla had guessed right that people would be quick to place her latest conquest inside the carefully cultivated "Persis Flake" narrative. And why not? Persis had spent the last six months concocting her reputation in the princess's court. It was for this she'd sacrificed school, for this she'd reinvented her image, for this she'd scandalized half the residents of Scintillans, who'd gone from thinking that Torin Blake was right in naming as heir his only daughter to wondering what in the world had happened to the clever, hardworking girl they'd grown up with. But what choice did Persis have? She had to protect the Wild Poppy. She had to help Isla. She had to save New Pacifica.

If they didn't take you seriously, they would never see you coming. Persis was the most stylish, the most glittering, the most frivolous girl in Albion. There was no way she was secretly orchestrating a spy ring.

Eventually they came across an older couple, two aristos whose Galatean origins were clear by their natural hair and more sedate wardrobe. Justen greeted them stiffly, and Persis followed suit, though in truth she knew them intimately, even if they weren't aware of that fact. Lord and Lady Seri had been the spoils of one of the Wild Poppy's first raids. They looked much better now, compared to the miserable, Reduced wretches she'd plucked from their ancestral home.

"Justen Helo," said Lord Seri, shaking Justen's hand, "welcome to Albion. It is an honor to make your acquaintance. I knew your grandmother well."

"Yes," Justen replied in a tone like the depths of the sea. "You argued with her mightily over the universal distribution of her cure."

But the old aristo merely chuckled and nodded. "Yes, I did. And lost. We will not argue now over who was right, despite the repercussions that have come of her work."

"If you mean the revolution," Justen said, his tone even and firm, "it was not a foregone conclusion. It was caused by the mistreatment of the Galatean regs by their aristo masters. You'll note there's no revolution in Albion as a result of the cure."

"No revolution—*yet*," Lord Seri replied.

Persis groaned. Loudly. "All this talk of politics makes my head hurt. Lady Seri, your dress is lovely. That silk is so rich I think I could drown in it. Does it come in any color but black?" She hadn't rescued these aristos so that they could export their snobbery to her homeland. And Isla hadn't granted Justen's request so he could act like some kind of revolutionary firebrand. His political leanings were obvious—even understandable given the old system in Galatea. But their plan wouldn't work if he couldn't keep his mouth shut in front of the court's more conservative elements.

"Besides," Lord Seri continued, "I wasn't necessarily talking about the *revolution*. Darkening is a more than sufficient consequence to call the entire experiment into question, is it not? What's the percentage of Helo-cured regs who suffer and die from that little side effect? Five? Ten?"

Justen's grip on her arm tightened. Had he felt her tense? She searched the old lord's face, but he barely seemed to notice she was there. His comment was pointed, but not at Persis. No one at court knew about her mother. Yet.

"One percent," Justen said, his voice clipped. "But I think even those would rather suffer from DAR than live their lives Reduced."

Lord Seri looked amused as he leaned in toward Justen. "And how do you know that, young man? It's not like you can ask them once they're comatose."

Persis saw Justen's jaw twitch. She rather felt like vomiting, herself.

"Oh look," she said quickly. "There's Andrine. Let's catch her." She tugged him away before more harm could be done.

Andrine had limited time to spend at court since she was still in school—or, as Persis's father had put it, Andrine "had her priorities in order." She'd already devoted most of her spare time to Wild Poppy escapades. And Persis didn't begrudge her those other commitments. After all, unlike herself, the fifteen-year-old reg did not have an estate to inherit. Andrine and Persis had been friends all their lives, though Persis never would have suspected that their antics on the cliffs and beaches of Scintillans would have so well prepared them for risking their lives in Galatea . . . and in the only slightly less treacherous environment of the Albian court.

"Citizen Helo!" Andrine exclaimed as soon as she saw them. Today, she wore a dress to match her wild blue hair. "I'm glad to see you're still among us. And what's this I hear about you planning to stay awhile?"

A gesture from Persis and Andrine offered to introduce Justen to her older brother. "Two sciency types like you should definitely chat," Andrine trilled, taking him by the arm. "You can tell him all about the dangers of genetemps sickness, right, Persis?"

She rolled her eyes. Justen would certainly disapprove of Tero's more frivolous science, from Slippy to palmports to badly coded genetemps. But she was more than ready to let Tero be the object of Justen's revolutionary contempt for a few minutes. He deserved it after what he'd done to her.

Once Persis was alone, she sought out Isla.

"A word, Your Highness?" Persis hissed through her teeth.

"Don't be silly, Persis," quipped Isla. "You've never kept a statement to a single word in your life." She swept past her friend and toward a break in the bougainvillea. "Keep it quick."

As soon as they were hidden by the fall of leaves and petals, Persis said, "This is a terrible idea."

"You're only saying that because, for once in our long acquaintance, you weren't the one to come up with it."

"Forget about giving him secret asylum." Persis eyed the famous Galatean through the blossoms. "I can go fetch his sister if that's the fear. Your real trouble is controlling him. He's a Helo, yes, but he's certainly a rebel as well. You think his presence will help prevent revolution? If you listen to him talk for five minutes, you'd guess he was here to incite it."

"What do you want me to do, Persis? Put him in an induced coma like that little revolutionary soldier you kidnapped last week? She's nobody, and she could still get us in a lot of trouble. Justen is a *Helo*." Isla fixed her with a very penetrating look. "A Helo, Persis. If he were imprisoned in Galatea for speaking out against the revolution's atrocities, you'd be moving the very Earth to get him out, and you know it."

Persis hated when her friend acted as clever as she actually was. It meant admitting she was right.

Life had been so much easier when they had nothing more to worry about than who was getting top scores at school—usually Persis, though Isla always beat her at botany. Had that only been a year ago? Then Isla's parents and older brother had died, and Persis's mother had gotten sick, and the Galateans had overthrown their government, and the Wild Poppy had been born. She hardly remembered the girls they'd once been. Day by day, the superficial mask she'd donned chafed more and more; and no matter how many disguises Persis took on as the Poppy, she couldn't help but feel they fit her better than the one she wore at home.

THE FRANGIPANI-SHAPED FLUTTER THAT melted into Persis's palmport was delicate to the point of fragility. The message that whispered into her head a split second later was anything but.

*Persis, darling. I've been hearing some very odd reports about a strange houseguest you entertained in our absence. Return home at once. Love and duty, Torin Blake*

Persis scrunched up her face. Her father always sounded so formal in his flutters, like he couldn't quite break out of the message etiquette he'd learned in his youth.

*At once, Papa. Kisses.*

She retrieved Justen and herded him back to the *Daydream* as quickly as the crush of the court would allow.

"My parents found out you spent the night," she explained as Slipstream swirled in excitement around her feet. He hated the court and was always relieved to get back into the ocean. "And now they're burning to make your acquaintance." Perhaps the name alone was enough to make up for her going against their wishes and bringing a stranger to their home. Perhaps her mother had rested all day in preparation for Justen.

"I look forward to meeting them," was all the Galatean said. Was all he said almost the whole trip back, as they skirted the coastline on their way to the far southwestern point of Albion that served as the seaward entrance to her father's estate. As the cliffs rose above them, turning the water a shadowed shade of teal and blocking out the glare of the sun, Persis watched her passenger stare up in wonder.

"Scintillans pali takes some getting used to," she said, using the ancestral name of the precipice, "but you saw it when you brought me home, right?"

"No," Justen replied. "I was down below with you. You were . . . convulsing."

"How embarrassing," Persis said, her tone carefully crafted to reveal only shards of her true humiliation. "I can't apologize enough."

"Don't worry about it." He was fixated by the rock rising above them. "I'm a medic. Besides, you're doing me a huge favor by agreeing to this subterfuge. Call us even."

"Does that mean I can't count on you for any more

medical assistance?" she asked coyly.

He cast her a dark look over his shoulder. "If you mean concocting more genetemps drugs, absolutely not."

"Humph." She slouched in disappointment as he shook his head in disgust or contempt or something bordering on frustration.

Well, he wasn't the only one frustrated. She had a Helo medic, who'd grown up in Citizen Aldred's house, sitting on her very own boat and she was unable to ask him anything important. The Wild Poppy's mission depended on her ability to hide her true identity, to present herself as shallow and disinterested. And it was vital to do so in front of this Galatean revolutionary. He may have asked for asylum, but that didn't mean she could trust him.

Which reminded her, it was time to school Justen on proper court behavior. "Back at the court, those Galateans you were talking to—"

"The Seris?" He snorted.

"Yes." In another time, another guise, she might have snorted herself. Horrible Lord Seri, to suggest that the Darkened would have been better off just staying Reduced! For a man who'd been temporarily Reduced himself, it was an astonishing assertion. Of course, he was one of those aristos who would have preferred that the cure had never happened. It was good the Seris had lost any claim they once held to control the lives of others. And yet, they still held influence among the Albian aristos on the Council. "You know, you shouldn't be so hard on them. I heard they were tortured. Given that Reduction drug."

"I know," he said softly. "And I regret—that my fellow countrymen did that. But they are safe now, and I will argue to the death against their bigoted beliefs. People like them are the reason Galatea was driven to revolution."

*Not people like the revolutionaries?* Persis longed to say but could not. She'd never get Justen to change his mind—and she didn't truly want to. Most Galatean aristos *had* been horrid to their population after the cure had been administered. Though the people were born reg, most had still been treated like Reduced slaves. Many weren't paid for their work or educated or allowed control of property, and the aristos and more fortunate regs who'd campaigned for equal rights had been shouted down by the queen and her supporters—or worse.

Desire for change was more than justified. Persis couldn't deny that. But the revolution was changing things in all the wrong ways. More slavery wasn't the right solution, and torture was torture.

Besides, if Justen was going to be an asset to Isla, he'd need to learn how to tread lightly on the mines scattered about the Albian aristocracy.

"Have you heard their story?" she asked. "I have. They were enslaved on their own ancestral lands, put to hard labor for the amusement of their prison guards." Until the Wild Poppy rescued them.

"Oh, the horror," Justen grumbled without turning around. "To have to *labor*. Like all their servants did for generations. Like your servants do now."

Persis bristled. "My servants do their *jobs*. They work

fair hours and are paid fair wages. They aren't enslaved or imprisoned"—she hesitated, framing the words more carefully, more like Persis Blake ought—"and we don't give them drugs to make them stupid, either."

"But what of the Reduced servants Lord Seri didn't want to give the cure to?" Justen asked, turning to look at Persis at the helm. "Choosing to withhold the cure from them would have enslaved them forever—in body and in their own minds."

Persis gripped the wheel tightly as a shudder skimmed beneath her skin. That's what was happening to the prisoners in Galatea. And it wasn't only the revolution that held such horrible fates for its people. Even here in Albion, some were enslaved in their minds, and some had that future looming before them, with no possible escape. There was nothing Persis could do for the Darkened—nothing at all. But even if such inevitabilities were written into her genetic code, she wouldn't let that kind of suffering befall anyone it didn't have to. The Reduction was over. She wouldn't let the revolutionaries bring it back with their appalling pink pills.

"But the cure wasn't withheld, in the end," she said at last. That was safe enough. A point even Persis Blake could make. "The queen who ruled then made its application universal, just as the king here did. Did your revolutionaries spare her descendant in gratitude?" Persis would never forget the night of Queen Gala's death. Her Reduction had been the first blow, but even then Persis—and all Albion—had been naive enough to believe that it was a temporary insanity and would all be resolved. But when she'd died and her body had been desecrated by an angry mob, Persis could think only of her own princess. Her own best friend, young and ruling and without the power to prevent these things from happening.

It was the night the Wild Poppy had been born.

"No." Justen lowered his head. "We made many errors. I told you, I no longer believe in the way the revolution is playing out. But that doesn't make the goals that brought us to this point any less valid. Sometimes bad things happen when you try to do something good."

Persis knew that all too well, as had her namesake. Since symptoms of the illness didn't manifest until the victims were around forty, Persistence Helo had been old when Dementia of Acquired Regularity had first appeared among the population of the Helo-Cured regs. She'd spent the remainder of her life in seclusion. Some said it was from embarrassment, but Persis often wondered if she'd been researching, trying to find a way to fix the problem she'd unwittingly created.

Persis would ask Justen, except she wasn't supposed to be curious about things like that.

"Whatever you believe," she said at last, "you ought to watch your tone in the Albian court. Not everyone is as sympathetic to the ideals of your revolution as the princess is, and you don't want to make enemies in your position." He was staring at her now, so she flipped her hair behind her shoulder and gave a careless, flirty shrug. "I'm no politician, but I know how to get by at court."

Justen nodded. "You're right. I'm too used to the

attitudes back home. I'll . . . try harder." He gave her what was surely meant to be a hopeful smile. "I am aware not all aristos are evil, you know."

"I do?" She cocked her head. He *was* cute when he smiled. It softened his whole face, making his eyes crinkle up a bit at the corners and turning those cheekbones of his from severe and serious to . . . well, surely *sexy* was well beside the point.

"*You're* all right. I mean, except for that thing on your head. Anything with that many feathers that can't fly is definitely evil."

She touched the fascinator and pouted. "I'll have you know this is my second-best hat."

The *Daydream* glided into its berth and Slipstream clattered onto the dock, catapulting his long body off the side and into the clear green water beneath.

"Oysters," Persis explained to Justen. "There's nothing Slippy likes better."

The cliff face rose before them, vertical and seemingly sheer. They strolled down the dock toward the lift and Persis peeled off her wristlock so her palmport could tell the door to open.

Justen chuckled.

"What?" she asked.

"Just a memory from last night," he said. "Andrine and I had a horrible time trying to activate your port long enough to key in the passcode on the lift. Neither of us liked the idea of hauling you up the switchbacks."

Persis glanced up at the ancient, zigzag road carved

into the cliff. It was the remnant of another time, a long-ago owner of Scintillans who'd populated the switchback trail with Reduced servants acting as beasts of burden. But the lift had been installed long before the cure. The Blakes had been progressive aristos for generations. "I suppose if you're going to stay here, we should get you your own passcode."

"Am I?" Justen asked as the doors to the lift opened and they entered.

"Well," said Persis, "it depends on how well you impress my father." The round room was large enough for ten passengers at a time, but Justen pressed his hands against the windows as if trying to escape as the lift rose into the air. She stayed where she was, in the center of the lift, watching him. The seaward walls bowed outward, large panes of glass revealing the vast, glittery channel beyond. Sometimes, when the weather was clear enough, you could almost make out Galatea, but though her companion scanned the horizon diligently, a haze blocked the southern view.

"Homesick already?"

Justen didn't respond.

With a jolt, the lift came to a halt and the solid back doors curled open like petals, revealing the Scintillans front lawn and every last one of its inhabitants, arrayed in their holiday best and standing at attention.

Her parents were stationed at the head of this ostentatious display. Persis stifled a groan. She knew what was coming.

"Justen Helo," said her father, spreading his arms and grinning broadly. "Welcome to Scintillans. It is an honor and a privilege to have you here as our guest." Her mother, holding tightly to her husband's arm, smiled as well. Every servant in the household looked ready to break into song, and if Persis knew her papa, they'd been rehearsing all morning.

Justen turned to Persis and raised his eyebrows. She shrugged. "Don't look at me. If there's one thing Papa likes, it's going overboard."

"Oh," said Justen with a wry smile. "It's genetic, then?"

# Seven

BEFORE THE REVOLUTION, THE royal palace in Halahou had been a monument to the selfish extravagance of its inhabitants. While peasants fought for equal rights against their cruel aristo masters, Queen Gala and her cronies knew no lack, experienced no injustice, and suffered from none of the problems that formed the daily fabric of life for every other Galatean. Was there a sickness? A legal dispute? A case of an aristo terribly mistreating a reg? The queen didn't care. She didn't even notice. She did nothing—nothing at all to help the people she ruled.

Vania Aldred reminded herself of this every time she walked past the old queen's portrait. She knew her father hadn't painted over the mural in the public courtyard for that very reason. The only alteration he'd made were the words in nanopaint that now flashed across the monarch's frescoed face.

*TYRANT*

Vania spit on the ground in front of the portrait as she

entered the gates. Queen Gala, the tyrant. Queen Gala, who had died too soon to fulfill the promise of the punishment her father had devised. The other aristos would suffer in her place—them and any other enemy of the revolution.

And that included that stupid, flowery Albian spy. Leave it to some aristocratic idiot to come up with such a deplorable and embarrassing code name. It was a wonder anyone took him seriously at all.

But they did. And her father would take it especially seriously once Vania reported that she'd lost the Ford children to the Wild Poppy.

The interior courtyard was occupied by a small group of police trainees in the midst of hand-to-hand combat practice. As she passed, Vania straightened. Most of her classmates were still in the program, while she'd sped through training and was already rising up the ranks of her father's military order.

"Citizen Aldred!" the instructor called to her. "You're just in time. I'm teaching a few maneuvers you'll remember from your own training days. Care to favor us with a demonstration?"

Vania smiled at him. This instructor was a bit of a suck-up, always looking for preferment from her father, but at the same time, her combat ranking was an objective fact. "Certainly." She slipped off her jacket and joined the group.

The cadets lined up, and Vania took her place in the courtyard. Her first opponent was clumsy and slow. She dispatched him easily. The second cadet was skilled at defending herself from blows but had no offense to match.

After thirty seconds, she, too, was lying in the dust.

The third, a tall, slim woman, approached with a determined look on her face. She had at least ten centimeters on Vania, and probably a few years, too. At eighteen, Vania was the youngest officer in the entire Republic of Galatea, just as Justen was the youngest scientist in the royal—rather, the republic's—labs. Vania tossed her hair over her shoulder as the cadet, Sargent, took a stance opposite her. She couldn't afford to lose these sparring matches—not today. Not after her error at the Ford estate. To get beaten by a mere cadet would just lend fuel to the fiery rumors that Vania held her position only because of her father.

With a swift kick at her midsection, the fight began. Vania deflected the kick with the padded calf of her uniform pants, then ducked out of the way when Sargent followed it up with a punch. They circled each other, swiping and jabbing ineffectually. The cadet had excellent form and good instincts. She seemed to know exactly how Vania planned to defend herself from each attack. Vania moved in, changing her approach. Sargent, being taller, had a longer reach and could more easily protect her body, but Vania had a lower center of gravity. She made herself as small a target as possible and darted in, aiming her blows at Sargent's knees to try to knock her off balance.

The cadet jumped back, then landed a punch to the side of Vania's head. Breathless, Vania landed hard on her back, her hair momentarily obscuring her view. She pushed her bangs from her eyes to find Sargent standing over her, triumphant.

No, she refused to let it end like this. Vania quickly twisted the bracelet she wore and grabbed Sargent by the ankle. The cadet let out a cry of pain as every nerve from hip to toe shut down and she collapsed.

Vania calmly sat up and brushed dust from the sleeves of her jacket. She pushed herself to her feet.

"Cheater!" the cadet gasped between whimpers of pain. "That was a pricker—you didn't say we could use weapons!"

Vania blinked innocently. "I'm sorry, Cadet. Question: Do you think the royalists I fight are polite enough to refrain from using whatever weapon they have at their disposal?"

The instructor gave a nervous chuckle. "And let that be a lesson to all of you. Citizen Aldred has a very good point."

Another cadet came to help Sargent up. Her leg was twitching, and Vania averted her eyes. The pricker contained only a little cone snail neurotoxin, but the cadet wouldn't be in control of her muscles for a good hour. The other cadets looked on, silent and skeptical, despite their instructor's ruling that her tactics had been fine.

Who cared what they thought? Vania was right—the royalist resistors wouldn't play fair in fights, so why should the revolutionaries? The point was to win, not to be fair.

VANIA HAD HOPED TO see Justen or Remy before dinner, but it didn't happen. Apparently, neither of her foster siblings had been in the palace since before last weekend. Remy was on some sort of school trip and Justen was no doubt buried waist-deep in research at the lab. Ever since the revolution started, they'd hardly spent any time together. Remy, especially, bore the brunt of Justen's and Vania's dedication to their work. It was good she was more mature than most fourteen-year-olds. And, of course, she understood the importance of the revolution.

Showered and dressed for dinner, Vania took the seat at the foot of the table, the one that had once been reserved for her mother. On her left sat two of her father's most trusted advisers, and on her right were the two empty chairs belonging to the Helos.

Vania gave a quick shake of her head, her black bangs shivering on her brow. If Remy was out east on her field trip, that was one thing, but what excuse did Justen have to miss dinner yet again? His lab was right here in Halahou, but his absences were par for the course of late. He was glued to his chair at the lab—either that or performing genetic counseling sessions for families of the Darkened in sanitariums. Miserable wretches. Vania didn't know how Justen could stand even being near them. If she were to find out she would Darken, she'd throw herself off the nearest cliff rather than wait for the end to come naturally. Word on the streets was that the Reduction drug was better . . . but not by much.

There was the sound of a throat being cleared at the other end of the table and Vania raised her eyes. Her father had come at last. Citizen Aldred presided over the head of the table, his back straight, his coat buttoned to the neck and bearing every medal and insignia the old queen had ever awarded him when he was just the head of the reg militia.

Vania had asked him once why he still wore them, since the old queen and indeed the entire old system of government were such a disgrace.

"Symbols are important, Vania," her father had explained. And right now, the populace clung to symbols of the old regime. They trusted Aldred both for his long service to the old country and for his promises about their new one.

Symbols, like those stupid leis and nanotech wild poppies Vania kept finding everywhere. It wasn't just that the Wild Poppy was snatching the odd aristo out of the work camps. It was that he had to be so ostentatious about it. It appealed to vain aristo hearts and undermined the purity of the revolution.

"Citizen Helo isn't gracing us with his presence again this evening?" Citizen Aldred asked wryly. "And with you home from your siege, too, Vania. We're to be a small party tonight, it seems."

Vania's brow creased. She'd been too busy with the Ford barricades to contact Justen, but if she thought about it, it had been almost a week since they'd exchanged words at all. Maybe this was what being grown-up was really all about. Justen was busy with his research; she was busy with her father's revolution. When they were younger, they'd shared everything, but they were no longer children, and they weren't like Vania's old schoolmates either, who spent most of their days wandering around Halahou, party-ing with genetemps and gossiping, as idle as any aristo. The last time she'd made an effort to socialize with them, they'd been more interested in discussing their various romantic entanglements than in the world-changing revolution happening around them.

Vania and Justen were above all that. They had serious matters on their minds.

The company at the table joined hands and bowed their heads as Vania's father began to speak.

"We gathered here tonight to give thanks to those who came before us: Darwin and Persistence Helo, who witnessed the suffering of the Reduced and devised the cure."

Vania smiled into her plate. Even without her foster siblings' presence at the table, the Helos were not to be forgotten. Remy and Justen were both understandably proud of their heritage. Vania's father encouraged them to be, and he always claimed the Helos were the best regs who ever lived—at least until now. Vania was sure that people would start exalting the Aldred name in the same way soon enough. After all, the Aldreds were the ones to finally free the regs from their aristo enslavement.

"We are also eternally grateful to the creator of New Pacifica, he whose name is lost to history due to the tyranny of the monarchs and the enslavement of the people. Without the work of this unknown genius, humanity would have never survived the wars."

There was a chorus of nods and murmured agreement around the table. Vania was glad that, since the revolution, the true story was coming out. When she'd been growing up, she'd been forced to learn the monarchy-approved version: that the islands of New Pacifica had been terraformed and settled by the first Queen Gala and King Albie as a refuge after the Wars of the Lost had rendered every other land on Earth uninhabitable.

But it was far more important to emphasize the truth—that the land itself had been created by the last general, the one who'd won the last War of the Lost by cracking open the Earth and killing all his enemies. Had he not done that—whoever that brave man was—there would have been no New Pacifica in the first place.

The aristos who'd ruled the land for so long were nobodies—probably descended from janitors or servants on the Lost General's ship. The only reason they hadn't ended up Reduced was that they'd been too poor to get the genetic enhancements that had accidentally caused Reduction. And then they'd taken advantage of the Reduced descendants of the people who'd really won the war.

Like the Lost General. No one knew what had become of him and his family. They were Lost, their children Reduced, and the aristos had never kept records about that sort of thing. It could even be the Aldreds. Probably was, considering that Damos Aldred was such a great military mastermind, too.

And Vania was determined to be just the same.

As the first course was served, Citizen Aldred directed his attention to his daughter. "How is the siege of the Ford plantation progressing, Vania?"

"Very well, sir. I'm told the fortifications will fall in less than a week."

"Excellent." Her father smiled. At his right, General Gawnt rolled his bulbous eyes, but Vania did her best to ignore it, as she did all his snide remarks and badly hidden whispers of "nepotism" and "brat." Vania was young to be captain, and some people had a problem with that. But she didn't know why anyone should be surprised. She had an aptitude for leadership and politics, like her father. Just because they had the same talents and went into the same line of work did not make them like the aristos, whose hereditary positions and privileges had been the bane of Galatea. It would have been wasteful of her father not to take advantage of her natural talents over some quibble about favoritism, just as it would have been wasteful of him not to utilize Justen's scientific genius, just because his name was Helo. The revolution would never have been this successful without Justen's contribution.

She wished Justen were here. She doubted Gawnt would be making these comments if Justen Helo were looking him in the eye.

"I heard a report that you were using unconventional methods to convince the Fords to surrender," said another of the lieutenants. "How did that work out?"

Vania grimaced. "Unfortunately, it didn't. We bribed the nanny to smuggle the children beyond the barricade, believing that the parents would surrender themselves for their offspring's sake."

"Good idea, Vania," said her father, and she beamed.

General Gawnt cleared his throat, and Vania's smile withered.

"Unfortunately, the nanny was a moron and lost the younger ones to the Wild Poppy."

"The Poppy!" General Gawnt snorted. "Again?"

Vania took a deep breath. "However, there is good news. The nanny failed to retrieve the heir, so there's no real harm done. Lord and Lady Ford will surrender eventually, and when they do, we'll have them, the heir to the Ford estate, and their entire inner circle."

"Why didn't you tell me about this before, Vania?" her father asked.

"I handled it." Vania clenched her hands beneath the table as all eyes turned in her direction. "The servant has been appropriately punished, only the youngest children escaped, and the siege remains on schedule."

"*Appropriately punished?*" echoed Gawnt. "How?"

"Reduction, of course."

"Did you interrogate her first?" he asked. Vania wondered whether or not the man was capable of speaking without spittle flying from his lips. "Did she give any information that might help us track down this Poppy?"

"She was an idiot!" Vania insisted. "She didn't even need the Reduction pill, she was so stupid. She handed those children off to a random old woman who gave her counterfeit money. She knew nothing of consequence."

"Well, we'll never know now, will we, *Captain* Aldred?" Spittle, spittle.

Vania bristled, and bristled even more when her father, of all people, came to her rescue.

"The salient point here is that this Albian spy is stepping up his activities on our soil," her father said, and all other conversation ceased. "It is time we respond with force and shut him down for good. We need to find out his identity and neutralize him."

"Which is why an interrogation of witnesses might have been prudent," Gawnt murmured. Louder, he said, "Is there any doubt about the kind of person we're looking for? Clearly, this is the case of an Albian aristo who is frustrated by what he feels is the utter uselessness of the child princess currently ruling their country." He sneered in Vania's direction.

She imagined all the instruments on the dinner table that might make a suitable weapon. How dare he liken her to Princess Isla of Albion? Some inbred, spoiled-brat, empty-headed aristo who wouldn't even be allowed the *appearance* of ruling if the infant king were old enough to take the throne? They were nothing alike at all.

"Do we keep any records of what aristos have been visiting the island?" Citizen Aldred asked.

"If they pass through the Halahou docks," said the general. "But there are plenty of unregistered moorings all over the island. It's unlikely that the spy is going through the city unless he has to."

"I think it's time to go to the source," said Vania. "The Albians are sending spies to us. Perhaps it's time we send our own spies to their shores, find out who's responsible for the raids. There must be gossip in the Albian court—"

"Enough, Vania," said her father. "Just because you're sitting at this table does not mean you can forget your rank. General Gawnt knows what he's doing here."

"But, Papa—"

"I said enough!" Citizen Aldred brought his hand down on the table.

Vania stared at her father, her eyes wide and unblinking. She would not cry in front of these people. Under the table, she twisted her napkin until it tore.

Gawnt proceeded to drone on, outlining his plan to ensnare the Albian spy and getting in quite a few jabs at Vania's expense. After a while, she tuned him out. She tuned them all out. Instead, she thought of her long-ago ancestor, the military leader who'd cracked apart the Earth and killed every person he hated in one fell swoop.

# Eight

THE GALATEAN PERSIS HAD brought home to her parents strode forward and bowed to the Blakes. Persis trailed behind, concerned both about how Justen planned to behave and what her parents must be thinking.

"Lord and Lady Blake, thank you so much for your hospitality—"

"Not at all," said her father. "Had my daughter truly been hospitable, you wouldn't have spent last night in some back bedroom. I don't know what Persis was thinking."

Oh, that was easy. She hadn't been. She'd been unconscious. Persis was half surprised—and fully relieved—that Justen said nothing. She was in enough trouble for bringing a boy home, Helo or otherwise.

"Papa!" she exclaimed. "Justen isn't fancy—"

"Please," her father continued, "we have a suite reserved for our most illustrious guests. You must take it. The king has stayed there."

And the princess had camped out on the lanai with

Persis when they were six. It was hardly hallowed ground.

"Thank you, but your 'back bedroom,' as you put it, is more than comfortable. It's the finest place I've ever slept."

That, Persis realized, was a lie. The Aldreds had been living in the royal palace since the queen had been deposed, which meant Justen must have been living there, too.

"Then you're welcome to remain there," said her mother, her voice soft as a sea breeze. She was as stunning as ever—the jewel of the Albian court, the joy of her husband's eye. Theirs had been a romance of fairy-tale proportions: the beautiful reg who'd won the heart of the richest lord in Albion. But Persis knew the truth. Not only had the heroine of the story been beautiful, but she'd been clever and resourceful, too, and her brains had attracted the handsome hero every bit as much as her lovely face.

If you only looked, you'd think nothing had ever changed.

"Our home is yours, Citizen Helo."

Beside her, Justen gave a tiny jolt. It wasn't the first time Persis had noticed it. It happened whenever someone called him "Citizen." Curious. No matter what arguments he made about the purity of his imaginary revolution, he clearly hated its reality. He hated his new title, and he'd abandoned the homeland that had given it to him. And yet there was no doubt he and his egalitarian ideals would have trouble adapting to the lifestyle of Albion. She recalled his treatment of the Seris and his disdain of her clothing and palmport. For Justen, opulence and snobbery went hand in hand.

"Mama, Papa," Persis said, "Justen is overwhelmed by all this. You forget, he's a proud reg."

"Not too proud," Justen clarified, "to accept the gracious hospitality of my new friend's parents." He bowed again, this time over her mother's extended hand, and deposited a kiss on her skin. "Your home is stunning, Lady Heloise, and its beauty and good nature are eclipsed only by the people who live here. Persis and I apologize that you were not told earlier of my arrival. It was unexpected. Your daughter took ill on a trip to—on her yacht—and I was fortunate to be in the right place to offer her assistance. I decided it was my duty to watch over her until she recovered. Since then, we have become fast friends."

Persis raised her eyebrows at him in surprise and approval. Her father was doing the same.

"We'll make up for our earlier lack now," her father said. "Come this way. We've planned a spectacular dinner. You do like tilaprawns, I hope?"

Justen nodded, and Torin dismissed the servants with a wave of his hand. They all started up the path that led back to the house. Justen walked ahead with her parents, chatting casually about the grounds, the meal, and whether or not he'd need a tailor sent over to make him more clothes for his stay. Whatever contempt he'd shown to Persis earlier, or to the Seris back at the court, seemed to have vanished completely. He was pleasant and engaged. Perhaps her little pep talk down on the boat had done some good, after all. Nice to know he'd been listening to her.

Wait, *was* it nice? She didn't want him thinking she was smart enough to dispense good advice on anything more complex than matching his shoes to his shirt, after all.

They ascended the wide, shallow steps of the terrace to the main building, where Persis noted that her parents had moved the formal dining table to the outdoor lanai and arrayed it with leis of frangipani and enough orchids to overwhelm a king. She covered her smile with her hand, sure that the more they went out of their way to impress Justen, the more he'd feel out of place.

"What a beautiful table," was what Justen said as they awaited their first course. He brushed a lei aside to examine the grain of the wood. "I've never seen anything like it." Hardwood like this was a rarity on the islands. Most furniture was made of polymer, stone, or bamboo. The majority of floors in Scintillans were composed of polished bamboo or crushed onyx, and the wide terraces that circled the main house like the lip of a mollusk shell were inlaid with stone in vast, undulating waves of black and red.

"It's called cherry," said Torin. He took a sip of his wine. "It's a relic my family has kept from before the Reduction. There isn't another one like it in all the islands."

"Beautiful," said Justen, his voice laced with proper appreciation. "I didn't realize the aristos could take anything so . . . bulky . . . with them in their escape from the old lands."

Persis gritted her teeth, but her father merely chuckled. "You are wondering, I suppose, if my ancestors denied a Reduced passage in order to fit the table into their cargo? I often wonder that myself. Sometimes I think it's a relief that so many of the records of the old time have been lost.

I cannot imagine I would like many of my own ancestors. If we let ourselves dwell on it too much, we'll end up like those Peccants on your island, in a constant state of punishment to atone for humanity's sins."

The Peccants were a tiny monastic order on Galatea that believed New Pacificans should not be allowed to live full lives after the dire fate that befell the rest of the world. Persis could understand why the notion hadn't ever made it to the mainstream.

"However," her father went on, "I am comforted, some, by an ancient saying: 'Every king springs from a race of slaves, and every slave had kings among his ancestors.'"

"That's Plato," said Justen. "I've read him."

"Ah!" Torin clapped his hands. "Then you and Persis must have plenty to talk about."

"Papa," Persis said lightly, "I just had to read him in school." No good could come of having Justen think she was up on ancient philosophy.

But Torin Blake wasn't to be swayed. "But, Persis, you couldn't stop talking about the classics! You made me take the Blake collection out of cryostorage so you could see them on real paper."

She rolled her eyes for Justen's benefit. "Three *years* ago," she said, as if Torin might as well be speaking of a time before the wars.

Still, she remembered the occasion fondly. She and her parents had spent hours poring over the stiff, cryoclaimed old volumes, reading the inky words on the dry, crumbly pages. Her mother had never seen real books before, and Persis knew only the few volumes they'd kept in cryostorage at school. Persis's favorite had been the poem about the clever, seafaring king who'd traveled around magical islands trying to find his way home to his loyal wife after winning a long, long war. Her father's had been a scary book about an aristo medic who'd gengineered a human out of corpses and lightning and was understandably horrified by the results. Her mother's had been the sad story about the farmhand with the Reduced brother he'd been forced to kill.

She wondered if her mother even remembered that story now.

"At any rate," Torin was saying to their guest, "I live in hope that people will judge me for myself and not any evils that may have been wrought by my ancestors."

Justen nodded solemnly. "I hope to be judged for myself, too, sir. But, as you see, we are both hampered. You by a heritage of aristos stretching back generations, and me by the name of Helo. If I were any simple reg who showed up at your door, I doubt you'd have prepared such a feast."

For a moment, Lord Blake just stared at Justen, then he threw back his head and guffawed, a sound so loud that his wife startled at it. "I think I like you, young man. There aren't many who would sit at my table and call out my own hypocrisy."

"Spend a little more time with Justen, Papa," said Persis. "You'll learn needling aristos is his favorite activity."

Justen looked scandalized. "I don't think you're a hypocrite, Lord Blake," he said quickly. "You and your family have shown me nothing but kindness since my arrival in

Albion. Even before. And it's obvious that, aristo or not, you have no prejudice against regs."

"Oh no," said Lady Blake softly and with a wry smile. "We always like regs."

"I wasn't speaking solely of you, Lady Blake. All the regs on Scintillans. I met Tero and Andrine Finch at court today, and they told me how your scholarships helped Tero get his gengineering degree. If the estates in Galatea invested in their people like you clearly do, I doubt there would have been a revolution at all."

How Persis longed to voice a response to that declaration. But her mother was speaking again, and such an occasion had become so rare that neither Persis nor her father dared interrupt.

"I think," said Lady Blake, "that Plato's words are apt. The aristos of these islands enslaved the Reduced for generations. They should have been their caretakers, and instead they became their tyrants. And yet, they're descended from the poorest and most disenfranchised of all in the old lands, which is why they never received the genetic enhancements that caused the Reduction in the first place. And it was the ancestors of the Reduced who began the wars, who destroyed the old lands. No one is innocent in the tide of history. Everyone has kings and slaves in his past. Everyone has saints and sinners. We are not to blame for the actions of our ancestors. We can only try to be the best we can, no matter what our heritage, to strive for a better future for all."

Even, thought Persis, if we are forced to pay our forefathers' debts.

Her father laid his hand gently on her mother's and squeezed. She smiled, but said nothing more for the remainder of the course, as if drained by that effort. Persis, as she had been for months, filled the silence with chatter of her own, tales of the goings-on at court or Slipstream's antics or news of the twins who had just been born in the Scintillans fishing village. Light, easy topics, suitable both for her mother's constitution and for the impression of herself she wanted Justen to have.

As the sun set over the edge of the western cliff and a lavender light descended on the lawn and the terrace, Torin asked Persis to go turn on the lights. She excused herself from the table and headed inside to find the controls, and there her father intercepted her.

"Where did you really find your new friend, young lady?" She turned to find him standing at the threshold to the terrace, arms crossed over his chest. His face was in shadow, and she couldn't tell from his voice exactly how angry he was. "And exactly how did you 'take ill' on your yacht?"

She mentally upgraded her assessment of her father's state of mind from moderately annoyed to highly disappointed. "Seasickness."

"I think not. You've been sailing since before you could walk, and I doubt a Galatean medic just happened to overtake you on the high seas."

"Papa—"

"What did I say about going to Galatea? Do you have any idea what's happening to aristos down there?"

"Yes, I do," Persis said. She had a better idea than almost anyone else in Albion. "But, Papa, the revolutionary government has given immunity to all Albians, and the princess would never let anything happen to me—"

"Something already happened to you, to hear Justen Helo's version of events. And you'll forgive me if I'm not willing to trust the announced promises of a man like Damos Aldred, a rebel leader who is torturing and killing his own people, when it comes to the relative safety of my daughter."

"Princess Isla—"

But her father cut her off. "I think we've done quite enough for Princess Isla around here, Persis. I know how much you love her, but you've already left school to become part of her official entourage or whatever nonsense you two girls are calling it. I'll not have you risking your life or your brain to get her a few yards of silk on top of that."

It was miracle enough that her father had let her quit school. But his mind was too full of care for her mother, and though she hadn't made it part of her argument, she'd let him believe that her mind was too full of it, too.

The excuse Persis had made at the time was that Isla needed her, that it was her patriotic duty to help her best friend as she recovered after her father's death and adjusted to life as the unexpected and very young ruler of Albion. The court was beautiful, but if the revolution in the south had proved anything, it was that it could be as deadly as a pod of mini-orcas to a young and inexperienced monarch. Isla needed to make sure there was at least one courtier she could trust completely.

"But you've been doing so well in school," her father had said back then. "I don't want you to lose yourself in the kind of idle pursuits that characterize most of the ladies at court." He'd never been much for Albian courtiers. Back when every young aristo girl in Albion had been throwing themselves at his feet, he'd fallen instead for a reg who could gut a fish as easily as read a sonnet. Together, he and Heloise had made history. Persis had no intention of letting the legacy die with her generation. "Gossip and court intrigue? Darling, you're the smartest girl on the island, not simply Isla's spy."

If only he knew that Persis's activities at court were the very smallest part of her spying. However, Persis would take each argument one at a time.

"Papa, there's a long tradition of such things. Look at that old story, where the student Horatio left school with Prince Hamlet after *his* father died and Hamlet needed help—"

"And how did that story turn out again? Maybe you *should* stay in school."

Well, Horatio had survived, even if Prince Hamlet hadn't. And anyway, Persis wouldn't be swayed. She had more important things to deal with than school—school where they taught her that the Reduction was over, that war was a thing of the past. School, where they argued these things even as Galateans were being Reduced by the score in a war her government refused to do anything about. She couldn't sit in a classroom while this was going on. She *couldn't*.

And she wasn't going to let a little bout of genetemps sickness stop her now, either.

"I can put a geographical lock on your boat, you know. You won't be able to sail beyond Remembrance Island without my say-so."

"Papa! You wouldn't!"

"I would, and what's more, I'm going to. I've never had to restrict you in this way before, Persis. You've always been so responsible. But I can't have you in Galatea. Listen to Justen Helo if you don't believe me. He has every reason in the world to be happy with the revolution and even *he* thinks it's unsafe there right now. If you get on someone's bad side down there, they won't care that your mother is a reg. They won't have any respect for the fact that you're a close personal friend of the princess. In fact, that might get you into even more trouble."

She started to protest but he cut her off.

"I don't care what Citizen Aldred's official policy is. You could get caught up by a mob and no policy in the world will help you. I don't want you in Galatea. Period."

Well, that was a nonstarter. Period. The Wild Poppy would just have to find alternative transport. The spy's missions had been doubly complicated by the day's events. Not only would she have to find a place to stow her new Galatean charge, now she'd have to find another way to cross the sea.

"Persis? Are we clear?"

She nodded. "Yes, Papa."

He smiled. "Good. Now that this is settled, let's discuss the rules about bringing strange young men into the house while we're not around. You're sixteen. I don't know what kind of nonsense is going on at court, but this is my *home*."

Persis rolled her eyes. "Ask the servants. Justen is a perfect gentleman."

Torin relinquished a smile. "I knew he would be. A Helo and all."

Her parents were both starstruck, Persis realized with a laugh and a shake of her head. Even if Justen *hadn't* been a perfect gentleman, she couldn't imagine her father getting too enraged. And that was a good thing, since the two of them were about to embark on their little cooked-up romance. Maybe it would serve as a distraction for her parents—the idea that she'd fallen for a Helo.

They desperately needed a distraction these days.

As they emerged back on the terrace, Persis was gripped by a moment of fear. They'd left Justen alone with her mother. But as soon as she saw them at the table, she relaxed. Justen was talking animatedly, and Heloise Blake was laughing, a light, musical sound that wasn't heard often enough around Scintillans these days. For a moment, Persis indulged herself with the vision of what this night might have been had everything been different. Maybe Justen Helo was the one from her fantasies: a young, talented medic she'd met on a trip to Galatea, a place where there wasn't a war. Maybe she was simply a schoolgirl studying politics, and she and Justen could be real friends. Maybe they were all having a nice family dinner, and her mother was well, and her father was happy, and all was right in New Pacifica.

Right. And maybe they weren't the only living land left on Earth. Fantasies were nothing more than that, and she wasted her time imagining otherwise. So instead she pasted her most enchanting smile on her face, poured herself a glass of kiwine, and joined them at the table for another round of being pretty and giggly and useless. Justen kept up his end of the conversation, and both her parents were utterly charmed.

"I do support gengineering," Justen said at one point, "but unlike your friend Tero who builds games and pets, I prefer to focus on its more therapeutic aspects—"

"Yes, but like Tero says, you never know what you might stumble across while working on something else," Torin pointed out. "Who knows if some breakthrough might be lurking inside the code for some silly palmport app."

Justen seemed to be having a hard time swallowing a bit of fish. "True," he said at last, coughing a bit. "Sometimes our discoveries are fortunate accidents. Or even unfortunate ones."

"Like with the genetic experiment that caused the Reduction in the first place, all those centuries ago." Heloise shook her head sadly.

Persis's father quickly moved to change the subject. "Tero is such a promising young man. He and Persis have been trying to one-up each other since they were children, you know."

Justen's brow furrowed.

"In collecting admirers, I'm far ahead," Persis said quickly, batting her eyelashes. "Tero is quite handsome with those broad shoulders of his. Like some sort of ancient warrior. But he does chatter on about the dullest subjects imaginable. All this nonsense about chemical reactions and DNA. It's deadly boring."

Her parents looked shocked, and Persis wanted to dive under the table when she imagined what they must be thinking of her. As dessert was served and kiwine flowed, she found it more and more difficult to restrain herself to flaky responses and interjections. Usually, dinners at Scintillans were one place where she could still be herself, still talk about politics and history and, yes, even gengineering like the girl who'd once beaten Tero and Isla and everyone else for top marks in school. But now, even that was taken from her. She ducked the odd looks she was getting from her father. Hopefully, he'd write her behavior off as trying to steer the conversation into a light, casual zone that would make it easy on her mother. But she could hardly bear the confused glances her mother sent in her direction. After all, how many more dinners would they have together? Could she really afford to waste the remaining ones masked as an empty-headed socialite?

After dinner ended, Justen said, "Which way is my room? I'm all turned around right now."

"I'll show him," said Persis and led him down the corridor toward the guest suites. But as soon as they rounded the corner, Justen put a hand on her arm. Persis stopped short.

"Your mother," he said abruptly, his face impassive

and somber. "How long has it been going on? Six months? More?"

"What are you talking about?" Persis asked, though dread trickled through her veins at his words.

"Persis, just stop. She's managing the symptoms well, but it's only going to go downhill from here."

"Honestly, Citizen, I haven't the foggiest—"

He hissed in frustration. "You might be able to hide it from your other silly aristo friends, but I'm a medic. I know DAR when I see it."

# Nine

No one had ever said it out loud to Persis before. Not her father, or her mother, or the family medic who shook her head and frowned during her weekly visits to Scintillans. The word was verboten. Talk of Darkening was banished from the grounds. Never mind that she saw it echoed in the eyes of each servant on the estate. Never mind that she dreaded every time she visited the court that today would be the day the whispers began. That today would be the day the story escaped and became fodder for the gossips. The day it became spoken. The day it became real.

*Did you hear about Lady Heloise Blake? Darkened. Guess that's what comes of Lord Blake marrying a reg. Can you imagine? All that beauty, all that cleverness, drained away like water down a hole. I wonder if their daughter's got it, too?*

For hundreds of years, the survivors of the wars that had cracked open the Earth and destroyed every place and person except those on New Pacifica had lived as two populations: aristo and Reduced. The few natural regs born were viewed as aberrations. Then the Helo Cure came along, promising that every child born would be regular. The cure was adopted by both nations, and the Reduction ended in a single generation. But as with the Reduction itself, the side effects were discovered too late. Dementia of Acquired Regularity was the dark underbelly of the cure, the shadow that lay over the salvation of the human race.

It was inescapable. Gengineers could make fantastic beasts and nanotechnologists could customize every material under the stars, but no one could solve this puzzle. Just like Reduction, Darkening defied science; and again, there were those who wondered if the victims deserved their fate—if they should have been content to remain Reduced.

Without the Helo Cure, Heloise Blake would never have grown into the brilliant, perceptive woman she once was, would never have met Torin, would never have had Persis or lived so many happy years in Scintillans. Some days, when Persis was gripped by the terror of what was to come, she remembered something her mother had said to her long ago. Something she hadn't understood at the time.

"Better a short life lived well."

At first, you might dismiss the symptoms as mere forgetfulness, a slightly spaced-out look in the eyes. But that was just the first few months. Full-blown senility followed, along with loss of muscle control, as more and more areas of the brain were compromised. The year after that came loss of speech, loss of sight, loss of hearing. Most victims wound up motionless vegetables, trapped in a prison of their minds and bodies for the final months before their brains broke down completely and they passed away at last.

The Darkened were usually sent away to sanitariums—that is, if they didn't take their own lives first. They'd escaped Reduction—the worst fate in the world was to be dragged back into its depths before they died.

Which was why the word was forbidden in Scintillans. Her mother was . . . sick. That was all. It wasn't Darkening. It couldn't be. As Heloise's parents had both died young in an accident, there was no proof that either of them had it. No proof that this was, indeed, what ailed Lady Blake.

And since it wasn't Darkening, there was no reason for Persis to get tested. No reason at all for her to learn whether or not she'd lose her mind and die in less than twenty-five years. No reason at all to think about what might lie in her future every single time she looked deep into a Reduced prisoner's eyes and wondered what, if anything, they retained of their former selves while trapped in their mindless hell.

"Persis?" Justen passed a hand before her eyes. His voice was filled with a concern Persis resented at that moment. "You *do* know, right?"

"Shh!" She opened the door to Justen's guest room and yanked him inside. "What part of 'watch your tone' makes you think it's acceptable to start tossing around accusations in my home?"

"Accusations?" Justen asked, incredulous. "It's DAR. She didn't do anything wrong. It's not her fault."

"No," Persis said without thinking. "It's Persistence Helo's."

Justen didn't look away, didn't flinch as she expected.

He met her eyes, his face grave. "Yes, it is. It's horrible. Persis, I'm so sorry."

Now she turned from him, from the pity on his face. They'd hidden it so well for so many months, but it had taken him seconds in her mother's presence to see the truth. If this was the case, soon they wouldn't be able to hide from anyone. Heloise Blake, once the darling of the Albian court, would vanish, and in her place would be a story about some reg who thought she was good enough to marry an aristo and infect the family line. Her mother would die in ignominy, the victim of a disease most aristos liked to pretend didn't exist, because it would never touch them.

And then what? How could Persis go on, pretending to be the perfect aristo daughter, the perfect heir to her mother's place in court, once the truth was known? Would she even be able to keep her position? What would Isla think when she knew what kind of secret Persis had been keeping?

"How long?" he asked again.

"A year." What was the point of lying anymore?

He gave a single nod. "If so, she's doing well. Her symptoms are exceedingly subtle. I trained in a dementia sanitarium. I know exactly what to look for in patients. I doubt the average person would even notice yet."

"That's indeed a comfort," she replied drily.

His mouth quirked up in a rueful little smile.

"What!" She pounced. "What is so funny about our situation?"

Justen sobered instantly. "I'm sorry. I'm so sorry. That was incredibly inappropriate of me. It's just—all the times

I've counseled families about a loved one with DAR—it's never been an aristo before. You sound so haughty. 'Indeed.'"

"*You* are *not* counseling me." He wanted haughty? She could reduce him to a cinder. How dare he come into her house and use forbidden words and ask forbidden questions and raise forbidden concerns? Helo or no, she wouldn't allow it.

"Has anyone been?" he pressed. "Is anyone treating her? What about you, Persis? Have you been tested?"

To what end? What good could possibly come of knowing she had twenty-five years left to live? That she could risk her life saving Reduced aristos and end up just like one herself? That every day she spent pretending she was stupid was just a prelude to the horrible, true mental incapacity she might, like her mother, be doomed to face? "None of your business."

"Actually," said Justen, straightening, "it is. It is, quite literally, my business. Or rather, my life's work. That's what I want to do, Persis. That's why I became a medic, that's why I trained in a sanitarium. My grandmother—she did something wonderful, something that saved so many people—but every time someone honors her for it, every time someone honors *me*, I remember DAR. I think about the people who are dying *because* of the cure. I want to stop it. Forever."

He went to his bedside table and pulled out several oblets. They were old and their surfaces were scratched and dull with age, like scuffed stones. He held them out.

"These were Persistence Helo's. They contain all her work. At the end of her life, she devoted every resource she could to trying to find a cure for the curse she'd unwittingly unleashed upon humanity."

Persis touched the oblets with a tentative hand. So the old medic Helo had been working on a solution, just as Persis had suspected. Just as she'd hoped. And here it was. In Scintillans! "How did you get these? I thought Persistence Helo left all her research to the Galatean Royal Laboratory."

"Which is—thanks to the revolution—under the control of Citizen Aldred. He gave me access to them, back when we were on better terms. I never gave them back."

"You stole them?" Persis dragged her gaze up from the precious oblets to Justen's face, afraid to even contemplate what this might mean. Yesterday, Justen Helo had saved her life. Today, he was promising to save her mother's.

"I had to. Unc— Citizen Aldred isn't interested in DAR. I'm beginning to wonder if he's even interested in helping the regs in general. Right now, the whole revolution is focused on one thing and one thing only—punishing the aristos."

And anyone else who got in Aldred's way, Persis wanted to point out.

"I can't do the work I need to do there. That's why I've come here."

"With stolen oblets."

"No one will notice they're gone, trust me," said Justen. "No one thinks they're even of use, except me. I'm the only person on the lab staff who even cares about this stuff. And if I could have done the research back home, I would have stayed in Galatea."

So he hadn't told them the entire truth. He wasn't seeking asylum because of some vague philosophical objections to the shape of the revolution.

"Galatea," said Persis, heedless of her tone. This was not the time to play flake. She needed answers from him. *All* the answers. "Where you told *my* princess that you no longer believe in what they're doing? Tell me, Citizen Helo, is it the torture you disagree with, or the fact that they aren't giving your research sufficient attention?"

His eyes met hers, keen and so intense that Persis felt the instinct to toss her hair or bat her eyes or do something to deflect the impression she was getting that Justen Helo was seeing her—really seeing *her*—for the first time.

And worse, she almost wanted him to.

But he said nothing for a long moment. "It's both," he whispered at last. He tore his eyes away from hers, and faced the bed. His grip on the oblets was so strong his knuckles had gone pale. "It's all . . . mixed up together."

Persis frowned, an expression she rarely indulged in outside of missions. If what he was saying was true, he could be holding in his hands the key to helping her mother. To helping *her*. If what he was saying was true, then Justen Helo was no ordinary refugee. He wasn't even a simple celebrity refugee. He was a spy, with the potential to save even more people than the Wild Poppy.

Even if he didn't know it yet.

When Justen had first set off for Albion, his grandmother's oblets concealed in his pockets, he knew he'd have to share the secrets to be found within. With Princess Isla perhaps, or more than likely, one of her science advisers. If he hoped to be put to work in the research labs of Albion, he'd certainly be forced to tell the scientists there what he was working on.

But he hadn't expected the first person he'd confide in would be an empty-headed aristo he was supposed to be having a relationship with. Then again, he was no longer entirely sure that Persis Blake was empty-headed. Shallow, sure, and woefully ignorant about every weighty topic affecting both her nation and his own—but she wasn't an idiot. She knew her way around the court. She knew where her loyalties lay. And despite the ridiculous head-in-the-sand approach her family seemed to be taking to Lady Heloise's illness, she wasn't stupid about DAR, either.

There was an unmistakable hunger in the way Persis had asked him for information. It made sense, especially if her family was just trying to ignore the problem, as if that would make it go away. Persis might be flighty, but she was no fool. Her mother was sick, and Persis wanted to do anything possible to help her.

Which meant she might help him as well.

And he had a lot less to fear from Persis than he might from actual scientists. Actual scientists who might start reading more into the research than she would, who would start putting two and two together and figuring out the *real* reason he'd been forced to flee Galatea. Justen still hadn't quite worked out what would happen if the Albians figured that part out.

He was even afraid to face it himself.

"You really think the information in here will help?" she asked now, still examining the oblets.

He nodded. "I do. I think my grandmother was close to a breakthrough when she died. And we've collected so much more data in the last two generations about DAR."

But Persis looked skeptical. "If she was so close, then why wasn't anyone in Galatea able to solve the problem before now?" She shook her head, a furrow appearing on her brow. "I mean, I'm sure you're very smart, Justen, but there are other scientists in your country who have been treating DAR for decades."

"Until the revolution," said Justen, "no one had access to these oblets. They were kept under lock and key by the royal house of Galatea."

Persis looked up at him, her expression unreadable.

Silly aristo. "DAR is a sickness of *regs*," he explained, frustrated. "No one in power in Galatea cared what happened to them." He regarded her carefully. "Can you honestly say it's any different in Albion?"

"We have very nice sanitariums—" Persis began half-heartedly.

"Let me guess. Beautiful gardens, impeccable grounds, bars on every window?" he scoffed. "Don't tell me what they're like. I trained in one. And you know very well it's the same here. There's a reason your family wants your mother's condition kept secret."

Persis said nothing, just stared at him with a defiantly raised chin.

"Your Princess Isla talks about avoiding a revolution,"

he said. "Perhaps she should start by admitting things in her country aren't as different from those in Galatea as she wants everyone to believe."

She pursed her lips. "I wouldn't know much about that," was all she said. "And I don't really care, either."

"Then what do you care about?" he practically shouted.

Persis was silent again. "I care about my mother's future. I know someone who works at the west coast sanitarium. Noemi Dorric. She's a brilliant medic," she added, though Justen wasn't sure he should take Persis's word on the matter. Still . . . "If you're serious about this, I can arrange to have you installed in a laboratory there as soon as tomorrow."

He looked at Persis. "You can do that?"

She rolled her eyes. "Justen, I'm one of those aristos whose crushing power you're always deriding. We can work it for good, too."

"True," he allowed with a chagrined smirk.

She lifted her shoulders. "Besides, even if that weren't the case, you're a Helo and under the protection of Princess Isla. Your only challenge will be finding time to turn down all the invitations you're about to get for your medic services."

"True again. Shall I rely on you to be my social secretary, then?"

At that, the aristo graced him again with one of her dazzling smiles. "You couldn't have chosen better if you tried."

# Ten

FOR A LONG TIME, the soldier called Trina Delmar floated—
weightless, senseless, like she used to at the bottom of the tide
pools in the cove where she and her brother played when she
was younger. Back then, she used to dream she was a fish, and
wished she had the money to get a gengineered sea pony like
the aristo girl up the bay had. But then the revolution had come
and the aristo girl and her parents had disappeared and one
day, Trina had seen the pony washed up on the shore, its marvelous coral flippers ragged and torn, its big, faceted golden
eyes lifeless and swarming with blackflies.

The revolution. It was supposed to save them all.
But then her brother had told her of impossible treasons
and she'd tried to help him, only to be confronted with
bleeding old men and guards who didn't seem to care as
much for equality as for making people pay and a cliff top
where the last person she'd expected to voiced the same
fears as her brother had—fears she didn't even want to
admit were possible.

Senses began to intrude on her solitude. The muffled sound of people talking, far, far away. A light, white and creamy, soft and blurry. The smell of orchids in the air. A soft, melodic tinkle that sounded almost like water in a fountain, but was far too musical for that. And, most of all, the ropes binding her ankles and her arms.

Her eyes shot open to see a bright dome above her head, framed at the edges by palm fronds strung with orchid leis. She sat up, and a wave of dizziness overtook her, but she tensed her muscles and blinked her eyes until her vision cleared.

"Hello, Citizen Delmar," said the woman—or rather, the girl—seated on the dais before her. She was all white from the tips of her high-piled hair to the sculpted white eyebrows against her golden-brown skin to her long cape and shimmering gown. At her feet knelt two handmaidens, both swathed in hooded robes of silvery gray. The princess regent of Albion, Isla. A royal, an aristo, and an enemy of the revolution. "Welcome to my kingdom."

In a rush, the memories flooded back. The Wild Poppy. She'd been captured by the Wild Poppy. She looked desperately around the room for an escape route, for a weapon of some sort. The white cushions and rugs wouldn't help her. The enormous planters would be too heavy to lift, even if she could break free. She tested the bonds and they tightened further.

"Trina," the princess admonished, in a tone that meant she'd probably said the word a few times already. Right. Her name. So they didn't know. That could be useful. "Don't waste your time, dear. You can't escape from nanothread ropes."

"What do you want?" Trina asked. Her voice trembled on the words, which was not ideal behavior for a revolutionary soldier, but it's not as if she'd had much training in that area. She might have skills with a gun, but she was no Vania Aldred.

"To talk to you," said the princess serenely. "Though, to be honest, I personally don't see the value in it. You were captured by a sea mink. You're hardly a crack soldier."

*Just a child*, echoed her brother's voice in her head. *You can't possibly help.* She'd hoped to prove him wrong, and now . . .

"But the Wild Poppy assures me you have potential, and his is an opinion I trust."

"Hers," Trina corrected before she could stop herself. "I saw her. She's a girl."

The princess regarded Trina, her eyes half-lowered, as if she was bored by the whole proceeding. "Nothing wrong with her memory, I see."

Trina felt the urge to cower. It must be that she was effectively at this woman's mercy, bound and imprisoned. After all, she'd not been raised to feel inferior to aristos, to bow her head before royalty.

"This is a waste of time," Princess Isla said now, her tone almost thoughtful. "Let's just kill her where she lies. I have some gengineered neuroeels in my dungeon I've been dying to put to use."

Trina's blood ran cold. She'd seen neuroeels once, while diving for abalone with her brother down at the cove. A whole flock of them had descended upon a manta ray nearby. Her brother had held tightly to her arm as they watched the fight in horror. Not that it had been much of a fight. The ray was big enough to ride on, yet a few seconds into the attack the eels' neurotoxin sent its muscles into spasms. The ray had bolted toward the surface, its massive, seizing wings churning the sea into a froth. Shudders had run the length of the manta ray's body, making its smooth gray skin look like ripples on a pond. The neuroeels clung fast to its white underside, little more than deadly black strings on the wings of a dying angel.

They'd never known what triggered the attack. Her brother had explained that neuroeels generally didn't go for large prey, despite the strength of their poison. He'd wondered, later, if they hadn't been escaped guard beasts, trained to torture people. One never knew what the queen had kept in her dungeons. At least, not until the revolution.

"Please . . ." she whispered. "Please don't." If she died here, her brother would never even know what had happened to her. No one would. Even if there was a record of "Trina Delmar" being captured by the Poppy, she'd still disappear without a trace.

And then her brother would be truly alone in the world.

The princess blew out a breath of air through her nostrils. "And you think this girl would make a good spy? Please. What will happen the first time Citizen Aldred threatens her with a Reduction pill?"

At the sound of the name, Trina flinched again. Citizen Aldred would never Reduce her. Ground her for life, possibly. It was her brother who would kill her for getting into this mess—that is, if she did get out alive.

All she'd wanted to do was help him before his moment of temporary insanity branded him an enemy of the revolution. What did she care about some Reduced aristos? But then she'd gone east and seen what was happening to old men, little children. Somehow, *seeing* the Reduced made all the difference in the world. And she'd started to understand why her brother had risked it all.

A flash of gold hovered near the princess's hand, and she turned over her palm and closed her eyes for a moment. "A bandage on Lord Lacan's thumb," she murmured to no one in particular, "is hardly evidence of sympathy to our cause."

Trina could certainly agree with that. She was not the one trying to stop the revolution. That was all on her brother. The idiot.

Then she cringed, remembering the way the guards had laughed when Lacan had cut his thumb. Remembering the way his grandchildren—*real* children, not practically grown teens like her—had been stumbling about in the field, their voices silenced, their brains wiped. What could they have done to deserve Reduction?

But that didn't mean she was on the side of the Wild Poppy.

One of the handmaidens cleared her throat. Another golden flower buzzed at the princess out of nowhere. Flutternotes, Trina realized. She'd never seen them in person before.

"Perhaps she just wanted to keep him alive to suffer longer," said the first handmaiden, lifting her head. Trina recognized the blue-haired girl from the attack.

"Of course I wouldn't do that!" she snapped.

"Oh, so you wanted him dead?" the princess asked.

"No! I—" Why were they asking her these questions? What did it matter? "I wasn't even supposed to be there, all right?"

Now the second handmaiden raised her head, and Trina saw the face of the girl dressed as a boy who'd attacked her on the skimmer. The face of the Wild Poppy.

"You," she whispered.

"You," the girl who was the Wild Poppy replied, "are not a soldier at all. I knew it. I knew there was something off about you."

"You don't know anything," Trina spat at her. "Especially not how much trouble you're about to be in."

"Oh?" said the princess. "And why is that?"

And then she released her most powerful weapon of all. "Because I'm not Trina Delmar. My name is Remy Helo, granddaughter of Darwin and Persistence Helo, and I'm no traitor to Galatea."

She expected shock, and she got it. She expected disbelief, and she got some of that, too, especially from the princess. But she didn't expect the bark of laughter that the blue-haired one let out.

"She's lying," said the princess. "Remy Helo is a schoolgirl."

"*We* were schoolgirls a few months ago," said the Wild Poppy. She peered out from beneath her hood, her amber eyes keen and penetrating. "She *may* be Remy. I see a family resemblance. And of course, we could always do a quick genetest."

"Family resemblance?" Remy asked, confused.

"Silence." The princess raised her hand. "Speak only when you are ordered to, prisoner."

The Wild Poppy gave the princess a look. "Assuming this story is true, and I'm inclined to believe it, do you think that behavior is going to get you anywhere?"

The princess sighed. "At least this makes the entire operation simpler."

"Does that mean I'm off the hook?" the Poppy said. "I mean, technically, I already fetched her."

"If you mean the public relations aspect, no," replied the princess. "The romance will still be useful."

What were they talking about? They were supposed to fall all over themselves to apologize. She was a *Helo*. "Pardon me, Princess, but I must insist upon my immediate release. I am the foster daughter of Citizen Aldred, the Protector of the interim government of—"

The princess waved her hand at her. "Oh, we know who you are, brat. We just wish you truly were Trina Delmar. She was useful to us, and *you* are an inconvenience."

"One thing is certain," the blue-haired handmaiden said. "We shall not be returning her to Citizen Aldred."

"Oh no?" Remy scoffed. "You think he'll let a Helo remain in your aristocratic hands?"

This seemed to amuse all three young women.

"Here's a question," said the Wild Poppy. "Does anyone in your family know you're here?"

Remy hadn't thought of that. How was Uncle Damos supposed to fight for her return if he didn't know she was imprisoned?

The princess cocked her head at Remy. "Maybe I should use those neuroeels."

This time, however, the threat held no weight at all.

"Why did you take a false name and join the army?" the Wild Poppy asked her.

"None of your business." The only good to come out of this mess was that with Lacan and his family spirited away to Albion, there was a chance Uncle Damos would never discover her brother's betrayal. If the prisoners on the Lacan estate were no longer in custody, no one would ever find out that their pinks hadn't worked properly.

As far as she knew, Justen hadn't sabotaged anyone else's drugs.

"Bet I can guess."

Remy was quite sure the smug aristo spy could not.

"You had plenty of political power as one of Aldred's inner circle. You had no need to take a false name unless whatever it is you wanted to learn was something you figured your foster father would disapprove of. Am I correct?"

Remy swallowed.

"And there you were at the Lacan estate, of all places in Galatea, watching over the aristo who might have been your grandmother's greatest ally. Watching him suffer, watching him bleed. Watching his children and his grandchildren tortured . . . and why?"

Remy could barely meet the older girl's gaze. Her eyes watered with shameful tears.

"So here's what I think. You hated what they were doing to the aristos on the Lacan estate," the Wild Poppy said to her, rising and coming forward. Her hood fell back, revealing hair the color of frangipani and eyes as bright as the scales on that long-dead sea pony. "You don't want to admit it, but deep down, you know your guardian is no longer interested in helping Galateans. He just wants to punish his enemies."

Enemies like Lacan. Enemies like Justen would be if Uncle Damos found out what he'd done. . . .

"The revolution has betrayed you, has betrayed your whole nation. You are not a traitor, it's true. But your loyalty lies not to the leaders destroying your country but to its citizens—all its citizens—who have the power to make it great."

Remy found she could muster no response to this enemy of the revolution. It made no sense at all. This woman—this girl, really—stood for everything Remy hated. She rescued aristos. She was an aristo herself. She undermined the revolution. How often had Remy heard Vania and the other soldiers complaining about the Wild Poppy?

So why was she saying things Remy agreed with?

The Wild Poppy made a quick motion with her left hand, and Remy's ropes fell loose. If she wanted to flee, now was the time. But her heart thrummed in her chest as the spy's words settled into the space between the two girls. How did this Albian know exactly what had happened to her? She looked only a year or two older than Remy, she was clearly an aristo, and yet it seemed she could see right through to Remy's soul.

All she'd wanted was to save her brother, and this was where she'd ended up. In the throne room of a monarch, kneeling before a young girl who was the embodiment of the aristocracy Remy had wanted so hard to fight, the embodiment of the spy Remy had tried so hard to be. This girl who was making her question everything. Everything.

All she'd wanted was to help her brother, but now she wanted more. To help the people the revolution had harmed.

The Poppy held out her hand, and Remy saw the flash of her palmport. No wonder she'd been hiding it under her glove when they'd met in Galatea. There was no way folks would fail to recognize her as an aristo with that hardware in her hand.

"Will you join us?"

"Yes," Remy said, though it was more like a sob. "Yes, I'll help you. Tell me what I have to do."

# Eleven

"THAT WENT WELL," PERSIS said as Andrine led the sister of Justen Helo away.

"It went somewhat differently than expected," said Isla, "but at least you got a well-connected spy."

"I mean for your first interrogation," said Persis, smiling at her friend. "You scared her cold." Remy would never have given them her name if she weren't certain they were going to kill her otherwise.

"Do you think?" said Isla. "I was afraid I sounded a bit comical with all my threats. As if I needed a mustache to twirl like some sort of ancient villain."

"Oh no," Persis said. "It was perfect."

"Really?"

"Yes. Don't change a thing—except maybe . . ."

"What?"

"The eels."

"Too over-the-top?"

"Not at all. The only thing was, you threatened to kill

her where she lay, and then you mentioned eels down in the dungeons—it was confusing. To a prisoner. They can't be intimidated if they're busy trying to parse your geography."

Isla waved her hand. "Semantics." She plopped back on a cushion. "My father used to make threats look so easy."

"Kill many people, did he?"

"Oh no, he was a softie." Isla shrugged. "Then again, he didn't rule in the midst of a war where he had to send his best friend to rescue tortured prisoners, so . . . who knows what he might have done?"

Persis smiled. "Would you really avenge me with neuroeels, Isla?"

"For you, darling, I'd gengineer a neuro*shark*."

"Aww." Persis pressed a hand to her chest. "That's very sweet."

"Well, you're very special to me, Persis. I hope you realize that." Isla's voice was serious—true serious, not the royal serious she'd used on Remy, and Persis's smile slid off her face.

Rescuing the Galatean prisoners was a worthy mission, and Persis bore no illusions that, were she to be caught by the revolutionaries, her punishment would be Reduction or worse, but she'd always figured she was only risking herself and those who'd chosen to join her cause. This was something they were doing to help the people of Galatea. To help Isla, who couldn't manage to convince the Royal Council that war could come no matter how much you tried to pretend it wouldn't, and that helping the Galatean people didn't necessarily mean bringing war to their shores as well.

But Isla's words had cast doubt in her mind. If she was captured by the enemy, what would Isla do? Would the ruler of Albion fight to free her? Might Persis be reason enough for her to defy the Council and jeopardize the very makeup of the government?

"Neurosharks might be overkill," she said at last. "What's the point of their teeth, if their bite contains neurotoxins?"

"True," Isla replied. "Well, I'll leave the details to the gengineers."

Persis wanted to say, "Isla, if they catch me, don't you dare do anything rash."

She wanted to say, "Isla, I know what I'm doing, so think of our country and not our friendship."

She wanted to say, "If I thought this might cause a problem for Albion, I'd stop."

But she didn't. Especially that last one, because the truth was, Persis didn't know if she could. People were being hurt. Innocents. Children. Aristos and regulars alike. Maybe Isla *should* force Albion to take a stand against the atrocities happening in the south.

But until she did, the Wild Poppy would do what she could.

Isla saved her by changing the topic. "Do you really think we can trust her?"

"Yes." Remy Helo was a lot like her brother. Persis remembered what Justen had said last night. How passionate he'd been about his hopes for his country, for a cure for the Darkened. The propaganda from Galatea said the Helos were model revolutionary citizens, but Aldred had no idea how accurate that was. They were *true* revolutionaries. They believed in justice for all Galateans, regular and aristo.

"And are you sure we shouldn't keep her here to appease your little boyfriend?"

"Does he even have to be my boyfriend now?" Persis asked. "There's no need to keep Justen's reasons for being here a secret if we have his sister safe." Persis could already visualize the look of joy on Justen's face once he was reunited with his sister. And it would make everything easier on her, too, if she was no longer forced to squire him around and keep her mask on at home.

"Oh, Persis. Don't tell me you aren't enjoying his company just a little bit. Justen is handsome, politically motivated, and the grandson of the savior of New Pacifica." Isla tapped her finger against her lips thoughtfully. "Isn't that pretty much your dream boy?"

Persis found it highly aggravating how well the princess regent of Albion knew her. "Yes, but I'm Persis Flake, remember? He can barely tolerate me."

"Give him time. He'll fall prey to your charm, just like everyone else."

Persis shook her head. No, not Justen. He needed something more than she was allowed to show him.

"Fine," Isla said. "Beyond trusting her, do you think Remy can actually help us?"

"Living in the palace with Citizen Aldred?" Persis pointed out. "Definitely. She'll have information about new prisoners before anyone else. And you heard Justen. He thinks his sister is a helpless little girl. He doesn't have the slightest idea what she's been up to."

And maybe that was the most useful thing Remy Helo had to offer. She'd already shown herself to be resourceful beyond her years—hacking the military records to give herself a position in the army. She was a spy long before she ever met the Poppy. And no one in her household seemed to know what she was capable of: not her brother and not the Aldreds, either. The best spies were those everyone underestimated. Persis knew that better than anyone.

"And she's so young," Isla added. "Even if she got caught snooping, how could Aldred risk harming her? A child and a Helo? He'd lose too much support with the Galateans."

Persis wasn't sure about that. She'd seen Reduced children—aristos, yes, but still innocents—and the Galateans didn't seem to have too much trouble with that. Still, a Helo was another matter.

"She's not so very little," said Persis. "A year younger than Andrine and every bit as brilliant as her brother, it seems."

"Her brother is 'brilliant'?" Isla said, raising her eyebrows. "From you, that's high praise indeed. The very highest." She nudged Persis. "Maybe you are enjoying playing the devoted girlfriend!"

She might be, if she wasn't forced to pretend to be someone else. She might not even think of it as playing at all. Persis unclasped her gray robe and dropped it to the cushion behind her, shaking out the candle-flame-yellow skirt of her gown. "It's not just me who thinks so. Noemi has been so pleased to have him at the sanitarium this past week. She's as starry-eyed as everyone else when it comes to the Helos."

Noemi Dorric was the de facto head of the DAR sanitarium nearest Scintillans. She was also the chief medic for the League of the Wild Poppy and the Blake family's private—*very* private—nurse. And she'd practically done backflips when she heard Justen was coming and bringing along Persistence Helo's own research.

Isla sighed. "I can't believe he wants to hide away in a sanitarium. It's not exactly the high-profile position I'd prefer for him."

Persis bit her lip, but it did little to lessen the sting of Isla's words. Justen's arguments came back to her then. Maybe they weren't as enlightened as they thought in Albion. Darkening shouldn't be an embarrassment to any family, even an aristo family, so why were they keeping her mother's condition a secret? Why wasn't working in a sanitarium a more honorable, high-profile job? There was an argument to be made that Justen was behaving in the only honorable way a Helo could. Instead of sitting back and enjoying the celebrity Persistence had won for his family, he was devoting his life to fixing the single mistake she left behind. Why didn't Isla get that? Would Persis, too, fail to see its importance if she hadn't been touched by the ravages of DAR?

"Speaking of Noemi, how are her *extremely* low-profile patients doing?" Isla asked. "Have Lord Lacan's grandchildren recovered?"

Persis shook her head. "Still compromised. Detox drugs don't seem to work quite as rapidly on the younger ones."

Noemi and the other medics had expected the opposite to be true. Young minds were more elastic and so they should bounce back more quickly from their ordeal. But after detoxing so many of the Poppy's rescued refugees, Noemi was developing a new theory on how the drug worked. Now, Noemi guessed the gap was due to the way the Reduction drug the Galateans were using not only blocked neural pathways but also prevented new ones from forming. The older victims recovered more quickly as they regained access to pathways their unhindered brains had long used first, then more-recent neural pathways later. But in young minds, the pathways weren't as familiar, and there were fewer. It took longer for children's minds to remember what they'd once known and to start forming new pathways again.

Isla grimaced and fell into step beside Persis. "That can't be easy for the Lacans to see. When I think of someone doing that to Albie—Persis, in that case, I *would* be out for blood. Neuroeels would be too swift a death for Citizen Aldred."

Now there was a sentiment Persis could get behind. "Would you like to come to the clinic and see them? I know it would mean a lot to the Lacans, and you could drop in on your newest medic, too."

The sanitarium was the perfect hiding spot for the recovering Galatean refugees. Since so many of the symptoms suffered by the Reduced were similar to those of the Darkened, the sanitarium already had resources to deal with them. And Persis knew well that Noemi could be trusted to remain discreet. She was one of the few who knew about Persis's mother, one of the even fewer who knew Persis was the Wild Poppy.

Isla made a face. "I have no particular desire to see Justen at work. I'd much rather you spent some time dragging him out in the open. Canoodle a little, my friend. You could start by taking him out and getting him some nicer clothes. Everyone expects you to, anyway."

They exited the throne room and emerged into the bright sunlight of the Albion court. "If I do, you won't get public canoodling. It'll be a public fight."

She'd already tried once to get Justen some new outfits. He'd come to Albion with nothing other than the clothes on his back, and they were in such a severe, revolutionary style that even the Scintillans servants were snickering at the laundry. Justen didn't care.

"I haven't come here for a shopping trip, Persis," he'd said, his tone as dour as his suit.

"Of course not," she'd replied. "Everyone knows the best silks are Galatean."

Justen had not been amused, and after being the recipient of yet another of his contemptuous glares, she hadn't seen much to laugh at, either. In another time, another life, she could have talked to him for hours about what he had come to Galatea for—about politics, about medical research, about everything they truly did have in common. She could have admired him for what he was, and maybe he'd do the same. But what was the point in this world, where he seemed uninterested in the only parts of herself she could risk showing him? From what she'd seen, Justen hardly noticed her appearance and found her taste in Albian fashion faintly ridiculous. She could hardly get to know the attractive Galatean medic better if she couldn't risk being anything other than a silly, spoiled aristo in his presence.

She shrugged. "I have other things on my plate, you know." Sending Justen to work in the sanitarium had a two-fold benefit as far as Persis was concerned. He'd be kept busy enough that he wouldn't question when she disappeared for a day or two at a time on her secret trips south. With Remy in the League now, it was likely she'd see the sister more even than the brother.

"I know you have commitments," Isla said, "but you *really* mustn't neglect your social life." She nodded mean-ingfully in the direction of Councilmen Blocking and Shift, who were standing in the courtyard below, deep in conver-sation. Shift caught sight of Isla and started up the stairs toward her.

"Uh-oh," said Persis's friend.

"Your Highness," Shift blustered at her. "There you are. Your aides said you were sequestered all morning. Another fitting with Lady Blake, I see?"

"What do you wish to discuss, sir?" Isla said, ignoring his dig.

"Princess, it's imperative that we deal with the situ-ation in the east. The regs in Sunrise Village have been blatantly trading with the Galateans, despite the local aristo governor's warnings."

The eastern governor was Councilman Shift's brother, Lord Shift. Persis knew the Council chief didn't think much of Isla, but underestimating her wasn't going to be useful to his cause, either.

"The Lord Shift's embargo is not approved by the Council or the monarchy, Councilman, as well you know," Isla replied smoothly. "And Sunrise Village is an independent township. They are not required to adhere to the advice of the governor."

"But—"

"I can certainly craft a letter of disapproval if you think I ought to, Councilman, but as it happens, I was just discussing this issue with the Galatean lord Lacan—who as you might recall, was recently rescued by the Wild Poppy and brought to our country. He knows well the denizens of Sunrise Village, as they are the closest Albian outpost to his lands. Now that he's here, he wishes to settle in Sunrise Village, as he has many friends in that area due to his family's long association of trading taro for Sunrise Village's milk and cheese across the strait."

"But, Princess—"

"Your brother owns a taro farm, does he not, Councilman? How he would gain if the villagers were required to buy all their taro from him instead. Perhaps he should seek to compete in a more forthright manner."

Persis wanted to cheer for her friend as Councilman Shift's face turned red and he cast about for a response. Isla dismissed him with a nod of her head, then turned to go.

"You ignore regs at your own peril, Princess," he said

to her back. "The more they think they can make decisions independently from you, the more they will. And the more they collude with their revolutionary friends in the south, the more likely they are to decide they don't need you at all."

Persis saw Isla stiffen, but her friend did not stop walking.

"You think they like you because you're soft on them. But all you're teaching them is that you're soft."

Now Isla did turn, and fixed Councilman Shift with her most royal glare. "And if I let your insult pass unpunished, sir? What am I teaching *you*?"

Shift's mouth snapped shut.

Isla walked on, and Persis followed, dying to speak, but knowing they'd have to be well out of earshot of any Council spies.

"Isla," she whispered at last, "that was amazing."

"I don't need your *approval*, Persis," Isla snarled under her breath. "I need your *cooperation*. I rule a nation of free people, and I cannot have the aristos and the regs at one another's throats. They need to know we're all on the same side. You and Justen are going to do that for me. And you're going to do it soon. Do you understand?"

Persis paused, then lowered her head in deference. Isla was her friend and her protector. She was also her ruler, and Persis couldn't fail to support what she'd been encouraging her friend to do for months. "Yes, Your Highness."

# Twelve

JUSTEN WAS OBSERVING THE patients on the sanitarium lawn when he caught sight of Persis strolling up the hill toward the main building. Today, she was swathed in a golden confection that fluttered in strips from her shoulders and around her thighs, revealing enticing glimpses of her warm brown skin. As she moved toward him, the breeze off the bay caught the material so that every strip blew out behind her like a flag.

He averted his eyes. Perhaps it was not so very unrealistic that people would believe he was madly in love. Like her mother had clearly been before her, Persis Blake was extremely attractive. For most people, that would be enough.

And even for Justen, it was extremely distracting. She descended upon him like a flock of very colorful, very loud parakeets. "Justen! How was your day? How are things here? Have you spoken to Noemi much at all? Has she filled your schedule with too many projects? I do hope you aren't booked solid, as I thought we might go for a sail before supper." She threw her arms around his neck and hugged him. The patients, and their visitors, looked on.

Today, most of Persis's hair was worn down, its yellow and white locks and braids swirling around her shoulders and arms like the strips of her unusual dress. She'd twisted a few strands of her hair into a circlet on top of her head, studded here and there with tiny, brightly polished enamel flowers bearing spiky green leaves. Wild poppies, he realized. Every Albian on the island was wearing things like this in support of their most infamous spy.

As usual, the effect was stunning. He hadn't seen Persis with her hair down since the morning after they'd met, when he'd helped her off the bathroom floor when she'd tried to use her palmport too soon. She looked younger this way, more natural, despite the strange hair colors that were, now that he'd spent several days in Albion, not looking quite so strange anymore. As always, she smelled of frangipani, all sweetness and sunshine and soft, pampered skin. As always, she hugged him too tightly and too long, as if they truly were the blossoming lovers they portrayed. And, as always, Justen found he liked it just a tad too much.

He gave her a perfunctory hug in return, then stepped back. "She has certainly put me to work. I appreciate your help in getting me this position. The last thing I'd want is to be a burden on Albian society."

Persis giggled. "Don't worry—besides, you're our guest at Scintillans. We can afford a dozen burdens like you."

He cleared his throat. "I have a lot of work to do, Persis. Is there something specific you wanted?"

She blinked at him, an enigmatic smile playing about her mouth. "It depends," she said coyly. "What are you offering?"

His lips drew into a tight line. Oh, so it was to be play-acting, then. But for whom? The patients here were not in a condition to spread the word about their ersatz romance.

He saw Noemi emerge from the main building and head in their direction. All right, one witness. Madam Noemi Dorric was a skilled medic in her own right, but had taken a job as the head administrator of the sanitarium, rather than the chief medic, for reasons Justen found bizarre. These Albians might be fair to their regs, but they were quite prejudiced against their women. The chief medic was a man Justen had yet to see; and, despite the official roles, as far as Justen could tell, every employee in the place deferred to Madam Dorric.

Justen had followed suit. He liked the woman enormously and was thankful that Persis had made the introduction. The aristo did seem to know enough to surround herself with clever people, even as she bragged about dropping out of school and not caring at all about anything that didn't button or zip. But this was the privilege of wealth and position, Justen supposed. After all, with very little effort, she'd managed to add him to her entourage as well.

Noemi, though, was one of the most no-nonsense people he'd met since landing on Albion. Even her clothes were simple, her hair natural. Her only concession to Albian fashion seemed to be her palmport. He had been surprised to find one installed on an older woman, not to mention a medic, as most he knew disapproved of the device and the way it leeched nutrients and minerals from its owners. But Noemi had explained that she found it very convenient and didn't mind taking the required supplements to keep it operational. Though he'd yet to see her actually use the thing. She usually kept it locked away under one of the ubiquitous leather wristlocks all palmport users wore to protect their devices.

"You're here," she said when she reached them. Justen had learned in the last few days that the middle-aged woman was not much one for small talk. "Good. There's something I need you to see."

"Need *me* to see?" Persis pressed a hand to her chest and laughed. "Goodness, no. I can't imagine what sort of help *I'd* be to you in an awful place like this."

Noemi rolled her eyes. Justen could understand the sentiment. And he was surprised to see Persis acting so flippant about it, given the seriousness with which she'd addressed the subject when it came to her own mother. Maybe this was the way she'd compartmentalized things in her head. After all, Persis had explained that they were refusing to call Lady Heloise Blake's illness what it was. Maybe Persis preferred to pretend that these people here were nothing like her mother. She took the usual aristo position: hide DAR victims away in sanitariums and never think about them again.

Noemi tried again. "I was actually talking to my new recruit, Medic Helo."

"That's better." Persis looked relieved.

"What can I do for you, Citizen— I mean, Madam Dorric?" He'd been catching himself like this ever since he'd been working at the sanitarium. The day he sailed away from Galatea, he thought he never wanted to hear the word again, but now, spending days in the sanitarium, surrounded by reg medics and the reg patients they served, he found the word sprouting unbidden from his mouth. Here he could forget what the revolution had done to him and to his country, how everything he'd ever wanted had been perverted, and recall instead what he'd once so loved about its principles.

"I—" Noemi looked at him for a second, then turned to Persis, looking flummoxed and, as far as Justen knew her, uncharacteristically tongue-tied. Was Persis's ribbon dress rendering her speechless as well? Finally, she sighed. "I really don't have time for this."

"Sorry?" Justen said. Was she letting him go so soon? Did she doubt his commitment to his work given Persis's unannounced arrival? "Madam Dorric, I was not aware that Lady Blake was coming here today—"

But, as always, Noemi got right to the point. "I find you very skilled, medic, and seeing as you're from Galatea, I think you might be able to provide us with some fresh insight."

"What?" Justen asked.

"*What?*" Persis echoed.

"There are a few patients on the lower level I'd like a consult for."

"The *lower level*?" said Persis, sounding skeptical. Her

mouth made a perfect, rose-colored O. "Surely there can be no cause to drag my poor Justen out of all this glorious sunlight simply to look in on a few silly patients."

Noemi cast Persis a weary look and Persis glared at her.

Justen laid a hand on her arm. "Persis, please. This is my job." He looked at her face to find her eyes blazing with . . . was that anger? That he couldn't run off and join her for a sail at the drop of a hat? The girl needed to find some sort of occupation. Her only commitments might be keeping up with her wardrobe and pretending to be in love with him, but Justen had serious work to do. The elder Blakes seemed like intelligent, hardworking people. It mystified him that they'd produced such a shallow daughter.

"Lady Blake, I am sorry to disagree with you," Noemi said, "but whatever *your* priorities are, I am a medic, and my highest duty is to my patients. I've come to the conclusion that Medic Helo here is in a unique position to help them, and so I'm going to ask for his help, whether you approve or not."

Justen wanted to laugh out loud as the medic scolded the aristo like a child. He wondered if anyone had ever been so strict with Persis in all her life. Of course, Persis had said that she and Noemi were old acquaintances. Maybe that's why his new boss felt so free with the aristo.

As he watched, Persis's forehead smoothed out, and she slipped them both a dazzling smile. "Well, I guess we have no choice but to delay our outing."

Justen and Persis followed Noemi into the building and down a hall to a reinforced door she unlocked with her palmport. As she ushered them inside and down a long staircase punctuated by several other locked doors, she explained.

"This is a very sensitive situation, Medic Helo, and I'm sure you understand why I require your absolute silence on what I'm about to show you."

Justen frowned. So much security. Was there some sort of unknown plague going on in Albion? What had he agreed to? And why was Noemi letting Persis tag along? Surely if something was supposed to be a secret, you didn't take the biggest gossip at court to see it. Then again, he supposed Noemi knew how well Persis had kept the secret of her mother's illness. She probably trusted the aristo to do the same here.

Finally, they passed through the last door and into a large chamber. It had clearly been meant as storage when the sanitarium was first built, but Justen saw that someone had put an effort into making it comfortable. There were many cots in the room, and curtains had been erected to separate sleeping and living areas and to give the occupants more privacy. There were touches of decor, too, colorful cushions and vases of flowers, plants and geothermal lights to make up for the lack of windows. There were more than a dozen patients, all ages, all sexes, some lying on their cots; some being entertained by therapeutic oblets or other games; and some stumbling around, talking to walls or swaying in place. That part was normal enough. DAR patients often passed through these phases. But why the young people? Why were there children in a sanitarium? It was impossible that they could be affected so young. And then, he took notice of something even stranger—every one of these people had natural hair. He hadn't noted it at first, since he was used to seeing such things in Galatea.

And then it struck him and he reeled back in horror as the full weight of his crimes smacked him in the face.

These *were* Galateans. They didn't have DAR.

They were Reduced.

Persis had been trying to get Noemi's attention for several minutes, but the medic was studiously ignoring her as she showed Justen around the facility and introduced him to the patients. The older woman must be getting desperate for assistance in solving the problems that plagued the Galatean refugees.

That could be the only reason she'd brought Justen into the fold this quickly. Surely Noemi didn't think this whole campaign Isla dreamed up meant that Persis trusted the Galatean revolutionary with all her secrets. He definitely disapproved of the revolutionaries' tactics, but he had no love for the displaced aristos. That much Justen had made abundantly clear when he'd met the Seris.

Still, he was a medic, and Persis supposed that, just like Noemi, he subscribed to all those old oaths by which medics swore to put aside all personal feelings and treat sick patients to the best of their abilities. Justen, thanks to his training, might be able to sew up the mortal wounds of his worst enemy.

Persis, if she happened upon a bleeding Citizen Aldred, would be hard-pressed not to kick him around a bit more. Well, as long as she could make sure he wouldn't survive to tell the tale and wreck her cover.

"The problems with detoxification have been twofold," Noemi was explaining as she activated an oblet on the nearest tabletop. It sparked to life, emitting a holographic replica of the human brain, colored to indicate areas of damage. "The first is that the younger aristo victims, especially those who were subjected to the drug for long periods of time, have been sluggish in their recovery." She went on to describe the symptoms and difficulties that the children had been experiencing, and Justen listened, his expression somber and impassive. He nodded from time to time as she spoke, and asked Noemi for details about particular cases. But when Persis lowered her gaze to his broad, skilled medic's hands, she saw the way he clenched and unclenched them into fists and the stiffness with which he held his arms slightly out from his sides, as if filled with a tension he dare not let loose.

He looked like he wanted to punch something.

"The bigger problem we have recently discovered lies with the reg victims." She poked at the glowing controls floating before her, and the oblet's display switched to a new brain model.

The tension migrated up to Justen's face. "What do you mean?" he asked softly.

Persis moved closer as well. She was no scientist, but she'd accepted responsibility for the refugees long after the Poppy had seen them safely to Albion.

"We've only recently received victims of reg origins," Noemi explained. "While your government began by torturing only aristos, they've apparently expanded their reign of terror."

"Yes," Justen whispered. "I heard rumors . . ."

"And the regs—they aren't recovering from the drug."

Persis's jaw dropped. In the muffled, blurry distance, she saw Justen nod again, heard him ask indistinct questions of Noemi, heard the older medic's equally indistinct answers. She barely realized she was backing up until she felt the warm, geoheated wall of the room against her bare spine.

They weren't recovering. They weren't detoxing. She was saving them from Galatea, but it was too late—the damage had been done.

"While there appears to be some increase in brain and motor function after a week of detox, they show no signs of regaining their language, motor control, or memories. It's not just that they seem slower to recover, as the aristo children do. The detoxification is having no effect at all."

Those poor people. Those poor, poor regs who'd done nothing worse than speak out against the current regime's cruel methods, only to have that very cruelty foisted upon them in an infinitely worse way. Brain damage. *Permanent* brain damage.

As bad as Darkening.

And the revolutionaries were doing it to everyone. Adults, children. For crimes and disagreements and even petty revenge plots. If any of her spies were captured, it's what would happen to them. To *her*. Persis had thought the Poppy could save them. She'd been wrong.

Persis took several deep breaths and schooled her features into her signature vapidity. Panicking wouldn't help anything now. She joined Justen and Noemi as they discussed the lab results, keeping her mouth shut and her ears open.

Noemi slid the first brain model up beside the second. "We've postulated that the Reduction drug hinders neural pathway functioning and development in the aristo brain, but if you look here"—she pointed at the other—"you can see that the response in the reg's brain shows a marked difference. Here there is a chemical binding of nerve endings. It seals off neural pathways permanently."

Justen was simply nodding as if this all made perfect sense. Perhaps to a medic, it did. "What does that mean?" Persis asked. For once, she didn't have to play stupid. She really did feel out of the loop.

Noemi looked at her, and from the question in the older woman's eyes, Persis could tell Noemi was wondering how much of Persis's behavior was just for show. The medic had never had much patience with the subterfuge aspects of the Wild Poppy, but then again, Noemi knew from firsthand experience how difficult it could be for a woman to get things done on this island. Though she was obviously the most talented medic at the sanitarium, she was kept in the role of administrative official while a man was given the chief title. Noemi held a place of sympathy in her practical little heart for Isla and Persis and their conundrum.

"It's the biological equivalent of putting a bit of resin at the tip of a rope to keep it from unraveling," she explained. "In an aristo brain, we've seen that recovery from the drug involves creating new pathways—basically rerouting neurons around the damaged parts. But when the Reduction drug enters the regs' systems, it changes their brains' ability to reroute those pathways—forever."

"And this is happening to all of them?" Justen asked.

"We've genetested them for DAR, of course," Noemi replied, "given the similarity of symptoms. None are susceptible."

"Are the patients lucid enough to give you a medical history?" he asked. "Do you know if they're natural or Helo Cured?"

"If they're natural regs, they can't Darken," Persis broke in before she even realized what she was doing.

Justen looked at her, his lips compressed into a tight line. He looked as stricken as she felt, as lost. There was no danger, in this moment, that he might see beneath her mask. Whatever he was thinking, his head was too full of it for anything else. "Yes. DAR only affects those regs whose ancestors took the Helo Cure. That's why it's called Dementia of *Acquired* Regularity. Not natural regularity."

"We haven't tried to get that information out of them," Noemi said. "But even if they aren't capable of telling us, we can test for it. Do you think it might be relevant?"

Justen jerked his head up and down. His jaw twitched as if he was clenching every muscle in his face. "Relevant, yes, but not helpful. We should test, just to make sure, but I think you'll find that all your patients are descended from Helo-Cured regs. If my hypothesis is correct, a natural reg wouldn't have this problem."

"Why not?" Persis asked, honestly curious this time.

Noemi looked grave as she put the pieces together. "He's saying the problem is connected to how the cure works, Persis. The reason Reduction was so insidious for all those centuries is that it couldn't be gengineered out of our genetic code. No matter what people tried, the genes would mutate right back into place in the developing embryo."

"Right, but Persistence did something different." Everyone knew that.

"Yes," said Noemi. "The Helo Cure didn't seek to *fix* the flawed code. It merely bypassed the architecture of Reduction, changing the way the brain developed in the womb. And that changes the way it functions. A natural reg, whose genetic code mutated the flaw of Reduction out, has a brain like an aristo's. But a Helo-Cured reg has an— Well, I don't want to call it an artificial boost. But it's a different kind of brain from other humans."

Justen gave Persis a curious look. "Does this really interest you?"

"How my brain might work?" Persis snapped. "A little." Let him think she cared on behalf of her mother. That she was still thinking about DAR. He could allow Persis Blake to be serious about that, at least.

"All right. Imagine a road that's perpetually flooded," Justen said. "That's Reduction. The road exists, but it's useless. With aristos and natural regs, the road's built on higher ground. It doesn't get flooded. With the Helo Cure, we built a bridge. However, the flooded road is still there. The flaw that causes Reduction still exists in the reg's genetic code, but there's a workaround now. That's what Persistence Helo did. She gengineered an early end to the Reduction."

Before Persistence Helo and her cure, only one in twenty Reduced births resulted in a naturally reg offspring. If they waited around for generations, Reduction would have died out eventually. But Persistence Helo, like Persis, didn't have that kind of patience. She fixed the entire population in one fell swoop.

Even though that meant side effects.

"There are some," Justen said, "who argue that DAR is more common in genetic lines that were farther away from producing natural regs. But there's no way to know now."

"And that's not relevant to this case," Noemi added, practical and focused as always. This is why Persis had wanted her so badly for the League. She was older than most of her other confidants, and she rolled her eyes at many of Persis's ideas, but her heart was true. Like everyone in the League of the Wild Poppy, Noemi Dorric cared only that Galateans were being tortured, and that it was wrong. She wasn't political; she wasn't snobby. She just wanted to stop people from being hurt.

And now it looked like that was a lot harder than anyone had imagined.

"So the damage being done to the reg refugees is connected to the way their brains work?" Persis asked.

Justen nodded. "We'd know for sure if the Poppy comes across a Reduced prisoner who's a natural reg. And they're much rarer."

If the Wild Poppy had her way, she'd start rescuing Galateans long before they became victims of this terrible drug.

Justen was still studying the lab results, his gaze intense, almost manic. Persis knew that look—it's the one she wore when the Wild Poppy was in charge. It was the one where everything fell away except a singular focus on her quest. There was no chance of taking him on a splashy public outing this evening, no matter what Isla wanted. Tonight, people needed him.

It was a glory to behold, actually. She'd agreed to host Justen the way she'd support anyone who wished to take refuge from the revolution, but she hadn't expected what she'd find in him. His medical skills might be a boon to her mother and now a boon to these poor Galateans, too. But even more than that, Justen had taught her the truth about the revolution.

All the other refugees she'd talked to after their detox so far had been real enemies of the revolution. Their feelings about it were purely negative, which was understandable, given their experiences. Upon meeting Justen, she saw a different side entirely, a side that she might have sympathized with before everything had gone so terribly wrong. Persis never would have understood Remy's mindset had she not seen it in her brother first.

These were the true revolutionaries, these Helos, these citizens who believed that things in Galatea had been bad, that they had to change—but were horrified at the way Citizen Aldred had perverted their desires into cruelty, revenge, and torture. And the fact that Justen and Remy could hold these feelings while being raised in Aldred's house—it was a testament to their inner strength.

There must be others in Galatea who thought the same way but were too frightened to act, given Citizen Aldred's swift and severe punishments. Unlike the Helos, they didn't have the protection of their names. But if others could be reached, if people who thought like Justen and Remy could be marshaled to pose a challenge to the reign of terror, then maybe they could find a way to stop all of it, and then no one would need asylum.

Or the Wild Poppy.

Could she ever be satisfied with merely running the estate and being a dutiful daughter to her parents after these months of adventures? Persis didn't know. But once the Galateans were no longer in danger, there would be no need for her alter ego, or for the mask she wore when playacting as Persis Blake. Maybe then she could finally talk to Justen as an equal.

Or maybe even sooner than that. After all, he was already helping the League of the Wild Poppy by assisting the refugees. And even his sister was taking part in the operations.

Maybe it was time to tell Justen who she really was. This latest development should kill any remaining loyalty he had left for the twisted travesty his revolution had become. Justen, who held so much respect for his grandmother's work, who had dedicated his life to fixing every flaw in her great achievement—he couldn't stand by and watch his leaders take it apart. Couldn't let them threaten his fellow citizens like that.

His fellow citizens, but not himself. Justen was a natural reg, she remembered with a sudden chill. He was natural, and she, though an aristo, might have a Helo-Cured brain. If either of them were ever captured by the Galateans and dosed with this drug, Justen would recover, while Persis—

She might learn what it was like to Darken a few decades early.

# Thirteen

SEVERAL HOURS LATER, PERSIS and Justen were still at the sanitarium, with no sign of departure on the horizon. Justen and Noemi had tested the regs in the facility and learned that Justen's hypothesis was correct—every one of them was descended from those who'd received the Helo Cure. The next step was seeing if there was a way to counteract or overcome the effects. To pass the time, Persis was playing chess on the floor with a few of the recovering patients. But she wasn't paying careful enough attention. She kept accidentally winning.

She'd also fired off a few flutternotes whenever she was sure no one was watching. She fluttered Isla that a problem at the refugee base was keeping her from fulfilling the princess's public relations quest, but that she and Justen were working on it together. She fluttered Andrine to get an update on Remy's transport back to Galatea. Andrine had been charged with giving the girl some very explicit instructions as to what she was to do when she arrived home, since Persis didn't want to place Justen's sister in the path of danger. Remy was to gather information, not hunt it down.

Finally, she fluttered her parents—on a frangipani flutter, naturally—saying she and Justen would be late for supper.

And she thought. Was it possible that the Galateans were not aware of what they were doing to their people with this drug? They'd begun by using it solely on aristos, a symbolic punishment meant to enslave the upper class as the aristos had once enslaved the masses. The revolutionaries' first victim had been the old Queen Gala, followed by her entourage. It was only recently that they'd expanded to punishing regs who ran afoul of the revolution in this manner. Did they mean the sentences to be for life?

"Excuse me, Lady Blake?"

Persis looked up from her most recent game to see Lord Lacan standing there, his face grave. Lord Lacan was the first aristo she'd rescued who was aware of her true identity, thanks to Remy's unmasking her during the man's rescue. The other aristos in his party, thankfully, had been out of sight when Remy had knocked off her cap. Though every new person who knew her secret was one more node of danger, she was glad it had been Lacan and not someone like Lord or Lady Seri.

She excused herself from the board—a good thing, too, as she was two moves away from another checkmate—and retreated with him into a quiet corner.

"Rumors have been flying around the facility like your little spun-sugar flower messages," the old man said to her.

"There's a problem, I understand, with the reg refugees?"

"It's not of concern to you or your family, sir—"

"You're wrong," Lacan replied. "The regs you rescued along with me are my friends. Anything that hurts my countrymen hurts me as well. May I see them?"

Persis blinked, surprised by the vehemence in his voice. Then again, even Reduced, Lacan had a presence about him. He'd been one of the most powerful voices for reform before the revolution, which is why she was so mystified that Aldred made him a target for imprisonment and Reduction. Even Remy Helo seemed to have been curious. Lord Lacan was responsible for changing at least one Galatean reg's mind about the revolution—and one who'd been raised to believe in it more strongly than anyone. Maybe that's why Aldred found him so dangerous. He was one of the only pro-reg forces out there who could challenge Aldred's despotic rule. Lacan was an aristo, but not the kind the revolution was meant to challenge.

Persis led him into the next chamber. There were seven refugees here, all regs. Lacan observed them for a moment, their sullen, confused faces, their clumsy movements and mumbled groans.

"This is an abomination," he said at last. "We must tell my countrymen what is being done to them, what they truly risk the longer they allow Aldred to control the island. Everything I fought for, the integrity of the Helo Cure itself—" The old man's voice broke on the words, and he shook his head.

"I know." Persis put a hand on his arm.

He looked at her hand, at the yellow leather wristlock covering her palmport. "You are a very young person to be taking this on all on your own."

"I'm not on my own," she replied in defense. "I have helpers, and Noemi, and the support of the princess—"

He cut her off, his tone contemplative, as if he hadn't even heard her. "This is what I've been thinking ever since I came back to myself. How young you are. How young you and that little soldier girl looked as you grappled on the ground in Galatea. How young Princess Isla is." The Lord Lacan looked down at his wrinkled hands, at the bandage covering his thumb. "I was ten years old when I took over my family estate. Twelve when Persistence Helo came to me and told me about her cure, when I decided to give it to every Reduced person on my land. My neighbors, all those people older and wiser than I, they all told me how foolish it was to listen to some reg who managed to get herself a medic's training. Said even if it did work, I'd have a lot harder time managing an estate full of regs than I would if they were Reduced."

"And you were right, in the end."

He chuckled. "Yes, I was. At twelve years old, I was young and idealistic and lucky that I happened to be right. So that's why I know it's foolish to tell you how dangerous this whole Wild Poppy business is and utterly pointless to say you're too young to pull it off. Because I know from experience that sometimes it's only the young ones who are crazy enough to change the world."

∞ ∞ ∞

VANIA SCOWLED AS SHE scrolled through the files on her oblet. General Gawnt's new strategy of beefing up the security at the work camps meant far more administrative work than Vania liked. He was doing this to annoy her, of that she was certain. Now, instead of being at the front lines of the Ford siege, waiting for the moment she could watch the final barriers fall, she was stuck in an office in the Halahou royal palace, reviewing files on troop movements.

Annoyed, she flipped back to his memo. His fat face looked like little more than a smear in the oblet display.

"With these new measures in place, we feel certain that the menace of the Wild Poppy will soon be apprehended."

What nonsense. The Wild Poppy was not intimidated by guards. He'd waltzed into a heavily armed estate and tricked an officer and all his soldiers into releasing Lord Lacan and his family. She'd reviewed all the witness interviews there.

Well, all except the missing guard's. The young one who'd apparently showed up out of nowhere then disappeared along with the Poppy. A plant? A spy? Her records were obviously faked and led nowhere. And it seemed the Poppy had done something to the surveillance records when he showed up, as the entire block of time had been erased.

Vania wasn't giving up, though. While Gawnt attempted to unmask the Poppy with brute force, she would do it with finesse, and she would start by tracking down every person who'd ever interacted with the spy—even if that meant detoxing the idiot nanny who'd let the Ford children slip through her fingers.

"Captain Aldred?" came the voice of her assistant. "You have a visitor. It's Citizen Helo." As always, there was a reverent hitch in the woman's voice as she pronounced the name. *Helo*. Vania wondered if her own name would hold such importance to future generations.

Also: finally! Justen hadn't been answering her messages for a week. She knew he was devoted to his research, but this was ridiculous. "Send him in," she called.

But the figure who came through the door wasn't Justen. It was Remy.

"Oh." Vania pasted a smile on her face to hide the disappointment. "You're back from your school trip at last?"

Remy's eyes widened and her hand went to her smooth cap of dark hair. "Yes. Glad you didn't miss me too much."

Vania chuckled. "Of course I missed you, squirt. Especially at dinner. You wouldn't believe how boring it gets without you or your brother to distract from General Gawnt's speeches."

"You haven't seen Justen, either?" Remy said. "He's not at the lab, you know."

"Oh?" Vania said, distracted. "Well, you know Justen. He's probably sequestered in some sanitarium somewhere, mopping the brows of pathetic Darkened."

"I don't know. We . . . haven't spoken in a while," Remy pressed. "We had a fight before I left. And he hasn't answered my message to talk in person."

"Probably forgot his oblet somewhere." Vania shrugged. "If ever someone needed a palmport, it's your brother."

Remy nodded. "He never would, though."

Vania made a sour face. "For good reason. They're disgusting and decadent . . . and dangerous."

Though the combination of nanotechnology and gengineering was all the rage in Albion and was starting to catch on even among aristos in Galatea before the revolution, Citizen Aldred had held the practice up as an example of the needless, wasteful indulgences that characterized the upper class, then outlawed the technology before it became popular among regs. Vania remembered how Justen had helped her father prepare tracts that railed against the unknown ravages palmports might be doing to the body's systems as it drained resources to power itself.

Vania had only ever seen them, dead and useless, on the palms of Reduced prisoners, but she'd watched videos of palmports in action—marvelous, spun-sugar flutternotes that carried encoded messages and applications that would generate small items, toys, or even chemicals if you'd taken the proper supplements.

Sometimes, when she ran out of neurotoxin prickers in her weapons bracelet, she wondered if some enterprising gengineer might write a palmport application for them. You know, if it wasn't illegal. Imagine not having to carry poisons around. Imagine just *being* poisonous, at the press of a button and the downing of a supplement. . . .

"Vania!" Remy waved her hand before Vania's eyes. "Are you even listening to me?"

She looked up at her little foster sister. Up—when had Remy gotten so tall? She was no longer the child who'd always tagged along behind Vania and Justen, begging to be part—any part—of their activities.

"Sorry, squirt," she said. "I've just had my hands so full with the Ford siege, and now Gawnt's got me trying to track down the Wild Poppy . . ."

"Really?" Remy said, her eyes alight with interest. "What have you found so far?"

Vania bit back a sigh. She really didn't have time to explain this to a little girl. "Not much, but more than I'll be reporting to General Gawnt, that's for sure. If anyone is going to catch the Poppy, it'll be me."

"Can I help?"

"Maybe in a few years."

Remy blinked, hurt, and now Vania did sigh. Justen was much better at putting his little sister off than she'd ever been. That was probably why he was working his bedside manner in a sanitarium and she was interrogating royalists as part of the military police.

"All right, squirt," she conceded. "Here's a way you can help. There's this story coming out of the Lacan estate about a missing soldier—some young recruit who apparently ran off with the Poppy. But no one seems to know where she came from. I've got tons of military recruit records to go through. Maybe you can help track this girl down." She handed Remy the oblet.

"Trina Delmar," Remy read on the display. "Yes, I think this is something I can handle."

Good. That would keep her busy, and it was doubtful Remy could cause much trouble combing through some static records. It was odd that Remy and Justen hadn't been in contact—though sometimes Justen and Vania spent weeks without talking, Remy and her brother were much closer. At least, Vania thought they were.

Maybe she'd missed a message from him explaining his extended absence? She checked again. Nothing from Justen, but in her queue was a message from a former classmate. She clicked on it and her oblet sparked up a video from a popular gossip source.

*Justen Helo, hero to the revolution, spotted getting cozy with an Albian aristo? Oh, Helo, say it isn't so!*

Jaw hanging like a fish, Vania played the video over and over in disbelief. The gossip sweeping Halahou was that Justen Helo was over in Albion romancing one of the most ridiculous aristocrats around.

The girl's name was Persis Blake, and according to the story, she was one of the richest, prettiest, and stupidest girls on the whole island. Her father, who probably also had pumice for brains, had defied Albian tradition to name her his heir, which made her one of the most eligible bachelorettes in New Pacifica.

Vania didn't understand. This had to be some sort of misunderstanding. Or maybe a vicious lie perpetrated by Galatean royalists. Justen wouldn't run off to Albion without telling them first. And he certainly, certainly wouldn't fall in love with someone as shallow as this Blake girl was.

Justen had always been uninterested in romance. Too

much work to do. Hadn't they had the conversation a hundred times, while their silly classmates got tied up in unproductive and melodramatic relationships that burned quickly and left nothing but anger and hurt feelings in their wakes? Vania had used these hurt feelings in her missions—one old classmate had been more than ready to reveal to Vania that an ex-lover was attending royalist meetings. Poor boy had been two months in his work camp, thanks in part to the bitterness born of a failed romance. Those sorts of feelings were beneath people like Justen and Vania. At least, that's what Vania had always thought.

But even if Justen decided at last to take notice of something other than his precious research, he would never have taken up with an aristo, even if she was obviously named for his famous grandmother. Not an aristo. Not her Justen. No matter how beautiful or charming or rich this girl was. Justen didn't care about that stuff.

If he had been sighted in Albion—well, Vania was sure there was an explanation. Sometimes Justen got so caught up with his research that he grew absentminded. Maybe he was collecting data at a sanitarium in Albion, thinking he'd only be gone on a day trip. That would explain the lack of messages. Justen would go to the moon if he thought it might help him in his research. And maybe he'd found the trip so fruitful, he'd extended it and neglected to message them. And maybe this aristo was . . .

Well, Vania couldn't quite imagine what an aristo would have to do with a sanitarium. None of the aristos in Galatea ever got their hands dirty with the reg disease.

And she couldn't imagine where someone might have gotten the idea that Justen would ever fall for an aristo, no matter how pretty she was. He'd have to be Reduced to be that stupid.

Or maybe Vania was the one acting Reduced. After all, aristos lived to be charming and flattering and seductive. Maybe Justen wasn't too smart to fall for their ways at all. Maybe, because he'd always been too busy to get involved with anyone before, he was completely blindsided by this Albian aristo's seduction techniques.

And of course the Albian aristos would want him on their side, if they could get him. He was far too valuable to the revolution to leave in their hands. Even Vania's father would agree with that. Hadn't he often said that Justen was one of their best assets?

This took precedence over any silly record combing. Vania needed to find out where Justen was and what he was doing. She'd message him, and if there was no reasonable response to these ridiculous rumors, if he didn't have a good answer for why he needed to stay on that aristo-infested island of Albion a moment longer than absolutely necessary, well then, she'd just go and bring him home herself.

And she could look for the Wild Poppy on the way.

# Fourteen

AS SO OFTEN HAPPENED to him in the labs at home, it was a persistent rumbling in his stomach that finally distracted Justen from his work. He looked up from the latest data stream to find rays of sunlight penetrating the skylights of Noemi's subterranean office. He exited into the residence room of the facility to discover the patients all gone to lunch and Persis nowhere to be found.

He stretched his back and blinked his dry, itchy eyes, momentarily disoriented. How many hours had he spent working? The patients' test results had come back by sundown, and it had taken him at least six hours to analyze the first lot of brain scans. Noemi had already started the victims on the current recommended therapeutics for DAR patients, and Justen figured that, to overcome suspicion, he would have to put together a reasonable body of research showing why it wouldn't help before he could suggest an alternate form of treatment. And he needed to do so quickly, as the longer these poor people remained in this state, the more damage would be done.

His jaw tightened. It wasn't supposed to be this way. It was never, ever supposed to be this way. Justen rested his head against his hands, massaging the tension out of his forehead. He'd never actually seen the Reduced in person before, and when he met refugees like the Seris, fully recovered and as loathsome as ever, it was easy to pretend that things weren't quite as awful as he imagined.

There was no escaping it now.

"Medic Helo?" He looked up to see Noemi waiting with the next round of brain scans. "Do you want me to make you up a cot? I think you should call it a day. You made a lot of progress last night, and we won't know much more until we can see the results of the new treatments."

"Because the current treatments are so effective?" he replied, his tone angrier than he'd intended. He knew already from his short stay at the sanitarium that DAR treatments in Albion were not so different from the standard regimens they used in Galatea. They could delay the progression of the disease for maybe six months, but they were incapable of gaining back any brain functionality. Once you began showing symptoms, there was nothing any medic on the islands could do to stop it.

But with the help of his grandmother's records, Justen had sought to change that. His research attempted to stop the mechanics that triggered DAR before they began. And he'd been on the right track six months ago. He had the mechanics down—it was everything else that was backward.

"You're not going to invent a new treatment today, Justen," Noemi said softly. "You may be talented, and you may be a Helo, but you're still human. An eighteen-year-old human. And you're no use to me unless you get some sleep."

He nodded stiffly. "Sleep." A lack of conscious thought that would rejuvenate him, while it only further damaged the people he'd hurt. He'd come to Albion to get away from what he'd done, and here he saw its full, gruesome effects. He'd asked Princess Isla for asylum, when really he should have turned himself in and begged for mercy. The paltry sabotage of the pills he'd attempted when he was still back in Galatea—the sabotage that had caused the fight between him and his sister—that was hardly enough to atone for the damage he saw before him.

This was his fault, all of it. The queen, the revolution, the suffering of his countrymen. He'd invented the Reduction drug that was tearing his homeland apart. How could he sleep? How could he ever sleep again now that he knew the extent of the damage he'd done?

He looked into Noemi's kind, intelligent eyes. Here, in Albion, he was all alone. Persis, stupid as she was, had practically torn him to pieces at the mention of having an alternate motivation for leaving Galatea. What would she think if she knew the real depths of his deception? How could he explain to someone like her the complexities of the trap he'd fallen into back home?

Uncle Damos had been his guardian since he was ten years old. He'd encouraged Justen's scientific mind, his research, his intention to help those with DAR. He'd arranged for Justen to do research before he'd even finished his degree, and had been so enthusiastic about every breakthrough.

Uncle Damos had been especially excited six months back by early test results from a treatment Justen had developed after studying his grandmother's notes. It showed wholly unexpected side effects when applied to a control brain model—an aristo brain model. The test drug hadn't halted the process of dementia. Instead, it had caused it. Justen had been distraught, disappointed at how his latest avenue of research had led to a useless dead end, but his uncle Damos had comforted him, reminding him that even Persistence Helo had suffered setbacks in her search for the cure and that no effort was ever *truly* wasted.

And how right he'd been in the end. His research wasn't wasted at all. It had been put to wider use than he'd ever dreamed. And it had led the entire revolution down a dark and twisted path.

Justen had been a fool to think escaping Galatea meant escaping his demons. Here he was, standing in a place the Wild Poppy created, viewing the results of his handiwork that the Wild Poppy had rescued. Forget what *Persis* might do if she learned the truth about Justen. What he really had to concern himself with was that Noemi—and by extension, the brilliant spy she worked for—never learned that Justen had invented the Reduction drug. It was clear the spy was a man of action who wouldn't rest until he'd righted all the wrongs happening in Galatea. The Poppy must be very clever and resourceful to secretly put all this together while his figurehead of a princess regent fooled around with creating fake romances between Justen and her favorite stylist. If Justen didn't tread carefully, he might inadvertently reveal the truth and find himself the next target of the Wild Poppy's activities.

But it was a risk Justen would have to take. He couldn't abandon the victims he'd created, even if it meant putting himself in as much trouble as he'd been when he'd fled Galatea.

"You're right," Justen said to Noemi at last. "Maybe I should rest." Someplace far from where the Wild Poppy might find him before he had a chance to redeem himself by figuring out a solution to the problem he'd caused. Someplace like Scintillans. "Do you know if Persis is still here? Or did she get bored and leave last night?"

Noemi smiled. "She's been entertaining the children with that weasel of hers."

Well, if there was anything that might distract from the specter of permanent brain damage, it was Slipstream. He set off to track down the girl and her sea mink, and followed the sound of laughter and splashes into an underground bathing chamber.

Carved from the same rock as the rest of the facility, the baths were lit by submerged lights in various shades that color coded each pool's temperature—a blue glow in the cold bath, a soft amber in the tepid one, and a fiery red for the hottest. The air was filled with clouds of steam and the voices of children, and Justen smiled, remembering his last visit to the public baths in Halahou. They'd been closed ever since the death of Queen Gala, when a riot had broken out that resulted in the drowning of several aristos sympathetic to the crown. Citizen Aldred had deemed them too dangerous in this period of unrest. It wasn't such a loss if you had a private geothermal pool in your home, as they'd had, living in the royal palace, but now Justen wondered exactly how many Galatean citizens had been deprived of the baths.

So many things he hadn't questioned when he should have.

As he walked farther into the baths, the din of the children's voices settled into coherency.

"Make him do it again!"

"Me next! Me next!"

Before him, the curtain of steam dissipated to reveal Persis seated on the ledge of one of the tepid pools, her skin and yellow dress shimmering like gold in the amber-tinted light. Around her stood a half dozen refugee children, squealing with delight at the antics of Slipstream, who was flipping into the water and performing marine acrobatics in return for the morsels of food the children tossed to him.

Justen smiled despite his exhaustion. "Surrounded by a crowd of admirers, as usual, Persis."

She looked in his direction and beckoned wearily through the steam. "Citizen Helo," she said. "At last you emerge from your lab. Discover anything interesting?"

"We have a few leads," he replied. He took a seat beside her. "Have you been here all night?"

"*I* slept." She looked like it. Her golden-brown skin glistened with vitality and maybe the steam as well. Justen found himself mesmerized by the sheen of moisture along her collarbone, in the hollow of her throat, cresting her jaw and the top of her lips.

He dragged his gaze away and yawned. He must be more exhausted than he realized. "I've been instructed to do the same."

"Are you sure you wouldn't be more comfortable here? Noemi would be more than happy to find you a bed." Slipstream finished his latest circuit and returned to his mistress for more food.

"If it's all right by you, I think I'll go back to Scintillans. It'll give me a break. A chance to clear my head." A chance, but not a large one. His dreams would probably be haunted by the faces of his victims wherever he slept.

Persis ran her hands through Slippy's wet fur and touched the creature's nose with her own. "I suppose spending any length of time around the people whose lives your guardian destroyed is terribly exhausting." She didn't know the half of it. "I can't imagine how you manage."

He wasn't entirely sure about that. Persis could be—well, if not serious, at least caring—when the situation warranted. She clearly took care of her mother, and here she was, distracting the children from their troubles with her silly pet. "It's my job. As a medic, I'm trained not to get emotional about my patients but to concentrate on their diseases and the science."

"You're excellently trained," she responded, and sent Slipstream out on another quest, to the delight of the children. "How beneficial it must be to be able to stay so detached and clinical when there's so much suffering around you."

That was a far more pointed comment than he'd expected from her. "Believe me, I'm very affected by what I learned today. But what good will my getting emotional do for these people? Nothing. I can't fix anything by getting angry. I have to act."

She gave him a look that cut right through the steam. Her lips parted and for a moment, he thought she was going to say something. He leaned in, and she seemed to shake herself free of the notion. Instead, she gave him her usual carefree smile. It must be a trick of the steam that it didn't quite reach her eyes.

She rose and snapped her fingers once. Slipstream glided to her side. "I'm so sorry, but Slippy and I have to go now," she said to the children. A wave of whines and pleas for "just five more minutes" rose up from the assembled crowd. "I promise we'll come back soon and you can play some more. There's nothing Slipstream likes better than doing tricks for treats."

"Are you serious?" he asked. "You're going to make room in your crowded social schedule to entertain a few refugee children?"

"Why, Justen Helo, I'm surprised at you. Do you really think I'd pass up the chance to share with these impressionable young newcomers to Albion the importance of proper hair color techniques?"

PERSIS TOOK THEM BACK to Scintillans via a land route, skimming inches over the lush green landscape of the western peninsula at speeds that would have kept Justen awake even if they hadn't been sitting in an open-air cab.

"Do you always drive like this?" he asked, squinting at her through the afternoon sunlight.

She slowed down a fraction, and the fans lowered to a dull roar. "Are you always such a stick-in-the-mud?"

He chuckled. "By your measurement, I think the answer to that is definitely yes. For instance, did you know I own only three pairs of pants?"

She cast him a horrified glance. "Please don't tell anyone else that. It's embarrassing enough to be in your company." She flicked on her palmport. "I'm making a note to get you an appointment with my tailor as soon as possible."

At that, he sobered. "Don't be too hasty. I'm likely to be spending a lot of time at the lab."

"Darling," Persis scoffed, "my tailor comes to *you*."

When they got back to Scintillans, Persis hopped out of the skimmer and skipped up the terrace. Fredan, the butler Justen had met his first morning, stopped them both in the front room. "Lady Blake, your parents have retired early today, but I can prepare you and Citizen Helo supper on the back terrace."

"How about the lawn beyond my room?" Persis asked. "The sunset is so lovely from that side of the house."

Fredan cleared his throat. "Lord Blake wished for me to remind you that Citizen Helo's room is at the *other* end of the house."

Justen's jaw dropped, but Persis laughed. "He's teasing me," she explained. "Papa's not going to let me get away with hosting you here without a little needling." She waved Fredan off and the older man shrugged and retreated.

"We should tell them," Justen said, "about the princess's plan."

"Not a chance," she said. "There's a reason my father's sticking to joking warnings rather than setting up a guard around the perimeter of my room. I think there's nothing my parents would like more than if you really did fall head over heels in love with their daughter." But her own tone was mocking, and Justen was relieved. They were on the same page, then. "So act devoted, if you please."

"Whatever you say, Lady Blake."

She paused on the path and gave him an appreciative smirk. "That was impressive, Justen. You almost sound . . . unrevolutionary."

They ended up eating on Persis's lanai anyway. It was a sumptuous meal of roasted taro and noodles and salads of star papaya and edible orchids, with vanilla foams for dessert. Despite the obvious care the Scintillans chef had taken, it tasted like sand to Justen. His thoughts were far away, in Galatea. He'd finally gotten a message from Remy, asking to meet him in person to talk, and he wasn't quite sure how to tell her that would be impossible. Halfway through the meal, a second message flared up on his oblet: Vania, wondering where he was, disturbed by rumors she'd heard about him and an aristo in Albion.

Guess he wouldn't have to tell Remy why they couldn't meet, after all. Justen ran a hand through his hair. How could he muster a reasonable response to either of his sisters' concerns right now, when he was exhausted and appalled and more certain than ever that he'd made the right choice in leaving Galatea? How could he even risk responding without breaking down and telling Vania everything he'd learned about what the Reduction drug was doing to its citizens, everything he'd realized about the way her father had been manipulating him? And if he'd thought Remy had reacted poorly last time, who knew what she'd say when he told her he'd defected and he wanted her to join him?

No, he wouldn't message either of them back until he'd had some rest and could organize his thoughts.

The sun dipped low in the sky, and Justen noticed a dark streak darting toward them across the lawn. Moments later, Slipstream scurried up the steps and clawed at the hem of Persis's gown. His fur was streaked with seawater, and droplets still glistened on his whiskers.

"Hello, sweet thing," said Persis, and heedless of the silks she was wearing, she scooped the animal up in her arms. "Did you have a good dinner, too? Yes, you did!" Slipstream nuzzled his face into the crook of Persis's neck and purred contentedly. Splotches and streaks of water smeared, ignored, down Persis's gown.

Justen didn't get it. In one breath, she acted like nothing mattered more than her precious clothes, and in the next, she let Slipstream or refugee children ruin them. He supposed it was because their obvious expense meant nothing to her. Everything was a game. Here she was, in her fine house, with her servants and her feasts and her fancy gengineered pet, and across the sea and up the road, people's lives were scorched earth. How could he sit here with a pretty girl and eat foam and flowers while that was going on? He pushed away from the table and rose, mind whirling. Noemi wanted him to sleep, but how could he when he could barely even sit still?

Persis caught up to him, still clutching her expensive, slimy sea mink. Bits of seaweed clung to its fur. "What's on your mind?" she asked him.

"This estate," he said honestly. "I'm too much a reg to ever feel comfortable in a place like this."

She blinked at him in confusion. "So then what are all the regs who call Scintillans their home?"

"Like your mother?"

She nodded. "And Fredan and his wife and children, and all the people I grew up with—"

"Your servants don't eat like this, Persis."

"You aren't my servant. You're my guest."

"And what makes me different from them?" he asked, turning.

She shook her head, and the edge of her mouth quirked up. "Nothing. But you're the one who's my guest right now."

"Because I'm a Helo."

Persis sighed. "Honestly, Justen, it's just a name. And it's just a dinner. It doesn't always have to be a political statement."

That was easy for the socialite to say. He shrugged and took a deep breath. "That isn't how things work in Galatea. And given that your princess is using me for her political ends right now, I wouldn't be so sure that's not how it works here in Albion, either."

Persis said nothing for a few moments. She bowed her head over Slipstream, breathing in the scent of salt from his fur. Then she raised her head and smiled. "I want to show you something. It's the perfect time."

"What?"

She set the sea mink on the lanai and grabbed his hand in her damp one, tugging him down the steps toward the cliffs. "Come on."

She went racing across the lawn, the sea mink cantering to keep up, its stubby legs a blur in the slanted light of the setting sun. Justen sighed and took off after them. The skirt of Persis's dress was flying out behind her, and the meters between them only lengthened despite Justen's attempts to keep up. For a socialite, she sure could sprint.

And as she approached the edge of the cliff, she didn't slow down a bit.

"Persis!" he shouted, but his voice was caught by the wind and ripped away from him. Seconds later, he saw her disappear over the edge. "Persis!" He thundered up to the very edge of the cliff and stopped short. There, a few meters beneath the lip of the cliff, Persis and her sea mink lay sprawled out against a wide net of silk, swinging slightly against the breeze.

She laughed wildly and beckoned to him. "Jump. There's plenty of room."

Room wasn't his concern. Toppling through the gossamer hammock swinging below his feet was closer to the truth.

"Come on," she cried. "We have to zip-line or we'll never get there in time."

"Get where?" he asked. But she gave him no response, just giggled again and held up her hands as if she'd somehow be able to catch him.

He sighed. Here he was, alone at the edge of the world, an island away from everything he'd ever known, a thief, a traitor to his country and, worse, to the values he'd been taught all his life. Here he was offering to play pantomime for a foreign princess's political benefit, to defer to the knowledge of a spoiled aristo, to deny the revolution he'd once have spilled his lifeblood to defend.

He hoped it was worth it.

All this rested on his head, had rested there since the moment he'd first boarded the *Daydream*. And he had no one to talk to, no one to ask for advice, for reassurance that he'd made the right choice. His only protector in this strange land was a pumice-brained, giggling girl who—

He stared down at Persis. A silly, spoiled aristo who was keeping the secret of her mother's illness from those in her society who might use the knowledge as a weapon. A flighty, shallow young woman who steadfastly filled the weighted silence at her family dinners with meaningless chatter about fashion and court scandals. An ignorant girl who was so terrified that she might die from an inheritable disease that she took genetemps and sailed yachts and drove skimmers like a maniac and threw herself off the sides of cliffs for fun.

"Move," Justen called down at her.

And then he jumped.

# Fifteen

"Ever travel by zip before?" Persis asked, fooling with some sort of contraption up near where the hammock attached to a wire.

"Can't say I have," he replied. "I grew up on the southwest coast of Galatea. More sandbanks, fewer cliffs." He often wondered how much control the creators had when terraforming these islands. The explosion that had split the skin of the Earth hadn't been designed with habitat creation in mind. The fact that there were two islands, one for the first King Albie and one for the first Queen Gala, had been a lucky accident. And so much about that time was lost to history. Maybe there were other creators who didn't get a country of their own. Maybe they'd never meant for the nations they'd founded to develop as they had, never meant for the regime of aristo and Reduced to become the dominant society for hundreds of years.

All thoughts instantly fled, however, as Persis pulled a release cord, and they dropped toward the sea. Justen felt his stomach leap into his throat. He clutched at the silk hugging him from all sides, its thin weave seeming too insubstantial to hold him. Near his feet, the sea mink lay calmly, and Persis squealed with delight as they zipped down, down, down, gliding through the air, silk billowing out behind them like the sail on a ship. The water rushed toward them, deep blue and closer than he would have liked, until he was almost sure he could reach down and touch it, then the line leveled and they flew across the water like a sea bird skimming for fish.

"Hang on," said Persis a tad breathless. "There's a bit of a jolt at the end."

"What?" Justen asked, then was thrown violently forward as the hammock caught on a block at the end of the wire. The bottom swung up, throwing him back again, right into Persis's lap. Slipstream squeaked in protest.

"Well, hello there," she said coyly, brushing her bare fingers through the bristly strands of his hair. Her smile was broad and inviting, and his left arm had somehow gotten entangled all the way under her skirt. He scrambled up and tumbled out of the hammock, apologizing while inwardly berating himself for not hanging on a little tighter while Persis dropped him off a cliff face.

"You didn't hurt me, darling." She shot him a grin and slid out of the folds of silk herself, as Justen looked around, trying desperately to silence the parts of his brain engaged in deducing which particular swath of her leg he'd been pressed up against. They were standing on a tiny patch of moss and sand that looked to be the only real land on the length of the narrow, rocky tide breaker leading out from the cliffs. Nearby was a stone shack. The cliffs rose over them, huge and nearly vertical. He followed the line of rocks back to where it met the mainland and spotted a minuscule, steep set of stairs carved into the rock.

"Is that how we're supposed to get back?" He nodded to the path.

She chuckled. "Don't be silly. I'll call for a boat." She peeled off her wristlock and, moments later, a flutternote flitted off her palm and was caught by the wind. "I told them to come in an hour. That'll give us plenty of time."

"For what?"

Persis grabbed his hand. "For me to show you why they call it Scintillans."

She pulled him along the narrow path to the shack, then disappeared inside. A moment later, she tossed a pair of dark blue swim trunks at him. "If you go around the shack to the east side, you're less likely to be seen from the fishing village. But," she said, wiggling her eyebrows, "I can't make any promises."

He looked at the dark blue trunks in his hands. "We're going swimming?"

Persis poked her head out of the shack. From what he could see, she was no longer dressed. "Please tell me they haven't outlawed that in Galatea, too."

"I can swim."

"Good." Back in she went.

Perhaps a swim would help clear his mind. He'd been envying Slipstream in the sanitarium bath. By the time

Justen had changed his clothes, Persis was lounging on a rock, basking in the coral glow of the setting sun. Her suit, also dark blue, was two pieces—a simple band knotted over her breasts and a brief bottom covered with a translucent blue scarf. It was the plainest thing he'd ever seen her wear. Justen wondered idly whose bathing trunks he was wearing, or if the Blake family kept a stash of blue suits in their shack—just in case.

As soon as she saw him, she popped up and onto the sand. Her hair was still mostly down, the mass of yellow and white curls and braids and locks twisted in a loose knot at the nape of her neck. For a moment, he could pretend she was like any other girl he'd known growing up. Her skin practically glowed in the slanted sunlight. She must know what a tempting sight she made, there on the rock. She must know it, because she had never concerned herself with anything more important in all her silly, shallow life. It was vital to keep such things in mind, before he totally forgot the real nature of their relationship. It was fake. All fake.

She held out her bare hand, and he saw the flash of gold from her palmport.

That should help some.

"Hurry!" she called. "We've got to get there before the sun sets." And again she took off, down the rocks to a tiny, shockingly clear-bottomed cove nestled at the base of the cliff. She plunged into the water and Justen followed her to the shoreline, bracing himself for the cold sea.

But he was surprised, for the water was as warm as a bath. The cove must be a natural geothermal pool. He sunk into the water up to his chest, sighing in pleasure. Though both islands were largely powered by the geothermal energy derived from the volcano, and Justen knew of several thermal pools inland in Galatea, it was rare to find a natural sea cove such as this—protected enough from the tides for the water to seem warmer where it emerged from the heated earth.

Persis paddled across the cove, and he followed her, noting how the sun must be very close to the horizon now, as the surface of the sea had turned to molten gold. Persis had reached the edge of the cliff and had situated herself on a ledge that seemed to have been carved out of the rock wall. A moment later he joined her, settling into the seat and letting his arms float before him in the warm water.

"I could sleep right here," he said, surprised to find it was the truth. Perhaps his all-nighter was finally catching up to him.

"It is tempting," Persis agreed, waving her hands through the water and watching gold drip from her fingers. "Of course, you'd drown. And wouldn't *that* be a tragedy? A celebrated young medic, a darling of Galatea, young, clever, handsome—struck down before his time. . . ."

More like struck down before he could ruin any more lives. He grimaced. What right did he have to relax in a geo-thermal pool while the refugees suffered in the sanitarium, while prisoners were tortured in Galatea? There was a rule that medics had abided by since time immemorial: first, do no harm.

He needed to fix his mistake. There was nothing more important than that right now. He'd sleep for a few hours, then head back to the lab.

Ahead of them, to the west, the sun melted into the sea, and already, the dusk had gathered here in the shadows on either side of the cove cliffs. "So why do they call it Scintillans?" he asked, more to change the subject than anything else.

"Wait."

He waited. It wasn't difficult to do, snug on the rocks with the warm seawater all around him. Persis didn't speak for once, and when he looked, she wasn't consulting her palmport, either, just sitting and watching the sun set, her expression devoid of its usual false cheer. Her hair was wet and plastered to her head, making her look like an actual mortal for once, as well as the two years younger than Justen that she really was. He wondered what she might have been like had she not been born an aristo in Albion. Like his sister Remy, perhaps. She wasn't stupid, just unconcerned with any weighty matters.

Then he thought of what she'd be like had she been born an aristo in Galatea. How she'd probably even now be Reduced, imprisoned, working herself to death in a field, her silly giggle extinguished like the mischievous spark in her cinnamon eyes.

And it would be his fault.

He was staring. He stopped, and returned his attention to the sun. Persis Blake was beautiful, but she wasn't a sunset.

A moment later, the sun sank below the surface. Justen made a hissing sound before he could catch himself.

But Persis was already grinning. "What was that?"

He shrugged, sending the water into eddies around his shoulders. "Something my sister and I always do, ever since we were kids. When the ocean puts out the sun, it hisses, like water on a hot pan."

"I like it." Persis nodded, as if giving him permission to hiss in her cove. "You must miss her."

"Remy's the only family I have left. Of course I miss her." Missed her and wanted to take back everything he'd said the last time he'd seen her. Remy was just a kid. Of course she wouldn't take kindly to his doubts about the revolution. Of course she would be shocked to learn that he was trying to undo the damage he'd caused.

What had he been thinking, leaving her alone in Galatea? He wanted to believe nothing would happen to her there—that no matter what, Uncle Damos would be kind to her. But he realized more each day how little he truly knew about the man who'd raised them since their parents died.

Now the midnight blue of the night sky was rushing after the coral line of the setting sun. The trail of sparkling gold across the surface of the water narrowed, and the waves turned dark. He felt her hand, warm from the water, in his hair again.

"It feels so weird," she said, brushing it back against its natural direction. "Prickly. Fuzzy. Like Slipstream."

Justen jerked his head away. "I feel like your *rodent*?"

She pursed her lips, considering it. "Your hair does. A little. Slipstream is softer."

"Thanks a lot."

"He's gengineered that way. To be soft, to be fast, to be

playful and clever and cute. To be perfect for me."

"Sorry I can't oblige." Unlike so many of his friends, Justen had never indulged in the gengineering that had become so popular since the revolution. There wasn't enough regulation right now—as he'd argued to Persis when she'd been messing with her genetemps. Human gengineering was a dicey prospect. He knew that better than anyone.

"I'll live." She looked at him, eyes narrowed, then shook her head in confusion. "Why do men wear it so short in Galatea? And everyone so dark. Don't you get bored, having everyone's hair just be black like that?"

"I like black."

"As your wardrobe proves," she scoffed.

"Don't you get tired of bleaching yours all the time?"

"I'll endure a little boredom for the sake of beauty." She pulled her hair over her shoulder. "If only we were all lucky enough to have juvenile canities like Isla's royal line."

Justen rolled his eyes. "Give them a few years, and the gengineers will make an argument for it."

"Not in Albion—the royals would never allow it. It's become such a signature." Persis shrugged. "This color is new—or relatively. I've only had it about a year. Used to be a lovely deep magenta, but I found it was clashing with Slippy's coat."

"Can't have that," Justen murmured. "Where is your sea mink anyway?"

"On the cold side. It's too hot over here for him." Persis slipped off the ledge and treaded water in front of him. "Why? Do you find conversations about hairstyles that dull?"

"Deadly dull."

"Then I fear you won't have much fun pretending to be in love with me." She shifted closer. "Since, to sell our ruse, you're going to have to pretend every word out of my mouth is utterly fascinating."

He leaned in, too. "I think there are enough people who think that around here, Lady Blake. Maybe what you find so fascinating about *me* is that I don't fall all over myself the second you speak."

She murmured something incoherent.

"What?"

"I do find that fascinating," she said more loudly. "If annoying."

He shrugged.

She glided back and forth through the water inches from his legs, every bit as graceful and sinuous as Slipstream. "But we should figure it out. What could someone like *you*, with all your revolutionary ways, find so wonderful about me?"

He shrugged again. There were some, he supposed, who would fall for this silken, silly goddess.

"That'll never do. We have to find something."

"You're rich and beautiful and the heir to this entire estate," Justen pointed out. "That should be enough."

She looked skeptical. "Not a very revolutionary senti-ment."

"Well, I'm a traitor to the revolution, so—"

Suddenly, Persis lunged forward, hooked her arm around his neck, and pressed her lips to his.

"Guh—" he said against her mouth.

"Kiss me," she whispered, her tone urgent.

He did. Her lips were as full and lush as he'd expected. She tasted of sea salt and flowers. His hands skimmed her sides, bare and slippery, and the wet hem of her suit as he steadied her in the current. Her skin was firm and smooth, just as he'd imagined. She moaned a little as his fingers pressed into her thighs, holding her just the tiniest bit away from his body for his own sake. Her lips parted and she slid her tongue along his bottom lip.

Justen jerked away. Enough was enough. "Per—"

She laughed again and splashed him. "What's wrong, Galatean?" she asked loudly. Very loudly. "Am I moving too fast for you?"

Even over the sound of the surf, he heard snickers. He looked back to see a group of figures huddled on the steps near the entrance to the cove. As soon as they realized he'd spotted them, they turned and, laughing, scampered back up the steps.

"Who—" he asked under his breath as he watched them go, neck craned to peer over the lip of rock.

"Some children from the village," Persis whispered, still on his lap. She sounded oddly breathless, as if the kiss had taken her as much by surprise as it had him. "Naturally they're spying. But don't worry, you put on a good show. This will help our case significantly." He felt her slide off his lap and turned to face her, then gasped.

For Persis was floating in a sea full of stars. He watched in wonder as she twirled in place, then submerged herself entirely for a moment, only to burst out of the water, scattering sparkles off her skin and hair. She caught him staring openmouthed, and smiled broadly.

"Welcome," she said, "to Scintillans Cove."

"What is it?" he asked in wonder.

"What are *they*," she corrected, lifting another palmful of starry water and letting it trickle back down her hands. "They are phosphorescent coral spawn, and they love the warmth here in the cove."

Before he knew what he was doing, Justen had pushed off his perch and joined Persis in the water. The stars sparkled in the wake of his movements and he waved his arms and kicked his legs, just for the pure pleasure of watching galaxies wing out in the eddies. He dove and opened his eyes beneath the surface, ignoring the sting of salt to see the marine universe unfold all around. In the silence, he thought he might be in space. When he was young, he and Vania had discovered a book in her father's library that described outer space missions in ancient times, missions like the one that had kept all their ancestors safe during the wars. He'd wondered then what it had been like for those people to float alone among the stars while the world burned.

This was exactly what he'd imagined.

When his lungs could take no more, he surfaced, blinded by the seawater for a moment. He rubbed his eyes and found Persis floating calmly beside him.

"Have you any place like this in Galatea?" She was on her back, staring up at the real stars appearing in the sky. They were surrounded. Stars above, stars below, and Persis, floating a few inches away, her arms and legs brushing against his in the water, sparkling everywhere they touched. Her hair flowed, pale and ghostly, in the water, the curves of her body like little shimmering islands peeking above the surface. Even after his swim, he could taste her in his mouth.

Somehow, he found his voice. "No, we don't, and I grew up on the shore. I've heard of sea phosphorescence before but . . ."

"This cove is pretty special," Persis said. "All Scintillans is."

"Yes." Seawater dripped onto his face. Was he swallowing stars? Or—coral spawn. He shouldn't think this a miracle. He shouldn't find it so impressive. A simple chemical reaction in the juvenile body of the . . . they sparkled and swirled in the water before him.

All right. Stars.

"And you're right, I'm the heir."

He blinked. Had he missed some part of the conversation while underwater? Then he remembered. They were talking about what it was he'd say he loved about Persis.

But that was before the stars. Before the kiss. He doubted he'd have to say anything now. Those kids on the steps would be convinced. Everyone would.

"Which is why," she went on, still looking up, while the real stars flickered to life in the slice of sky they could see beyond the cliffs, "it's important who I'm with. It's important that he be someone I can trust, because if I marry—he'll get it all."

# Sixteen

For the first time since donning the mask that had defined her life for months, Persis found she didn't resent the shallow, playful role she'd taken on. Here in the cove, with stars winking above the cliff top and weaving in and out of the knots in her hair, she could be the part of herself that wasn't at odds with her faked persona. The part that entertained her mother with village chatter, who sailed her yacht in high winds and played with Slipstream on the shore. Justen had spent a day and a night fighting against the evils perpetuated by his fellow countrymen. He needed to relax. He needed laughter and splashing and . . . yes, even kisses. Who knew that better than a girl who'd spent months risking everything for the same purpose?

The kiss they'd shared had affected her more than she'd expected. It wasn't her first kiss, or even the first time she'd kissed a boy for less than honest reasons. However, it might have been the first time she'd ever kissed someone who didn't *want* her to.

Now that she knew how awful being on the receiving end of fake kisses felt, she never wanted to indulge in the practice again—though with her new duty as the object of Justen's false affections, she doubted that was going to happen. She'd figured he'd enjoy it, what with him being a teenage boy and her being a pretty girl in a bathing suit. She'd thought he *was* enjoying it, and then, just as things had started getting interesting, he'd pushed her away.

And it had been here, in the star cove, where the greatest love story she knew had begun.

Two decades earlier, the young, idealistic heir to Scintillans had met his secret lover in this cove and told her that he didn't care what it meant for his future in Albian society, that he didn't even care if he was disowned by his parents or shunned by his king—he wouldn't go another day without her by his side. Torin was rebellious and resolute, and Heloise was clever and charming, and theirs was a love story that won the hearts of the entire island.

Persis was the happily ever after of that story. It was her proud legacy and the cloud that hung over her head. She wondered how much longer her mother would remember that night, the one that Persis had been told about like a bedtime story all her life. The night her parents swam in the star cove and promised to defy every rule they knew. What if Persis fell in love like that, what if she married and had children and ended up as sick as her mother? She couldn't do that to another family. Persis closed her eyes until she could breathe again. Love and duty, as the Blake family motto went.

For months now, the latter trumped the former.

"Are you saying that your future husband will be in charge here?" Justen asked, appalled.

"Yes, of course."

"Of course?" Justen scoffed. "That's ridiculous. You were born here. This land is yours."

Well, if that wasn't the least revolutionary thing she'd ever heard him say. "Well, lucky for me, I have no interest in such boring pursuits as land ownership. I'd be happy to let my future husband handle that sort of thing."

"I find that hard to believe, Persis. I bet you won't even let your future husband pick out his own clothes."

She smiled in spite of herself. He had her there. "The laws of Albion state that a woman and her holdings are the property of her father, her husband, her brother, or her son. Women can't inherit unless there's no man in the picture at all."

"Then if I were you," Justen said, "I'd never marry at all. Stay single and control your land as you see fit."

She laughed and splashed at him. "You wouldn't condemn the villagers to a life of foolishness and fashion, would you?"

"No, but I doubt you would either. You love the people here too much. You can't fool me, Lady Blake."

That stopped her in her tracks. She had *better* fool him. She might be forgetting herself here in the star cove, but her mission was still all-important. Then again, maybe it was time to stop lying to Justen. If he was working to help the refugees, he was halfway in the League already.

And what would he do if she did tell him? Would he even believe her? Would he fight by her side? Would he kiss her for real?

She cleared her throat. "It's how things work in Albion, though. Men make the decisions. This is why Isla is only the princess regent, and her infant brother is the king. If Albie had never been born, they'd be pressuring Isla to marry as soon as possible, so the country could get a proper king."

Justen snorted. "Some hereditary rule. You can take control of the country just by marrying the princess?"

"I suppose you prefer taking control of the country through a military coup, Citizen Helo?" she snapped.

Justen squeezed his eyes shut in embarrassment. "No. That's not what I meant."

And Persis had not meant to turn to such a serious topic. That wasn't how the flaky, shallow girl she pretended to be would act if she had brought a handsome young man down to the star cove. Even one she was just pretending to like for Isla's sake. She mustn't forget herself, no matter how many stars sparked against her skin, no matter what Justen had done today for the people the Poppy had rescued. This was a mission—same as any other. She was used to the role of Persis Flake. She needed to remember that the role of starry-eyed admirer of Justen Helo was just as false.

"I had wanted the queen removed from office," he said quietly, returning to the ledge. "She was cruel to her subjects and unfair to the regs. Personally, I'd already argued with her more than a year ago about access to my grandmother's research. She . . . patronized me. Acted like I was a child playing scientist instead of a student doing legitimate research. It was right of the people of Galatea to seek to remove her from power. I will not deny that. But—everything else. It wasn't motivated by justice. It was something much darker."

"Revenge," Persis whispered, though she wasn't sure if he heard. Revenge for all the cruelty and the dismissals and the wrongs done to an entire people.

"I wasn't there when the queen was sentenced," Justen said. "But I was there the night she died. I saw . . . what happened afterward."

He was weighing his words carefully, Persis noted. And with good reason, for "what happened afterward" was that a mob had formed, and they'd taken their desire for revenge into their own hands, stealing the queen's body and tossing it into her private cove to be devoured by her own mini-orcas.

He shook his head. "It got out of hand. All of it. No one deserves the punishment of Reduction. No one deserves to have their body desecrated as the queen's was. This is not the world we've fought to create here on New Pacifica. This isn't the life Persistence Helo wanted the regs to have."

Persis ducked her head beneath the warm water then, as the only other option would have been to throw herself on him and kiss him again. Justen Helo was handsome and smart and was trying to be the hero his famous name required, but she had a job to do, too. He wouldn't ever kiss her by choice. He didn't even know who she was.

When she surfaced, he continued. "I thought, perhaps, it was all a terrible mistake. I didn't think it would continue. I've been proved wrong again and again these last six months, but I never thought it would get as bad as what I saw in the sanitarium yesterday." He ran his hands across his short, prickly hair, starlight flowing from his fingers and down his arms in streams.

Persis nodded. It's what everyone thought. And everyone had been wrong. That's why the Poppy had been born.

"I don't know how we'll ever recover from this. I don't know how to make it better."

She glided to his side on the bench. "There is only one way to recover from the evil humanity does to itself: overcome it. It's like my mother said at dinner the other night. We can only be responsible for what we ourselves do. Bad things happen in this world, and we are judged on how we respond. Do we take part in evil, or do we fight against it with all we have?"

Justen made no response to that at all.

Emboldened by the darkness, Persis continued. "Bad things have happened everywhere, even at my beloved Scintillans. My ancestors kept Reduced as slaves. My ancestors *were* Reduced slaves. But now things are different. When my father had the chance, he worked to make the lives of the regs here whatever they wanted them to be."

"Oh, and they want to be servants and fishermen?" Justen asked, skeptical.

"Not all of them, and not all of them are," she replied. "Look at Tero. He's a gengineer, though his father is our butler, Fredan." She shrugged. "Regs like Tero have more choice than I do about what course they want to take in life."

Justen's eyes were so wide, Persis could make them out by starlight. "Andrine and Tero's father is your butler? Andrine's a friend of the princess and the daughter of a servant?"

For once, Persis did not have to pretend to be clueless. She was honestly baffled. "Who's the snob now, Justen Helo? Your grandmother was the daughter of Reduced slaves, and she invented the cure."

"Yes, and fought almost every aristo on her island to do so." Justen shrugged. "I'm sorry. I'm not used to such things being encouraged by aristos."

"And I'm not used to men telling me I should lead my estate like an equal." Well, except her father. "Perhaps if more men took that approach with me, I wouldn't be available to help you and Isla with your little romantic subterfuge."

And that, Persis decided, was as honest as she could risk being with Justen Helo. She cast him a furtive glance, but if he was at all affected by her words, he didn't show it. And why should he? If there was anything she understood about the revolutionary she'd invited into her home, it was that he was impervious to Persis's infamous charm. He was too smart to be seduced by her stupidity, too industrious to be impressed by her idleness.

She wondered if he'd feel differently about the girl who was the Wild Poppy. Then again, he didn't even know the Wild Poppy was a girl. Everyone, from this equality-minded Galatean to the most sexist aristo in Albion, thought the spy was a man.

"What would you be doing right now, if you weren't helping Isla and me?" Justen asked her, rousing her from her thoughts.

What an apt question. Persis smiled. Planning more raids to his homeland, mostly.

"I mean, would you be looking for a real husband?"

Her mouth snapped shut. Oh, of course. Because the Persis she'd presented to him could do nothing more useful than find a husband.

He pressed on. "Did you have anyone in mind? Have you broken any hearts at court?"

She laughed aloud as an image of her confessing the truth to an incredulous Justen reared up in her head. She could tell him right now what she really did with her time, and he'd never believe her. Not a girl in a bikini in the star cove. Not the spoiled, stupid aristo she'd convinced him she was. Persis tossed a lock of wet hair behind her shoulder. "I've broken a dozen hearts this week. Don't you know? I'm Persis Blake."

He chuckled softly. "Fair enough. You know, we made a list of why I might have fallen for you, but we didn't figure out what it is you see in me."

"You're Justen Helo. A man with a famous name. Wherever you go, people are impressed. That's enough."

"So that's what you look for in a man?" Justen asked. "Fame?"

Sure. Fame would do for Persis Flake. "You're easy on the eyes, too."

"I'm not as beautiful as you."

"Another bonus, as far as I'm concerned," she replied,

letting the compliment roll off her like so much star-studded water. She waved her hand at him. "Your fashion sense we can fix."

"That can't be all you care about, especially if you're giving him your home. Especially if . . ." He trailed off.

Especially if she was going to Darken. Well, there was an argument for getting tested. If she had a reg brain, she would Darken like her mother, which meant she had a vastly compressed timeline to get married and start a family. That was, if any aristo would risk reproducing with someone, even an aristo heiress, coded for DAR.

And there, also, was an argument *not* to get tested. If she was going to die and leave Scintillans to a stranger, better that it be someone she considered long and hard first, rather than whatever young man just happened along.

And if you spent any time at all working in a sanitarium, as Justen had, you already knew every side of the debate about getting tested for DAR. Some wanted to know so they could plan accordingly. Some didn't, so they could live their lives without the specter of death.

"Persis," he murmured, and it felt like a hug. "I just meant . . . with your parents' example, you shouldn't sell yourself short. You should marry someone who can be a true partner."

The two sides of Persis Blake warred within her. It had been a long time since she'd considered—*truly* considered—what she wanted in a romantic partner, in the husband she would one day have to have. Isla could make as many jokes as she wanted about Persis's dream boy, but the reality was much harder to pin down. Someone as clever as she was. Someone who cared as much as she did. Someone who saw the real her and loved her *because* of it, not in spite of it, the way everyone—even her parents, even Isla—did. It's what she wanted, but it was impossible.

"When I marry," she said at last, "it will not be a love story like my parents had. I relinquished any fantasy of that long ago."

Love was magma, shooting from the Earth. It had the potential to form pillars of rock that would last for a thousand years or plumes of ash that choked the sky. She would never love like her father, never let herself be loved like her mother. She would never suffer what her parents were suffering now.

"Do not concern yourself, therefore, in pretending to be my perfect man. Your focus should be on the refugees now. They're the ones in real need."

This was, Persis decided, reason enough not to burden him with revelations about her true identity and the fact that she'd just put his sister in a rather precarious position. Though Persis knew that Remy was capable of the tasks they'd set before her, Justen seemed to consider his sister little more than a child.

Justen leaned back against the stone, as constellations swirled around and above them. "Oh, look," he said. "You have a message."

A fludternote flitted above their heads in Andrine's preferred form of a flying fish. Persis lifted her hand out of the water and it dropped down, melting into her palmport.

*I have received a message from our new young operative.*
*The Ford barricades have fallen and the rebels have taken*
*prisoner what remains of the family and their reg supporters.*
*Immediate rescue required. The Fords are being transferred to*
*Halahou city prison, with sentencing scheduled for sundown*
*tomorrow.*

Persis caught her breath. Remy Helo was already paying off. And with what Persis knew about the Reduction
drug, it was imperative that the Poppy liberate the reg prisoners before they were dosed, or they'd suffer permanent
damage.

"What does it say?" Justen asked.

She forced a giggle. "News travels fast on this island.
Apparently it's more than the village children who know
about our kiss."

"How CAN WE KNOW that this intelligence is true?" The image
of Isla's face, flickering in the lights coming in the window
from Scintillans Village, looked skeptical. Andrine, Tero,
and Persis were huddled around Tero's oblet in Andrine's
bedroom, discussing the mission with the princess. Persis
thought she'd spent more time here since becoming the
Wild Poppy than she'd ever done growing up. They'd always
played outside or up in Scintillans proper. Andrine's room
wasn't . . . cramped exactly, but it was certainly smaller and
less comfortable than Persis's apartments at home.

All things she hadn't thought of much before spending time with Justen Helo.

"Remy Helo has been back home for what—a day? Terribly convenient for her to have delivered such news so quickly."

"I agree," said Tero, sitting beside his sister on a bamboo trunk. "The timing of this is suspect. We could be walking into a trap. I mean, Persis and Andrine could. Wild mini-orcas couldn't drag me to Galatea these days."

Andrine shook her head. "I've talked to her at length. I trust her. She's not the devious sort. She believes in the revolution, but she believes just as strongly that it's gone astray. In that capacity, she's willing to help us."

Isla appeared nonplussed. "She's not devious, you say, yet we've sent her into the arms of Citizen Aldred bearing our biggest secrets? Wonderful. I knew this was a bad idea. We'll be at war within a week."

"She doesn't need to be devious," said Persis. Remy's best disguise was that she was undervalued. They couldn't imagine her useful as anything, and certainly not as a spy. Persis did have *some* experience in that arena. "All she needs to do is keep her ears open. Andrine is right; Remy is as trustworthy as her brother."

And, it seemed, just as interested in fixing the problems the revolution had wrought. It was good the information had come in when it had. Persis had been close to losing herself in the star cove. Or rather, close to *being* herself, which was just as dangerous.

"The fact that the Ford barricades have fallen has been verified by propaganda out of Galatea. In a few hours, I'm sure they'll be telling us exactly what Remy has—that the

Fords are to be sentenced in Halahou prison."

"So what's the rush?" asked Tero. "Why not rescue them after their sentencing, as you have with all the others? Security will be much more lax if they only have Reduced prisoners to guard. Don't get cocky, Persis. I still remember the days when you couldn't make it up the pali without scraping your knees."

"Were those the days when you thought the height of chivalry was to burst cuttle jellies on Isla and me?" she replied.

"I remember that," Isla said with a smirk. "My hair was sienna for a week, until the dye wore off."

Tero fell silent, which was fine by Persis, since she didn't plan to budge on this point. She couldn't risk permanent damage being done to the regs who'd been captured along with the Ford family. But she also didn't want to scare Tero and Andrine.

"Remy says that General Gawnt has been increasing security at the estate work camps in response to our activities. They will be expecting us at the Fords if we wait to get them once they've been Reduced and returned to their estate. But they won't be expecting us at the prison." She touched the oblet to pull up a file on the Halahou prison. "Since the revolution, the inmates and guards have changed, but the supply schedule has not. If we were to pose as one of their usual supply deliveries, we could infiltrate the grounds very easily."

"More genetemps?" came Isla's dry rejoinder. "Are you up for that, Tero?"

All three women looked at him and he clenched

his jaw. "Am I ever going to live it down? Yes, I messed up Persis's coding that one time. I'm not a genetemper, sorry. Have you ever had a problem with one of my palmport apps? Your knockout drug's working fine, right, Perse?"

She shrugged. "So far."

"And you, Your Highness? I've been keeping you and your brother in nonstop toys and I don't recall a single complaint." He glared at the image of Isla hovering over the oblet, and she looked down and away. An odd response, Persis thought. As if she was really hurt by his accusation.

"Yes." Andrine rolled her eyes. "You're brilliant. We get it. But you almost killed the Wild Poppy. If it wasn't for Justen—"

Tero snorted. "Fine. Get your precious Helo to cook you up some genetemps, then."

Persis expected New Pacifica would freeze over before that happened.

"I'll stick to cuttle jellies and other life-forms on my own, *low* level."

"What's burning you?" Andrine asked her brother. "I'm just teasing."

Persis, too, was taken aback by her friend's tone. Was she really acting high-and-mighty? Andrine didn't seem to think so, so what was Tero's problem?

"Come on," Persis said sweetly. "You know you're our favorite gengineer, even if you did try to kill me that one time."

"I didn't try to," he corrected, and the teasing was back in his tone. So whatever he was angry about, it wasn't her fault. "If I'd actually tried, your little revolutionary boyfriend wouldn't even have had a chance to save you."

"He's not really my boyfriend," Persis said automatically.

"No," he grumbled, grouchy again. "None of us have *real* boyfriends or girlfriends, do we?"

Andrine looked confused. Persis was sure she was wearing a similar expression.

"For a moment, let's talk about something other than our love lives," Isla cut in.

"That's rich, coming from you," Persis said. For the last week, she'd been trying to get Isla to realize she had better things to do than go on a public relations campaign with Justen.

"Thank you!" Tero cried to Persis. She stared at him, baffled. There was something she was missing here, and that hardly ever happened.

"Look, we're sorry for making fun of you," she said at last. "Obviously, we think you're a very talented gengineer, and that the unfortunate incident was just a mistake, or we wouldn't ask you again. But we *are* asking. Can you do it?"

Tero's lips made a thin, stern line. "Yes. I'll do it. For you, Persis, and for Andrine. For the League."

"Thank you," Andrine said, exasperated.

"But not," he added, "for you, Your Highness." And he reached over and tapped the oblet off.

In the split second before the connection ended, Isla's eyes met Persis's.

The princess regent of Albion looked guilty.

# Seventeen

PERSIS STARED DOWN AT the pricker in her hand. She doubted very highly that Justen Helo would approve of what she was about to do. Not that his opinion should matter. She was only pretending that he was her boyfriend, after all.

She gritted her teeth and rolled up her sleeve, remembering all too well the last time she'd attempted genetemps. Tero promised he'd filtered out all the bugs. He swore he'd gotten it right this time.

But he also seemed to have a lot of stuff on his mind.

"Persis?" said Andrine, huddled close by her side on the narrow cabin bench. She, too, held a pricker, but seemed to be waiting for Persis to go first. The boat they'd borrowed from the fishing village smelled of salt and seaweed. "We're still going through with this, right?"

"Of course. I trust your brother, don't you?"

"Sure. As far as I can throw him."

"Slipstream is great," Persis argued.

"We're humans, Persis. Not weasels."

"Sea minks," she corrected.

"Whatever." Andrine stared at the pricker in distaste. "You don't think—you don't think anything's going on with Tero and Isla, do you?"

Persis had vaguely suspected that Tero had a crush on her best friend. His palmport apps, his adoption of "your highness" when all her other friends were still calling her Isla, his ability to use any excuse at all to run errands from the Royal College of Gengineers' lab to the court . . . and that was fine. But his anger and Isla's guilty expressions yesterday—had things moved beyond unrequited crush? With the ruler of the realm? Was this what came of Tero growing up in Scintillans and seeing Persis's parents live happily ever after? There was a huge difference between a reg marrying a random aristo and one falling for the princess regent. Maybe Persis should have been paying more attention to what was going on with her friends.

And maybe if Justen Helo knew what she was thinking, he'd get all revolutionary again.

She took a deep breath and jabbed the pricker in her arm. "Tero is always making her those palmport apps." The burn began deep in her muscles and she winced and reached out for the pallet shoved in the corner of the cabin.

Andrine followed suit. "That might prove he *doesn't* like her. I mean have you *seen* the supplement she has to take to run that jumping threads application? It's like drinking rock slurry."

Tero had warned them there might be dizziness in the half hour it took the genes to reach maximum expression in her system. She stumbled over to the rough linen cushion and collapsed, and the boat pitched beneath her feet as Andrine joined her.

"Too bad your father geolocked the *Daydream*," she slurred to Persis. "At least there we could be sick in comfort."

"Sick," Persis agreed through chattering teeth, "but also far more suspicious. I think this particular genetemps will be harder to explain away as a party drug gone foul, and they've stepped up their monitoring of all boats from Albion."

Papa's restrictions might be a blessing in disguise. Someone in Galatea would eventually correlate the appearance of the *Daydream* with a visit from the Wild Poppy. There were enough commonplace fishing boats in the Scintillans Village that Andrine and Persis could commandeer one without anyone getting wise. A new round of tremors overtook her and Persis hugged herself and clenched her jaw to ease the pain.

"This . . . had . . . better . . . be . . . worth it, Persis," said Andrine, who sounded similarly pained.

Persis reached over to give her friend a comforting pat, but every move sent arrows of agony through her flesh. "Don't worry," she ground out. "If it goes wrong, I'll treat you to a full body wax."

Andrine forced a laugh, and everything went dark.

WHEN SHE WOKE, PERSIS could tell by the angle of the sun that at least an hour had passed. She stood up, her muscles stiff and slightly sore from the spasming. Andrine was still asleep, but the evidence of the drug's effectiveness was there on her face. Persis crossed to the mirror they'd hung above the cabin door.

"Well, Tero," she whispered, and her voice came out deep and gruff. "Good job."

A fine, downy black hair covered Persis's face from the bottom of her nose down past the collar of her shirt. Her hands, when she reached up to touch her face, seemed swollen—the palms were wide, the fingers broad, and the knuckles far more evident. Her feet felt tight inside her slippers, and she was sure she'd find the same changes wrought there. Her amber eyes seemed darkened to a muddy brown and even her complexion appeared darker, though it was difficult to tell beneath her new beard.

What would everyone think of her now? Stylish, feminine aristo Persis Blake had been wiped off the map, and in her place was a rough-looking man. She couldn't picture the image before her as the toast of Albion society, couldn't picture him luring Justen into the water and kissing him against a rock wall. A giggle escaped her lips; but in her new rough voice, it came out sounding more like a grunt. Here she was, rough and furry, and freer than she'd been in days.

She ran her fingertips over her mouth. It remained much the same. These were the lips Justen had kissed. Would he even recognize them now, surrounded by so much hair? Maybe, if she looked like this, she'd never be put in the position of having to kiss people she didn't want to in the first place. If she looked like this, she could be a Council member. If Isla looked like her father, she could be a king.

But she still couldn't date Tero Finch.

Last night, as Persis swam in the star cove and trumpeted the great opportunity to be found for regs in Albion, Justen had reminded her that they weren't spread out equally. Noemi would never run her own sanitarium. Tero had grown up to be a gengineer, but his sister, Andrine, despite her service to the princess, would never be a Council member. And a princess regent could never rule the country or marry a reg.

Just because things were better in Albion didn't make them perfect.

But that was neither here nor there at the moment. She needed to rescue Lady Ford and the others, who were in far more immediate danger than any women or regs in Albion.

Quickly, she gathered up supplies to complete the transformation. When she was finished, her hair had been painted with dark temporary dye and arranged in a flat, unobtrusive tail down her back. The fuzz on her face had been transformed into a trailing mustache and a neatly kept beard. Dressed in a squarish coat, cropped trousers, and cylindrical cap, she looked every inch the part of a salt miner from Galatea's southern shores.

A moan at her back gave her pause, but when Persis looked around, Andrine was still deeply asleep. The sedative Persis had added to Andrine's dose of genetemps should last for several hours. She double-checked, but the moan appeared to be a false alarm. Persis took a breath, then let it out. Andrine would no doubt be furious when she awoke, but until Justen figured out how to fix the problems with detoxing the regs who got Reduced, Persis refused to let her friend be put in more danger than strictly necessary.

Andrine's family was Helo-cured. If she was caught and Reduced, she might never recover, and Persis would definitely never forgive herself. Andrine, so young and so brilliant—doing all this because of her loyalty to Persis? No, it wasn't worth it.

Then again, Persis had never been tested. She might have an aristo mind and never even have to worry about Darkening, or she might be a reg through and through. If she were caught and Reduced, she might never escape, either.

But that was a risk she'd have to take.

FEW PLACES IN THE islands were as dismal as the Halahou city prison. The golden sunlight that bathed the rest of New Pacifica didn't penetrate its interior courtyards, and the gray basalt walls were devoid of color or decoration. The moans and wails of the Reduced ricocheted down corridors and bounced off the ceilings of the cells. The sound was relentless. Those who visited the prison often wondered if even Reduction was worse than the punishment of waiting for sentencing in your cell and listening to the unintelligible chorus that you, too, would make once your brain was scuttled by the drug. Was this the sound that their ancestors had made for generations? Was this the noise that permeated the islands before the cure? Such a notable aspect of Reduction would surely have made it into the histories, right?

But it was silly to question whether or not the Reduction drug was different from actual Reduction. Dangerous, too.

Those who questioned the revolution would soon get caught in its crosshairs.

Today, the prison was more chaotic than usual, with all the excitement surrounding the triumph over the evil Lady Ford and her army of royalists. The Fords had waged a month-long battle of resistance against the revolution, barricading their estate against the military police and enlisting the help of loyal regs against their best interest. As the siege had drawn out over days and weeks, the fiasco had become a thorn in Citizen Aldred's side. The regs loyal to the Fords had spoken out against the revolution, disseminating royalist propaganda and undermining the populace's support of the new republic. It was not to be borne. The Fords would have to pay, and so would anyone who'd dared side with them.

But, at last, the barricades had fallen and the Ford estate belonged to the people of Galatea, thanks in no small part to the tireless efforts of Citizen Aldred's own daughter, Captain Vania Aldred. The Fords and their supporters had been transferred to Halahou prison to receive a public Reduction, which would be broadcast at sunset all over the island. Along with the Fords had come a host of new guards, mostly transfers from the siege. They wouldn't need nearly so many forces at the estate once it was a work camp, even with the new guidelines that General Gawnt had put in place to root out the Wild Poppy.

All this was perfectly understood by the bearded figure who was slowly driving a service skimmer filled with barrels of salt up to the gate of the Halahou city prison.

"What took you so long?" the head gate guard asked as the salter handed over an oblet with the inventory and order list. "You were supposed to make this delivery several hours ago."

"Lava flow cut off the road," the salter grunted. "Don't have heat shields on the lifters."

The guard whistled through his teeth. "What is going on down in the southern lowlands? It's a good thing Citizen Aldred's in charge now. We regs will get the public works we deserve."

"Long live the revolution," the salter said, lifting a gloved fist.

Once inside the prison, the salter made a big show of unloading the prison's barrels, then trying and failing to restart his skimmer.

"Looks like it needs a fresh battery," the salter said, in case anyone was listening.

He wandered down one corridor and then another, the dead battery in his arms, as if searching for a geo-charging station.

After the third turn, he found what he was looking for. A young girl in a military uniform sat in the shadow of a wall, far away from security imagers.

"Private Delmar," he said, his smile hidden behind his beard. "You're looking well."

Remy Helo stood and smoothed down her chin-length hair. "Not too loud. I've been recognized once already and said I was looking for my uncle. But most people just see the uniform and ignore my face. There are so many new guards today from the Ford estate, no one knows anyone."

"That's what we're counting on."

Remy peered through the shadows at the salter. "Are you . . . *her*? Or someone else?"

"What does it matter?" said Persis. "You know what I'm here for."

Remy regarded the beard and the other changes. "This is a much better disguise than the last one you used."

"I'm glad you approve. Now let's get going."

Persis quickly dispatched the two guards monitoring the cells holding the Fords.

"Is that the drug you used on me?" Remy whispered as she watched the knockout drugs spinning from Persis's palmport and smacking the guards in the face.

Persis didn't answer. She inserted the nanotech key into the panel and it quickly scrambled the locking mechanism. With the cell unlocked, she pressed a lever on the skimmer battery. It began to droop and sag, looking less every moment like a piece of machinery and more like a sack of some sort. Inside were the items Remy would need to complete the mission.

Persis handed the sack to Remy and gestured to the cell. "The rest is up to you," she said. "Welcome to the League."

Remy nodded and took a deep breath. "Wait—" she said. "Aren't you forgetting something?"

"What?"

"I need a wild poppy. They'll never believe I'm here to help them without one."

Persis laughed despite herself. When a wild poppy

could be found on the side of every road in Galatea, it was hardly a certificate of authenticity. Nevertheless, she pointed at the edge of the battery-turned-bag. "Everything you need is there."

There, on the side, glowed the outline of a wild poppy in shimmery nanotech gold.

Remy beamed and headed for the cells.

Back at the skimmer, Persis managed to reassemble, then start her engine again with little trouble. She hovered out to the gate once more, relieved to find a bit of a backup. Everything was going according to plan. The guard transfer at the gate seemed to be somewhat chaotic, with a tangle of new guards coming in and going out—not all of whom seemed to understand the protocol. When everything was sorted, she let out a deep breath and moved up to take her place.

"I apologize for the delay," said the head guard as Persis handed over her inventory oblet once more. "Some of these new transfers aren't especially well trained."

"I see that," she replied. "Almost wondered if Citizen Aldred has taken to Reducing his own."

The guard shrugged. "Heard those rumors, too, huh? These lot are probably untouchable. The Ford estate transfers are all under the command of Captain Vania Aldred, you know."

Persis swallowed. "The daughter?"

"Explains why they're such a mess, huh?" the guard said with a snort. "She's not old enough for her own command, if you ask me. Course, I never said such a thing."

"Right." Persis and her genetemps-enhanced vocal

cords gave a deep, throaty, salter chuckle as the guard pressed the lever to open the gate. Persis started to move out, but there was a figure blocking her path, a medic by the look of the uniform.

"Citizen Fisher," the medic called and waved at the guard.

"Citizen Paint," the guard replied. "Back again? Another problem with the latest batch of pinks?"

Persis decided it was time for her skimmer to break down again. She ground the gears to a halt and the engine died, thumping the machine to the ground.

"What's this about?" cried the guard. "Get a move on. You're blocking the gate."

"So sorry, Citizen!" Persis jumped out of the cab and went around to mess with the fans. "It's been giving me problems all day."

The guard gave her an exasperated sneer and turned back to his medic friend. "So what's wrong now? We had a bit of a fright last week when the last batch turned out to be a dud. Prisoners waking up all over the island."

Persis bit her lip to conceal a delighted smile. Could this be possible?

"Well, it's either the pills or the prisoners are building up a resistance to its effects."

She'd have to inform Noemi of this as soon as she got home.

The medic turned to Persis and snorted. "Need a push, man?" He looked back at the guard. "Apparently not everyone needs a pink to be an idiot, right, Fisher? Anyway, the lab guys are flummoxed, and it's not like they've got the Helo wonder kid around to fix things up anymore. Have you heard he's run off to Albion? Taken up with some aristo girl, apparently."

"You never can tell about a person, can you?" said the guard.

Persis pressed a button on the side of the skimmer and the fans clanked together, emitting a shower of sparks.

The medic jumped. "Watch what you're doing, man! Don't you know this is a prison? You're liable to get shot if you start a fire."

"Yes, sir," she said meekly. "You're right about that. Say, did you say you knew a Helo? A real live Helo?"

The guard grunted. "Don't know how much of a 'real Helo' he is to run off with an aristo."

But the medic puffed out his chest as he replied. "I know him pretty well, actually. He was a few years below me in school. Of course, I didn't have Citizen Aldred giving me special assignments like Justen Helo did. Smart as a whip, that kid, but he does put on airs. Thinks he's way too good to just sit in a lab all day and mix up pinks, so we've got to do it."

"That doesn't surprise me," the guard admitted. "Aldred's daughter is the same way. Went right to the top, that one. Regs that think they're aristos, if you ask me."

Persis risked speaking up again. "But it was Persistence Helo what ended Reduction. Her grandson probably doesn't want to be involved in starting it up again."

"What is that supposed to mean?" The guard scowled at Persis. "You'd better watch your tongue, salter. You have no idea what you're talking about."

The medic laughed in agreement. "You sure don't! Helo's the one who invented pinks in the first place."

Persis's heart dropped somewhere into the vicinity of her kneecaps.

"That's why he's so high on himself," the medic went on. "That's why he's Aldred's right-hand man—or was until he wandered off island."

But Justen was helping the refugees. Justen hated what was happening to the Galatean prisoners. Justen had defected from Galatea because of how evil the revolution had become.

It wasn't true. This medic was full of bitterness toward Justen. He was lying to make Justen look bad. Except . . .

The medic had nothing at all against pinks. He thought that was the best thing Justen ever did. He wasn't criticizing him—in fact, he was praising Justen. She restarted the skimmer and got out of the prison as quickly as she could, her mind erupting with anxiety.

Could she have left her refugees in the hands of the man responsible for their torture?

REMY HELO WAITED WITH her charges at the rendezvous point. The Wild Poppy hadn't given her any instructions on what to do once the prisoners were clear of the city limits, so she was pleased that Lady Ford had the presence of mind to corral her people out of sight until the Poppy rejoined them.

When she did, she appeared frazzled. Already, the genetemps of the spy's disguise was fading, and she looked more like a woman in a fake beard than the salter who'd shown up at the prison.

"Is there a problem?" Remy asked.

"Not at all," the Poppy replied. "As expected, the prison guards followed me, searched my skimmer, and found nothing." She looked at the escaped prisoners in their prison guard uniforms and blinked twice as if forgetting for a moment why she was there.

This was not the cool-headed spy who'd wrestled her gun away with a devil-may-care smile on her face. This wasn't the elegant handmaiden who'd laid bare Remy's soul on the floor of Princess Isla's throne room. Something was wrong.

"Are all the Ford prisoners accounted for?" she asked at last.

"We are," said Lady Ford. She took off her guard's cap and shook her hair free. "And you must be the famous Wild Poppy. Younger than I'd thought. And . . . more feminine."

The Poppy inclined her head. "My lady. We're not out of the danger zone yet. I need you and your companions to board my ship for the journey back to Albion."

"I'm eternally grateful for all you've done for me and my people, Poppy," Lady Ford replied, "but I would never be able to live with myself if I abandoned my country in its time of need. My place is where it's always been, on the Ford estate, protecting my lands and those who live there."

"Madam," said the Poppy, "it's dangerous for you here."

"It's dangerous for *you* here," said Lady Ford, then gestured to Remy. "It's dangerous for this revolutionary soldier who led us from the prison. But that doesn't absolve any of us from our duties. I will give my people the option to go with you if they choose. Some already have children in Albion and may wish to be reunited with them."

"Three of your children await you in Albion, too," the Poppy argued.

"My children know that my separation from them is in service to our homeland." Lady Ford shook her head. "It's no use arguing with me, young lady. You aren't alone in fighting to save Galatea. I have other friends on this island. We'll find ways to hide. And we can be more of a help to you here than we could hiding out in Albion."

The Poppy's bushy, mannish eyebrows furrowed, but she relented, and Lady Ford left to speak to her people about who was leaving and who was staying behind.

"Now I see," said Remy, "why the revolution thinks the Fords are so dangerous."

"Indeed," replied the Poppy. "Maybe one day we'll grow up to be like her."

Remy raised her eyebrows at the Poppy. It was easy to forget, sometimes, that the spy was only a little older than she was. "Oh, I think you're plenty like her already. Probably even more so, since, unlike Lady Ford, you've never made a mistake and gotten caught."

Beneath her beard, the Wild Poppy frowned. "No, I never have been caught. But we've all made mistakes." She shrugged it off. "And everything is going well for you?"

"Yes. No one even noticed I was gone." Remy shrugged. "They don't even care if I'm at school or not."

"Have you spoken to your brother?" she asked now.

Remy shook her head. "No. I— We had a fight before I left, and since I got back, I've been caught up in collecting information about the Ford transfer. He's hard to get in touch with, you know. He's either living at the royal labs or out at a sanitarium in the middle of nowhere."

"He's in Albion," the spy said abruptly. "Has been for a week."

This did surprise Remy. Justen had been there at the same time as she? And he hadn't even left her a message saying he was going? She recalled his fear in their last conversation, his certainty that he was about to bring the wrath of Uncle Damos down on his head. Had he done something even more foolish while she was away? "Do you know what he's doing there?"

"I was hoping that you, as his sister, might tell me. Furthering his research, perhaps, on the Reduction drug that's ravaging your countrymen?"

Remy clamped her mouth shut.

The spy eyed her, eyes blazing. "You do not deny, then, that it was your brother who developed the method Aldred is using to torture his citizens?"

Remy's heart pounded in her chest. A week ago, she'd been terrified that Justen had succeeded in sabotaging the Reduction program Uncle Damos was basing his rule on. Now, she feared the opposite. What might the Wild Poppy do to her brother now that she knew the truth?

"Please," she said softly. "Don't hurt him. He's the only family I have left. And he's not a bad person, I promise. I don't think he had any idea how far this would go. None of us did. And Uncle Damos—Citizen Aldred—he was so encouraging of Justen's research, in a way that the queen never was. You have to understand that. To Justen, the science is everything. And Uncle Damos was the one who made it possible."

"Naturally," said the Poppy, her voice soft and strangely sad. "I imagine that to Citizen Aldred, Justen Helo is quite the hero."

# Eighteen

JUSTEN SIGHED AT THE pile of half-assembled nanorectors littering his desk. The brain stem model the minuscule computers were in the process of constructing was getting him nowhere. Might as well start from scratch. One downside of not having a palmport like the other medics at the lab—while they could wave their hands at the nanorectors and dissolve them into blocks again, he had to type his instructions into an oblet.

He chuckled to himself. He'd better watch it—he was beginning to sound like Persis. Next he'd be calling typing "primitive."

Not that he was going to get a palmport. He'd already had quite enough of Albian fashion, thank you very much. He'd woken this morning to find his clothes either hidden or—if he knew Persis—destroyed and several new outfits hanging ready for him in his closet. As Persis had been nowhere to be found, he hadn't yet had the opportunity to complain that her idea of proper attire included collars that chafed his neck and inappropriately shiny trousers cut entirely too tightly at the crotch.

Even Fredan hadn't been able to hold back a chuckle when Justen had emerged in his new outfit and asked to borrow a skimmer to drive to the lab.

The clothes might be appropriate for a cocktail party or lounging about in court, but after ten hours on a stool in the laboratory, Justen was ready to strip naked. Why Persis preferred such clothing was beyond him. Maybe they should stick to bathing suits.

They got along a lot better in those, anyway.

Justen had done his best to push the memory of Persis's kiss from his mind while he worked today. It meant nothing—just a publicity stunt, like everything else they did together. And it hadn't been the taste of her mouth or the feel of her skin that had flitted around the edges of his mind while he worked to save the refugees. Instead, it had been her words.

*We can only be responsible for what we ourselves do. Bad things happen in this world, and we are judged on how we respond. Do we take part in evil, or do we fight against it with all we have?*

He was truly off course if Persis Blake was the one talking real sense. Though, make no mistake, Persis Blake was not as stupid as she'd first appeared. Maybe Justen had underestimated her, the same way he'd dismissed every aristo. Sure, they were spoiled and could be silly and shallow. But they weren't all like that, and that's not all they were, either. Persis was certainly frivolous and overprivileged, but she was also charming and playful and kind. Not everyone was made for saving the world. It didn't necessarily make them bad people. And maybe some aristos in Galatea deserved to be removed from power, but none of them deserved to be tortured as the revolutionaries were torturing their prisoners. *None* of them deserved Reduction.

If Justen was to be judged for what he did, he'd like it to be for fixing the problem he'd created and curing the refugees before it was too late.

He punched a code into his oblet, and watched the brain model on his desk disintegrate. But it wouldn't be tonight.

Instead, he shut down his oblet and headed out of the facility. On his way, he stopped by the refugees' chamber. All those months in Galatea, he'd avoided the lab where they made the pinks, he'd avoided the prisons and the labor camps, as if not seeing the victims of his work would somehow lessen his own responsibility.

Never again. Standing before him, the people he'd hurt were impossible to forget, impossible to ignore. He wouldn't rest until he'd helped them. What Justen had done was an accident, but he was to blame for failing to stop it before people's lives were destroyed.

Today, a few Reduced were sitting before a large music keyboard, plonking out random notes. An older man sat before them, clapping heartily—for encouragement, Justen figured, since he couldn't really be impressed by the atonal noise. After a few minutes, he seemed to notice Justen's presence and joined him at the threshold.

"Good evening. Are you here to visit friends or family?"

Taken aback, Justen replied, "Neither. I—I work here, actually."

"Oh." The old man's eyes widened. "Forgive me. With your hair and lack of palmport, I mistook you for a Galatean."

"I am," Justen replied. "I'm also a medic. I'm trying to help the refugees—"

"How wonderful!" he exclaimed, and held out his hand. "I'm Lord Benzo Lacan of Galatea. What's your name?"

"Justen," he mumbled. Just Justen. So here was Lacan, the man he'd tried to save by sabotaging the pinks sent to his estate. He'd failed—but the Wild Poppy had succeeded. Justen knew this aristo had been an ally of his grandmother's. His Reduction had been proof Justen could no longer ignore regarding how perverted the revolution had become.

"So they put you to work right away, did they?" Lord Lacan went on. "That's good. These Albians need all the help they can get it seems, especially given the problems we're facing. This Reduction drug"—the lord's voice turned dark—"it's the worst evil to be visited on the world since the wars, I think. Reduction almost destroyed the human race. The fact that the revolutionaries have resurrected it to achieve their political goals—I can think of no punishment severe enough to repay them, can you?"

"No," Justen said softly. "I can't."

VANIA HAD BEEN WAITING on the outlandish inlaid-stone terrace belonging to Justen's aristo girlfriend for a full hour by the time she heard the unmistakable whirr of skimmer lifters over gravel out front. She could hear the abominably rude butler who'd shown her in—he of the appalling orange-dyed hair—greeting Justen at the front door, then informing him stiffly that a young woman from Galatea was here for him. There was a pounding of feet as Justen rushed toward the terrace.

Poor boy. Vania had been right. He must be positively suffocated by these Albian aristos. She smiled as he came out into the sunlight. He frowned and skidded to a dead stop on the terrace before he reached her.

"Vania." Justen's tone was flat.

Vania swallowed and lifted her chin, resisting the temptation to smooth her hair. It had been, perhaps, a bit of a rough journey across the sea. And there was quite the wind down on the docks. But he should have been far happier to see her. Had Albion corrupted him already?

"Justen." She eyed his outfit. A little shinier than he'd been wont to wear back home but not too outlandish. Judging by what she'd learned about this Persis Blake girl, Vania had been half expecting feathers. Had they no idea how ridiculous they looked? Even the workers she'd met at the base of the cliff had dyed hair. No wonder the Wild Poppy was so skilled in the art of disguise. It seemed every Albian, from the lowliest servant on up, cared too much about fashion. "Been keeping yourself busy here in foreign lands? Where is your aristo girlfriend?"

As she hoped, Justen flinched at that. Good. So he hadn't lost all his revolutionary principles.

"Vania. This is . . . a surprise."

She lifted one shoulder. "Well, I'm visiting Albion

anyway, so I thought I'd drop in on my dear friend, meet his fine lady—"

"Persis is a friend," Justen said quickly. Again, very good. "And why are you here? I thought you were stationed at the Ford barricade."

Vania smiled. "It fell yesterday. The Fords, their heir, and any of their servants still foolish enough to stand by their side are imprisoned in Halahou, awaiting their sentencing. They will all be properly punished."

"You mean Reduced," Justen replied in a low voice.

"Of course. What else?"

Justen said nothing for a long moment, as if carefully weighing his words. "Do you think the revolutionary government is overusing that form of punishment? It was never meant for regs. It was never meant—"

"Don't be so modest!" Vania laughed. "Pretty soon, we won't have to use it at all, ever. Just the threat of Reduction is usually enough to make people realize the importance of supporting our policies. Once everyone is in agreement, things are going to be so much more harmonious back home. For everyone. The revolution won't last forever, Justen. It's a little violent right now, but it's all in the service of creating a better future."

"A better future for whom?" Justen said. "The regs you're about to Reduce from the Ford estate?"

"They were royalists," Vania pointed out. "They're enemies of the revolution."

"And the heir?" He wouldn't let up, would he? "She's a child. What's her crime?"

"She's an aristo!" Was this what came of being in Albion for any length of time? You started siding with royalists? You took up with some aristo whose greatest skill in life was coordinating her jewelry with her dress? Why were they even *having* this conversation? The old Justen would have congratulated her on a successful campaign.

Though honestly, Vania didn't think she'd heard one word of praise out of his mouth about her work since Queen Gala died. He'd been far too caught up in his research, in all that he'd been doing for the revolution.

"Look, Justen," she said, annoyed, "I came here with nothing but good intentions. I want to congratulate you. I want to meet this girl who—aristo though she is—has apparently stolen your heart."

Justen's expression softened. "I'm glad you're here, Vania. You've always been such a good friend to me and—I need a friend right now."

"These Albians you're so enamored with don't fit the bill?" she scoffed.

"You know me better than that."

She groaned aloud. "Then what are you doing here, Justen? Research? What hold can these aristos possibly have on you?"

"Vania—" Justen's voice dropped to a whisper and he moved in close.

Vania inhaled, waiting for the familiar scent of Justen to hit her nostrils—but he smelled different, too. Probably perfumed with the Blake family flower. Revolting.

His voice was little more than a breath. "Do we really

know what we're doing with the Reduction drug? What if we're hurting people?"

She frowned, incredulous. Of course they were hurting people. That was the *whole point*. What kind of punishment didn't involve pain? "They're traitors. Enemies of the revolution. Do you think we should give them a parade?"

"I think we should stop using the drug," Justen replied, his voice louder now and steady as the cliffs themselves. "We have no idea what the long-term effects are. It hasn't undergone the proper testing—"

"You should have thought of that before." Vania sniffed and backed away. So he was turning his back on the revolution. It was good he *was* here, then. This kind of talk back home would have cast a dark light of suspicion on Justen, Helo name or no. "And if you plan to stay in Albion, then I can't imagine what happens with the revolution should actually concern you so much anymore."

"I'd better stay in Albion," Justen replied. "If I go to Galatea, one wrong word might see me Reduced as well."

How astute he was! "Don't worry about yourself," Vania snapped, "but do take a care for your aristo girlfriend."

Justen gave her a murderous glare and Vania bit her tongue. Perhaps that last part had been over the line. "I'll ask again, Vania." Any trace of friendship had left his tone. "What are you doing here?"

Fine. Two could play that way. She stood up as straight as she could, though she was still a few inches shorter than Justen. "I'm here in service to my country. I'm trying to track down the Wild Poppy."

Justen appeared nonplussed. "Any leads?"

"None of your business."

Justen sighed and shook his head. "Well, I'd wish you luck, but . . . I actually don't. The Wild Poppy is the only man on Earth who seems capable of stemming the tide of destruction this revolution has caused."

Vania's mouth dropped open. "Treason. Open treason? Justen, what's become of you?"

"What's become of *you*!" Justen cried. "Listen to yourself. Celebrating the Reduction of the Ford child. It's disgusting."

"Disgusting?" Vania clenched her fists around the hem of her coat to keep from punching Justen right in his silk-clad stomach. "I'm sorry the revolution isn't as pretty as one of your girlfriend's soirees. I'm sorry it's not all flutternotes and luaus. And I'm sorry that you can't handle the reality. This is what it takes to make a better future, Justen. There are people who are going to fight against what we're trying to do in Galatea. There are people who are going to try to stop us if we don't stop them first. You'd think, after all those years with my father, you'd understand that better."

"I understand a lot of things. I understand that we have no hope for a better future if it's built on a foundation of torturing our fellow citizens over political disagreements. We're torturing *children*, Vania. *Children*. I have no love for cruel aristos. I've met some Galatean refugees here—"

Vania pounced on this. "Who?"

He waved her off with a distracted "the Seris."

She made a face. "They're terrible. The Poppy will pay for kidnapping them!"

"That's not the point. I hate the Seris. I will always hate them. They hate me. They hated Persistence Helo. But when they disagreed with her, they debated her, they voted against her, they argued and fought like civilized people. They didn't torture her or give her drugs to destroy her brain. And that's what *we're* doing, Vania. We're worse than people like the Seris ever thought of being."

Vania stared at him, jaw clenched, eyes blazing with anger and what she absolutely refused to admit might be the seeds of tears. This could not be Justen. Her best friend. Practically her brother. If he'd been back in Galatea, would she have the strength to report his words to her father? Since he was in Albion, she could afford to be lenient. After all, he couldn't damage the revolution from here. But it still broke her heart.

If he couldn't understand the difference, she didn't know how to explain it to him. The Seris had the luxury of avoiding violence. Their power was centralized, firm, absolute. They were aristos from a long line of aristos. They were certain of their position. Until the revolutionary government had complete control of the island, had the respect and recognition of Albion, had consolidated its sovereignty—things were too fragile to allow dissidence.

"The Ford heir was dangerous to our cause," Vania said at last, "not necessarily because of anything she did herself but because of what she represented. She has power because of who she would be allowed to become, unchecked. An aristo, the head of an estate. Given power for no reason other than her birth. It's a difficult decision but unfortunately she has to suffer the consequences. She has to bear the punishment for the crimes committed by her ancestors."

"And when our children are judged for *our* crimes?" Justen asked coldly.

"Justen—"

But he wouldn't listen. "Before the cure," he said, "when aristos treated our Reduced forefathers poorly, they said we deserved it. We deserved it because it was our ancestors who'd ruined the world. Our ancestors who performed the gengineering that caused the Reduction, who started the wars, who cracked open the Earth."

"Yes," she said. "And now the aristos are being repaid for their cruelty." How was this not obvious to him?

"And then we will be repaid for ours, and then the cycle will start all over again. When does it end, Vania? Does the world have to be completely destroyed?"

"I hope not," came a silky voice from the far end of the terrace. "I rather think we've destroyed enough of it already."

Vania turned, and was confronted with a figure who could be no one but Lady Persis Blake. She was swathed from chin to toe in what looked like form-fitting chain mail, and despite herself, Vania's first thought was of some ancient female knight.

What seemed like acres of yellow and white hair was piled up on top of the girl's head, making her tall, slim figure even more towering. Her features could not be seen clearly, as her face was obscured by a tight silver veil embroidered thickly across her cheeks with silver beading in a starburst design.

Vania blinked. It was late afternoon. This was Persis Blake's daytime wear? She was more ridiculous even than Vania's research had led her to believe.

"Justen." Persis glided toward them. "You didn't tell me you were expecting a guest."

"I wasn't," he grumbled. "This is Vania Aldred, an old friend from Galatea."

"Lady Blake," said Vania, inclining her head a full millimeter, which was more than her father would want and more than this glittering statue deserved. "I'm Captain Aldred of the revolutionary army."

Persis laughed, a musical sound that instantly grated on Vania's nerves. "How fascinating. A captain! Who knew that my Justen was friends with members of the military?" She smiled so broadly, Vania could make it out even through the mesh of her clinging veil. "And what brings you to my home? Merely here to visit Justen, or are you opening diplomatic relations with our princess regent?"

"She's looking for the Wild Poppy," Justen muttered.

Persis pressed a gloved hand against her chain mail–encased throat. "How extraordinary! And here I'd been under the impression that the revolutionaries thought our celebrated spy was an actual threat to them. He won't be half so much fun to gossip about if the Galateans don't even care."

"We *do* care," Vania snapped. "That's why I'm here to find him."

Persis cocked her head. "They can't care too much, if all they sent was a little girl."

Justen groaned and stepped between them before

Vania could do what she wanted. "You're going to have to indulge Persis, Vania. She's Albian, remember? She doesn't really understand the concept of women having leadership positions."

"Oh? I thought she was friends with the princess," Vania growled.

"I am," Persis trilled. "She wouldn't dare leave her dressing room without getting my approval on her footwear."

Justen turned to Vania with a look on his face that said *see?*

Except Vania didn't see. She didn't see at all what Justen could possibly find attractive about this empty-headed, shallow, crazily clothed aristo. She looked on in horror as Justen tried explaining to Persis that Vania actually had a very important job back home. He spoke to her as one might to a child.

"Persis, you know that's not how things work in Galatea. Vania is a very well-respected captain of the military police."

What sort of affection could possibly grow from this? Was this what men liked? Was this what *Justen* liked? No, she'd never believe that. Justen needed someone who could match him intellectually.

"And because she's Citizen Aldred's daughter, she has much more experience than most her age."

Well, he needn't have added *that* part.

"I suppose," Persis said at last, "that's good news for the Poppy. And for any aristos he might wish to save."

"I assure you it is not," Vania stated. "I will stop the Wild Poppy from undermining my homeland's new government."

Beneath the veil, Vania saw Persis's eyes slide in her direction. "Shall you? I'll be curious to see that." Then the aristo addressed Justen. "How *fierce* you all are in Galatea. Tell me, Justen, is this what most men of your nationality prefer in a woman?"

Finally, a good question. Vania turned to her old friend, who looked like he wanted to sink through the polished stone floor.

"Persis," he said with a sigh, "not now."

Ah, so all was not perfect in his aristocratic paradise. And, really, how could it be? As they liked to say in Galatea, his aristo girlfriend didn't need pinks to be an idiot.

The girl shrugged. "Well," she conceded, "I suppose it must be their fierceness. It certainly isn't their sense of fashion. Will your friend be staying long, Justen?"

"No," said Justen with a definitive shake of his head. "She won't be staying at all."

Persis nodded regally. "It was nice to meet you, Captain." She sashayed off.

Vania congratulated herself on her remarkable restraint. She hadn't even rolled her eyes. "Justen," she said, "you've gone mad. Aristos? Albion? This moronic, spoiled brat? I don't even know you anymore."

"No, you don't. And I don't know you. When the revolution began, it was about making a better Galatea. Is this better? Torturing and imprisoning your own citizens? Threatening your best friends?"

To be fair, she hadn't threatened him, just the spoiled aristo brat he'd taken up with. And it hadn't even been a *threat* so much as a statement of fact. "Stop being so dramatic. It's impossible that you've changed so much so quickly. What's happened to you, Justen? Don't you remember the day the old queen was sentenced? Don't you remember how happy we were? Finally, we'd been able to change the world."

"We changed it," he agreed. "But not for the better."

Vania sighed. This was going nowhere. Justen must have had his brains sucked out by his new girlfriend. She gathered her strength for another argument, but was interrupted by a message ping. She pulled out her oblet.

Captain Aldred,

Report: There's been a break-in at the prison and the entire Ford family and their servants escaped. Their cells were left empty except for the sign of the Wild Poppy.

Where are you?

Long live the revolution,

General Gawnt

# Nineteen

PERSIS MANAGED TO KEEP it together until she'd reached her bedroom, until she'd engaged the privacy screens, until she'd sat down at her vanity, unwound her mesh veil, and stared in the mirror at the rashy burns all over her face.

She met her angry, amber gaze in the glass, and her eyes began to sting.

"I did it," she grumbled to her reflection, "though I'd rather have tossed him off the pali."

The whole way back from Galatea, she'd been planning to do just that. Capture Justen as she'd captured his sister, drag him to the throne room for interrogation—maybe even utilize those neuroeels Isla claimed to have in the dungeon.

Six months as the Wild Poppy, and she'd never felt such an urge to get violent. Six months playing dumb, and she'd never felt as stupid as she did right now. She'd invited Justen into her home. She'd introduced him to the princess. She'd told him all about her mother's illness. She'd kissed him in the star cove. And, worst of all, she'd shown him the refugees in the sanitarium—the poor, broken people *he* was responsible for creating. And all the time, Justen had been lying to her. All the time, he was a worse enemy than Citizen Aldred himself.

Here she was, the most celebrated and loathed spy in New Pacifica, and she'd been taken in by a freshly cooled medic with a kind face and a famous name.

She'd planned to confront him with all that the very second she got home to Scintillans, but then she walked onto the terrace and saw him talking to Vania Aldred. *Captain* Vania Aldred, his "old friend." Captain Vania Aldred who'd toppled the Ford estate, and who'd apparently come to Albion specifically to seek out the Wild Poppy. Possibly with Justen's help.

Persis needed a plan. A good spy would neutralize her enemy as soon as possible. A great spy would go a step further. If Justen was working for the revolution in Albion, it would be better to play his game and use his position against him. She just had to find out if he suspected her first.

She looked at the girl in the mirror. Her eyes were glassy with unshed tears, bloodshot and baggy with exhaustion from the mission and the genetemps. Her face was swollen and red, her lips set in an angry line. Not the beautiful socialite any longer and not the skillfully disguised spy with the masculine features and corresponding beard. In this moment she was Persis, raw and unfiltered. The scared girl with the sick mother and the best friend trying single-handedly to yank her country back from the brink of revolution. The silly teenager with a crush on a famous boy who'd made her promises so convincing she'd almost risked it all in the star cove. And she could scrub and primp and style and none of that would change.

But she'd learned her lesson. She smoothed her expression as well as she could. She could do this. She was the greatest spy in New Pacifica. Bit by bit, she vanished, leaving only the steely determination of the Wild Poppy.

The screen pulsed. "Persis?" came Justen's voice.

She pasted on her most vacant smile, until even the Wild Poppy was hidden beneath the mask of Persis Flake, and disengaged the screen.

Justen strode into her room, and it was all Persis could do to keep her eyes on her reflection and her mask in place. "Where have you been all day? You were gone when I got up this morning."

"Oh, I'm sorry, darling. Andrine and I went to a spa and I turned off my palmport for relaxation purposes . . ." She gestured to the rash. "As you can see, it wasn't quite as relaxing as I'd hoped."

In the mirror, she saw the annoyance on his face evaporate. "Oh, Persis. What did you do to yourself this time? Have you put any ointments on it yet?" He reached for her cheek, but she jerked away from his touch.

"A slight allergic reaction." To him. "I'm managing." She always managed. She'd do it again, and he'd keep his war criminal medic's hands off her.

"Allergic reaction to what?"

She rolled her eyes. Were they really talking about

her pretend spa treatments? "My facial scrub, of course. I think . . . hibiscus? Can't remember. Anyway, what do you want?"

"Nothing. I"—he sounded almost sheepish—"I was wondering if maybe we could go swimming again."

Persis almost gasped. Was he serious? She really had melted in the star cove, then. And before that, too, when she'd led him right to the heart of the refugees. Even if he didn't suspect her of being anything more than Persis Blake, he'd managed to get quite a few secrets out of her already. And maybe he wasn't even after information, but just hoping to relax with a pretty, stupid aristo who would kiss him on command.

Either way, he could forget it.

"Are you sure you wouldn't rather take your Galatean friend?"

"Excuse me?" Justen spluttered.

Now Persis did face him, and let just a sliver of the rage she felt show on her face. "I know you think I'm stupid, Justen, and you're probably right. But if there's any hope for you at court, it might help if you weren't openly consorting with Citizen Aldred's daughter." She turned back to the mirror. "Especially since you're supposed to be madly in love with *me*."

In the reflection, she saw Justen blink in astonishment. "Persis, are you . . . jealous?"

Not even the girl she pretended to be would fall that fast. She rolled her eyes. "What I am is very concerned about our image as a couple. The moment I leave you alone on the estate, you start inviting your Galatean lover by?"

"I didn't know Vania was coming," Justen said. Or lied.

Persis whirled around. "Wrong answer again, Justen. My goodness, you're dreadful at public relations. You'd think, living with a propaganda machine like Citizen Aldred, you'd have picked up a few tips."

He shook his head in confusion. "What are you talking about?"

"The correct response to my accusation is 'She's not my lover. We're just old friends. I actually think of Vania more as a sister.'" Persis dropped her Justen impression. "That's the sort of thing people expect you to say. You should practice, you know, in case we have one of these spats when gossips are listening. Honestly, Justen, if someone like me can manage this, I don't understand why *you're* having trouble."

Justen plopped onto Persis's hammock. The golden silk fanned up around him, bringing with it a cloud of Persis's signature flowery scent. "Because I'm not a courtier, Persis. I'm not good at being political and charming. I'm a medic. All I want to do is work in my lab and make sick people well."

Liar. Liar, liar, liar. How she wished she could scream it at him. He was reclining on her bed and he was staring at her with that infuriatingly earnest expression, as if every word from his mouth were pure as fire. She'd fallen for it once. She'd wanted to believe him so badly she'd almost endangered the refugees all over again. She'd almost endangered herself.

She hadn't realized how hard she'd been hoping the prison medic was lying until she heard Remy confirm it:

Justen had invented the Reduction drug. He was responsible for this entire nightmare. On the boat, she'd almost managed to convince herself that Justen might have been telling Persis and Isla the truth, or at least part of it. That he *did* regret the direction the revolution had gone in. And maybe that meant he regretted the part he'd played in creating the pinks.

Except that didn't add up, either. If Justen Helo had honestly wanted to defect to Albion and atone for the sins of making the Reduction drug, then he would have told them so at once. He certainly would have brought up his special knowledge of the drug when he'd been shown the damaged refugees. He seemed deeply disturbed by what he saw, to be sure, but Persis knew all too well how something like that could be faked.

And then she'd seen him entertaining Vania Aldred.

If he truly was working for the revolution, the best thing Persis could do was make him think everything was going according to plan. If he truly was their enemy, capturing him—branding a *Helo* a war criminal—would only ignite the aristo-reg conflicts Isla was trying to avoid. For a moment, Persis stood at the edge of a precipice every bit as high as the Scintillans pali. But here, there was no glass-walled lift, here there was no zip line and the safety of a silk hammock. Here she was about to embark on the most important mission the Wild Poppy had ever undertaken.

"I spent all day in the lab," he said now, "while you've been getting your skin flayed off for fun. And I plan to go back first thing tomorrow morning, too."

"If you really cared," she said, her tone as smoothly

superior as possible, "you'd still be there, helping them move the facility, instead of talking to your *dear old friend*."

"They're moving the refugees?" Justen asked.

No, but let him report to Vania that they were. That would buy Persis some time to find a new safe house with Noemi. And it would also give her the opportunity to find out what Justen might be leaking to the Galateans.

"Darling, if you'd just get a palmport. They're the only way to stay in the loop in Albion. Noemi fluttered me when she couldn't get in contact with you." That sounded believable. Justen knew how her countrymen depended on their palmports.

"Where are they going?" he asked. Too quickly? Maybe even frantically? Was Justen understandably upset that he hadn't been told, or concerned that he'd given bad information to his revolutionary buddy?

"Oh"—Persis flicked her hand in the air—"somewhere inland. Such a hassle, really. You're going to spend so much time traveling to and fro, you'll hardly have any left to spend with me." And she planned to keep a much closer eye on him from now on.

"I'm not here for a vacation. I have to have my work. Otherwise this is all for nothing. I can't stand by while my countrymen keep suffering."

"I beg to differ, Justen." He'd stood by just fine for six months now. "As we discussed, part of your bargain with Isla was that you spend time with me—"

"I don't expect you to understand, Persis," he replied coldly. "Just tell me where they're moving the lab."

Not likely. Fake Persis may pretend she didn't care, and real Persis might not fully understand all the intricacies of Justen's work and the further damage he might potentially do, but both of them could unite under the banner of keeping him as far away from the refugees as humanly possible.

Fredan appeared in the doorway, his face drawn, his usual butler's air of indifferent formality utterly absent. "Persis. You're needed in your mother's room."

She took off without another word.

Outside, dusk had descended on the lawn, but the sound of evening insects gave way to screams and crashes that ricocheted across the stone and crystal columns and polished floors. Persis was relieved they'd be swept away by the wind as soon as they reached the lanai. At the door to her mother's room, she saw the extent of the damage. Every piece of furniture was overthrown, every item of clothing ripped from the cupboards. Her mother, wild-eyed and wailing, was digging through a trunk of monsoon gear, shouting hoarsely.

"Where is it! Where did you put it! Give it back!"

In the corner stood two maids, wringing their hands and looking on in horror.

"Where's my father?" Persis asked.

"Down in the village," said one of the maids. "Fredan sent a flutter."

"And the night nurse?"

"Not here yet."

Persis swallowed and crossed to her mother, recalling the advice Noemi had given her and her father. Keep her calm, talk her back into rationality. She could do this. If there was anything she was good at, it was making people behave the way she wanted.

Heloise's hair had escaped its clips, sending bronze spirals cascading down her back. Persis brushed one aside. "Mama?" she asked softly. "I'm here to help you. What are you looking for?"

Heloise Blake turned and her eyes went even wider, if that was possible. "You."

"Yes, Mama—" Persis began, when her mother grabbed her by the throat and threw her against the wall.

"You!" Heloise growled, shoving her against the stone. "You stole it! Who are you?"

"Mama!" Persis said, though her voice tripped over the syllables. "It's me, Persis."

"*You stole my face.*"

Her muscles relaxed. Here was the heart of the episode. She'd seen this one before. "Yes, Mama," she said calmly, blinking until the threatening tears subsided. "I'm your daughter. We've heard that all my life, remember?"

Heloise's hands crept up to Persis's cheeks, her fingers curved into claws. "Give me my face back."

Persis neatly caught her mother's wrists before she did any more damage to her inflamed face. "Mama, please. Look at me. I'm Persis." She moved Heloise's hand to her own face, let it caress her own cheek. "We look alike. We always have. You're the most beautiful woman in all Albion, and I'm lucky that anyone thinks I resemble you."

Sometimes this worked. Sometimes her mother

remembered. But Heloise's eyes were still wide, her pupils constricted to tiny points. Her nails were now raking across her own skin. And then, suddenly, she slumped against Persis. Justen stood behind her, a pricker in his hand.

"What did you do?" Persis cried as the maids rushed to help support her unconscious mother.

"Sedated her," Justen said. "She needed it. You did your best, Persis, but—"

"You had no right to medicate my mother," she said, her tone low and dangerous. She'd been getting there. She just needed more time. And Justen Helo was never, never allowed to give anyone she loved a drug.

She swept by him and followed her servants to the bed, where they were laying Heloise down. At the edge of the platform lay the cracked remnants of a hand mirror, its rotating lifters bent and clicking as they tried to turn. That was probably what had set the whole spell off. Sometimes her mother lost track of the passage of years and failed to recognize her own reflection. She tapped the mirror off, swallowed, and said in as steady a voice as she could muster, "You may be a medic, but you aren't ours."

"I have a little more experience dealing with DAR than you do," he replied. "When they reach a certain point of confusion, they can't be reasoned with. There's a feedback loop that happens in their brains, and—"

"Save it for your lab reports." The maids had wisely retreated, and Persis took her mother's limp hand. Her parents' bed was suspended from the ceiling on long lengths of silk, and swayed slightly as she perched on the edge. Her mother was sleeping, her face so relaxed in repose that she looked much younger than forty. She looked, indeed, like Persis herself. "You don't know her."

"Do you think that's the first time a member of a patient's family has said that to me?" he asked softly. "It's true. I don't know your mother. I wish I'd known her when she was well, when she was all the things she wanted to be, all the things you love about her." His voice came from very close now, but Persis would not turn toward him. "I don't know—I can't know—how you and your mother feel. But I have seen people go through this before, and I do know the best ways to help."

Her heart pounded in her chest and her skin burned from more than the chemicals she'd used to remove her genetemps facial hair. Justen's voice was sweet and soothing. He was surely trained for that—bedside manner, they called it. He knew just how to talk to patients and their families. Just how to keep them calm.

He was a bigger liar than she was.

"You can go now," she intoned, still focused on her mother. "My father and the night nurse will be along shortly."

"I can stay." She felt his hand on her shoulder, pressure and heat searing right through the silvery fabric. "This is what I'm good at, Persis. Let me help."

She bit her lip. A day ago, that would have been all she wanted. The grandson of Persistence Helo, dedicated to the cause of helping Darkened. Ministering to her mother. Recruited into the League of the Wild Poppy. Kissing her in the star cove. But it was all a lie. Justen wasn't here to help—he was her enemy, and he had no idea what Persis was truly capable of.

"Here," Justen said, though she'd offered him no answer. He had a tube of ointment in his hands, and he was dabbing it on the scratches marring her mother's perfect cheeks. He offered her another cloth. "You could use some of this on your rash, too."

She took it, but the words "thank you" stuck in her throat, the aristocratic manners of Persis Blake warring strongly with the Wild Poppy's need to flatten this man.

"She'll sleep for at least four hours with this sedative," he said. "When the nurse gets here, I'd like to consult with him about what just happened. My observations are from a clinical standpoint, so they might be more useful—"

"Than mine," Persis finished. "I understand." Like it or not, Justen knew how to care for Heloise far better than Persis did. "Excuse me while I see how soon my father can be expected." She also needed to send in a maid to clean up the room before her father returned. It would upset him far more than necessary.

Torin Blake always put on a brave face, but his wife's bad spells were destroying him, and there was nothing, absolutely nothing that Persis could do to help. If anything, he would rather not see her whenever things got bad, as if dreading the day Persis followed the same path.

Secretly, Persis wondered if that was why her father had let her drop out of school and was indulging what he called her current "phase" of parties and dresses and silly court intrigue. After all, the prospect of losing one's intellectual capacity hurt somewhat less if you'd spent your life wasting it anyway.

Her mother, on her better days, was less understanding. "Fashion is certainly art, Persis," she'd told her the last time they'd discussed her sudden apathy toward intellectual pursuits, "and worthy of your time. But I always thought you were more interested in politics. I'd hoped, someday, you could finally become the female voice we need on the Council."

Persis couldn't pursue politics. At least not until she was done being the Wild Poppy. But she could hardly explain that to either of her parents. If Papa wouldn't let her go to Galatea on shopping trips, he'd flip if he learned she was risking life and mind every time she crossed the sea. No, they'd just have to spend a little while longer being utterly baffled that their previously book-ravenous daughter refused to talk about anything in public except her ever-expanding wardrobe.

Lies upon lies. She lied to her enemies as the Wild Poppy and to her friends who didn't know her secret identity. She lied to her parents when they asked her why she no longer wanted to join Albion's intellectual salons or continue her studies at school, and to Isla when she explained away her mother's absences from court. She lied when she pretended to the public that she was in love with Justen Helo, and to Justen when she pretended that she didn't know exactly what he'd done to his countrymen. There was almost no one left now who Persis could tell the truth to.

The night breeze blew across her heated face, bringing

with it the scent of sea spray and frangipani. She heard a few playful barks and Slipstream darted up the stone path threading down the pali. His coat was wet from the sea as she scooped him into her arms.

"You know it all, though, Slippy." His big otter eyes shone in the starlight, his fish-scented whiskers tickled her cheeks as she nuzzled him. "Now tell me what to do."

Instead he stretched out his long neck to sniff at the golden flutter that had halted above their heads and was drifting slowly downward. An orchid. Persis opened her palm.

*Dearest Persis,*

*I have decided that tomorrow would be an excellent opportunity for you to throw a small party for our friends on the Daydream. It's been quite a while since you have used the yacht for any social events, which apparently seems strange to some of the courtiers. I believe you shall invite me, the Finches, Lord and Lady Blocking, Councilman Shift's nephew Dwyer, and of course your darling Justen must attend.*

*It would please me very much if you were to pick us all up at the docks near the court tomorrow morning. Perhaps a sail out to Remembrance Island is in order?*

*Princess Isla, Regent of Albion*

Persis grimaced, imagining Isla composing this flutter under duress from Councilman Shift. Its tone was so stiff and formal she wondered if Shift had made Isla type it out in front of him on a wallport. Setting the flutter to her usual Blake frangipani, she thought out her reply.

*Of course, if you insist, I'd be happy to throw a boating party tomorrow. However, I feel as if there may be a better way to spend our time at the moment. I have very important news about Justen and me.*

The princess fluttered back in record time.

*I insist.*

# Twenty

BY THE TIME VANIA got back to Halahou, she'd reviewed every bit of information she could find on the prison break-in. She'd also gotten sick over the side of the boat. In a single burst, the Wild Poppy had managed to destroy not only her long campaign against the Fords but also the week she'd spent rearranging the troops according to General Gawnt's orders, which she knew he'd somehow manage to blame on her. And the spy had done it all while Vania had been off in Albion, failing to talk sense into a clearly lunatic Justen Helo.

How was she ever going to explain this to her father?

She was surprised to find Remy waiting for her on the docks, her short black hair mussed in the breeze.

"What are you doing here?" Vania snapped at her foster sister, disembarking before the sailors finished setting the nanoropes. "It's not safe in this neighborhood so late."

Remy pouted. "Moral support, of course. Do you have any idea what they're saying about this fiasco at the palace?"

Vania wasn't sure she wanted to know, but then again, forewarned was forearmed. "Thanks, squirt." She ruffled the girl's hair a little as they headed for a waiting skimmer. "I imagine it's not particularly good."

At first, no one seemed to know how the Poppy had pulled it off. After they discovered the Fords' prison cells were empty, troops had been sent after all deliveries and repairmen who'd entered the palace that day. One guard recalled a suspicious salter whose skimmer had broken down right at the gate, but though he'd been located, detained, and thoroughly searched along with his skimmer, there was no sign that anything was amiss. With a lack of any evidence and the clearly innocent and distraught salt miner beginning to draw a crowd on the public road, the guards let him go. All the other visitors to the prison that day had been similarly cleared.

It was all so mysterious.

It wasn't until the guards reconvened at the prison to review the records of all comings and goings that they'd noticed the exodus of a crew of military personnel without any movement orders to match.

Vania groaned. "So no one recognized the guards as prisoners? No one thought, 'Well, I haven't seen these people before'?"

Remy shrugged. "Apparently, with all the staffing changes, as well as the influx of soldiers who'd previously been assigned to the Ford estate barricades . . . I was down there today looking for Uncle Damos and I barely recognized anyone."

"I told Gawnt increased staffing wouldn't help," Vania muttered, mostly to herself. "If anything, it's backfired." She looked at Remy. "You have no idea how frustrating it is not to be taken seriously."

"I can't imagine," Remy replied, and for a second, Vania was almost positive she heard an edge in the girl's voice. "Did you find anything worthwhile in Albion?"

Vania remained silent. How much should she say about Justen's behavior? She didn't want to upset the girl, but it would be better for Remy to hear it from Vania than get shocked if things went bad for Justen later on. Vania couldn't quite picture her father being kind if Justen's treasonous ravings made it across the sea.

Stupid Justen. If he really felt so guilty about all of this, then he shouldn't have gone to Albion. He should have simply joined those weird Peccants and spent the rest of his life whipping himself and combing the beach on Remembrance Island. At least then everyone would have just written him off as crazy.

"Not much on the Wild Poppy, no," she said at last.

"Did you see Justen?" Remy pressed. "I heard he's gone to Albion."

"Yes." They passed through the gates to the palace, the sound of the lifter fans echoing off the massive walls of the courtyard.

"Did he tell you why he left?"

Vania rubbed her temples with her fingers. She didn't have time for a big dramatic scene with Remy. She needed to arrange her thoughts around this break-in. Like it or not, the Wild Poppy took precedence over whether or not her foster brother had decided to betray everything he'd ever believed in for some stupid rich girl.

"I don't know," she snapped. "The gossip all says he's in love with some idiot aristo." There. That excuse would hold Remy for a little bit, until she had time to explain all the complex political philosophies involved. Hearts and flowers a girl her age could understand. "Her name is Persis Blake."

"An aristo?" Remy sounded skeptical. "That doesn't sound like him, and an idiot even less so." She laughed awkwardly. "You know Justen—he'd sooner Reduce an aristo than kiss one, right?"

Vania looked at the younger girl. There was something odd in her tone—grasping and almost desperate, as if she was trying to convince herself of something she didn't really believe. Had Justen already infected her with some of his traitorous ideas? Vania made a note in her oblet to screen all Remy's messages from Justen. For now, let the girl think Justen was being guided by lust.

"This aristo's especially rich and especially pretty," Vania said. She accessed an image of the lady in question and turned the oblet's display toward Remy. "Here. Take a look at her and tell me your brother's thinking with his head."

The display sparked to life, revealing Persis Blake in all her splendor. She was at some event or another, in a gown that sparkled like a sunlit sea, her wild yellow and white hair floating above her in a cloudy puff. She was holding a crystal glass of kiwine in her hand, and she had her head thrown back, laughing.

Not a care in the world. Spoiled brat. Vania started feeling sick again. She rolled her eyes and turned to Remy. "See what I mean?"

"That's Persis Blake?" Remy asked quietly. Her eyes were wide, her mouth open.

Oh no, not Remy, too! They were supposed to be above all this awe-of-aristos nonsense. "That's her. And believe me, she's every bit as stupid as she looks. Don't be too impressed, Remy. Trust me, your brother has made a huge mistake."

Remy looked from the display to Vania and back again. "That, I believe," she said at last.

THE *DAYDREAM* WAS AT full sail, the party was at full tilt, and they were halfway to Remembrance Island, but Persis was certain this trip would go down as the worst event a Blake had ever hosted. Half the attendees weren't speaking to one another, and the other half couldn't figure out why.

"Darling," Isla cooed in Persis's ear. Persis turned to see the princess wearing a diaphanous white wrap and her most disapproving frown. "You're neglecting the party, and, worse, you're neglecting Justen."

"I'm sorry," Persis replied. The poison-green petals of her skirt swirled around her knees in the sea breeze, and her split sleeves flapped like angry snakes at her shoulders. "Would you prefer I livened things up by dumping him overboard?"

Isla sighed. In deference to the bright sun, she'd donned an enormous white floppy hat with a hole in the middle that allowed her to pull her hair through and arrange it in layers around the brim. When Persis had picked up the royal entourage at court, she'd said Isla looked like a child's shell art. Isla had said Persis looked like a clump of seaweed.

The party, in Persis's opinion, had gone downhill from there.

Justen sat like a lump in the extreme aft, giving monosyllabic answers to every attempt at conversation. He was deeply unhappy that he'd been dragged out on the boat instead of being allowed to return to the lab, though he'd only registered his complaint once to Persis. Noemi, however, had reported to Persis that he'd sent her several messages overnight about the "new address of the refugees."

Forget dropping him off the side of the *Daydream*. She'd wait until they got back to Scintillans and push him off the pali itself.

"You're supposed to throw the best parties on the island, Persis," Isla reminded her, "so act like you're having fun or people are going to start to suspect you have something else on your mind."

Which she did. And it wasn't like Isla wanted to be here, either. "Fine," she said. "Shall I arrange a game of spin the shell with, say, you, me, Justen, and Tero?"

Isla gave her a queenly look. "Tero and I have made up."

"*Kissed* and made up?"

"Don't start with me right now."

"Then don't complain about me and Justen," she replied in as low a voice as she dared out here in the wind. "Those pictures of us kissing in the star cove probably did more for your campaign of equality than any five royal balls."

Isla turned on her heel and went to talk to the other aristos aboard. The princess had invited Lady Blocking and her stick-in-the-sandflats Council-member husband in what was supposed to look like a show of support for the Council. They'd at first acted thrilled to finally score a ride on the *Daydream*, then dialed down their enthusiasm as the festive atmosphere failed to materialize. Then there was Dwyer Shift, who seemed much happier about attending than Isla was about putting him on the guest list. Dwyer was every bit as exasperating as his powerful uncle, and his unctuous behavior was not a particularly welcome change. His tangerine hair had been arranged in an artful swoop, and he'd chosen to dress from head to toe in a material that made him look for all the world like a molting brass crab. He'd spent the party either offering Isla an endless parade of sweets or telling Justen that it must be exceedingly wonderful to be descended from Persistence Helo.

Persis was quite sure neither recipient enjoyed his attentions and, quite frankly, she thought they both deserved it—Isla for forcing her to host this event, and Justen because being bothered by Dwyer Shift was the least of the punishments she fantasized for him.

Andrine and Tero rounded out the party, but neither was in the mood to help. Andrine had been giving Persis the silent treatment ever since waking up in her own bed, totally feminine and completely clueless as to how she'd wound up there, rather than in the middle of a spy mission on Galatea.

Persis was surprised she'd even accepted the invitation, given how angry she was.

"Oh, don't worry," Tero had informed Persis as they'd boarded. "She's got plenty to say to you later. But my sister, unlike a few people I can mention, knows the proper time to impart her feelings on issues. Which is not, I'd like to add, in the middle of a mission."

"The beginning of one is better?" Persis had said. "Like that temper tantrum you threw with the princess the other day?"

"I didn't slip her drugs." Tero crossed his arms, probably because he knew how large and intimidating it made him look. "You know there's a big difference."

"There are complications that are making it particularly dangerous for regs to be in the League of the Wild Poppy."

"Oh, so I can drop out, then?"

"You're not that lucky, Tero."

Her friend sighed and handed her a pill. "No, not as lucky as you. Because while you were off drugging my sister and causing a ruckus in Galatea, I've made you a new palm-port application. Allows for hand-to-hand exchange—no flutters necessary. I've got one for Slippy, too. It'll record input to his optic nerves. You'll be the only one in Albion with a surveillance sea mink."

"Fantastic," Persis said, and downed the app. "Perhaps it'll start a new fashion."

Tero watched her swallow, and then with a slow, dangerous smile said, "You're awfully trusting, Perse. What if

I'd decided to take revenge for what you did to Andrine yesterday? That could be a knockout drug."

Persis started coughing, and he laughed.

"Joking. But if you mess with mixtures intended for my sister again, it's the last genetemps you'll ever get from me, Lady Blake."

*Lady Blake?* "Well, at least you're respecting rank today."

Tero narrowed his eyes at her. "Don't start with me, Persis, or I'll make you eat sand like I did when you were four."

"Funny," said Persis. "That's exactly what Isla said."

How in the world was she supposed to throw a party when she hated half the guests and the other half hated her? Persis fed Slipstream the surveillance app pill Tero had given her for the sea mink, then camped out near the wheel, running diagnostics on the program—which was, admittedly, amazing, though it was too bad neither Tero nor Andrine was willing to try it out with her—and hoping it would all be over soon, and she could go back to playing the part of the daring spy, rather than the foolish socialite.

Now, at Isla's urging, she lifted her voice above the wind and called out, "My friends, it'll be another half an hour before we reach our picnic on Remembrance Island. What shall we do to entertain ourselves until then? A poetry reading, perhaps? A game of questions?"

"Oh, please no poetry," said Lady Blocking as everyone on the yacht gathered in the center of the lower deck. "Don't we get enough of that at court?" Her husband elbowed her in the side and she went quiet.

"I love poetry," said Dwyer. "I've attended every

reading that the princess has held since taking the throne."

"Tell me," Isla drawled, "were you such a fan of the art before I became regent?"

The Blockings looked scandalized, but Tero snickered behind his cup of punch, earning a radiant smile from the princess. Persis shook her head. Isla could afford to be openly cynical about Councilman Shift's obvious attempts to throw his nephew in her path, but not if she was going to openly flirt with a reg gengineer. Whatever was going on between her two friends, it wouldn't end well.

"Citizen Helo!" Isla called. "Have you heard Persis's poetry? She had quite a reputation for it at school, though I think she's fallen out of practice since."

Justen, still moping, lifted his head. "I have not had the pleasure, no."

Isla clapped her hands. "Well, you shall today. Persis? Grace us with a ditty."

Persis stared evenly at her friend. "I don't think I'm in the mood for extemporaneous composition."

"Of course you are," the princess insisted. "I'll take topics now." She pointed at Tero.

"Love," he said, and Isla rolled her eyes.

Persis sighed. As soon as this party was over, she and Isla were going to have to have a serious talk. There was a reason Persis had quit composing poetry after she'd left school. Cultivating a reputation as a wit was not conducive to her goals. But as long as she was being forced to perform like the princess's pet parrosprey, she could get in a few digs of her own. *Lady Blake*, indeed! After a moment, she responded:

> The fool says "Love," but I confess,
> I'd rather have a nice new dress.
> He may be strong of build and fair of face
> But I prefer a frock's embrace.

The group chuckled appropriately, and Isla pointed next at Lady Blocking.

"Oh!" the woman said, stirring her beverage with a stick of sugarcane. "Um . . . oh, I know. The Wild Poppy!"

"Of course." Persis nodded, and flashed a glance at Isla, who shrugged almost imperceptibly.

Very well. But they were playing with fire:

> Across the sea and up the stair,
> The Wild Poppy's everywhere.
> Though southmen search until they're blind,
> They know not what they seek to find.

"Wry, Persis," Isla drawled with a warning glare. Well, *she* had started it. Persis cast a glance at Justen, but he barely seemed to be paying attention. How disappointed his dear Vania would be in him. Here she was, dropping clues like jewels, and he hardly noticed.

"I don't get it," said Lady Blocking, her head cocked, her mouth slack. Perhaps Persis should spend more time studying the woman's behavior to make sure her own act achieved proper authenticity. She was never quite successful at playing dumb.

"Unfortunately, they can't all be works of art," Persis said, lifting her shoulders in pretty defeat. "And I did warn you I was out of practice."

"Better luck next time." Isla pointed at Justen. "Your turn, Justen. Challenge our girl."

His expression was as flat as his voice as he replied, "Reduction."

The guests began to fidget with their cups and plates.

"I—ah—don't know if that's quite the topic we're looking for, Citizen. A little serious, perhaps, for our purpose." Isla gave an apologetic smile. "Perhaps a different topic springs to mind?"

"No," he said. "I can't think of anything else right now."

Good, thought Persis. When it came to Justen Helo, neither could she. Persis lifted her hand. "Oh no, I've got this one." She stared straight at Justen and began to recite.

*Though long forgotten by the kind,*
*Lucky enough to keep their minds,*
*The threat sadly, remains most keen,*
*To those who are called Galatean.*

Justen rose, not breaking eye contact, and recited back,

*The world's content to sit and wait,*
*While those in need suffer sad fates.*

*And while we laugh and ride the waves*
*Our negligence will dig their graves.*

Persis blinked. Well, that was unexpected. Who knew Galatean medic students had time to fit in lyric lessons amid RNA transcription classes?

Whatever had remained of the party atmosphere, however, had vanished. Andrine chuckled nervously. "We seem to have gone far off course."

Persis narrowed her eyes at Justen. "My dear Justen is, perhaps, not entirely used to the way we do things in Albion."

"But he's so well-suited for it," said Dwyer. "A Helo *and* a poet. Almost as good as a real aristo!"

At least three of the people on the deck rolled their eyes.

Persis smiled broadly at the guests. "Please excuse me. I'm going to pass my turn along to Andrine, who I recall spent many a night at school keeping us in stitches with her limericks."

She crossed the deck, took Justen by the arm, and led him to the upper deck, out of earshot of the rest of the party.

"Your agreement with Isla demands not only that you accompany me to social events but that you look happy about it," she reminded him softly but firmly.

"You first."

She drew back. Who would have thought he was paying so much attention?

Justen looked out over the water in the direction of Galatea. "Those refugees are suffering and every moment

I spend here playing your devoted admirer, I'm not able to help them."

And every moment she was forced to spend playing hostess was one she couldn't use to get to the bottom of Justen's lies.

He turned back to her. "Does Isla really think she's impressing the regs of Albion by setting off on a yachting trip with a bunch of aristos and a few token court regs? Is that what she thinks is going to keep the populace happy? Wouldn't they be much happier to know that we've found a way to protect the regs in Galatea?"

"Shh!" she hissed. "Lower your voice." The last thing she needed was for the Finches to find out the real reason she'd drugged Andrine. She leaned up against the rail and drew Justen against her. "People are watching."

"So?" He leaned his body toward hers. "We're supposed to be arguing."

She draped her arms about his shoulders and arched her back. Behind her, the sea spray frosted her skin, but heat radiated from Justen's body. The last time she'd held him this close had been in the star cove. It seemed like a world away. Then, she'd let down her guard, acted almost like herself, imagined that Justen was the sort of person she could tell things to. It had been her most serious lapse in judgment in a week that seemed full of them.

"Well, now we're making up. Isla hasn't authorized any fights." More's the pity. How she'd like to have it out with him here and now. How she'd like to pitch him over the side of the *Daydream* and sail away, no matter what secrets he might discover in his grandmother's files to help her mother. If Justen could find a cure in them, someone else could, too.

"I don't care what she's authorized," he whispered. "All I care about is my countrymen. I can't stand by and watch them suffer."

"You were happy enough to do so before." The words slipped out, unfiltered. He began to jerk away from her but she held him tight. "When you were in Galatea, there were citizens being Reduced all around you. Why was that all right?"

"It wasn't," he replied. "And there was very little I could do in Galatea with my uncle breathing down my neck. Here I can help the refugees in that sanitarium."

Persis was sure that was a great comfort to those regs already damaged by Justen's pinks. She lifted her hand and caressed his cheek, when what she'd rather do was smack it.

"Oh, lovebirds," called Lady Blocking, "are you going to rejoin the party or find someplace more private?"

He looked into her eyes, pain furrowing his brow. "You sound angry with me, Persis. If I've done something to hurt you, I'm sorry. I'm sorry Vania came to your house. I didn't invite her, believe me. I respect your family's privacy."

"And what about the princess's good opinion?" Persis said. "Entertaining her enemies—"

"Don't worry about Vania. All she cares about is the Wild Poppy."

That was plenty to start with.

"I thought," he said, "that we were becoming friends. In the star cove—"

"I made it clear what we're doing here," she finished. "At least, I thought I had. If there was any confusion . . ." She shrugged. "This is a role, Justen. *Play it*."

He glared at her, his jaw set, his dark eyes burning. And then he kissed her.

She couldn't pull away, not with half the party watching and the other half judging. And after a second, she didn't want to. There was something desperate and wild about the kiss, about Justen himself. In the star cove, he'd touched her gently, tentatively. Now he cupped her face in one hand, tangling his fingers in the windswept strands of her hair, while he slipped the other around the small of her back, pulling her up from the rails and holding her against his body.

This was not the Galatean medic she knew, cautious and serious and sarcastic. The petals of her skirt whipped in the wind, molding about his hips as tightly as her arms wrapped around his back. He moved his mouth over hers, hot and hard and hungry for understanding or absolution or something else entirely unexpected.

And then, just as suddenly, he lifted his head, and there was no pleasure in his face. "There," he said. "Satisfied?"

Not even a little. Persis caught her breath before speaking, afraid of how she might sound otherwise. "It's . . . a definite improvement."

Down on the main deck, Princess Isla pointed at the sky and screamed.

# Twenty-one

EVERYTHING DISSOLVED INTO CHAOS. Persis vanished from his side, hurrying to her princess. Justen tried to focus, taking in the situation. Moments ago, he'd been kissing Persis Blake like his life depended on it. Now, everyone was pointing up into the sky, gasping and chattering.

"What is it!" cried Lady Blocking. "What is it?"

Justen shielded his eyes and peered into the cloudless blue. It took a moment, but he found it, a tiny, golden glitter in the sky. At first, he thought it was a flutternote, but its movements were too measured for that. Flutters moved in lazy floating motions only to a certain height, and then they zipped off at maximum speed to their intended recipients. This . . . thing, whatever it was, was circling. Also, he got the sense that it was a lot larger, and a lot higher up, than any flutter ever went.

Persis reappeared in front of him. "Do you know anything about this?" she spat at him. "Is this one of Citizen Aldred's new tricks? Attack the princess regent of Albion from the air?"

Justen shook his head, baffled.

"I thought," Isla said, her voice faint and a little lost, "I thought it was just a flutternote gone astray. But it's not. It's high, and big . . ."

Tero took the princess by the arm. "Your Highness, we must go below for your safety."

"Um," said Lord Blocking, "maybe we should all go below. We're the perfect targets out here."

Andrine was staring up at the object hanging in the sky. "For a sniper, I suppose. But if they wish to bomb us, we're as much in danger in the cabin as we would be on the deck."

"No one is bombing anyone," Isla insisted. "Not even Citizen Aldred would dare such a move."

"And if he did?" said Lord Blocking. "What would be your response?"

Princess Isla shot the aristo a poisonous glare and went below. Persis was still on deck, staring at the thing as if she could bring it down by will alone. Justen couldn't decide what was more unusual: Persis or the object that held her transfixed. All the other women had gone below, but she remained, in her silly green dress, like some ancient sea nymph defying the sky.

Flying machines. He'd read about them, of course, and seen the images. In the last war, unmanned flying machines had been the ones to carry the explosives that had torn apart the world. It was his ancestors who'd done that—his and all the other regs'. Safe and secure in their own, giant flying machine, they'd sat far above the Earth and destroyed the rest of it.

When the creators landed on the pristine soil of New Pacifica, they'd made a pact: no more flying machines. Even skimmers hovered less than a meter above the surface. Never again would mankind be able to destroy the world from a distance. It was inconvenient for travel but worth it for the preservation of the scraps of humanity who remained alive.

What if Uncle Damos had broken the creators' pact? After all, he could argue that it was a limitation set by the aristos, and the revolutionaries were not bound to follow it.

"Whatever it is," Persis said, still staring upward, "it's leaving." Her tone was clipped and businesslike, nothing at all like the husky, breathless whisper she'd graced him with after their last kiss.

They were the only two left on deck. She strode to the side, dipped her head over and called out, "Slipstream, up!" The mink came scrambling up the hull and onto the deck. He shook himself until his sleek fur stood out in all directions in damp spikes, chattered once at Persis, then rolled over.

"Good boy, Slippy."

Justen rolled his eyes. This was a time to practice pet tricks? "So are we turning around?"

"And ruining the party?" Persis asked. "Just as it was livening up?"

"Persis. There are flying machines. Shouldn't we . . . I don't know, *warn* someone?"

She rolled her eyes. "I'm sure Isla, the actual ruler of our nation, handled sending a warning quite neatly. How can we, a socialite and an unemployed medic, do any better?"

Above them, the flying machine faded from sight. It hadn't gone south, though. If anything, it seemed to have gone west—same as they were headed.

"Persis?"

She threw open the door of the cabin. "All clear! Next stop, Remembrance Island!"

The rest of the party emerged, some looking visibly shaken by the events, and a few, like Lady Blocking and Dwyer Shift, looking relieved that the commotion had ended and they could return to their useless, silly existences. Persis had adopted the attitude of the latter group, much to Justen's dismay and a little to his surprise. He supposed he should be used to the idea now that, despite flashes that Persis could think of serious things, she'd shown a marked preference for *not* doing so. For a few brief moments—in his bedroom after he'd first met her parents, in the cove when she'd told him about her inheritance, with her mother the previous night, and even just now when she held him on the deck—he'd thought that maybe, just maybe, there was something in Persis, dormant, atrophied from disuse, that they had in common.

She had passion for the plight of DAR victims, due, no doubt, to her mother's situation. But, like so many aristos, she seemed to want to keep it buried, as if not talking about it would make it go away. Her reg heritage did nothing to change that, and the fact that she refused to have herself tested for the potential to develop DAR only underscored it. Persis preferred to live in ignorance. She preferred to devote herself to silly, useless pursuits like clothes and parties and playing courtship games.

And yet he couldn't dismiss her entirely, either. Justen had never felt so unmoored. When he was younger, it was easy to pick out the worthy people of his acquaintance. They weren't the ones who cared about fashion or social status or parties or romance. They were people like him and Vania, who were smart and well-read and ambitious and wanted to change the world.

But what had they changed it into? Vania was off imprisoning and torturing her own countrymen; and Justen had helped, then run away to hide. Compared to the damage they'd done, perhaps Persis's idle concerns were the better ones. In her shallowness, she was harmless, and when she did use the brain she liked to pretend she didn't have, it was to create beauty or to comfort her mother with silly stories, to compose entertaining poems or to playact a romance that would help the princess she so obviously loved avoid the same kind of war that he'd fled in Galatea.

Persis—silly, superficial, genetemps-partying Persis— was a far better person than he was. And if he ever hoped to correct the damage he'd caused, he needed to learn to emulate *her*.

There were no docks on Remembrance Island, but several mooring balls had been sunk near the shallowest bay, and it was to one of these that the *Daydream* attached. While most of the guests chose to travel to shore in the dingy,

Persis defied the odds again, leaping over the side, dress and all, to swim in with her sea mink at her side. By the time the boat reached them on the beach, Persis had repinned stray locks of her wet hair, and Slipstream was shaking himself dry. Justen watched Persis make a sign to the animal, who snapped to attention and scampered off.

"What was that command?" he asked her, as Andrine and Tero began unloading the picnic supplies.

Persis shimmied her hips, and the seaweed-green petals of her skirt unstuck from her thighs. "Oh, you know, don't go too far, be back after lunch."

"He knows all those commands?"

"Don't underestimate Slippy, Justen. You'd be surprised what he knows." She clapped her hands and raised her voice to the rest of the party. "All right, what's first? Food? Historical lecture and exploration? Cocktails?"

"I vote cocktails before any lecturing," said Lady Blocking. "Otherwise I might not survive it."

"Agreed," said Persis. "Besides, we all know the story." She turned back to Justen. "Though I'm curious as to the Galatean revolutionaries' take on Remembrance Island."

"We're revolutionaries," he replied smoothly, "not revisionist historians."

Remembrance Island—a tiny speck situated halfway between the westernmost points of New Pacifica's two main islands—was a sanctuary, a monument. It had been left completely barren and uncultivated but for a single ceramic obelisk, a remnant of the ship that all their ancestors had once lived on. Generations ago, when they marooned themselves on New Pacifica and destroyed their ship, they'd kept this one piece and inscribed it with a memorial to the Earth they had destroyed and the societies they had lost, promising to carry on, to live in the world that they'd made and to commit themselves to someday atoning for it all.

It was this promise that Justen's grandmother Persistence Helo had used when trying to convince the old Queen Gala, the old King Albie, and all the aristos of her generation to distribute the cure she'd created. It was this promise, one of moving on and protecting the humanity they'd almost destroyed, which eventually led to the widespread adoption of the cure and the end of the Reduction that had triggered the almost total destruction of mankind in the first place. The Helo Cure had saved the world.

And in only two generations, they were trying to wreck it again.

Justen shook his head. He had to fix the refugees. He *had* to. He couldn't let his family legacy be destroyed because he'd been too naive to understand his uncle's true purpose.

Armed with kiwine cocktails as if the Albians viewed them as some sort of vital hiking accessory, the party began the ascent to the island's summit, where the monument stood. The path was narrow and rocky, requiring the group to walk in a line of ones and twos, and explained the uncharacteristically simple outfits and shoes the Albians had chosen. He had never seen Isla without her towering high heels before, and it had been a surprise to realize how short she really was. She barely reached Tero's chest, and they made a comical pair as they hiked beside each other.

Persis was the tallest woman in the group; even in flats, she was only a few centimeters shorter than Justen.

As they went, they shared stories about their first visit to Remembrance Island. Justen was surprised to learn that most Albian aristos made it a yearly pilgrimage. He'd been once or twice on field trips in school, but the Galateans had never thought it such a vital part of their culture. Only the Peccants visited regularly, but they were generally considered a tiny and bizarre fringe.

"Perhaps," said Isla when he shared this information with the group, "that is why your people were willing, once more, to go to war." She didn't sound superior when she said it, however, only sad. At the moment, she was walking near him, at the very head of the group. "Growing up, my father took my brother and me here many more times than yearly. We were constantly reminded of our duty. Whenever Albie— my older brother Albie—whenever he got particularly hotheaded on some matter of diplomacy or other, Father would pack us up and sail out here to reflect on what anger and strife can do to humanity. On how there should always be another solution."

Lord Blocking, behind them with his lady, snorted. "Is that why you are so reluctant to help put an end to the atrocities happening in the south, Princess? Because you have interpreted your father's teachings as a call to passive inaction?"

"No," replied the princess smoothly. "It is because I govern by the will of the people and shall not go to war, risking who knows how many of my own citizens' lives in the process, until the people of Albion will it."

"And if the people of Albion will a revolution? If the people of Albion will you stripped of your power?"

For a moment, Justen wondered how far the man planned to go with this.

"Oh, come now," said Andrine, who seemed annoyed equally at the direction the conversation had gone and the fact that she was walking alongside Dwyer. Somehow, in the last few minutes, Persis and Tero had fallen way behind the rest. Andrine kept looking back at them and scowling. "Surely the fact that our leaders bother to take into account their people's opinions is an argument for *not* revolting. What do you say, Citizen Helo?"

Justen started. Despite being the only Galatean present, he'd not expected to be put on the spot in this way. "Queen Gala was a distant and indifferent ruler," he said.

"Oh, and you knew the queen so well?" asked Lord Blocking.

"I met her a few times," Justen admitted. "The first was when my parents died ten years ago and there was a question of where my sister and I would go. It was suggested by some that the queen take us in herself, given the debt the Galateans felt they owed our family."

"What happened?" asked Dwyer Shift.

Justen forced a smile. "I was not raised by Queen Gala."

"No," said Persis, who'd at last caught up to the group. "She pawned you off on her trusted military general Damos Aldred."

The group fell silent. Isla paused on the trail, causing everyone else to stop short as well, and turned to Persis. "So what are you saying, Persis? That I'm safe from a military revolution as long as I don't stick any of my councilmen with a bunch of orphans to raise?"

Persis smiled sweetly. "Couldn't hurt."

A few of the guests chuckled, and, just like that, the tension diffused. How was it that Persis was so good at this? Maybe he should have left her to deal with her mother as she wished last night.

Slipstream appeared out of nowhere, hurrying to his mistress's side. When he got there, he lifted himself up on his hind legs and proceeded to do a strange little dance, hopping back and forth, then dropping, rolling over, and repeating the process again.

"What's he doing?" Dwyer asked, incredulous.

"He's glad to see me," said Persis. She stripped off her wristlock and leaned over to pet the sea mink, running her fingers deeply through his fur. "Aren't you, boy? What a good, good boy you are." Something gold glinted near the animal's green collar, but Justen figured it must be sunlight reflecting off the buckle.

"Let's just get to the stupid monument," grumbled Lord Blocking.

"*Stupid?*" Isla drew herself up, looking quite majestic and almost supernaturally grand all of a sudden. It appeared to be part of royal training. Justen would never understand. "I'm sure you meant to say *dumb*—as in *silent*—as in magnificent and lonely and ever so sacred."

The man looked away.

Isla appeared satisfied. "Perhaps in the next election

cycle, it shall be the will of the people in your district to revisit the wisdom of placing you on the Council." She strode off, and only Justen heard as she passed close, "And then I'll no longer be forced to place you on my guest lists."

"Princess," Justen said, jumping on his first opportunity to be out of earshot of the others. "I need to speak to you. I know we'd originally agreed that I'd be available for your publicity purposes, but I feel my true purpose in Albion lies elsewhere."

"Oh?" Isla responded. "So you want to be relieved of the duty of sucking my friend's face off like you were back there on the boat?"

"Yes—"

"Didn't look like it." She walked on.

Justen caught up. "I've had the opportunity to see the Galatean refugees. As a medic, I know my place belongs in the labs, helping your scientists develop a treatment for their condition. I can be so much more useful to you there. Even Persis will agree . . ."

Isla groaned and pressed her fist against her brow. "Certainly, Citizen Helo. I shall look into it as soon as I've managed to prevent the imminent uprising in my own country."

Justen drew back, chagrined. "I know you're busy, but—"

"I'm not happy about you hiding away in some Darkened sanitarium, and switching that up for a secret refugee lab is even less appealing. However, if you'd like to do a few propaganda videos for me about the importance of stopping the Reduction of your people, I'd be more than happy to arrange it. All right?"

No. Not all right. Not all right at all. He needed to keep a low profile until his sister was secured. Vania's visit had proved that. After all, she'd as good as threatened Persis yesterday.

And Justen had almost bitten her head off for it.

"Please, Princess—"

At the rear of the party, Persis rose and for a minute, it looked like she'd lost her balance. Tero grabbed her hand, and they held on to each other until she regained her footing.

"Are you hurt?" Justen called.

"Fine." Persis dropped Tero's hand and strode up to where Justen stood. "Why, are you jealous you aren't walking with me?" She batted her eyelashes at him and tossed a few ropes of her hair behind her shoulder. Lady Blocking ducked to avoid being hit in the face with them.

"I think," Tero said, "that I'm going to do a quick survey of the beach. Given the day's events, we can't be too safe." Bizarrely, he shook his sister's hand in farewell before vanishing down the trail.

"Let's keep going up!" Persis cried. "Up, up, up! The sooner we get to the monument, the sooner we can get back to lunch—am I right, Lady Blocking?" Not waiting for an answer, she rushed forward, past Justen, past Isla, and kept up the pace until she reached the next curve in the path, far above their heads. Isla also quickened her pace, and the rest dutifully followed. As they passed the curve, Justen looked down at the beach and stopped dead on the path.

"Who is that?" Far below them stood a figure. From here, he could make out little more than orangey hair and a dull brown dress.

Persis practically ran down to meet him. "Oh, look, another Albian, out to pay her respects to the monument. How lovely. Who knew this would be such a popular trip? Of course, the weather's so lovely today. Everything is *so* lovely. All right, onward—" She tugged at his hand, but Justen was riveted by the girl on the beach.

There was something strange, and yet oddly familiar, about her movements. He struggled to place it. Perhaps the distance was just playing tricks on him. But as he peered closer, he saw her joined by another woman, whose hair was a color he'd never seen outside history books and videos. Not yellow like some of Persis's, but a soft, sunshiny gold. "Blond," he said to himself. It was called blond. He'd yet to see any Albian who'd chosen to dye their hair a color that had once appeared on humans in nature.

"Come *on*," Persis insisted, and pulled him away. "Stop spying. I don't know how they do things in Galatea, but in Albion, it's considered rude."

"Odd," he replied. "Since the most famous spy in the world is Albian."

Persis allotted him a pity chuckle.

Two more turns, if memory served, and they'd reach the summit of the island and the ceramic obelisk that marked the sanctuary. Isla still led the way, her pace now almost as fast as her friend's. Everyone had stopped talking, concentrating mostly on keeping up.

"And here we are!" Isla announced, a bit breathless, as they rounded the last turn. "The monument of Remembrance I—" and here words failed her.

There were two people already there. At first glance, the strangers standing before them appeared Galatean, to judge by their natural, dark hair and more somber dress. Except "somber" wasn't the right word for it. The young woman wore a simple, faded shirt and patched trousers hardly fit for the most downtrodden of Galatean peasants before the revolution. Her hair hung down her back in a braid almost long enough to skim the earth as she knelt and examined the writing at the base of the monument. The young man, dressed notably better, almost like an aristo or at least a rich reg, stood facing them, as if he already knew they'd arrived, though he couldn't possibly have heard them over the wind here at the peak. Justen wanted to say the strangers were nearly the same age as he was, but that didn't seem right, either. Surely he'd remember a Galatean of his social class who looked like this. The other boy's skin was paler than Justen was used to, and the shape of his eyes and cheekbones gave him pause. But though the stranger looked on their party with extreme wariness, he couldn't hide his expression of unmitigated delight.

"Hello."

At the sound of his voice, the girl looked around, then jumped to her feet in shock. Quick as a flash, the boy maneuvered until he stood between her and the rest of them, his hand stretched back toward her in a gesture of both comfort and protection.

"Hello," said Isla, pausing haughtily in expectation of a bow that never came. She shot Justen a look. "Galateans, I see. Well, we're on neutral ground. I won't stand on ceremony."

But Justen, the only Galatean in the group, felt in his bones that he wasn't looking at his countrymen.

The young man came forward, his back straight, his head high and his eyes, Justen could now see, glittering with a light no one on Earth had seen for generations.

"My name is Captain Malakai Wentforth of the ship *Argos*," he said, his words so distorted and odd sounding that they were practically unintelligible. "We have come from the end of the world to search for other survivors. You are the first we've met. Tell me, what is this place, and why does it not appear on any map?"

# Twenty-two

ON THE ONE HAND, the picnic would forever be remembered as the most disastrous party that the Lady Persis Blake had ever thrown. On the other hand, every guest was present to see history made, so that was a point in its favor.

The established mode, according to the old stories Persis and her father used to read before bedtime, was for the impossible aliens to ask the natives they encounter to take them to their leader. However, in this case, the leader in question, Princess Isla, was already one of the party. And she wasted no time getting the full story out of the two visitors, who called themselves Captain Wentforth and Chancellor Boatwright, as if the titles weren't utter nonsense and the way they pronounced the words almost impossible to understand.

It was called an "accent," if Persis remembered correctly; a change in vowels or pronunciation in a language, like you sometimes saw in history videos. And, in this strange accent, the strangers told Isla they meant no harm, and as their story emerged, even Persis was inclined to believe them.

And yet it was impossible that they were here. There were no survivors elsewhere. The population of New Pacifica was utterly alone on the world. Everyone knew that. They'd always known that. It was the whole point of Remembrance Island. And if there were, surely they would not come to New Pacifica with any purpose other than revenge—revenge against the descendants of those who'd destroyed the world to begin with. Right?

Persis would have loved to take part in the interview, but she was trapped in hostess mode, in Persis Flake mode, shuttling the whole party down the mountain. Isla had already fluttered Tero, who Persis had earlier sent off to investigate the empty golden glider that Slipstream's new surveillance app had shown the sea mink finding on the beach. When Justen had seen the two figures below them on the trail, Persis had deduced that they'd found the owners of the illegal glider, though she'd been surprised to see by their hair that they were Albian. But apparently in that, too, she'd been mistaken.

They weren't Albians with illegal gliders and dyed hair. They weren't Galatean revolutionaries planning a sneak attack. Instead, they were something far more shocking and infinitely more dangerous.

And Persis was stuck playing a stupid aristo while Isla and Tero got to have all the fun.

By the time they'd reached the beach, Tero had rounded up the other two strangers, and was waiting with them.

"Ro!" The one who called herself Chancellor Boatwright ran toward the one with the orangey hair. Tero tensed but otherwise did nothing. "Are you all right?"

"Of course she is," drawled the light-haired one. They were both dressed in the same simple, homespun fashions of the two they'd met at the monument. "Do you really think I'd let anyone hurt her?"

The girl in question, Ro, shrank back from the group, pointing in fear at their hair and clothes. She said nothing, but the gestures continued, fluid, graceful, and utterly silent. Was she mute? No one was mute, except . . .

"She's Reduced," Isla whispered in amazement. "I mean—*really* Reduced."

There was a chorus of oohs from the Blockings and Dwyer Shift.

The other three strangers all exchanged glances. "Are there no Reduced here?" asked the one who'd identified himself as the captain.

Justen looked away, Persis noticed immediately.

"Not real Reduced," Lady Blocking blurted. "Not for about two generations, since the cure."

The male stranger's bright eyes got even brighter. "There's a cure?" He looked at the dark-haired Chancellor Boatwright. "There's a cure."

The girl was already nodding, her severe face utterly transformed by a breathtaking smile. "There's a cure. You did it, Kai." Her voice was breathless, ecstatic. Persis imagined this is what Darwin and Persistence Helo must have once looked like, when they realized what they had on their hands. The dark-haired strangers were facing each other, gazes locked, hands floating out toward each other, like they'd completely forgotten there was anyone else on the beach, anyone else in the world.

"Oh, please," groaned the blonde, looking nauseated. "Not this again. Honestly, I'm glad we've found land, if only because it means I'm not trapped on a boat with you two."

Isla cleared her throat, understandably baffled by how this revelatory meeting had somehow turned into a discussion about the visitors' interpersonal relationships. "Persis, if you would be so good as to return your guests to Albion? I have already called for a royal guard ship to escort our visitors—"

"We're not getting on any of your *guard* ships," said the light-haired one. She turned to Captain Wentforth, who had drawn away from Chancellor Boatwright, though their hands were now clasped tightly. "Tell her, Malakai."

Captain Wentforth sighed. "I agree with Captain Phoenix." *Phoenix*. What ridiculous name was next? "We've come to find other survivors of the war, not be imprisoned by them. If you want us to come with you, we will do so in our own vessels."

"Absolutely not," said Lord Blocking. "We don't allow flying machines in New Pacifica. Yours will be destroyed."

"Oh, no they won't!" said Chancellor Boatwright. "We don't know your laws. If you won't allow the gliders, we'll just remove them. Boats, I assume, are all right? We'll just go back to our sailing ship."

Isla turned to her. "And how many more of you are there . . . on your ship?"

Chancellor Boatwright shut her mouth and cast a long look at Captain Wentforth.

He swallowed. "We mean you no harm, but we must insist that we be allowed our freedom."

"By what means," said Lord Blocking, "are you insisting? What weapons have you got?"

A flutternote buzzed against Persis's palm. She shifted the edge of her wristlock to allow it entrance to her palmport. It was from Isla.

*This is a disaster. We must keep the visitors a secret from the court until we learn their full story. I wish to agree to their autonomy, but I can't show weakness in front of the Council members. What do you advise?*

Persis advised a diversion. Quickly, she manufactured the Poppy's knockout dose. It was a stretch of her resources, but as long as she got back to the *Daydream* soon, she had the proper supplements to counteract any negative effects. Once made, she instructed the nanos to aim it at Lord Blocking. He was as good a victim as any, and deserved to be shut up.

Seconds later, he slumped to the sand.

"Oh dear!" Persis exclaimed as Lady Blocking screamed. "I do believe the hike was too much for our dear Lord Blocking. He needs a medic!"

"He has a medic," Justen growled. He was already kneeling at the man's side, fingers of one hand pressed against the aristo's neck, while his other hand pried open the man's mouth. "Odd. He's asleep. No sign of tachycardia or obstruction of his airway—"

"Oh! Oh!" Lady Blocking squealed. "They did it! They hurt him! My poor husband! They—they—"

"They made him go to sleep?" asked Andrine, her tone mocking. "Oh, the unmitigated horror. What a tragedy." She glanced at Persis, who shrugged. If Andrine wasn't speaking to her, then she wasn't getting kept in the loop when Persis deployed her knockout drugs.

"We did nothing of the sort!" the one called Captain Phoenix cried.

"He needs medical attention I can't give him here," said Justen. "Persis, I need the wallport on the *Daydream*. Perhaps we should transport everyone back to the yacht, as the princess requested. The sooner, the better, for Lord Blocking's sake."

Persis narrowed her eyes at him, but his expression was utterly guileless. A medic would recognize drugged sleep. A medic as skilled as Justen would recognize exactly the nanodrug Persis had used. Which must mean—

He was *helping* them?

"Right away," was all she said, and rounded up the others.

"I'll stay with my brother," Andrine said, and Persis nodded. It wasn't quite a conversation, not exactly a reconciliation, but they didn't have time for anything else.

Andrine knew what to do, and neither of them wanted Isla left alone with the newcomers with only Tero for protection.

After all, Andrine's brother was an excellent gengineer, but it was Persis and Andrine who were the spies.

And it was Persis who assisted Justen into the cabin with the unconscious Lord Blocking, while Dwyer walked beside them, aristocratic and useless. Persis and Justen dumped the sleeping lord on the nearest hammock belowdecks and engaged the privacy screens before Lady Blocking could slip in, too.

"The wallport is right here." Persis pointed it out for Justen, while she checked her supply of supplements in the cabinet. The one for the knockout dose was there, and she grabbed it, patting away the sheen of sweat that had sprung up on her face.

Justen smirked. "I don't really need it. Blocking will be fine once he sleeps it off. I suspect Tero slipped him a knockout drug through his palmport to shut him up, since he was making the situation with the visitors so much worse. He probably has all the latest applications, as well as access to the supplements to run them."

"Tero." Persis nodded and popped the cap. "I suppose that makes the most sense." And as long as Justen was the one coming up with her alibis, she had no business disagreeing with him.

"Though I do worry about leaving them alone out there. Even though that one with the orange hair is Reduced, our party is still outnumbered. I'm surprised Tero didn't knock them all out."

She took a long draft. "Maybe he didn't take enough supplements to make more than one dose."

Justen made a noncommittal hmmm. "Or maybe he thought that knocking them out is no way to respect their autonomy." He looked down at his sleeping patient. "Though it's not as if Blocking's has been respected, either."

"Well." Persis lifted her shoulders. "He didn't deserve respect."

"That's where you're wrong, Persis," Justen said sadly. "We all deserve it. We all deserve to live in a world where our rights aren't violated at the whim of our leaders. It doesn't matter if our leaders are kings and queens, or the people who claim to save us from them."

Persis blinked at him, unsure how to respond, no matter who she was pretending to be at that moment. All of a sudden her luxurious cabin on her fabulous yacht felt very stuffy and cramped. Justen stood an arm's length away. His face shone with perspiration and his short hair stood in black spikes all over his head. She recalled quite vividly that they still had not had a chance to talk about the urgent way he'd kissed her the last time they were on this boat.

They still hadn't had a chance to discuss the way he'd invented a terrible pharmaceutical weapon, either.

Justen wore an expression that switched between disappointment and apprehension. "I didn't say anything back on the beach—not because I agree with what Tero did but because I didn't want to cause a scene. These people, these visitors . . . they're going to be difficult enough to deal with."

Persis couldn't argue with that. Justen might be her

enemy, but right now he was the only New Pacifican she could talk to about what they'd just seen. "Is it possible that their story is true? Could they really be from elsewhere?"

Justen shrugged. "I don't know. There isn't supposed to *be* any elsewhere."

"Maybe they're descended from people who abandoned New Pacifica a long time ago." In school, Persis had learned of people who'd left the islands. Back when the creators had first landed, there'd been a few aristos here and there who'd threatened to secede, to pack up their plantations of Reduced and go elsewhere. The histories Persis had studied had made note of it. But the books also always maintained that those who'd left had led suicide missions. There was nowhere else to go.

Justen looked skeptical. "There was a lot of genetic variation among those four—did you see it? We don't have that here. Wherever they're from, it has a population much, much larger than ours. And they said they didn't expect New Pacifica to be here, which means they're using old maps. And their eyes—" But now Justen shook his head and chuckled dismissively.

"What?"

"Nothing." But Persis had learned to read that expression. He was lost in that brain of his. Unlike her, Justen had always had the luxury—indeed, the privilege—of letting people know when he was thinking hard and had never had to hide it. Right now, he was thinking very hard indeed, and it was all about the single realm where Persis's skills did not lie: the scientific.

Since the arrival of the visitors, she'd been strategizing about all the things this would mean to Isla, to her reign, to the country, to the entirety of New Pacifica and the revolution going on down south. She needed more information, of course. Who were these people and what did they want? And yet, even without his being privy to the questions the princess and her captain were no doubt asking the visitors back on the beach, Persis suspected that Justen was already drawing quite a few conclusions of his own.

"What is it, Justen?" she pressed.

"Nothing. Just—the very thought of other people, out there in the world. This changes everything."

His expression shone with excitement and Persis stared at him, wondering exactly how scared she should be.

WHILE THEY SAILED, DWYER Shift and Lady Blocking remained on deck, chatting about the newcomers. Persis rejoined them, the perfect hostess, while Justen chose to stay below with the still-unconscious Lord Blocking. That the councilman's wife hadn't chosen to do the same hadn't escaped Persis's notice. Perhaps their marriage was based on as much true affection as the arrangement she had with Justen. In fact, it probably was. Just because Persis's own parents were madly in love didn't mean any other couple on the island was. Aristos married for wealth and property, just as she'd explained to Justen in the star cove.

"It's so odd," Dwyer was saying. "I can't wait to hear what my uncle thinks of these people. I tried to message him, but this crummy palmport's been on the fritz since we left Remembrance Island."

"Oh, what a shame," Persis said. "Another kiwine cocktail?" The dampening agent she'd spiked the drinks with wouldn't last long, but it would render the aristos' palmports useless until Persis received further instructions from Isla. The last thing anyone needed was the Council discussing the visitors before Isla had even arrived with them.

"Perhaps your wallport—"

Persis's lower lip jutted out. "Sadly, Citizen Helo drained all the power making medicine for Lord Blocking. I've asked and asked my papa for a better port, but he's so stubborn about these things sometimes."

Lady Blocking gave a sympathetic tsk. "I feel for you. Listen to me, Persis. Before you marry this Galatean of yours, you'd better work out exactly what kind of say he gets in your pocket money. I didn't get that spelled out in my marriage contract with Blocking, and I'm still paying the price." She took another swill from her drink while Persis tried to hide her amusement. She'd have knocked out Lord Blocking long before this had she known it would make his lady infinitely more interesting.

"I for one think it's a good idea that a husband have a say in where his wife spends his money." Dwyer's tone was the type one uses when surrounded solely by those who already agree with your opinion. "Otherwise the entire estate may fall victim to her lack of proper decision-making skills. I think many of the political problems we're facing now can be attributed to the fact that the princess remains single."

"Your uncle thinks it best she marry soon, then?" Persis asked.

"Oh yes!" Dwyer nodded enthusiastically. "He talks of little else. The sooner she has a husband to take her in hand, the better."

"And naturally," she added innocently, "your uncle thinks it best that the husband she gets has firm opinions of his own?"

"Absolutely!"

Persis gave him a close-lipped smile as the sound of a chuckle carried across the deck on a breeze. She turned to see Justen standing at the cabin door, shaking his head. She excused herself from the party and joined him.

"Didn't think you'd find a member of the Albian court more stupid than me?" she asked him.

"I don't think you're stupid, Persis." Really? Well, that was an error she'd have to rectify. "Though to be completely honest, that man makes even Lady Blocking look clever. So it's not a fair standard."

"And yet a leader on the Royal Council thinks him an excellent match for Isla."

"Well, he has a different object in mind than you and I would."

Persis began to nod, then stopped. She didn't want to think that Justen shared any of her opinions about—anything. And she didn't want him laughing as she teased the idiots at court either. It was much easier to think of him solely as the person responsible for the Reduced refugees in Noemi's sanitarium. Anything more—his sense of humor, his medical talents, his obvious intelligence, his stated interest in curing DAR—well it may be true, but it didn't cancel out what he'd done in Galatea. They didn't have to disagree about everything for him to be her enemy.

And she still needed to learn more about his plans. The boating party had been a delay, and the visitors would be another one. If the Wild Poppy wanted to get to the bottom of Justen's story, she wasn't going to be able to count on Isla—or her neuroeels—for help.

"You know, Justen," she said, "I've been thinking about your visitor from last night. What's her name?"

"Vania." Justen sighed. "Persis, not this again. I—"

She raised her hand and he stopped. "I don't want to fight," she said, smiling sweetly. "I just wanted to say that if it's so easy for Vania to flit back and forth across the sea, maybe she can bring your sister on her next visit. Once you have Remy, you won't need to continue any sort of charade with me." Not that it would convince Isla, but Persis wasn't worried about that now. Her words were a test.

If Justen truly was concerned about the shape of the revolution and his sister's well-being back home, he'd surely leap at any chance to bring her to Albion. But if his presence here was a ruse, he wouldn't care.

He chuckled. "Thanks, but I'm pretty sure Vania would see right through that plan. She's suspicious enough about me being here." He gave her a patronizing shrug. "I think Vania's too smart to fall for something like that."

She simpered at him, which was probably preferable to giving him a good, hard smack. "If Vania is suspicious about your reasons for being here," and Persis didn't doubt it, "then your sister is no longer safe."

Justen considered this for a moment, while Persis read his face for any clues. "Remy is like a little sister to Vania. I'm sure . . ." he trailed off. "Actually, I'm not sure of anything anymore when it comes to Vania. She's so changed by the revolution."

"What if the Aldreds were to make an example of her!" Persis let out a little gasp, then covered her mouth with her hands and made her eyes as wide as they would go. "What if—oh, Justen! What if they were"—she lowered her voice to a breathless whisper—"to Reduce her, while you're here in Albion. Oh no."

*What if they were to Reduce her with your own drug?*

Persis watched as Justen's face changed, as real fear overtook his features. "You're right," he said, and couldn't quite hide the note of surprise in his voice that he thought she *was* right. "I need to talk to my sister."

"Don't let our guests know your oblet is in working order."

"Why does it matter?" he replied. "It's not compatible with your flutter system anyway. It's why I'm always forced to use wallports."

"I'm keeping them from contacting the shore until Isla has decided how she'd like to release the news about the visitors."

"You're doing *what*?"

She shrugged. "Royal orders." She didn't need to justify her activities to a war criminal like him.

Justen looked disgusted. "Do you and your princess believe you can do whatever you want?"

"Everyone believes that," she said flatly. "Or at least that they can do whatever they're able to get away with. Don't you agree, Justen?"

# Twenty-three

WHEN JUSTEN AND PERSIS arrived back in Scintillans, after dropping Dwyer, Lady Blocking, and her still-groggy husband off at the court, it was to find a royal guard ship docked at the base of the cliff. The visitors' golden gliders, their fragile arms tucked in like the wings of giant dragonflies, were lashed to the sides of the ship.

Persis fluttered Isla, but didn't have time to wait for a response. She cast Justen a look, which he mirrored back with equal concern as they hurried into the lift that would take them home.

Her father must have been alerted to her arrival, for he met her on the terrace.

"Persis. A word." A finger flick in her direction and she was at his side. Justen, thankfully, continued inside without her.

"Papa, I had no choice—"

"Half the royal guard is here, do you know that?"

"I didn't. Isla never—"

"And something about strangers—visitors from *else-where*? In my house?"

"I am as baffled as you are, Papa. Isla said—"

"'Isla said, Isla said,'" Torin repeated. "Isla may rule this island, but she does not own this estate. I've been allowing Justen Helo, because he's a refugee and a Helo and, frankly, because he's a medic. But I thought we'd agreed on this, Persis. No visitors. Not in your mother's condition. And certainly not the princess regent herself!"

Persis sighed. They had agreed, and he'd been so lenient with Justen. "Honestly, Papa, I had no idea she was coming here. But you shouldn't worry. There is so much else going on here, it's highly unlikely they'll notice—"

"They've noticed," Torin stated. "Your mother is having a very bad day."

Persis's stomach twisted like a typhoon. "*Oh, Papa.*"

He brushed her off, his rage quiet and bubbling. "The damage is done. Go deal with your guests."

Isla was waiting in the long, low-ceilinged sitting room where, years ago, they'd held countless games of high adventure. She lounged on a cushion, her right hand gripping a tall, slim supplement bottle, her eyes closed as she fired off flutter after flutter of royal orchids from her palmport.

At the sound of Persis's footfall on the stone, she opened her eyes. Her expression was unreadable.

"What are you doing here?" Persis asked.

"How long have you been lying to me?" was her friend's response. No, not her friend. For Isla's voice contained nothing of the girl who'd once known every one of Persis's secrets, the girl with whom Persis had once shared all her dreams. Instead, it was the voice solely of the princess, the royal, the monarch to her subject.

Never had Persis felt more like a revolutionary herself than when she said, "It isn't any of your business."

"This is it, isn't it?" Isla asked. "The reason for all of it. The Poppy—everything. You dress up and you run away to Galatea and you risk your life because you can't bear to stand the idea that you may Darken."

Persis looked away from the princess. That wasn't it. Or not all of it. Someone needed to do something, so it might as well be her. And at least, if she died as the Wild Poppy, at least she'd done something with the brain she'd been given before it was stolen away. One day, when DAR had her in its grip, would she forget everything? Would the Wild Poppy be just another legend to her, as it was to everyone else?

There was salt dried on her skin. She felt itchy from head to toe. She needed a bath; she needed a rest. She needed anything but to stand here and be judged by the person she always thought was her best friend.

"Tell me!" Isla demanded. "I deserve that. I've done everything you wanted."

"No, I've done everything *you* wanted," Persis snapped back. "I've helped you secretly assist the Galateans hurt in the revolution. I've carried on the charade with Justen so you can appeal to public interest. I've refrained from asking you questions about whatever is going on between you and Tero. I've drugged my fellow citizens . . ."

"Yes, you did!" Isla said. "And not just Blocking, either. Don't you dare try to pin Andrine on me."

"I stopped Andrine from going to Galatea to protect her."

"How noble and condescending of you. You'd think you were her aristo master, just like the old days. Well, guess what, Persis—Scintillans doesn't have subjects anymore, but I still do, and I actually *do* need to protect them from the shock of visitors from elsewhere. So don't you dare try to take the moral high ground with me."

"Oh no, Your Highness. I wouldn't dare to ever try to be higher than you," Persis snapped. "It's a good thing we all know our place around here. It's a good thing you're keeping Tero firmly in his."

Isla gave a delicate humph. "Maybe you've been spending too much time with your revolutionary. Even if you're lying to him, too."

The words came rushing out before she could stop herself. "Justen knows about my mother."

Isla was silent for a long moment, and even beneath her regal bearing, Persis could see she was deeply hurt. "Let me get this straight. You think he's responsible for the pinks, yet you're letting him care for your *mother*? Persis, have you gone mad?"

She rolled her eyes. "He's not going to Reduce my mother on the sly. She's already suffering enough." She was halfway to Reduction under her own steam. "Whatever else he is, Justen is a good medic. And if it distracts him from wanting to go back to the sanitarium, all the better. Until I get to the bottom of his story, I'm not letting him within fifty meters of one of my refugees."

"They aren't yours."

"They aren't yours either, but I'm sure that won't stop you from doing whatever you want with them, same as you've been with these visitors. They didn't even want to come to Albion, and you forced them here on this ship, and now you're forcing me to keep them?"

"What are my options, Persis? I can't take the visitors to court. Things are so delicate right now. I need to keep this quiet until I can figure out exactly how to introduce them. And I wouldn't have brought them here if I had known the kind of difficulties you were facing." She took a deep breath. "You should have told me."

"There's no way on Earth I'd tell the princess of Albion that my mother is Darkening."

"I'm your best friend."

Persis swallowed. "You're my ruler."

They stared at each other for a long moment. Finally, Persis continued. "We didn't tell anyone. The stigma . . . my parents didn't want to mar the image everyone had of them. The perfect couple. Blindingly in love, living happily ever after."

"Persis, that's so silly—"

"Is it?" she asked coldly, pulling away from the princess. "You, who are ordering me into this ridiculous charade with a Galatean revolutionary, just so you can promote the dream of an aristo/reg romance. You think that somehow the story of a gorgeous love affair is going to stop your people from rioting. So what happens to the people of this nation when a famous romance falls to pieces?"

Isla stared at her, shaking her head. "Is *that* what you're afraid of?"

Persis turned away, running her hands over the grit on her arms.

Her friend's voice sounded incredulous. "It hasn't fallen to pieces. Torin loves Heloise—worships the ground she walks on. Still. Always. She's not to blame for what is happening to her, and he's not shunning her because of it, either. This is a tragic accident, nothing more. If word got out, it would only strengthen the story of their—"

"*Don't you dare.*"

Isla held up her hands. "I totally respect your family's privacy."

Persis laughed mirthlessly. "Oh, you do? When you fill my house with strangers, you do?"

"I'm not your enemy!" Isla roared. She stopped and took a deep breath, but her white eyebrows were still drawn into a frown. "I'm not your enemy, Persis. We've always told each other everything. I thought I was one of the only people to know all your secrets."

No. No one knew them all anymore. And Persis wasn't about to let Isla off the hook for treating her like a subject instead of a friend. "I told you I didn't have time to take on Justen and your fake romance."

"I thought you meant because of your . . . other activities. But, Persis, don't you see? Justen is why I knew you'd be perfect for this assignment with the visitors. You've been keeping watch over him just fine. Without further information, why should I think this would be any different? I know they'll be safe here. No one is going to get in or out of Scintillans without your say-so."

And yet Vania Aldred had waltzed in just yesterday. Clearly, the Blakes were going to have to improve their security, for more reasons than one.

Isla crossed the room and laid a hand on Persis's arm. For a long moment, they stood like that, until Persis finally lifted her head to look her friend in the face.

"I'm sorry," they both said at once, then laughed. It was short-lived, though, like a seconds-long sun-shower from invisible clouds.

"I will take them away if you wish," Isla said. "Andrine and Tero, perhaps—though their home is not quite so secure—"

"No," Persis said, defeated. "You're already asking too much of him."

"I'm not asking anything of him," Isla said with a sigh. "Something happened, yes. Once. And we've talked about why nothing can happen anymore. He's a good friend, but—"

But it was impossible. Isla could champion an aristo/reg romance, but only if it was the right kind. Progressive aristo Torin marrying beautiful, brilliant Heloise. Persis, already half reg, snagging famous Justen Helo. But the princess regent of Albion could not be with a common servant's son like Tero. It might thrill all the regs, but she'd lose even more ground with the aristos who were already dismissing her.

Persis could already hear what Justen might make of that.

Isla's expression had grown concerned. "Have you been tested?"

She shook her head.

"Persis . . ."

"I don't want to know." Her tone was wild, but she didn't care. This was Isla. She'd been keeping this secret far too long. "We're all going to die one day, Isla. I could die next week on a mission. Maybe . . . later, after—" but she couldn't say anymore.

Isla understood anyway. She already knew what it was like to live in the *after* of a parent's death. The girls joined hands there, in the quiet, dim room where they'd once played as children, long ago in a world where their genetics meant no more than Isla's white hair and Persis's beauty and cleverness, where their heritage hadn't trapped the former into ruling a country that didn't want her and the latter into running away from a sickness that had no cure.

"I'll tell you one thing," Isla said at last. "Justen is going back into a sanitarium. He's here to work on finding a cure for DAR, and I'm not about to let his past keep you or your mother from a cure. I don't care what he might have done in Galatea. Remember learning about the ancients and how they first built nuclear weapons?"

"I don't think that's a good example for us to use."

"They didn't balk at hiring enemies if they could help. If I can take what I can get out of him in terms of public relations, which you have to admit he's pretty awful at, then I'll take what I can get out of him when it comes to his medical talents."

"Which he's pretty good at." Persis could begrudge him that.

"And we'll find out the truth about his past, too," said Isla. "Have you even spoken to Remy about it?"

"She knows he invented the drug. She believes he's a proper revolutionary, though, which doesn't help his case."

"Whatever Justen did, it's clear he's changed his ways. He wouldn't be here otherwise, desperate to help the refugees."

"If helping the refugees is really what he's after," Persis replied. "Of which we can't be sure. What if he's here, trying to ingratiate himself with us, so he can cause the escapees further harm?"

Isla considered this. "If he is, he's pretty bad at that, too. Persis, you have to stop thinking the worst of people. And that goes for me as well as Justen Helo."

"You haven't seen the Reduced, Isla. You haven't seen what the Galateans have done to them. If Justen is responsible for that—I don't care if he regrets it now. He deserves the worst punishment he can get."

"And what would that be, Persis? What sort of torture are you imagining for your fake lover? Dungeons? Neuroeels? Reduction?"

Persis looked away.

"Nothing?"

And she found that for once, she didn't have words to reply.

# Twenty-four

THE VISITORS HAD BEEN in Scintillans for an entire day with very little fanfare about their arrival. Though the Scintillans' servants were known for their discretion, it seemed impossible that no one would leak such a juicy story. After all, unlike word of Heloise Blake's condition, there was no one to hurt. Therefore, the fact that the presence of people from elsewhere remained a secret was a testament to Isla's ability to shut down conversation before it started. However, her quest might have been helped along just a tad by the rather shocking stories sweeping through court that Lady Blocking planned to divorce her husband, that Dwyer Shift had had a row with his councilman uncle over some unmentionable situation with a pair of fishermen from Sunrise Village, and that Persis Blake was considering cutting her hair.

It was rumored that she said long locks were *so* last winter.

And yet, no matter how long the visitors might stay, or how many conversations Justen Helo might have with them, he thought he'd never grow used to their very existence. Every time he saw them he was struck with a sense of wonder that left him unsettled—he should not feel the same about seeing a human being as he did upon seeing a sea pony or a mini-orca or a hogfish. They were not otherworldly creatures; they were fellow human beings. No matter what the strange genetics of these people—and almost without exception, they were very strange indeed—there was more to them than their scientific potential.

But without real patients to observe, it was hard to resist. He'd yet to hear back from Noemi, and Persis claimed not to know exactly where the refugees had been moved. Isla, of course, said she was too busy to concern herself with his scientific whims.

Justen had started out frustrated, but now he was just scared. Noemi wouldn't go to the trouble of moving an entire ward of patients without a good reason. What if Vania's visit the other day hadn't had anything to do with tracking down the Wild Poppy? What if it had been about finding the refugees? She'd left in such a hurry, and right after that was when Persis had told him about Noemi's plan to move the Galatean refugees.

If the revolutionaries tried anything on Albian soil—what would that mean for both nations?

And he hadn't heard anything from Remy since he'd left. In the first few days, he'd figured she was just angry with him, but her continued silence boded ill, especially since his fight with Vania. Then again, if she had turned against him completely, then maybe she'd be safe in Galatea.

Today he and the male visitor, Kai, were sitting in the shade of the terrace, overlooking the cliffs while the Reduced woman played on the lawn with Slipstream. She squealed with laughter as she chased the sea mink and it wove skillfully around her legs, chattering and dragging along the ground a faded green scarf Ro—whose real name, apparently, was Tomorrow—had been wearing around her hair. Neither sea mink nor girl seemed the least bit hampered by her heavy, long skirt. Justen had wondered why she'd wear such a thing in the equatorial heat of New Pacifica, but the other visitors had all shrugged and said that fighting with Tomorrow would not have been worth it. "She's a creature of habit," Chancellor Boatwright—or Elliot—had said at the time. "If she's hot enough, she'll ask for different clothes."

"Everyone here stares at her," Kai said now. "Is it so easy to forget, in two generations, what Reduction looks like?"

"Yes," said Justen. "Apparently it is." Now that he saw real Reduction, *born* Reduction, he regretted even more the name he'd offhandedly suggested to his uncle Damos of the effects he suspected his experimental drug would have on healthy patients. What was happening to the victims in Galatea—that was not Reduction. This girl had grown into and beyond her limitations. Her nature breathed in her and through her like a tree that springs from a rock. It might grow stunted because of the poor soil around its roots, but there was beauty and majesty in the way it clung to life and thrived in its own way.

By contrast, the drug was merely an artificial shade, smothering its victims. Tomorrow was beautiful, whole, human. People under the influence of the Reduction drug were broken. Broken by *him*.

"Everything all right?" asked the stranger.

"I wonder what my countrymen would think to see her. If they'd be reminded to honor our past, not exploit it."

"You're talking about the civil war." Kai nodded. "I have friends back home who wonder if that's where we're headed, too. In so many ways, your society is far advanced. But I guess some things don't change."

Justen turned to his companion with a knowing look. "Actually, about that. Most here won't recognize it, but I have medic training and couldn't help but notice. Your eyes . . . your reflexes. Your people still practice ERV?"

Kai started, a subtle movement, and his crystalline eyes widened. "No. Not usually. Our people don't practice much of anything."

They must not, if they were still using such quaint and clumsy gengineering. Extreme endogenous retroviral enhancement had been designed to push human capacity to its limits. It had caused the Reduction when it was first invented, and was better consigned to the waste bin of medical procedures, like trepanning, leeches, and systemic chemotherapy. The gengineering on Kai and the other captain, Andromeda Phoenix, was like looking at something out of an ancient history text.

Or a project that would flunk even an intro gengineering class.

"We don't do much in the way of science back home," the visitor added. "The things you have here are like something out of a dream. Those palmports look like magic."

Justen made a face. "They're an appalling perversion of science. Wasteful. Dangerous." No one yet knew the long-term effects that their nutrient leeching could have on the system. You couldn't fix everything with a supplement or two. Then again, who was he to talk? He regularly railed against palmports and genetemps, but it was his own achievements that had caused the most damage.

Kai chuckled. "Where I come from, it's the . . . well, I guess you'd call them the aristos who disdain science. It's strange to hear it from a Post's mouth."

"A Post?"

"A . . . what do you call yourself? Regular? Reg?" Kai shrugged. "Same thing. We say Post-Reductionist, or Post. The ERV was . . . a desperate move. My friends and I—we had very little choice. We needed to escape, and we needed enhancements to do it. Elliot is still terrified that we've single-handedly brought back the Reduction." He shook his head, frowning. "She's—you'd call her an aristo, I guess? Except not like the aristos here. They don't seem to have anything against technology."

Justen frowned. It was *he* who'd brought back the Reduction, not a bunch of primitive gengineers. "You mean she's afraid for your children?"

Kai looked away. "Not in so many words. Elliot . . . doesn't like to use so many words. But I know her, and I know she must be."

Justen smiled, the medic to the patient. "Well, you can tell her not to worry. You're a natural reg, right? That means your neurostructure has already bypassed the architecture of Reduction. ERV shouldn't undo that. But if you like, I can do some tests. If you're vulnerable, you can just take the Helo Cure and your offspring should be fine." There were no supplies of the cure lying around anymore, of course, but it was simple enough to compound a dose. The formula was universally known. If he were in Galatea, he could probably find some stock in the storage rooms of the royal labs along with the rest of Persistence Helo's belongings.

Except for the oblets he'd stolen, of course.

Kai laughed again, incredulous. "The things you say—I can't believe you're so casual about it. Where I come from, they hardly believe in surgery, let alone biotechnology."

"You sound like you lived in the Dark Ages."

"I did." Kai pointed at Tomorrow. "Back home, there are hundreds of thousands just like her. They're born and live and die in slavery, and there's no other choice for them."

Choice. What an interesting thought. Justen wondered if Tomorrow, offered the choice of the cure, would choose to take it. There was nothing in the histories of Reduced refusing the cure. Of even being given the option. He did recall reading about debates among natural regs with Reduced siblings about waiting, worrying that the cure was a second-rate solution to the regularity they were sure was going to come to their family within the next generation. Worrying that it might even set them back. He also recalled reading in the histories protests on estates where aristos forced even the natural-born regs to take the cure.

At any rate, it had no known effect on those who

weren't Reduced. Persistence Helo took the cure herself as a publicity stunt to show it was harmless to regs.

"Here on . . ." Kai faltered.

"New Pacifica," Justen offered.

"On New Pacifica," Kai said, amused, "you've cured everyone and ended the Reduction. But if we took your cure back to our homeland, it would be a battle to get it to the Reduced."

"It was a battle here, too," said Justen. "And it was only the first of many."

Kai looked around him. "This place seems like paradise."

Justen nodded. "Yes. *Seems*."

PERSIS HAD SPENT THE last few months as a spy and the last week as the admirer of Galatea's most celebrated mad scientist. But today, she played tour guide, taking the single aristo among the visitors for a trip around her estate. Apparently back in her homeland, Chancellor Boatwright—whose name was actually Elliot North—owned one estate and managed another, despite being an unmarried teenage girl. From Elliot's descriptions, Persis gathered the visitor's holdings were almost half as large as Albion.

It shouldn't be Persis this young woman was talking to. It should be Isla.

"Now, Chancellor, if you look down there, you'll see the fleet of fishing boats. This should be especially interesting to you given your family's traditions."

Elliot said nothing, but peered politely over the side of the skimmer and down the pali. "Is your diet mostly fish?"

These days, Persis's diet was mostly palmport supplements. "We're islanders, Chancellor. Of course we eat a lot of seafood."

All day long, Elliot had seemed very concerned with how the people of Scintillans—and of New Pacifica in general—ate. Persis had never thought as much about food production in her life as she had today. No one starved in New Pacifica. She had a difficult time imagining anyone living the way these visitors claimed to, with coal stoves and gas lanterns and hardly enough food to sustain the fields of Reduced slaves that labored in rags and died in their thirties. Practically all the visitors were wearing rags, especially this Elliot, who was supposed to be the highest born of all of them. Persis had offered them new clothes, but Elliot in particular had seemed scandalized by what Persis had considered very conservative garments.

"It'll be high summer back home," Elliot said wistfully, looking out over the fishing village and the fields that lay beyond. "My lands lie along the sea as well, but our islands are not quite so . . . lush."

"Do you miss your estate?" Persis asked politely. It was the most she'd heard Elliot speak in one go since they'd started out that morning, and she didn't want to scare the other girl.

"Yes," Elliot said. "I miss it desperately, but"—the older girl took a breath—"I spent four years missing Kai, and wishing I'd gone with him the last time he left us. So this time I made the other decision." She looked at Persis and her eyes shone. "And it was the right one. For four years, I'd hoped I could do something for the people who live on my estate. And now I can do so much more than I ever would have even with the changes I'd made on my farm. Now we know there is a cure. It's all Kai could have hoped."

"Captain Wentforth," Persis said. So far, their non-verbal communication and instant alliance on every issue had been the dominant personality traits she'd noticed in Kai and Elliot. Even the other captain, Andromeda, seemed powerless to argue against their combined force. "He chose that name himself, I hear?"

Elliot chuckled. "Yes. That's what Posts do, where I'm from."

Persis nodded. "It was a bit of a trend here among the regs before the cure as well. I'm named for one who did that. Persistence Helo, who invented the cure."

"Justen's grandmother, right?" Elliot looked impressed. "And he's a medic, too, just like her."

"Not entirely," was all Persis could trust herself to say.

They rode in silence for a few moments. "So . . ." Elliot began, "you don't do much farming on this estate?"

"Not this one, no," said Persis, "but I can arrange for you to tour others if agriculture is what interests you."

Elliot nodded. "And what do you do? Are you in school?"

"Not anymore." She didn't need to get into details with this foreigner.

"So you help your father with the fisheries?"

Persis laughed. "Not really. My father does serve an advisory position in the village, of course, but fishing isn't his interest, either." Her father had an excellent staff of biologists, gengineers, and aquaculturists working in the village and had always argued that the best landowners surrounded themselves with experts who were passionate about their pursuits. Torin himself was a scholar and had worked tirelessly in educational reform for as long as Persis could remember. More regs than ever were getting the chance to pursue the education and careers they desired, thanks to his and Heloise's efforts, though their duties were curtailed somewhat by her mother's illness at the moment.

"Oh." Elliot was quiet again. What an odd girl. She seemed so attached to her strange way of life, the customs and habits of her homeland. She was almost painfully shy, clearly homesick, and utterly without pretense. A less likely candidate for sailing off into nothingness on the whim of a teenage boy Persis could hardly imagine. Then again, Persis wasn't exactly what she appeared to be, either. Maybe this Elliot North had hidden depths. After all, there had to be something the dashing Captain Wentforth saw in her.

Unlike Persis and Justen, there seemed little reason for them to fake an affection for each other.

"I'm sorry if this all seems strange to you," Persis said at last.

"No," the visitor said. "It actually doesn't seem that strange at all, in the end."

THE LITTLE SKIFF THAT pulled up to the base of the Scintillans cliffs did not go unnoticed by the denizens of the fishing village. There was a guard posted at the main lift to the estate, and when Vania applied for admittance as "a friend of Justen Helo's" she was swiftly turned away. She eyed the switchback road with curiosity, but there didn't seem to be any entrance that wasn't being watched.

Fine. She'd approach the estate from the land side. There were plenty of ways into Scintillans, she was sure. Strange that they'd have increased the security so much since her last visit. Had they been plagued with spies and nanocams since the lovebirds' infamous little cove kiss? Figured. These Albians didn't have anything serious to employ their minds, like she did.

Returning to her skiff, she piloted it away from the docks and toward the west coast of the island, looking for an alternate entrance. The cliffs fell away on the convex coast of Albion, so perhaps she'd find an easier approach. She was rewarded about twenty minutes later when she reached the very farthest point of the peninsula and saw a tiny semicircular cove that looked dug from the cliff wall. A dark line zigzagged up the cliff face, and as she drew closer, she could see it was a staircase leading to the village beyond. Endlessly long ropes of vines fell down all around the staircase, tiny yellow flower heads looking ready to bloom any moment. When they did, the whole place would turn into some sort of enchanted bower. For a moment, Vania was struck dumb by its beauty. How long had it been since she'd stopped to consider how pretty anything was? Day after day, she'd traveled all over her own splendid island and seen nothing but whether or not the places she went were under her father's control or still resisting the revolution. Night after night, she went to sleep in a palace once infamous for its opulent beauty, but considered nothing but her own ambition.

She shook her head. Perhaps it took leisure to appreciate beauty. This Persis Blake had all the time in the world to look at flowers and wear pretty dresses. She had nothing else going on. And now Justen was following in his little girlfriend's useless footsteps. He'd probably forgotten all about his research in favor of . . . well, whatever it was he found to do with Persis Blake.

Vania was quite pleased she'd blocked Remy from sending or receiving messages from him on her oblet. The last thing she needed right now was to watch her little foster sister follow Justen's dangerous, worthless path. He could have his communication privileges back when he stopped being so infuriating.

As she pulled into the cove, she saw two figures splashing around in the shallows. Like all Albians, they had brilliantly colored hair, but even that seemed somehow off as she drew closer. One of the young women, a few years older than her, had hair like sand, and the other, younger one's was a dull, burnished red. Their skin was impossibly pale, and the red-haired one had a face full of freckles. They looked up at the sound of her engine, and kept staring as she ran her boat aground and tied a line to a rock.

"Hello," she said. "I'm trying to get to Scintillans."

"This is Scintillans," the sandy-haired one said, though her pronunciation was truly bizarre. "But I don't think you're supposed to bring boats into the bathing area."

The clear water lapping her toes was warmer than it

ought to be, and Vania bit her lip. "My mistake." She studied the two women. Neither had palmports in their pale, pinkish hands, and their clothes were certainly not the high fashions she'd seen Persis wearing. Their hair, too, was not the eye-melting shades so popular among the northern elite. They must be reg peasants, possibly with some sort of speech impediment. And the one had said "don't think you're supposed to" as if she didn't know for sure.

"Does that staircase go up to the estate?"

The sandy-haired one looked at her companion as if weighing her answer. "I believe they're looking for privacy now. If you want to visit, it's best to apply at the lift."

"I tried that," Vania said. The other woman's use of the word "they" had clinched it. Whoever these two were, they had no authority to stop her. "I'm here to visit my friend Justen Helo, but the last time I came, we had a bit of a fight. I've come to apologize, but I can't if he won't let me see him."

"What's your name?" the blonde asked.

"Vania. I'm an old friend of his from Galatea."

"The southern island?"

Vania's eyes narrowed. Where else?

"I'm Andromeda," the light-haired one said. "And this is Tomorrow." Bizarre names, for even stranger women. "I can give your message to Justen if you want."

The red-haired one, Tomorrow, still hadn't spoken, and as Vania watched, she wandered off without a word. Andromeda took no notice. Vania had never seen such odd behavior in a grown woman. Never seen it in anyone but a Reduced prisoner.

"Actually," Vania said, "I want to see him. So I can take these stairs?"

Quick as a flash, Andromeda stood between Vania and the staircase. "I don't think I'm supposed to let anyone up without permission. I understand we're already a big imposition on the Blakes."

Who were these two? Vania blinked at the other woman in shock. What kind of enhancements were they doing here in Albion? Andromeda's skin, her speed, her shallow sea-colored eyes? She'd never seen anything like it. She knew Albians colored their hair—were skin and eyes the new trend? Was she going to find Justen up on the pali with a lavender face and bright pink irises?

But no matter who this Andromeda was, she wouldn't distract Vania from her mission. "I'm afraid I was a little unfair to him the other day," she lied smoothly. "Ever since the revolution, I've been a tiny bit prejudiced against aristos, so when I heard he was involved with one . . ."

"You're one of those revolutionaries," Andromeda said.

Vania straightened. "Yes. But I'm here on personal business, so—"

"Tell me more." Andromeda leaned in. "The princess has been very forthcoming but also very uninterested in letting us see or talk to anyone else. And unlike a few other members of my party, I'm not the type to just blindly trust a lord, Luddite or otherwise."

Vania blinked at her. "Pardon?"

"No one will tell me anything about Galatea but that it's dangerous and we should steer clear."

Typical aristo propaganda. Vania had no doubt the princess was using quite a lot of it. It was the only possible explanation for why the revolution hadn't inspired their northern neighbors yet.

"No, indeed," Vania explained. "The revolution is a beautiful and cleansing thing. We regs have never been given a proper chance before. Finally, we're exerting our human rights. Honestly, do you think you've been given all the chances you ought, growing up here in Scintillans?"

Andromeda snorted. "I'm not from around here, but I agree with everything you say."

"Oh, well then wherever you are from in Albion."

"We're not from Albion, either." And then, as Vania's eyes got wide and her mouth dropped open, the woman told her the craziest story she'd ever heard. "We didn't even know these islands existed until a few days ago. We're explorers on a mission to find other survivors from the wars. A few days ago, we landed here, and that Princess Isla and her guards have us holed up so we don't cause a riot or something." She leaned in and dropped her voice. "But if they don't figure things out in a few more days, they're going to have another revolution to deal with, if you know what I mean."

Vania suppressed her look of shock and replaced it with a smile. "Oh, I so do. Please, tell me more."

# Twenty-five

IT WAS LATE IN the evening and the female captain and her Reduced friend were nowhere to be found on Scintillans. Their glider was still waiting on the lawn, but it didn't keep Elliot North from pacing and wringing her hands. Justen watched her concern grow, unsure of what he could do to help the stranger relax. He had a variety of antianxiety prickers in his supply bag, but from what he understood of the aristo visitor's personality, such a move would be tantamount to assault in her eyes. And then he'd have Captain Wentforth to deal with.

And Justen wasn't the only one who'd noticed Elliot's growing discomfort. Captain Wentforth's expression swelled from worry to anger as he watched his girlfriend. At last, he strode over to Persis and demanded answers. "We were promised that if we did what you said, we'd be safe here. Where are my friends?"

Persis's eyes were as round and innocent as an accomplished courtier like herself could manage as she answered.

"Sincerely, Captain Wentforth, I don't know. The last anyone saw them they were headed down to the sea to swim in our heated star cove—"

"So what?" Elliot broke in, her voice shuddering over the words. "Are you saying they were just swept out to sea?"

"Not from the cove," Justen jumped to Persis's defense. "It's completely protected from undertows. No currents at all. Maybe someone from the fishing village offered to give them a tour. I know there's a path cut into the rock that goes to the village—" He looked to Persis for assistance.

She closed her eyes. A moment later, several flutternotes erupted from her palm and zipped off to points unknown. Both Kai and Elliot stepped back.

"I'm sorry—did those scare you?" Persis asked.

"I will never get used to them," Elliot said. She looked a bit green around the gills.

"You're not alone," Justen said. "They've been around for years and they still make me sick."

"Oh, Justen!" cried Persis. "You're such a luddite."

Both visitors stiffened at her words. Persis cast Justen a confused glance.

"It's their word for 'aristos,' remember?" Justen said.

"Right. Droll name." She batted her eyelashes and Justen nearly groaned. "At any rate, I've just messaged Isla, as well as Andrine and Tero down in the village, to tell them that your friends have vanished. I'm sure we'll get word of their whereabouts soon. And don't concern yourself for another moment about that cove. Nothing could be safer in the world. I myself have been swimming there since I could barely walk."

Justen doubted this made Kai or Elliot feel any more comfortable.

When another hour passed with no reply from Persis's contacts, Elliot went from concerned to frantic. "I'm the one who took her with us, Kai. I'm the one who put her in this danger. She would have been safe back home on the North Estate with Dee. She would have—" She broke off.

"She's with Andromeda, Elliot. Nothing's going to happen to her—Andromeda will make sure of it."

Persis jumped into action, immediately offering to go down to the star cove and search herself, though Justen was sure the visitors found the idea as comical as he did. Persis Blake wasn't suited to the job of retrieving missing people.

Perhaps they should call the Wild Poppy.

Kai insisted he be allowed to take his glider and go as well. "It's fully charged since it's been sitting out all day. I can fly all night if necessary." He turned to Elliot and took her hands in his. "We'll find them. Trust Andromeda to take care of herself and Ro. You know how much experience she has."

Elliot gave a barely audible humph. "But what if they're separated? This place . . . the way they look at Ro here—"

"We stare at her," Persis said, "because we're not used to her. The same way you stare at our palmports." She paused, as if suddenly realizing it did little good to compare a human being to her flashy piece of technology. "You know what I mean. She's unusual here. You all are. But how many ways can I promise you we mean you no harm?"

Elliot turned to her, still holding tight to Kai's hands.

"What are your promises good for if my friend has disappeared?" She looked back at Kai. "I'll take the other glider."

He shook his head. "I don't think I like the idea of you flying at night. It's different with Andromeda and me. And all these cliffs? You don't have enough experience . . ."

"Experience?" Elliot laughed. "I've been flying your gliders since you first knew how to make them, Malakai Wentforth." Her voice was haughty, but the expression on her face was wry, and Kai was grinning at the way she pronounced his name. "Besides, everything you design looks like our old tractor, remember? I'll figure it out."

Quick as that, it was decided, and Elliot, Kai, and Persis all left Justen alone. Not one of them offered to take him along for the ride, or suggested a place he might look for the visitors himself. And since Torin and Heloise had used the arrival of the visitors as an excuse to go on a private retreat to their north shore cottage, Justen found himself, again, alone in the house. Most of the servants had already gone home for the evening.

Since he still hadn't received any response from Noemi about the new location of the refugees, he couldn't go to them. But that didn't mean he couldn't help. He still had his grandmother's research. Maybe, when cross-referenced with the recent tests he'd done, he could glean some new information. If only Noemi would write him back. He was sure she must be busy, but he needed to help his countrymen and undo some of the damage he'd caused.

Then again, she might let him come back to work and he'd just make a bigger mess of things than he had last time.

The pinks had been just such an accident, and seeing Kai and his rudimentary gengineering today reminded him of how much trouble humanity could get into while trying to help, let alone trying to harm. Even the great Persistence Helo had created DAR alongside the cure, and Justen bore no pretensions he was smarter than she.

He'd read Persistence's diaries a hundred times, and he couldn't find her mistake any more than she could. She'd followed every trail that might hold a hint of a solution, from genetic flaws that might have worked themselves into the cure to ways to stop the deterioration before it had started. Indeed, it had been one of Persistence Helo's hypotheses that had led him to create the Reduction drug.

Or whatever it really should be called, as Justen now knew what *real* Reduction looked like. That girl, Tomorrow— or Ro as her friend Elliot called her—embodied the past of most of the population of Earth. He'd never seen it in person before. But, of course, his grandmother had. She'd been surrounded by Reduced people. And yet, none of the research or history he'd studied could teach Justen what being Reduced really meant. Only Ro had had the power to show him.

In his grandmother's diaries, there had been points where she'd written, late in life, about her attempts to trace the genetic ancestry of those regs who seemed most affected by DAR. Since the side effect was still relatively new by the time of her death, she hadn't had a large enough sample size to test her hypothesis, but she had postulated that there was a genetic basis to natural regularity and that those whose family lines had achieved it by the time of the cure—even if individuals hadn't themselves—were less likely to develop DAR.

Justen, coming into the research a few generations later, was able to follow family backgrounds further and determine not only that his grandmother was correct but also how much more likely a reg was to develop DAR if, at the time of the cure, his or her ancestors had no siblings or cousins who were natural regs.

But if DAR susceptibility had some basis in the genetic predisposition of its victims toward naturally remaining Reduced, what would it mean for someone like Tomorrow? Someone his age, who was probably three or four or more generations younger than any Reduced that New Pacifica had ever seen?

Wasn't it far more likely that this Reduced girl had siblings or cousins who were natural regs than it had been at the time of the cure? Regularity grew, generation by generation. Even at the beginning of Persistence Helo's research, she'd mapped out a timeline, based on population and reproduction patterns, for a natural end of the Reduction. She just hadn't wanted to wait that long. But here was Tomorrow, much farther down the line. What possibilities lay in her genetic code? What would happen if Persistence Helo were doing the same research now, using Tomorrow as a model of a Reduced of her generation? Might Ro's descendants be immune to DAR completely?

And if so, might Justen be able to figure out how, and apply it to his own people?

As always, time blurred into a series of brain models, numbers, notes, and chemical equations. For a while, everything else was forgotten. He didn't even hear the voices on the lanai outside the sitting room where he was working. And he certainly didn't see when a figure entered the room at his back.

"It's nice to see you working so hard. I was afraid when you'd come to Albion you'd given up the use of your brain entirely."

The sound of Vania's voice snapped him out of his focus. He looked up to see her standing right behind him, her long hair drawn back in a dark tail over her shoulder, her black military jacket and trousers looking out of place against the Blakes' bright furnishings.

"What are you doing here, Vania? I thought we'd said all we needed to last time."

"If we hadn't, your striking me from the Scintillans approved guest list certainly got the message across."

"All evidence to the contrary." He tapped his fingers against the oblets to hide the displays. How long had she been standing there? How much had she seen? "As you're here."

"Yes, but not as *your* guest." She nodded to the terrace. "I made some new friends this afternoon. Nice people, if a bit . . . strange."

Justen craned his neck. Andromeda and Tomorrow were on the lanai, looking disheveled and confused. Justen understood the feeling. All this time everyone had been worried about the two missing visitors, they'd been off with Vania? What was his old friend up to?

"Where is everyone?" Andromeda called in to him.

"They're out looking for you. They even took the gliders."

"What?" Andromeda exclaimed angrily. "Malakai let Elliot use my glider?" She took off, Ro hot on her heels. Justen sighed, crossed to the nearest wallport, and sent out a barrage of messages to Persis, Isla, and Tero that the missing visitors were home. With any luck, Persis would find a way to flag down the other two.

He turned back to find Vania sneaking a peek at one of the oblets.

"Get away from that."

With a flourish of her hand, she made the files spin above the oblet's base. The smile on her face was keen and cunning. "What secrets you've been keeping, Justen! People from elsewhere. Natural Reduced. Flying machines . . ." She passed her fingers through the oblet's display. "Anything else I should know?"

He pushed past her and shut the machine's display down again. "I don't think you should know as much as you already do."

"So arrogant. I suppose you think like an aristo, now that you're such good friends with them. You think you and your pretty, stupid aristo and your pretty, stupid princess all deserve knowledge about the world that no one else is allowed to have. Is that why these visitors are being hidden away up here? Do you honestly believe that's why they came to New Pacifica in the first place? To be imprisoned in your girlfriend's gilded cage?"

Justen grimaced. He didn't need Vania putting a voice

to all the thoughts in his head. "It's a temporary situation." He'd never once made the argument that Isla's actions were faultless. But temporary discretion was not the same as imprisonment. She'd requested that the visitors wait, which they were happy to do for a day or two, until their friends arrived on their ship. And they were free to go—as Andromeda had just proved.

Vania was still talking. "Captain Andromeda Phoenix—next to her most fascinating name—has the most remarkable impression of our homeland, Justen. She's been told it's a vile place, full of danger and destruction. Wherever would she have gotten that idea?"

Justen shrugged in response. "Honestly, Vania, I don't have much to do with what the visitors are and are not told. I'm merely a guest here, like them."

"They're not like you, Justen. Not like anyone in all New Pacifica, and you know it. That one with the orange hair is Reduced. *Really* Reduced."

Her eyes practically glowed with promise. How much had she seen of his notes? Justen watched Vania the way one might a snake. She hadn't come here to chat this time. Vania was smart and ambitious, and because she'd once been like a sister to him, he knew she classified people into one of two camps: friend and foe.

Justen was pretty sure he'd slipped into the latter category at their last meeting.

"Well, you didn't come here looking for them, Vania, so what did you come for?"

"I came to enlist your help."

"In what?"

"Tracking down the Wild Poppy."

A sharp, staccato burst of laughter escaped his lips. Again with this? "What in the world would I know about the Wild Poppy?" He didn't even know where the spy hid the refugees. Not anymore.

"I'm not sure yet. That's why I'm here. After all, the Wild Poppy is undoubtedly an aristo, and you seem to be thriving among that community. Here you are, in the very heart of elite life in Albion, doing favors for the princess, going to parties with her— What exactly is your girlfriend's official position again, Justen? The royal stylist?"

"If you like," he replied. Hadn't he once thought the same of Persis? Now, of course, his opinion of her was— well, wasn't exactly sure. Persis was confusing. She was silly, and then she made the most sense of anyone he knew. She was sexy, but she wasn't anything like the type of girl he could feel something for. She was shallow, but she was also one of the most thoughtful, kindhearted, and generous people he'd ever met.

"And now"—Vania gestured to the work littering the desk—"it seems you're back to your favorite topic of research. Only this time, you're doing it for the Albians."

"I've always been doing it for the Albians and Galateans both. Just like my grandmother."

"Hmm." Vania shrugged, then moved away from the table. "And yet here you do it in your girlfriend's living room, whereas back home Papa gave you an entire lab and a staff of your own."

"That lab came with trappings I found . . . a bit constricting."

Her gaze dropped from his face to his feet and back up, studying one of the new outfits Persis had picked for him. "Actually, I find your new trappings much more *constricting*. But no matter how much you wish to talk about fashion, Justen, I have more important things in mind."

"Right, the Wild Poppy." Justen sighed and waved his hand. "Well, off you go."

She chuckled, but there was no amusement in it. "No, off *you* go. I am going to find the Poppy this time, and you're going to help me."

"I beg your pardon? We already went over this. I absolutely will not."

Vania was silent for a moment. "You haven't even asked after your sister, Justen. Don't you care to know how she's doing, all alone, in Galatea? Don't you wonder how knowledge of your treason is affecting her?"

Justen's blood chilled again, but he did his best not to let it show. "I think of my sister every day. I miss her tremendously." And he didn't think she'd received a single message he'd sent her since coming to Albion. His fears for her were starting to come to pass. At first he'd thought she was still angry from their argument, but now he feared worse, especially since Vania's last visit. After all, why would they let him contact Remy if they thought he'd betrayed the revolution? He needed Remy here.

"In fact, I'd appreciate it if you could give her a message for me."

"I think that will be difficult," Vania said, her expression utterly guileless, "unless of course you help me. After all, it's so hard to communicate anything to the Reduced—"

Justen didn't know how he did it, but it was as if he could move as fast as those visiting captains, for suddenly he was right on top of Vania, her narrow shoulders in his grip. "What have you done to Remy?" he shouted.

"Nothing." Her voice shook as she freed herself from his grasp. "But, Justen, you know that treason is a clear cause for arrest—not just of the traitor but of his entire family as well."

"You wouldn't—you couldn't do anything to Remy. She's living in your house." And yet wasn't that exactly what he'd been afraid of all along? He'd just never thought Vania—Vania of all people—could betray him. Betray them both. They'd grown up together; they'd loved each other as brother and sister—or so he'd always thought. Was this what the revolution had done to her?

Vania's eyes narrowed. "Are you accusing my father of favoritism? That would make him no better than the queen he had a role in deposing."

"Remy has done nothing. To ensure her safety, I've been keeping my feelings about the revolution private. Don't you think, if I'd wanted to, I could have argued long and loud against everything going on down there?"

She snorted. "You want me to admire how *ineffectual* your treason has been?"

"Vania, you love Remy. You can't let anything happen to her."

"That's precisely what I'm saying to you."

Justen ran his hands through his hair, paced away a few steps, then turned. "You won't do anything," he insisted, trying to convince himself. "You'd be foolish to. If word got out—Remy's a Helo. The people of Galatea wouldn't stand for it." To say nothing of the people of Albion. If Isla needed an excuse to invade, Remy Helo might be it.

"I hope you're right. But if you aren't, I doubt the Wild Poppy will find it so easy to break into Halahou prison again."

The Poppy had broken into the prison? The man was more adept even than Justen had thought. "Vania. Listen to yourself. Listen to what you're saying. You're coming to me and actually threatening to imprison Remy? Torture Remy? Reduce . . . *Remy*?"

There was the faintest flicker in Vania's eyes, but a second later it vanished, replaced by a serene expression. "It's not going to come to that. You're going to help me find the Poppy, Justen."

Justen shook his head in disbelief. Vania was perfectly calm, but it was the assuredness of a zealot. Justen remembered when things had seemed that simple to him. The revolution was a moral good, no matter its price. And then, even when he'd first come to Albion, he'd not given much thought to anything beyond putting up with Persis and the princess in order to get his research off the ground.

But now he'd seen a natural Reduced, now he'd talked to the Galatean victims, now nothing was as it seemed. He looked at Vania. At his friend Vania; at his ally Vania; at his foster sister, Vania, and he didn't even recognize her.

"I won't."

She stiffened and her expression turned stern. "Then I guess you're the one who will be Reducing Remy." She started to move away, and Justen tried to grab her.

"Stop! No, you can't."

But Justen, who spent his days in a lab and his nights with his nose buried in books, was no match for a top member of the Galatean military. Quick as anything, she swept his legs out from underneath him. He landed hard on his spine, the back of his head thunking against the inlaid stone floors. For a moment his vision blurred, and when it cleared, Vania was standing near the door.

"Though I suppose," she said, her tone thoughtful, "if you think about it, it was you all along."

# Twenty-six

PERSIS EXITED THE LIFT and approached the visitors clustered around the gliders on the lawn and chattering away, despite the late hour. As she drew closer, she saw there was an extra member of the party present. She peered through the darkness at the young woman in the dark clothes.

Vania Aldred. Again. She was about to have a very stern conversation with the guard staff.

An orchid flutter buzzed against her hand. She nudged aside her wristlock to let Isla's message in.

*I am glad to hear from Justen that no harm has come to our guests. I suppose you can't pen in explorers, now can you?*

*I have wonderful news. One of the Albian royal vessels has made contact with the* Argos, *and with messages from the captains and Chancellor Boatwright, has persuaded them to make landing at the royal court as early as tomorrow. In honor of their arrival, I plan to introduce the crew of the* Argos *to Albian society at a massive gala luau tomorrow night.*

*Do you think they have anything decent to wear?*

*All my love.*

Persis barely paid attention to the message, as all her focus was on the Galatean revolutionary who'd somehow managed to sneak past the guards she'd posted at both the lift and the landside entrances to the estate. The revolutionary who'd somehow, in the past hour, become close personal friends with the visitors from elsewhere.

Where was Justen while all this was going on? Had he been the one to let Vania in? Had he been the one to introduce her to the visitors?

"You're saying it snows where you live?" Vania was asking as Persis approached. "Real snow? Astonishing. Tell me what it's like in this . . . winter thing, when the days are only a few hours long."

"Dreadful," said Kai, as if that finished the matter.

"Well, what a surprise to see you again, Citizen Aldred," said Persis.

"Lady Blake." The dark-haired woman turned and affected a deep and oddly reverent bow, which instantly made the rest of the group uncomfortable.

Oh, so this was how she intended to play. Act the downtrodden reg, as if that would make a case for the revolution. Persis smiled. She could checkmate that.

"We must call each other 'Persis' and 'Vania' now," Persis said. "After all, we'll practically be sisters when Justen and I get married." The girl flinched ever so slightly. Interesting. "Besides, I never can remember whether it's more polite to call you by your military title or the one that you and your father share."

"'Citizen' is meant to denote our equality, Lady Blake."

"Is it now?" Persis giggled. "And yet, the truest equality lies not in names but in actions." She took the woman's hand and drew her away from the visitors. "What brings you to my estate at such a late hour?"

"That would be my fault, Lady Blake," called Andromeda. Curse the visitor's insanely good hearing. And *Lady Blake*? Andromeda had been calling her Persis since they met. And there was a sneer on the woman's pale face that Persis had never noticed before either. "Vania took Tomorrow and me on her boat all day. We toured the coast of Albion and she told us all about her country."

"Such a shame," Persis murmured. She continued, more loudly, "What's going on in Galatea, I mean. Luckily, we're safe from all that nastiness here."

"And what *we're* safe from in Galatea," Vania replied just as sweetly, "is the tyranny of stupid aristos who lord over us for no particular reason but their birth."

"I'd like to see a country where there are no lords," said Andromeda. "I used to read about them in books and wonder what such a place was like."

"I'm sure such a place could be most lovely," Persis said quickly. "But tyranny can come from those who aren't *called* lords as well."

"True," said Kai. "And it wouldn't have hurt for you and Ro to tell us where you were going, Andromeda. Elliot and I were worried sick."

"Fine," said Andromeda. "We'll decide as a group. I vote we leave here and head to Galatea. I'm tired of being told by a bunch of lords and princesses where I can and cannot be."

"Excellent decision!" Vania cried as Persis looked on, appalled. "We can leave right now if you wish. It's just a short trip from here to the northern tip of Galatea. . . ."

Persis refused to panic, though from Vania's smug grin, the Galatean was clearly waiting for such a response. Instead she said, "Oh, dear. Perhaps it would be best to delay the trip for a day or two. I've just received word from Isla that her ship met up with the *Argos* and is leading it back to Albion."

"Have your monarch message her ship again," suggested Vania, "and tell the *Argos* to divert to Galatea instead. We wouldn't want to keep the visitors here against their will, would we?"

Persis pouted. "Oh, but her highness the princess will be so disappointed. She was planning a luau for tomorrow night, to welcome the visitors to Albian society. It would mean so much to all the people of my country. You can leave for Galatea right after." Or never, as the case may be. "It's going to be ever so much fun. Feasting and music and dancing."

"Dance?" asked Tomorrow hopefully, looking at Elliot and Kai for confirmation.

"Now you've done it," said Andromeda with a snort. "Ro would kill for a dance."

Elliot was glancing back and forth between Persis and Vania. The chancellor, Persis had decided, said very little unless she absolutely had to, and yet Kai deferred to her whenever she did. In fact, the only thing she'd ever seen them disagree about, even temporarily, had been Elliot's insistence on flying her own glider to search for their friends. What must it be like to have a friend you always agreed with, to be in love with him besides? Persis was hardly ever in agreement with even her best friends, and the only person she'd ever come close to falling for turned out to be a liar and a war criminal. Maybe her problem was her taste in men.

Or the fact that she was a rather extreme liar herself.

"I think," Elliot said now, "that we should wait to visit the other island until we've rejoined the rest of the crew. And perhaps we do owe the princess attendance at her luau, if we're to be guests of honor."

"Leave it to the Luddite to stand on ceremony," grumbled Andromeda. At least, that's what Persis thought she'd said. "We can always count on you to side with the aristos."

"There's no side," said Elliot.

"Yes, there's no side," Persis agreed. "Naturally, I highly advise against visiting Galatea. My father won't even let me go anymore. He thinks it's dangerous. I suppose, however, with an escort like Vania here, you'd be relatively safe." Here she simpered in Vania's direction, who returned only a steely glare. "All we're requesting is that you stay an extra day to attend a party. Surely one day in Albion is no burden—especially since your friends are just arriving. The party will be spectacular—all Isla's luaus are. And she's instructed me to procure you each a suitable outfit for the event. Everybody who's anybody in Albion will be there."

"And how do you define 'anybody' in this place?" Andromeda asked drily.

"Andromeda!" Elliot said. "Would you lay off for once?"

"Would you?" the sandy-haired captain snapped back. She looked at Persis. "And while we're on the subject, how do you define 'outfit'?"

Vania smiled. "I'll stay, too, Andromeda, and that way we can be sure that Lady Blake here keeps her promise to let you all go when the luau is over."

"*Let* them go?" said Persis. "I'm not keeping them prisoner."

"The guards stationed at the lift would lead one to think otherwise."

"Well, you would know from guards."

Vania Aldred—a captain of the revolutionary army; a proponent of arresting aristos for imagined slights; a torturer of men, women, and children—calling her out for trying to keep a few nosy gossips from spying on the visitors before it was politically expedient? As it was, Persis nearly bit her tongue off keeping from saying anything more. After all, the guards were meant to keep *Vania* out, but voicing that fact wasn't about to win Persis or Isla points with the visitors.

And if Vania thought she was going to spend the night in Scintillans, Persis had a bit of news for her.

"Fantastic," she said when they had all agreed to stay. "I shall relay this wonderful news to Isla and then first thing tomorrow morning, we'll start in on your outfits." She turned to the Galatean. "Good night, dear Vania. I'm sure you know the way out."

"Yes," the revolutionary replied. "But I won't be going far."

AFTER PERSIS HAD TAKEN her leave of the visitors, fluttered Isla about the new developments, and made absolutely sure that Vania was off the estate, she found Justen slouched on a cushion in the sitting room. He wasn't paying attention to any of the oblets glowing around him. There were piles of nanorectors on the desk before him. Half were engaged in forming a quite complex model of what Persis assumed was a human brain. The others he was absentmindedly shifting into random shapes—a frangipani flower, a cyclone, a parasol, and a sea mink.

Persis stationed herself before him. "Isla will not be pleased that you failed to report who it was that spirited Captain Phoenix and Tomorrow away from here."

"The important thing is that they're back," he replied in a monotone.

"Yes. Their heads filled with all sorts of prejudice against the princess—not to mention *me*—and all kinds of fantasies about what it's really like in Galatea. She'd almost convinced them to leave with her tonight. And here you are, hiding away doing—what exactly?" She gestured to the nanorectors.

"I'm not a political operative," he said, grimacing. "I can't do this. I can't do all the court drama, like you do, Persis. Can't smile and be charming and pretend that nothing bothers me. I'd sooner throw Vania off the pali tonight than engage in a battle of words with her."

That would be acceptable, Persis thought. "Fine. Ignore Vania. But you of all people can speak freely about exactly what's happening in your country."

His shoulders lifted a centimeter or two in a barely there shrug, and his face and voice were every bit as glum. "Oh, yes. I'm quite a trustworthy source for the crew of the *Argos*. They're the bravest people I've ever heard of. They left their homeland in search of what might have been nothing at all. They fought their entire society in order to build their ship and sail away. They've found strange islands filled with people and animals and things that seem like they came from dreams. They *certainly* have reason to trust and like a cowardly runaway who's living as the kept man of an idle aristo."

His self-loathing oozed off him in waves. Persis almost wanted to step back before it dripped on her shoes.

"I don't know why I'm even trying to talk to you about this. I'm nothing but a performer for your princess. I can't help in the sanitarium, I can't help my sister—"

"What's wrong with your sister?" she broke in before she could stop herself. If Remy had been compromised, Persis needed to know.

"She's in Galatea. What else does she need to be in danger?" he snapped. He scrubbed his hands over his hair, his face cast down in deep contemplation. "I can't even talk to her. I think they're screening my messages or something. Imagine what she thinks of me now. All the stories that must be circulating about us—about me and some . . . aristo."

Some idiot aristo, he'd obviously been planning to say.

How sweet; he was concerned for her feelings. For once.

"And the truth's not much better, from her perspective. I am a traitor to everything she believes in."

If only he knew! "You think your sister is like Vania?"

"No, I think she's a child." He shrugged. "Citizen Aldred is the only father she's ever known. Of course she supports him. Maybe if I'd been there for her more, instead of being in the lab all the time . . ."

"She's fourteen," Persis said. "I don't think she's as much of a child as you imagine." But was she as grown-up as Persis had hoped? She knew Remy's family members underestimated her. Persis, of anyone, understood how easily something like that could happen. But Justen did know the girl better than she did. If pressure were put to bear on Remy Helo . . . if Vania got desperate . . . would she crack?

"You haven't met Remy," Justen said, smiling ruefully. "She was so young when our parents died—it makes her a little intense sometimes about family, about protecting the people she loves . . ." He trailed off. "And maybe I have some of that, too. I can't let anything happen to her. She's the only family I have left."

Curious. Remy had said precisely the same thing. And here stood Persis in the center of it. She couldn't say if Citizen Aldred would hurt Remy because of Justen's actions, but if Remy's work for the League were discovered, she'd surely be Reduced—or worse. And Persis couldn't vouch for Justen's safety in Albion, either. No matter what Isla had accused her of yesterday, Persis would find a way to make Justen answer for his work on the Reduction drug.

The biggest danger to both Helos was Persis herself.

What a strange family this was, who claimed to wish to protect each other but left each other in the company of people they suspected might hurt them. Then again, she'd allowed Justen to treat her mother, allowed it because she wanted to believe he wished to help the Darkened, rather than harm an aristo. Allowed it because, just as Isla had said, her hope that he might cure her mother—might cure *her*—trumped any hatred she had for what he'd done to the refugees. No matter what crimes he'd committed, if he held the secret to stopping DAR, he *had* to be allowed to work.

"I don't want Remy in Galatea any longer," Justen was saying now. "If my messages to her are being intercepted, I think it's time the Wild Poppy gets involved."

Persis's laugh was high, trilling, and not entirely faked. The Wild Poppy was very much involved. "I'm sure he'll be relieved that you've started making those decisions for him."

Justen blinked. "I didn't mean—"

"To sound like some bossy aristo?" Persis finished. "What if the Poppy's busy with something big? Or maybe he's decided to scrap the whole thing and take up cliff diving for fun and profit. Can't be any more dangerous, right?"

"Well, Isla said he liked challenges. And the royal palace in Halahou . . . that's a tricky prospect."

"I think you should leave actually planning events to the Poppy, Justen," she said, a trifle annoyed. She could get into the palace. If she wanted to. And she'd had quite enough of discussing the Wild Poppy with Justen. He could ask for

Remy's extraction until the islands cooled, but *she* would be the one to decide when her informant needed to get out of Galatea.

Justen shook his head. "If Noemi ever responds to me, I'll ask her to put me in touch with him. Or maybe the princess will do it."

Persis remained silent, fearing any response would connect the dots in Justen's head. The only person those two had in common was her.

"I wonder," Justen said, "do you think Tero is the Wild Poppy? I know all along we've been saying that the Poppy must be an aristo, but maybe he's not."

All right, her and her other friends from Scintillans village. But even that guess was too close for comfort.

"Tero?" She tossed her hair over her shoulder. "He has far too many gengineering duties at court. Besides, I've known him for ages. He's not the sneaky type. He can't even keep his feelings for the princess a secret."

"Yes, but remember how he knocked that lord out on Remembrance Island the other day?"

Right. She had let Justen think Tero was responsible for that.

"And if Isla was helping him, he'd have the money and the resources to make all the trips to Galatea that he needed. And the disguises! He's a gengineer, so he'd have access to the lab to code whatever genetemp he wanted. It makes a lot more sense than some bored Albian aristo who knows nothing of spy craft."

"It makes more sense that some freshly cooled

gengineer knows something of spy craft?" Persis acted as if she was holding back her laughter. "That's preposterous, Justen. Trust me, I've known that boy all my life." Which was why she trusted Tero in the League, and why she didn't want Justen sniffing around him. Why, after all this time, did he suddenly want the spy to fetch his sister? And why was he so curious who it was? "Besides, who cares who the Poppy is? Isn't the important thing that he is effective?"

Was Vania still trying to find the Wild Poppy? Had she enlisted Justen's help?

"Everyone cares, Persis," Justen said. "It's the only thing anyone talks about, on both sides of the sea."

*That* she knew. "Oh, Justen, I thought you weren't interested in gossip."

He paid her no mind. "It must be Tero. Look at the way he keeps his hair. No one here cuts their hair so short. It's for his disguises, maybe."

Now Persis really wanted to laugh. Yes, she supposed short hair would have been a boon to her in her disguises. Perhaps she should let that rumor about her new taste in hairstyles stand and go for it. "I look forward to seeing Tero's response when you ask him at the luau tomorrow." At Justen's confused expression, she explained Isla's plan as well as the fact that Vania had invited herself.

His face fell, which ignited an uncomfortable twinge in Persis's chest, one she firmly ignored. She didn't care if he was despondent. Or care about anything he did as long as it didn't hurt the refugees anymore.

"Another party," he said. "Another day away from the

lab. I don't know how any of you can celebrate with all this suffering. You most of all, Persis. How can you worry about clothes and hair and not think about the fact that this is going to be the first luau your mother's too sick to attend?"

She stiffened.

Justen paled. "I'm sorry. I didn't mean it."

"You did," she replied bluntly. "You look at me and you hate the fact that I can put my mother's sickness from my mind while I tell Isla what shoes will best match her dress."

"She wears white, Persis. It can't be that hard."

"It's not? *You* do it." She was safely back in her role now, but her mind erupted with ideas. He truly couldn't stomach having fun while people suffered. And yet he was asking questions about the Poppy like he'd been sent on a mission from her enemies. Which was it? Who was he? How could she find out the truth?

A flutter zipped into the room; halted above Persis's head; and switched to its lazy, lilting trajectory toward her palm. Orchid. Isla.

*We must discuss the visitors' clothing requirements. Call me immediately.*

She took a deep breath and fluttered back:

*Yes, Your Highness.*

JUSTEN HAD NO MEMORY of dropping off to sleep at his desk, nanorectors still hard at work, oblets burning bright, but when he woke, it was to find a kimono-wrapped Persis standing above him and shaking him by the shoulders.

"There's only four hours until we have to leave for court. Do you even know what you're wearing?"

"Pick something," he groaned, blinking. "I'm sure Isla would prefer our outfits matched anyway."

She rolled her eyes. "Oh, you, too? Must I single-handedly dress every person on this island?"

"I thought's that what you liked doing." There was something on the edge of his mind he couldn't quite grasp. Something about last night. After Persis had left, he'd fumed a bit, and then, unable to sleep and unable to do anything for his sister, he'd gone back to work. He scrubbed his hands across his face and toggled up his notes. "Fashion. Fun. Nothing that could remotely be construed as serious."

Persis fixed him with a glare. "You wouldn't like me serious, Justen. I promise you that."

The nanorectors on his desk were blinking blue and green, indicating they'd completed the task Justen had set. As Justen looked at the model they'd built from his program, rotating silently on the desktop, everything clicked into place.

Staring in fascination at the model, he waved her away. "I don't care what I wear, Persis. Put me in whatever you want. I have more important things on my mind."

Far more important. He may have found a way to stop it all.

# Twenty-seven

ELLIOT NORTH HAD ONCE thought the brightly colored velvets and silks the Posts wore back at home were garish and over-the-top. Now, thanks to the hours-long ministrations of Persis Blake, she realized how tiny her worldview had actually been. *Now* she knew garish. Even the brightest fabrics in Channel City had nothing on Albian fashions.

"I can't wear that," Elliot said when Persis showed her the gown she'd chosen for the party.

"I know, it looks terribly complicated," Persis had replied, "but the zip goes right here, and you step into it like so, and then we wind this piece around after you're inside."

That hadn't been exactly what Elliot meant, but somehow she'd found herself fastened into the outfit anyway. She gasped when she saw her reflection in the mirror. Her curves had been pushed and squeezed and lifted and restrained—harnessed, really—revealing the figure usually hidden underneath her work trousers and coveralls. Her hair had been pomaded and glittered and curled until it fell in sparkly ringlets halfway down her back.

"But for that truly exotic touch," Persis said, "I think we need makeup. Sit." Elliot, helpless to resist now, sat and let Persis go to work on her face with a palette the size of a dinner plate. The Albian aristo was an odd one, to be sure. When Elliot had first met her, she'd placed Persis in the same boat as her sister, Tatiana: pretty, rich, spoiled, and lazy. And though the first three were certainly true, she was beginning to have her doubts about the fourth.

"Persis?" she asked as her gorgeous host painted her lips a rich plum. "May I ask you something?"

"As long as you don't move your mouth too much."

Elliot took a deep breath and raised her eyes to the other girl's. "Why do you pretend to be stupid?"

The brush stilled on Elliot's lips. Persis turned away to the table, to find a blotter. "You think I'm stupid?"

"No. I don't." She'd seen Persis, her flashes of seriousness, her eagerness to help Elliot and Kai when they worried their friends had gone missing. She'd seen her go head-to-head with the black-clad revolutionary when Andromeda and Ro returned. Persis had acted like she hadn't a care in the world, but every word was carefully crafted for maximum impact. "But I see you pretend to be, and I don't know why. If you're the heir to this estate, wouldn't it be best to try to gain the respect of the people here?"

Persis shrugged. "Not really. I won't have any power once I'm married, so it's better not to spend my life regretting what was once mine."

What an odd way of doing things they had on this

island. Who cared if the heir was a boy or a girl? Still, Elliot knew something about managing without official power. "I ran my estate for years without any power at all. My father was supposed to be the one in charge, though you wouldn't know it from the inside."

"How nice for you, Chancellor. And yet, you gave it all up for a man, too, didn't you?" There was a sharp edge to Persis's pleasantness this time, and Elliot was taken aback. But she was no longer the frightened child living under her father's thumb. She was a Luddite lord and a Cloud Fleet explorer, and she knew that the paint and the clothes and the hair were more than fashion for Persis Blake. They were armor.

"See what I mean?" Elliot said. "If you didn't care, you wouldn't be cross."

"I'm *cross*," Persis drawled, as if it was a word from a foreign language, "because you're calling my life choices into question. In my house. While I dress you in clothes I bought for you. Now, hold still while I do your eyes."

Elliot sighed and closed her eyes while Persis began to paint them with gold. "I'm sorry," she said. "I'm not being a very good guest. It's just—where I'm from, a mind is a precious commodity. Our most precious commodity. One would never have one but pretend otherwise."

"You are saying I'm acting Reduced?"

"I'm saying when human intelligence is all that's keeping the world alive, we should use every bit we've got." Elliot blinked her eyes open. Persis was staring at her very seriously.

"Where *I'm* from," the beautiful aristo said, "a mind is precious but temporary. In Galatea, they destroy them as a means of punishment. And everywhere, there are those who will lose theirs in time, and there is no way to prevent it. I may be one of those, Elliot. I just may."

JUSTEN ENDED UP BEING almost physically dragged from his desk by two Scintillans servants who cared a tad too much about how the estate presented itself at a party they weren't even attending. He was bathed in perfumed water, shaved, styled, and arrayed in a pair of silk slacks and a dark blue long silk jacket with a mandarin collar. After it was all over, Justen stood before the mirror in his bedroom and admitted that Persis may actually have the marked talent for clothes she always claimed. The material was not quite as dark as his usual revolutionary black, but the richness of the blue didn't look alien on him, either. The lines of the suit were simple and snug, and the design lacked all the nonsensical embellishments favored by the men of the Albian court. The material was subtly shot through with a shimmery golden thread, and the jacket buttoned up the front with a row of round star sapphires.

He probably could have done without the star sapphires.

That being said, the party was the perfect opportunity. He'd see Isla again and be able to communicate to her the importance of being put in touch with the Wild Poppy as soon as possible. With the kind of information Justen had to give him about the prisoners, the spy would have to agree to put Justen's sister at the top of his priority list. For the first time since Uncle Damos had started using his drug, Justen felt a ray of hope.

As he exited onto the terrace, he saw the other guests waiting to depart for the royal court. His eyes went first to Tomorrow—pretty, carefree Tomorrow, who couldn't possibly comprehend what she meant to the human race. She was dressed in a swirly, sleeveless confection of emerald green with a high neck and a massive, bubbly skirt that floated about her feet as she bounced on her toes with excitement. Her hair had been arranged in a series of braided crowns that twisted around her head, studded with both rosy and yellow frangipani blossoms, which Justen found a nice touch on Persis's part.

Both captains were present—Andromeda in a gown of diaphanous deep red draped about her body like she was some ancient goddess. The voluminous folds were gathered at each hip, and girded with thick cords of twisted bronze material that Justen couldn't tell were metal or fabric. Her hair was swept back into a long tail banded intermittently with the same material—pulled back from her face like that, the foreign captain's most prominent feature was her unusual blue eyes, large and glittering with her ancient, radical gengineering. Persis was aiming to cause a sensation. He hoped Andromeda was prepared.

Captain Wentforth's outfit was similar to Justen's own, though the full, pleated lines of his basalt-gray frock coat were more like the foreign style he'd been wearing when Justen first met him. His shirt was a pale, silvery plum, open at the throat, with wide cuffs that extended past his wrists to cover a good chunk of his workman's hands, though, rather than concealing them, they drew the eye like a well-placed frame.

Of the lot, Elliot North looked most uncomfortable in Persis's choice. Her form-fitting violet creation was sleeveless, plunged deeply at the halter neck, then fell in straight, simple lines to her feet. At first, Justen thought that was all there was to the dress, and he was surprised by Persis's restraint. But then, the chancellor moved, and he saw that behind her, fanning out at either side of her hips like a vast set of wings, was a wide, structured train in a pleated, lavender-tinted rainbow of fabric. The wings varied in shade from cream to purple to the charcoal and plum tones that Kai wore, giving the pair a subtle visual tie that made explicit the connection Justen and everyone else had been noticing since the visitors arrived. Elliot's dark hair spilled down her back in curls and sported jewels Justen couldn't believe he actually recognized as belonging to Persis's own collection. That she'd lent them to the visitor took him by surprise, though he just as quickly realized it shouldn't have. As rich as she was, she seemed to prefer her pretty things be used rather than hoarded for herself, whether that meant letting refugee children manhandle Slipstream or lending jewelry to near strangers.

Justen nodded at the visitors. "Are we ready for our first Albian luau and all that entails?" He gestured to his own outfit with a rueful grin. Three of them chuckled, while Tomorrow bounced again.

"I think you all look wonderful," came a clear, soft voice at his side, and he turned to see Lady Heloise Blake standing with her husband. She wore a soft, draped dress of shimmering rose gold, which set off the color of her copper-bronze hair. Her husband, standing at her side, echoed his wife in a creamy yellow shirt and maroon brocade slacks. His only ornament was a lei of frangipani, which Justen had already been told was a tradition of the aristo houses. Each lord wore his official flower in a lei.

"Lord and Lady Blake," Justen said, with a deeper nod. "I wasn't aware you'd be attending."

"I wouldn't miss it," said Heloise, giving him a discreet squeeze of the hand. Justen understood. Like her daughter, Heloise must love a party, and given the progression of her illness, he doubted she'd be well enough to ever see another.

"You all look marvelous, if I do say so myself," came Persis's voice from somewhere behind him. Everyone's eyes turned to her.

As she no doubt had intended.

Justen ought to have guessed that if these were the outfits his false lady love had procured for her guests, her own would eclipse them in every way. But even with that understanding, as he heard the gasps around him, he barely avoided joining in. The tiniest of earthquakes seemed to rustle through him, the kind that shakes petals off flowers, as Justen became aware of the gulf between what he was supposed to feel for Persis Blake and what he actually did.

Maybe it was the way he'd first met her, ill with gene-temps sickness and wrinkly from the code. Maybe it was his own prejudices against aristos, even if his dismissal of Persis was slowly being worn down by her infuriating effervescence, her ingratiating pride in her family and her home, and her determined insistence that her life was perfectly fine just as it was. Maybe it was his own sense of self-preservation, seeing as he was supposed to pretend to be in love with her. Whatever it was, Justen had grown quite adept at ignoring how jaw-droppingly gorgeous Lady Persis Blake was.

Not tonight.

At first glance, her dress appeared to be the same deep sea blue as Justen's coat, but as she moved toward them, he saw a thousand shades of green and blue and black in the carefully ruched fabric that hugged her curves, then at her knees spread out in waves—there was no other word for it—that rippled around her as she moved, fading in color the way the sea does when it nears the shore until finally, at the floor-length hem, they exploded into frothy white. The crest of the bodice sported the same lacey froth, and her yellow and white hair was piled high on her head in an arrangement so complicated that Justen didn't even want to know how many people had to help her. In her hair and wound about her neck and arms were delicate strands of gold that twinkled—actually twinkled— with odd nanotech bursts of iridescent blue and green that reminded Justen of nothing more than . . .

"You're dressed as the star cove," he blurted.

She smiled and took his arm. "You noticed."

THE VISITORS WERE WHISKED away to rejoin their newly arrived companions as soon as they reached the court and, in truth, Persis wasn't sorry to see them go. She had as much curiosity about them as everyone else, but their arrival had complicated everything from her home life to her plans for the Poppy—and for Justen.

Her father had installed his wife at one of the garden tables near the water organ, which had been tuned to play lively, rippling music one might dance to. The water cascaded rapidly through the musical locks, the tempo creating rushes of white water and tiny waves. It was perfect positioning—away from crowds and too much conversation but not suspiciously withdrawn from the festivities. As soon as Persis was assured they wouldn't need her assistance, she set off to find Andrine and Tero . . . only to be led right back to the visitors.

"Can't it wait until after the luau?" Andrine begged. "People from elsewhere are about to be introduced at court. This is the most exciting thing to happen in centuries."

"This and the cure," Persis said, but relented, though she was sure Andrine would feel differently if she knew how time sensitive their rescues had become. For aristos, they could afford to wait—but regs were in serious danger from the moment they were arrested by the Galateans to the moment the League came to their aid.

But for now, she'd stand back and let Isla have her moment. Her best friend was standing on the dais above the court, her hair winged out in massive petals meant to invoke the royal orchid and her dress swirling about constantly thanks to the nanobots in the hem meant to make her skirt move like she stood in a breeze.

The visitors stood in an arc behind her. Aside from the four Persis knew, the ship brought with it a couple of natural regs older than Persis's parents named Admiral and Mrs. Innovation, as well as half a dozen crew members with equally silly names. Though Isla's courtiers had tried to dress the rest of the *Argos* crew before their introduction, Persis felt a little pleased that none were quite as successful in their mission to give the visitors more suitable Albian dress as she'd been.

In another life, Persis would have counted that a triumph and spent the rest of the evening listening raptly to their stories of the sea and their far-off home. She would have danced the night away with whatever boy asked nicely enough, gossiped with her friends, then sailed home with her parents—all equally exhausted and exhilarated by the party.

Instead, she waited impatiently for Isla to finish with the formal introductions, cast worried glances back at her parents on the terrace, kept an eye out for Vania Aldred, and tried to plot the Wild Poppy's next move.

The next move was Justen. It had to be. He had asked too many questions about the Poppy yesterday to be merely an interested bystander. And given what she knew about his history with the revolution, she could not afford to let him suspect how close he really was to the spy. It had been hard enough to act flattered and flirty during the trip to court on the boat, and—perhaps for the benefit of her parents—Justen had been doing exactly that. Gone was the glum, frustrated scientist she'd been dealing with ever since her last trip to Halahou. Justen had been as cheerful as a sea mink, displaying charm she hadn't seen since the night he'd first had dinner with her parents, and he hadn't mentioned Vania or the Wild Poppy even once.

Persis was suspicious, to say the least. She was no longer the trusting girl who'd taken him to the star cove for swimming and kissing. Whenever Justen acted light-hearted, he was hiding something.

After Isla introduced the visitors, and they repeated the story of their home island and the mission that had brought them to New Pacifica, the party started in earnest. Naturally, the visitors were mobbed by guests who wanted more information. Invitations to the luau had gone out to aristos and regs alike, and Isla stood by and watched with satisfaction at the way her subjects were interacting.

Persis joined her. "A successful party, Your Highness."

Isla rolled her eyes. "You never do use my title without a laugh in your voice. Even in your flutters, I can hear it."

"That's your interpretation," Persis replied. "I have nothing to do with the tone of my voice in your head. And, for what it's worth, your flutters always sound bossy to me."

"Oh no, that I intend," Isla replied drily. She frowned. "Speaking of bossy, here comes Shift."

The councilman was stuffed into a long, glittering frock coat loudly encrusted all over with hibiscus made from rubies. Persis longed to give the man a few fashion pointers. "Lovely party, Princess," he said. "You always can be counted on for an event like this."

"Thank you, sir." Isla nodded her head.

"Pity it's so crowded," he said airily, "but I guess that's what comes of inviting regs to court."

"Seeing as the visitors are almost exclusively regs themselves, I could hardly avoid it," Isla replied. Her dark eyes burned in her face, but her expression remained serene. Persis admired her friend's restraint.

Tero appeared, a tray with two flutes of kiwine in his hands. "Some refreshments, Isla?"

Shift scowled at him. "Don't interrupt your betters, boy." He swiped a glass off the tray as the three teenagers stood there in shock. "A good server will wait for a break in conversation."

"I'm not a—" Tero went silent as Shift drained his glass and turned away.

"As I was saying, these regulars are completely forgetting their place . . ." he trailed off. "I feel . . . odd."

"It's the app," said Tero with a roll of his eyes. "As I said, I'm not a waiter. I'm a gengineer and you just drank my latest surprise for the princess."

Isla looked at her own glass of kiwine. "What is it?"

"If you had taken it?" Tero shrugged. "Supposed to be a lie-detection app. But you already have that voice-modulation and heat-monitoring app I gave you last month. Without those installed, I'm not precisely sure how his will run."

Persis bit back a smile. Tero didn't look the least bit contrite, and who could blame him?

"You *drugged* me?" Shift looked as green as kiwine.

"Technically, you drugged yourself. I never offered you a drink . . . *sir*." He peered at the aristo's dilated eyes. "I think you should sit down."

Isla was openly grinning as she sipped from the other glass of kiwine. "Oh, Tero. I take back every mean thing I said about that time you messed up the genetemps. This is too, too entertaining."

"This is outrageous," Shift slurred. "Dealing with a child and her slum friends . . ."

"Interesting." Tero's tone was one of a scientist mid-observation. He and Justen had more in common than Persis would have thought. He took Shift gently by the arm and led him to a seat, and the girls clustered around.

"We aren't going to make the same mistake with the boy as we did with you," Shift was saying, to Persis's shock and Isla's open delight. "Without your fool father around, he won't be exposed to as many ridiculous ideas about reg equality."

"'Fool father,'" Isla repeated ecstatically. "Please tell me someone's recording this!"

"All scientific observations," Tero said. His oblet was in his palm, glowing red. "Royal College of Gengineers standard policy, Your Highness."

"Oh, Tero, I could kiss you." She looked at Persis. "And note that *he* says my title properly."

"Maybe because you kiss him," Persis replied. Shift was sweating profusely, his lips quivering and popping. "What's happening to him?"

"If I had to guess," said Tero, "it's that the app is working on him like a truth serum. Which is a bit like a lie detector but . . . backward?" He cocked his head.

Well, wasn't that handy. She knew a few people she'd like to try it on. And certainly easier than neuroeels.

"Best thing that ever happened was that accident," Shift was saying, his face all red as he glared at the princess.

"It's just too bad you weren't on the boat that day."

Persis hadn't realized her jaw could drop so far.

"I think that's all we're going to need," Isla said. "Any more insults and I'll demand more than his resignation. I'll need his head, too." But beneath her haughty face, Persis could tell the comment had hit more than Isla's political pride. She still missed her parents and brother immensely.

"Sir," said Tero, and there was the mocking note that was missing every time he addressed Isla as *Your Highness*, "I'm afraid you may be suffering from a faulty palmport application. I think it's best we find you a medic." That, too, was Royal College of Gengineers procedure. Tero had just taken his sweet time getting to it. A flutter spun from his hand, no doubt calling for a medic to take charge of the councilman.

"You," Shift growled as best he could. "Don't think I don't know what you're up to. Grasping, uppity little reg. You won't sleep your way onto the throne, I can promise you that."

Tero straightened, then looked down at the aristo darkly. "I think the poor man has suffered enough," he said, and opened his left palm again.

Isla put her hand in his, covering the port before the knockout drug could be released. "Don't," she said softly. "I'd like the soon-to-be ex-Councilman Shift to be awake to see me dance with my boyfriend."

Tero looked at Isla. Isla looked at Tero, a tiny smile on her face.

"You want to dance with me?" he whispered.

"Desperately," she whispered back, before looping her arm in his and walking out into the crowd.

Persis watched them go, unable to contain her smile. At least one romance on this island would end happily. "Convey my regrets to your nephew, Lord Shift," she said as the court medic arrived.

# Twenty-eight

For a good fifteen minutes after the visitors had been introduced, Justen saw no one he knew. The crowd of people seeking to get a glimpse of the visitors had kept him separated from them, and Persis and Isla were nowhere to be found. Then, when he finally did catch a glimpse of the princess, dancing with Tero Finch like it was the most natural thing in the world, he didn't want to interrupt. Thankfully, he was soon joined by Kai, Elliot, Andromeda, and Ro, who had found respite when the entire court had been distracted by the sight of the princess regent embracing a lowly gengineer.

Ah, Albion. Not as equal as they liked to imagine. But then again, if Isla and Tero were an official item, maybe they were headed places.

The visitors looked understandably overwhelmed. Though Justen was growing used to the typhoon of clothes, flowers, perfumes, and flutters at court, he knew the visitors, with their technologically backward origins, still had a long way to go.

"It's all I can do to keep watch over Tomorrow," Andromeda said, hitching up the train of her dress. "You'd think, with everything to look at here, they wouldn't be so fascinated by one girl."

"Oh, they aren't fascinated by one girl," said Kai, laughing. "You're just as captivating."

She stuck her tongue out at her fellow captain. "And you're lying low?"

"So far," he replied with a grin, but Justen could see how tightly he held Elliot's hand.

"I can't wear things like this. I'm too much of a Luddite," Elliot said now, dipping her head.

"A Luddite lord," Kai corrected, "and therefore, the only visiting dignitary on the *Argos*. Remember that." Elliot nodded but didn't lift her head. Sometime, Justen was going to have to get the entire rundown on the political system of their homeland. If Elliot was an aristo, she certainly didn't act it. "Also," Kai added, "you look lovely."

She lifted her chin to look at Kai now, and he leaned in, kissing her mouth softly enough not to mar her makeup.

Justen looked away. He'd never thought the foreign aristo—or Luddite lord, as she called herself—was a beautiful girl, but tonight, everything seemed different. Maybe it was because she was wearing Persis's clothes. Maybe it was the way she and Kai looked at each other. It reminded him of the looks he'd seen Persis's parents giving each other, the love Persis had claimed in the star cove was an impossible standard to meet.

At the time, Justen had agreed. Who even wanted a

love like that? Wouldn't it distract from everything else you wanted to do with your life? But looking at Kai and Elliot, Justen wondered if, instead, love was what made it possible. Torin and Heloise had defied the customs of their nation and helped bring about great social change in Albion. Kai and Elliot had sailed to a whole new world. He didn't know much about the intimate aspects of his grandparents' relationship, but he did know that Darwin Helo had worked tirelessly to help his wife bring the cure to all the people of New Pacifica. If Justen ever found someone like that, would he change his mind?

Of course, that couldn't happen, not while he was playing games with Persis. Persis, who'd looked so gorgeous tonight he'd almost forgotten the danger hanging over his head. Dreams of grand love and world-changing partnerships aside, it would be nice to get in one dance with his fake girlfriend before the night was over. After all, she'd put so much effort into their matching costumes.

Tomorrow took off through the crowd toward the water organ, and Andromeda followed, still scowling. The rest of them watched the party for a while, Justen keeping his eye out for Persis, Isla, or indeed, anyone who might be able to connect him to the Wild Poppy, and Kai and Elliot looking far more content to stand at the sidelines than brave the crush in the center of the court. The water organ cycled through several songs and servants lit bonfires around the dance floor for fire dancing, but he couldn't make out anyone he knew. Andromeda and Tomorrow never returned, and Elliot was starting to look overwhelmed again. Justen snagged a few glasses of kiwine from a passing waiter and offered it to the visitors. "This might help."

Elliot made a face at the pale green liquid, then took a sip and smiled, relieved. "It's wine."

"Kiwine."

"Kiwi . . . wine?" She laughed. "You people have the strangest foods. The strangest everything. I thought the Cloud Fleet clothes were crazy, but this is"—she tugged at her skirt—"this is like something out of an ancient book. Marie Antoinette, maybe?"

"I was always partial to the French Revolution." Vania swooped in on them, swiping Justen's glass of wine right out of his hand. "They certainly knew how to deal with their aristos. Good evening, everyone. How do you like my outfit, Justen? Does it meet with your aristocratic fashion taste?"

His eyes dropped from her sly, calculating smile to her clothing. Vania still wore revolutionary black, but tonight she was dressed in a slinky, glittery gown that wouldn't be out of place on any Albian aristo. Crisscrossed straps webbed up the bodice and down the sleeves, and there was a black cormorant-feathered cape tossed jauntily across her shoulders. The feathers shimmered with iridescence, and Justen realized how much he must have learned from his week with Albion's most fashionable aristo. Vania had chosen a feathered outfit specifically to ruffle aristo feathers.

"Are you *trying* to cause an eruption?" he asked her, eyebrows raised. Even if Isla hadn't chosen that fashion style this particular evening, feathered capes were usually reserved for royalty, in ancient tradition.

"Yes," Vania replied. "I am a revolutionary, unlike some people I know." She looked at the visitors. "Can I borrow him for just a moment?"

As soon as they were alone—or as alone as they could be in the crowd—Vania turned to him and took a deep breath. "I owe you an apology."

"You owe me my sister," he hissed at her.

"Remy is fine," Vania said with a shrug. "You honestly think I'd do something to her? Come on, Justen. That's what I wanted to apologize about. I was so angry at you, at the way you'd abandoned us, that I lashed out. I'm sorry."

He breathed a sigh of relief. This was the Vania he knew. And if Remy was safe, it was all that mattered. "I'm glad to hear it."

"Not as glad as I'll be when you come back to Galatea with me tonight."

He shook his head. "I can't go back, Vania. Not ever."

Her lips formed a scary little line. "Why, because of Persis? Justen, the clothes are nice and all, but let's be serious. You have work to do."

"I'll do it here."

"Oh, no you won't," she said. "That Reduced girl is going to Galatea, and she's not coming back. You think I'd miss an opportunity like that? I saw her name all over your notes the other night. Any work you want to do with her—and I know you well enough to tell you're just itching to start your little experiments—you can do in Galatea or not at all."

"Please," Justen scoffed. "Do you honestly think that the Albians are going to let you leave here with any of the visitors? They've learned their lesson after yesterday."

Now it was Vania's turn to laugh. "*Please*," she mocked. "They're already gone."

Justen's face drained of blood.

"Andromeda Phoenix knows aristo tricks. She couldn't talk Kai or his aristo sweetheart into coming along, but we don't need them anyway. The important one is the Reduced girl, and it was ever so easy to convince Captain Phoenix that these shiny, sparkly aristos do not have Tomorrow's best interests at heart. She didn't want that controlling princess or her stupid sidekick trying to stop us either." Vania gave him a simpering, closed-lip smile. "We're of such similar minds, Andromeda Phoenix and I. They're halfway there already, and I only stayed behind to give you one last chance to come along."

He stared at her in shock. "Vania, don't you think Andromeda's also smart enough to see through your ruse?"

"What ruse?" she looked mystified and a little hurt. "It's only Albians who think things are so very bad in our country, Justen. Well, Albians and you. *True* Galateans are much happier now."

"I know a lot of Galateans who would claim otherwise," he grumbled. "And Andromeda won't be happy at all when she hears about your plans for her friend."

"Why not?" Vania shrugged off his concerns. "We're not going to hurt the girl. It's not like we need to drink her blood, right? A few genetests. Besides, at least there she'll have friends of her own kind."

"The victims of the drug are *not* Reduced," he growled.

"Well, you'd know best. Please come," Vania said, placing her hand on his arm. "I don't want to be enemies with you anymore. I love you so much, Justen. You're my best friend. Please come back. We can smooth over everything with my father and the populace. I don't blame you for getting sidetracked here. Aristos can be . . . bewildering. And I know that Father wasn't letting you work on the projects you really wanted to. But we can convince him together. That Reduced girl will change everything—for DAR and . . . well, for the revolution, too."

"How so?"

Vania gave him a pitying smile. "I know how much guilt you've been feeling over the pinks, Justen. And, believe me, I feel the same. It's just not right for the aristos. And it's like you said. Seeing Tomorrow made me realize it—how perverted their form of Reduction is. It's not real Reduction at all, is it?"

Justen nodded, relieved, and took Vania by the hands. "I felt that way, too. Oh, Vania, thank you so much. Seeing Tomorrow, seeing how she lives, the light that shines out of her—I can't believe I was ever so crude as to call the effects of that drug Reduction."

"Exactly. For the aristos to truly get their just desserts, it's only right that they be *really* Reduced. Permanently. And now that there's a real Reduced in Galatea, we can figure out how to make it happen."

Justen must have dropped her hands. He must have stepped back. But he couldn't tell. His body seemed to go numb. "No," he whispered.

Vania looked confused, then angry.

There was a roaring in his ears. "You can't." He thought he said it. He must have said it, based on the rage that overtook Vania's features.

"It's our turn to win, Justen," she said, her voice sounding sad and a little lost. "How can you not understand that? We've been punished long enough for what our ancestors did. It's *their* turn for punishment now, and our turn to rule."

One night, not long ago, Justen had floated in a starlit cove with a girl who told him, *There is only one way to recover from the evil humanity does to itself: overcome it. We can only be held responsible for what we ourselves do. Bad things happen in this world, and we are judged on how we respond. Do we take part in evil, or do we fight against it with all we have?*

He had to fight. But he couldn't stop Vania on his own. There was only one man in New Pacifica who could.

The Wild Poppy.

JUSTEN GRABBED VANIA'S HAND and shouted for a guard. It had the effect of bringing at least three heads swerving in his direction, but no more. A crowd of hundreds, and dozens of fluternotes in the air above them—but not a single chance of calling for help.

"What are you—" She writhed in his grip, then brought the side of her palm down on his wrist.

He winced and his hold on her slipped. She slammed her knee against his groin.

"Are you trying to start a war?" she whispered in his

ear as he grunted. "Not so fast, Justen. There's plenty of time for that after we perfect our drug."

He grabbed at her again, but she easily evaded him, spun, then took his elbow in her hand. A lightning bolt of pain shot through his arm.

"Honestly, Justen, perhaps you should have spent a little time outside the lab. Have you any idea how much combat training I've had?" She let go of him and he stumbled back, gasping. "I'm going to assume that's a firm no to my offer. A shame." She bit her lip. "But at least now I know for sure. I've tried so hard to help you, but you've chosen your path."

"Vania, don't." The agony spread from his throat to his fingertips. This was no mere pressure point. He ran his other hand across his sleeve and pulled out a pricker. Empty. Justen turned his eyes to Vania. "What is this?" he gasped.

"Oh, don't look so betrayed," she said, annoyed. "It's just a mild neurotoxin. I could have used something way worse on you and you know it."

And with that, she melted into the crowd, leaving Justen fighting for breath. He needed to find the medic station. But more than that, he needed to find the Poppy. If the rumors were true, if he was an Albian aristo, then the spy must be at the luau. But he had no idea how to even begin searching.

Justen clutched at his arm and searched through the crowd with watering eyes, but he didn't even see anyone he recognized. Persis, Isla, Andrine—where were they all?

Persis was right. He should have gotten a palmport like everyone else in Albion. Instead, he stumbled toward the palace wall. If he remembered correctly, there was a public wallport near the restroom here. If he was lucky, there might even be a medic kit in the restroom.

The kit he found was standard, but it still contained an epinephrine pricker and a pain relief pricker. He utilized them both, then logged into the wallport, his fingers straining with every button he typed as the medicine took effect.

*Noemi, it's Justen. I need you to put me in touch with the Wild Poppy immediately on a matter of utmost importance.*

He watched the portal open and a sad little generic flutter zip out. How long would it take to reach Noemi? Should he try Isla, too? At least she was *here*.

Justen massaged his arm with his good hand, sweating as the pain radiated out from his elbow. How long would he have to wait? Could he even afford to wait? Slowly, feeling returned to his fingers and shoulders, and the pain subsided. He leaned his forehead against the cool stone wall, breathing heavily.

A tiny golden poppy flitted by his nose and sunk into the wallport. Justen turned back to read the screen.

*Hello, Justen Helo. What do you want from me?*

# Twenty-nine

Persis moved through the crowd as quickly as she could in her gown, the voluminous fabric undulating about her legs like real waves as she hurried, her eyes searching everywhere for a glimpse of Justen. The flutter Noemi had forwarded to her sounded desperate, but what could Justen possibly have to contact the Wild Poppy about so urgently at the party?

Another generic flutter buzzed her palm. Now that he had a flutter from the Wild Poppy, Justen could contact her directly. It was a risky move, but the chance that someone could follow a flutter back to her, especially in this crowd, was slim. She slipped her wristlock aside to allow his message entrance.

*I need to meet you.*

She laughed.

*I think not. I have a policy of not revealing myself to*

*Galatean revolutionaries. Tell me what you want. Your sister, I suppose?*

At last she saw him, leaning against a column by one of the public wallports. She stationed herself several yards away, on the outskirts of a group of people watching the fire dance. From the corner of her eye, Persis saw Justen read her flutter, then bang his right hand against the wallport in frustration. Persis narrowed her eyes. A moment later, she received:

*I'm not a revolutionary! Not that kind, anyway. Typing takes too long. Please, you have to believe me.*

Well, she had been telling him since he'd arrived to get a palmport. Now, perhaps, he'd learned his lesson. She sent back:

*Why would I ever trust the person who invented pinks? Why would I trust someone who takes secret meetings with Vania Aldred? You've lied to everyone who has tried to help you in Albion: Princess Isla, Noemi Dorric, even your little girlfriend Persis Blake. But I know who you are, I know what you've done, and you're lucky to be hearing from me at all.*

At last, the words she'd wanted to cast at him so long. At the wallport, she watched him read her flutter, and even from a distance, she could see his chest rise as he took a deep breath. He was gripping his arm, flexing the muscles of his left hand as if they bothered him. Clenching his jaw, he leaned over and began typing, while Persis waited impatiently.

Seriously, Justen. Palmport.

*There is no apology I can make that would be sufficient. Yet I swear to you that I never meant to hurt anyone. The Reduction drug was an accident. I was trying to make a new treatment for DAR, based on the architecture of the aristo brain, and I stumbled upon a compound that would, if administered to aristos, cause the effects you've seen. I made the mistake of telling my uncle.*

By the time the flutter reached her, Justen had started typing again, and another flutter soon zipped after the first.

*I promise I didn't know what he intended. The day Queen Gala died, and I saw her body desecrated and her whole court Reduced, I lost all faith in the revolution. I went to Aldred. I tried to get him to stop. When that didn't work, I even tried to sabotage the pills. He started to suspect what I was doing and restricted my access to the lab. That's when I ran away to Albion.*

She shot back:

*My heart breaks for the poor little mad scientist cut off from his lab.*

But then she remembered what the medic at the prison had said, about how the pills weren't working as well as they used to. Had that been due to Justen's sabotage? After a moment, he replied:

*You want to know why Lacan recovered as quickly as he did? It was because the pills he was getting weren't full strength. If you were to get my sister, she could tell you herself.*

Was that what Remy had been doing at the Lacan estate in the first place? Persis *would* ask the girl. Justen's flutter continued, its tone as frantic as his typing.

*Believe me or don't. It doesn't matter. But you need this information: Vania Aldred has taken two of the visitors back to Galatea, including the Reduced one, and she plans to keep them there. She believes that Galateans can use the Reduced girl to create a drug that will cause permanent Reduction . . . and I'm afraid she may be right.*
*This is the absolute truth. I have nothing to gain from telling you this—and nothing to lose, either.*

Persis frowned. Justen was a medic, and no one knew better than he how to create a Reduction drug. If he believed that scientists could use Tomorrow to make the effects permanent, then it was worth paying attention to. And yet, what if the whole story was a lie, engineered by Vania Aldred for the purpose of a trap?

She watched Justen wait by the wallport, growing increasingly agitated. She watched him pacing, foot tapping, then slamming his right hand against the wall in frustration. He turned around and their eyes met.

She smiled sweetly and waved at him.

He gave her a halfhearted wave in return. Did he honestly think the Wild Poppy owed him a response?

Persis beckoned to him, but he gave a little shake of his head and turned back to the port, typing furiously again. She waited as patiently as possible, but he seemed to be writing some kind of book over there.

Enough was enough. She marched over, the material of her skirt churning like the waves of a stormy sea. "What are you writing, dearest?" she cooed. "Love notes to a strange woman?"

He whirled around, blocking her view of the screen. "None of your business, Persis."

He had that wrong. "You've been avoiding me for the entire party and now you're melded to the wallport. People are going to think we're fighting. We can't have that."

He groaned. "Not now, Persis. I'm in the middle of— I can't. Not now."

She arced her neck to look behind him. "You always say that."

He slammed his hand over the display buttons and the port closed. "And I always mean it. Now leave me alone."

Persis looked at him, her gaze steady and dangerous. "Show me," she said slowly, "what you were typing."

Justen stared at her for a moment, then raised his voice. "Excuse me, sir?" he called over her shoulder. She whirled to find a young courtier who looked vaguely familiar turning in their direction. "My sweet lady Persis is wild to try the fire dance, but I'm afraid I have not yet had the chance to learn the Albian style. Would you do me the honor of dancing with her for a bit so that I might observe you and learn?"

Persis snapped her jaw shut. The little sea sponge. So he hadn't been ignoring all her lectures on courtly behavior.

The young aristo nodded. "Of course, Citizen Helo! It would be my pleasure."

Justen gave her a grim smile and handed her off to the courtier. Carvel? Carrell? His name hovered just beyond the reach of her memory. As the man led her toward the dancers, she cast a glance over her shoulder at Justen, but he'd returned to the port.

Oh well. She'd find out eventually.

She stepped into the dance with her partner and immediately began messaging the rest of the League. The courtier probably thought she was acting a little too familiar with the way she draped her wrists over his shoulders and closed her eyes. That Persis Blake—what a flirt.

She told Andrine to find the other visitors and confirm that Andromeda and Tomorrow had departed. She told Tero to load up a boat with as many supplements as he could think of, as well as at least three different types of genetemp doses, just in case. She told Isla that the party had taken a rather desperate turn.

She felt a tap on her shoulder and turned to see Justen standing there, his eyes glowing with the flames of the fire. "I think I've figured out the steps now."

He cut in, and the courtier departed. Persis's eyebrows

drew together. How did he get here before his flutter? Were they too close to the fire? Flutters would melt in high heat conditions. She danced a little way from the flames.

"I don't like arguing with you, Persis," said Justen as he spun her around. He still hadn't learned the moves of the fire dance. His motions were too large, his hands too rough.

She found she didn't really mind. "And I don't like you sending love notes to other girls right in front of me."

He gave her a wry smile. "What makes you think it's another girl?"

*What makes you think it isn't?* She almost asked him aloud. Common wisdom held the Wild Poppy was an Albian aristo, and to the Albians, that meant he must be a man. But the Galateans had been ruled by queens for centuries. Women there had as much power as men. Yet even Justen, whose friend Vania was a revolutionary captain, whose own grandmother had invented the cure, took the story at face value.

His flutter sunk into her palm.

*I understand now that you are the reason Noemi won't tell me where she's moved the refugees, as I am the reason they have probably been moved. And I don't blame you, either. I can never forgive myself for what I have done to my countrymen. I will spend the rest of my life trying to reverse the pain and suffering I've caused and to atone for the shame I've brought to a family name that once symbolized hope to all New Pacifica.*

*I give you this information so you can take it to Noemi, who will confirm that I'm telling the truth. I do not yet know how to heal those regs who have been damaged by Reduction, but I believe I know how to prevent anyone else from being hurt. The answer lies in the Helo Cure.*

*A few days ago, I offered the cure to one of the visitors, though he is a natural reg. He feared he might have made his offspring vulnerable due to his primitive gengineering. In the old days, it was thought that the cure had no effect on those who were not Reduced, but now I think it's something more. The cure won't heal a Reduced brain, which is why it doesn't fix the Reduced who take it. But it will prevent the damage of Reduction from ever taking place. In natural Reduction, this damage occurs in utero, in the developing brain of the fetus. The Helo Cure prevents that from happening. It will also, according to my models, prevent it from happening when one is given the Reduction drug.*

Persis gasped. Could it be that simple?

"Are you all right?" Justen asked.

She nodded, swallowing. Justen's message continued.

*Take this information and guard your friends and allies, here and in Galatea. It might take a while to produce enough of the Helo Cure to protect the entire nation, but if they all take it, they will be able to defend themselves, aristo and reg alike, from the revolutionaries' terrible weapon.*

*With your help, I can begin to atone for the harm I've caused my countrymen and keep anyone else from being hurt like this again. Once, Persistence Helo was the hope of all New Pacifica. I'd hoped to follow in her footsteps, but I recognize now that you are the one who will save us.*

*You are the hope of every true patriot of my homeland.*

Persis tightened her hands on Justen's shoulders and buried her face against his chest.

"You're not all right," he said. "Too near the fire?"

"Justen," she breathed. There was no question he was telling the truth. There was no possible purpose his lie would serve. Noemi could easily verify or dismiss his claims. She fluttered the medic at once, to be sure, but not a doubt remained in Persis's mind. Everything fit—it fit what she knew of what was happening in Galatea; it fit with Vania's befriending Andromeda and Tomorrow; it fit with the way Justen had been tied to his grandmother's oblets and his nanorector models for the last day and a half; and it fit, most of all, with what she knew about Justen—what she'd known all along, if she'd been completely honest with herself.

And maybe it was time to be honest with him, too. She took a deep, shuddering breath. *I'm the Wild Poppy. I'm the Wild Poppy. I'm the Wild Poppy.* "I'm—"

Another flutter slipped into her palm.

*Persis,*
*Your mother is ill. Bring Justen at once.*
*Love and duty,*
*Torin Blake*

Her head shot up. "We have to find my parents."

# Thirty

IT TOOK THE BETTER part of an hour to make sure Heloise was stabilized. Sedation would have been easier, but Torin was desperate to avoid it.

"Please," he'd said to Justen. The three of them were in Isla's private chambers, where Heloise could rest among the white pillows and swaying palm fronds. "This may be her last party. If there's any way I can let her have a final glimpse . . ."

These aristos sure had their priorities screwed up.

When he was done, Persis was nowhere to be found.

"She left a while ago," Torin explained. "Actually, I'm relieved. There are things she doesn't need to see."

"She's seen them," Justen argued, remembering the night Heloise had almost clawed her daughter's lovely face off. "You can't keep them from her. And you can't let her go on like this, either, pretending it's not happening. Do you know she hasn't even been tested?"

"Actually," said Heloise from the chaise, her voice so

hard for once, the woman reminded him of her daughter, "we do know that. And I strongly believe she should be given that right. If she is to die like me, then she doesn't need to know at sixteen."

Torin didn't respond, but his lips were pressed in a tight line. Justen could imagine his fear—that both his wife and daughter would die young, leaving him alone in Scintillans. If the Wild Poppy got Tomorrow back, Justen would make sure that never happened.

"She has too much life right now to dampen it with diagnoses," Heloise went on. "Look at her, young and beautiful and in love!"

Justen looked away. She wasn't in love. She was playing a game. A silly, stupid game to keep the peace on her island. She deserved more than that.

Torin took his wife's hand. "I am glad that she found you right now, Justen. You've been such a blessing to our family. Such a help to Heloise and, well, I think you're good for Persis, too. Before you came along, I was so worried for her. She's too smart for most of the boys in Albion, you know. They won't ever love a wife as clever as she, even if they'll take her for the estate. They won't love her, and she won't love them, either. She can't, with a mind like hers. She needs someone who will understand how brilliant she is, and love her for it."

Justen bit back his bark of laughter. Brilliant? Persis was occasionally witty with a bit of poetry, but—

"It got to the point that I worried this new phase of hers—the parties and the gossip and the dresses—was her way of trying to prove that she *wasn't* the smartest woman of her generation. Like she could be the perfect Albian social-ite if she tried hard enough. And, God help me, I indulged her in it. I even let her drop out of school, since at least it meant she'd spend more time home with us. I didn't want the last—" Here Torin broke down.

Heloise drew his hand to her chest. "It's all right, my love."

"Persis is very sweet," Justen said automatically. But "sweet" seemed somehow insufficient to describe her. She was beautiful and fun loving. She was kind and fiery. She'd been there to help him and to comfort him.

She'd even been the one to give him words to use against Vania.

He found he could not agree with Torin. Many men would fall for a woman like Persis. He might, if he didn't value more seriousness in his partners. Actually, it was quite touching to see a set of parents so smitten with their child that they'd excuse her faults and mistake her for bril-liant. He wondered if his own parents would have seen him that way, had they survived. If they would have told him he was forgiven for his mistakes and that he could make resti-tution for the things he'd done.

"I don't think sweet's the word for it." Heloise sighed, then laughed, as if remembering. "Oh, the arguments I've had with that girl. Inappropriate clothing, daredevil stunts on the pali, political debates . . ." She turned to her husband, eyes as lit up as her daughter's. "Oh, Torin, do you remember that campaign she started in the village when she was seven to change the Blake family flower from frangipani?"

"Yes!" Torin replied, chuckling. "What was it she wanted to change to again?"

Heloise shook her head, trying to recall. "I think . . . it was those poppies. The pua kala? Because they grow wild on the wall by the star cove . . ."

"Right." Torin nodded, grinning. "Something about how the pua kala was a far more interesting flower—"

"Stronger and more resilient," his wife said through giggles.

"With a more important history with the ancients as medicine." Torin threw back his head, laughing. "You ought to appreciate that one, Justen."

"She's right," Justen said slowly. "Pua kala was valued by the ancients for more than its beauty. It was a highly revered plant." Medicinal and spiny and wild. Useful and dangerous and tough.

Torin shrugged good-naturedly. "And since they're both yellow and white, we wouldn't even have to do any redecorating."

Heloise was laughing so hard, tears were streaming down her cheeks. "But if we'd changed it, whatever symbol would the Wild Poppy use now?"

All laughter stopped. All three of them fell silent.

*No.* It wasn't possible. Justen looked at the stunned faces of Persis's parents. Her rich aristo father, her brilliant reg mother. Both thought that Persis was strong willed and brave and the smartest girl in Albion. They'd raised her to be patriotic and kind, on an estate the farthest south of any in Albion, and they'd given her a swift yacht and a clever sea mink and an education alongside the princess of the island.

But it simply wasn't possible. He'd been living beside her for nearly two weeks. He knew her well, and more than well enough to know that Persis was too simple, too shallow, too . . .

*No.*

Justen had met her in Galatea. In disguise. She'd introduced him to the princess, and sat in her throne room. She'd introduced him to Noemi, and visited the refugees at his side. She'd prevented the Albian courtiers from sending out messages on her boat, and then been handed the visitors like she'd know what to do with them. She'd come to find him when he'd been fluttering with the Poppy, then disappeared the moment he was distracted.

She wasn't the most foolish person in Albion. *He* was, because he hadn't seen it before now.

Persis Blake was the Wild Poppy.

Her Highness Princess Regent Isla of Albion stood in the middle of her throne room, her head held high, the white swirls of her outrageous gown floating around her of their own accord, powered by tiny, buzzing nanobots. Her white hair was arrayed in enormous wings that shot out from her head. She looked very intimidating.

Torin Blake, however, was standing before her and he did not seem remotely impressed. All he'd been able to ascertain so far was that Persis, along with Andrine, was long gone from the royal court, and possibly from the island altogether. "You will tell me what you and my daughter have been up to," he stated firmly, "and you will do so right now."

"Will I?" Isla replied haughtily, looking from Torin to Justen to Heloise. "I think you will watch your tongue in my palace, sir."

He shook his head. "Don't you talk like that to me, young lady. You want to launch military operations against Galatea, I'm all for it. You want to use my daughter and my boats and my tenants to sneak around playing spy games, I'll have something to say about it."

"Officially," offered Tero sheepishly, arriving in the room with Kai and Elliot in tow, "it was Persis who used those things, which she technically has the right to, being a Blake and all."

"Tero!" Isla cried, exasperated.

The gengineer shrugged his shoulders. "What, you think we're going to get away with denying it? These are the *Blakes*, Isla, not the Blockings." But he flinched as he looked at his lord and lady anyway.

"So it's true," Justen said. "You two and Persis—"

"And my sister," Tero added matter-of-factly.

"You guys are the Wild Poppy?"

"The League of the Wild Poppy, yes."

"*Tero*," Isla tried again. "Shut. Up."

"Don't you dare shut up, Finch," said Torin Blake. "I may not be able to tell Her Highness here what to do, but *you'll* listen to me."

For the first time, Justen could appreciate an aristo's power. He wanted answers out of Tero, too.

The Blakes were looking from Isla to Tero, their faces drained of color. Kai and Elliot were remaining silent, clearly realizing that this matter was none of their business.

"You are saying," Heloise began slowly, and Justen was sure it took all her strength to speak aloud, "that my daughter, with the assistance of a few of her school friends, has been spending the last six months running back and forth from Galatea in disguise, defying Citizen Aldred and his entire army, in a foolhardy and possibly deadly attempt to liberate imprisoned Galatean aristos and other dissidents?"

Tero grimaced but nodded.

Heloise turned toward her husband. "I knew we spoiled her."

"Noemi Dorric is fired," Torin said. "*Fired*. She'll be lucky if she can get a job vaccinating cuttle jellies when I'm done with her."

"Sir," said Justen quickly, "Noemi Dorric is a skilled medic and—"

"And she had no business helping my daughter with such dangerous activities and not telling anyone!" Torin whirled on Justen. "And what, exactly, did *you* know about all this, Citizen Helo?"

Justen raised his hands in surrender. "Nothing! Believe me, I'm even more blown away by this than you are."

Completely blown away and more than a little fascinated. His mind reeled with replays of conversations he'd had with Persis that now overflowed with double meanings. When she'd comforted him in the sanitarium, confided in him in the star cove, scolded him on the *Daydream*—all those times, she was New Pacifica's most infamous spy.

She'd known all along that he was responsible for the Reduction drug, yet she'd welcomed him into her home. Why? To keep a closer eye on him? Why had she let him visit the refugees, if she only planned to rip him away? And what had she made of his confession an hour ago at the party? What had she been thinking while they danced . . .

Justen felt knocked sideways as if by a giant wave. Persis Blake was the most skilled actress he'd ever known. He'd handed her all that information, and she'd talked to him about *dancing*.

He looked at Tero. "When she left, what did she take with her in terms of drugs?"

"*Drugs*, now?" Torin Blake roared.

If Kai and Elliot had seemed out of their depths at the party, they looked completely lost now.

Tero appeared ill at ease. "The usual. Supplements for knockout doses. Enough genetemps for her and my sister and the targets."

"Genetemps!" Her father threw up his hands in despair. "This is a disaster." He turned to the princess. "I want you to send a security detail down there to get my daughter back. Now."

"Please," Isla scoffed. "Do you think for a moment that Persis would let a few paltry Albian soldiers stop her? She's outwitted the entire guard force of Halahou city prison."

That might have been the wrong thing to say. Heloise put her head in her hands. Her shoulders were shaking, though Justen couldn't tell if she was laughing or crying. His medic instincts warned him that the fragile woman should probably not be involved in this, but at the same time, he wasn't about to be the one to point it out. And he had other things on his mind, anyway—like what Persis had taken from his conversation with her as the Poppy.

"Did she request doses of the Helo Cure?" he asked Tero.

Tero's eyes narrowed. "Yes, she did, but I didn't have any on hand. Given the gengineering requirements, it would take a while to code. She did order some, though. Why?"

Justen shook his head. "Nothing." If she asked Tero for the cure, that meant she trusted his information. She did want to protect herself and Andrine should they be captured, and anyone else. But she hadn't told Tero why. Had she simply been in too much of a rush?

"You mean for Ro?" Elliot asked anxiously. "The cure. It's supposed to be for Reduced like Ro, right?" She looked at the others. "Does anyone here but Persis know what that Vania girl is planning to do to her?"

"She won't hurt her," Justen stated firmly. "All she needs from Ro is a genetic sample, but having her in Galatea is insurance."

"Insurance for what?" Elliot asked.

"That I won't bomb Halahou into oblivion, for a start," Isla muttered.

"Insurance for me," Justen clarified, as the visitors' eyes went wide. "Vania wants me back and she thinks if she has Ro, she'll get me, too."

"Why?" Elliot asked again.

Justen sighed. "Because I'm the one who wants to experiment on her."

Kai's face turned severe. Elliot's turned into that of an avenging goddess.

"Wait just a minute—" Kai said. "You can't simply kidnap people and run experiments on them without permission—"

"I wasn't going to," he said quickly. "I simply wanted a sample of her genetic material for my work. At most, a brain scan. Nothing invasive or painful, and naturally I was planning on asking for permission first, and explaining to all of you—"

Kai held up a hand. "I don't need the details right now. The important point here is that whatever it is that Vania is planning to do to my friends, clearly Persis—who is apparently quite learned in these matters, what with being such a good spy neither her *parents nor her lover* had the slightest inkling that's what she was doing—"

"I'm not her *lover*," Justen grumbled defensively. He especially didn't need Kai throwing around terms like that in front of the Blakes.

But Kai had also set Justen's thoughts on another track. Vania *knew* all he needed from Ro was some genetic material. Material he might already easily have had. A strand of hair, a scrape of cheek cells. It was all a Galatean scientist would need as well. Something Vania could have gotten from Ro just by asking nicely. Something she might have gotten from Ro without anyone ever being the wiser.

"Apparently Persis thought it was so important that

this not happen that she ran off to Galatea at a moment's notice," Kai finished. "Am I right?"

Justen's mind whirled. There was no pressing need to take Andromeda and Ro in the middle of the luau, to separate them from their friends.

"And now she's off," Kai went on, "alone but for Andrine, trying to rescue our friends. I don't know much about Galatea, but if someone is risking her life to rescue Andromeda and Ro, I feel duty bound to help."

But Vania had done it like that anyway, and she'd told Justen about her plans, too.

"Persis and my sister had to go quickly," Tero was explaining. "Persis believes it will be easier to intercept the visitors before they reach the Halahou city prison than try to get them out later. If that's where they're going."

And when Justen had refused to join Vania, she'd injured him, but she hadn't captured him. She hadn't silenced him. In fact, she'd left him alone, so he had time to . . .

Warn the Wild Poppy.

The truth hit him like the smack of a wave. Vania wasn't after Andromeda and Ro at all. They were merely perks of the process. She'd been laying a trap for the Wild Poppy. And Justen and Persis had fallen right into her hands.

# Thirty-one

IN THE SHELTER OF the cliffs below Fisherman's Rest, Persis and Andrine moored their boat and came ashore. The moon was high in the sky tonight, providing little cover as they hiked up to the road and turning the sea behind them into a single silver sheet that stretched all the way back to Albion. They huffed their way to the bluff, hampered by the long robes of the isolated Peccant order they were impersonating and Tero's last-minute genetemps, which had bloated them both into puffy, swollen versions of themselves. With their hair tamed and covered with dark hoods, and the excess bloat obscuring most of their facial features, they were decently concealed for a nighttime mission, though Persis wondered how much more extreme Tero's genetemping would have to get if Vania kept inviting herself to Albian social functions. If she gave them more than a passing glance, she'd probably recognize them.

"There might have been a more convenient disguise than this," Andrine gasped, her face soaked with sweat.

"Don't exert yourself too much," Persis replied. "You need as many fluids as you can retain for the disguise to work."

At last they reached the skimmer, which was charged and waiting for them, thanks to the help of the Ford resistance.

"Is the oblet working yet?" Persis asked as they put their supplies in the back and took off toward Halahou. She was never completely comfortable until they'd regained contact. Their palmports couldn't receive messages in Galatea, and their oblet had been inoperable since arriving on the island's shore.

"Not yet." Andrine slipped it back in her pocket. "But I hear Aldred's instituted dampening hours. It gives his operatives time to search for seditious messages and purge anything that might have gotten through from dissidents like the Fords. We'll have to work out a hack for it when we get a chance."

"Sure," said Persis drily. "We've got all the time in the world for that. I do wish Citizen Aldred would be a bit more respectful of our schedule."

Andrine chuckled, her eyes turning to slits in her swollen face as they sped through the clear, cool night.

Without warning, the car collided with some sort of unseen barrier, springing both girls out of their seats. Persis crashed hard against the dashboard. The controls slammed into her bloated body, knocking the wind out of her. Fighting for breath, she looked over at Andrine, who lay slumped in her seat, unconscious, blood dripping from a gash near her temple.

"Andrine, wake up!" She shook her friend.

"My, that looks nasty," said a familiar voice.

Persis turned to see Vania standing there in the dark, her fall of black hair hardly differentiated from the night itself. Several officers in military uniform stood at her back.

"Nanothread." The captain gestured vaguely into the darkness as she approached. "So strong for such a tiny thing, don't you think? I'm especially fond of it. So, Wild Poppy is it? Who is hiding underneath all that blubber?"

Persis reached for the wristlock covering her palmport and felt a sudden slash of pain traveling up her arm.

"No palmports, Albian," Vania scolded, wagging her finger and the empty pricker launch. "Don't you know they're bad for you?" She approached, and Persis could see she'd changed from her gown into her military uniform. The sparkly black makeup webbing out from her eyes remained, however, as did her dark lipstick. "It's nice to finally meet you."

*We've met*, thought Persis, but what she said through gritted teeth and the pain flowing out from her hand into the rest of her body was "Can't say the same."

"It was so easy, in the end," Vania said, as if bursting to share.

Pain shot through her heart, but Persis clenched her jaw and refused to show it as Vania blabbered on.

"I knew the first boat to land on my island would be yours. Every aristo on Albion was at that party. I knew Justen would find you." Her entire guard leaned forward as she gripped both Persis's chins in her hand and swept Persis's hood back from her face.

Persis could barely remain upright, but she mustered the wherewithal to bat her eyes coquettishly at Vania as her enemy's eyes widened with shocked recognition. Even captured, she was still Persis Blake.

"Well," Vania said, breathless with exultation, "*that* was unexpected."


THE *DAYDREAM* SPED SILENTLY across the moonlit sea that separated Albion from Galatea. Tero stood at the helm, while Justen twitched awake on the long bench nearest.

"Welcome back," Tero said. "For what it's worth, you look . . . stately."

Justen sat up, coughing a bit, then looked down at his arms. They didn't look much different. He brushed his hands over his face, feeling the crags and wrinkles Tero's genetemps had formed all over his skin.

"You promise you've worked out the kinks from last time?" he asked Tero, and his voice came out as a gruff grunt, like he'd spent sixty years barking orders at people.

"Pretty sure." At Justen's withering glare, he held up his hands in surrender. "I know how touchy you are about the whole operation. But I'm fresh out of fat coding and the male coding won't help you much."

Justen meant to laugh, but it came out sounding more like a growl. "This is going to take some getting used to," he grumbled. "How far are we from shore?"

"A good twenty minutes yet," Tero replied. "Don't worry too much. If we don't get to Andrine and Persis before Vania catches and doses them, Isla will get them back, even if she has to tear Galatea apart to do it."

Justen wondered if Tero would be so sanguine about the whole operation if he understood the extent to which his own sister was in danger from the drug. Though Tero had told Justen about a fight the Finches had had with Persis recently regarding her drugging Andrine to keep her away from a mission, the gengineer didn't seem to understand why Persis had made that choice, which must have happened after Justen explained to Persis how the drug worked differently for regs.

Every conversation he'd ever had with her had taken on whole oceans of new meanings, and every time he started thinking about that, his head hurt more than from the genetemps.

"That's not good enough," was all he said. No need to scare Tero at the moment.

Tero gave him a wry smile. "The things we do for love."

"Persis and I are not in love," Justen said automatically. "It was all for show."

The Albian gengineer remained skeptical. "I saw the images of you two kissing in the star cove, you know. Everyone did. Quite convincing."

"Persis is a consummate liar," Justen said in his gravelly old man's voice.

"And you share her expertise in the clandestine arts and other methods of spy craft?" Tero replied. "Impressive.

I guess medic training really is more comprehensive in Galatea than I'd thought."

"There's no need to be sarcastic."

"There's no need to deny it," Tero said, "especially not to me. I know what it's like to have completely inconvenient feelings for one of these girls. I tried to hide mine for months. It's hard."

Justen sighed. He liked the Albian gengineer, liked him even more now that he knew he was doing something more with his time than tinkering with Slipstream, but the last thing Justen needed was Tero, who'd only come out about his . . . whatever it was with the princess *tonight*, giving him relationship advice. Especially not when he was about to attempt the hardest thing he'd ever done.

"Persis and I are not in love," he repeated at last.

"Really," Tero said flatly. "Why not?"

"Excuse me?"

Tero raised his hands. "Look, I've known that girl my whole life. She's basically a kid sister. Used to follow me around the beach in the village, bugging me to play with her. But I'm not blind. I know what she looks like in a bathing suit these days, and I know what kind of brain she's got hidden under all that hair of hers, too. I would never have signed on to this whole Poppy nonsense otherwise. Because of who she is, she has to protect herself. I've never seen any guy who could match her. And then you came along and you didn't care one bit that she was the heir to Scintillans. You called her out, Justen. No one does that. And then, you helped her mom, you're helping the refugees, and you're taking genetemps to go rescue her." Tero shrugged. "I also saw you two making out on this very boat on that trip to Remembrance Island. There's something there."

"Believe me," Justen said ruefully, "it was faked." Mostly, at any rate.

Besides, Justen was pretty sure she hated him for his involvement in the Reduction drug. The Persis he'd thought he'd known might be able to forgive him, but the Wild Poppy, who risked her life to protect the victims of the revolution— no. Not her. She'd made it quite clear in the Poppy's flutters.

And Tero would never understand. He'd always known the real Persis, bathing suits or no. To Tero, someone developing real feelings for his brilliant, charming aristo friend was no big surprise. But Justen didn't have the right to feel the same. He'd spent the last two weeks dismissing every point Persis made because he'd idiotically decided that she wasn't smart enough to be correct about things. Yet even when she was acting her flakiest, she still managed to make more sense than his revolutionary friends back home in Galatea. He'd known it, even if he hadn't wanted to believe it. How odd that an array of gorgeous dresses and a few well-placed dumb comments were all it took to disguise her true self. Was it because she was a woman? Was it because Justen was actually far shallower than Persis had ever appeared to be?

He'd taken her at face value, because she was pretty and rich and dressed so nicely. He'd wanted to think the worst of an aristo, the same way everyone wanted to think the best of him because he was a Helo and a medic. He'd relied on his reputation to bring him to Albion, to get him an audience with the princess, to give him the lab space he'd needed. But the Wild Poppy—Persis—had seen through all that. As Persis she'd urged him to do better with the gifts he'd been given. As the Poppy, she'd neatly cut him off from all the things he'd used his borrowed reputation to gain. She was an aristo, but every member of her spy league other than Isla was a reg, and Persis was not using her aristo status to ply her trade.

It was Justen, the supposed revolutionary, who had thought he should be trusted merely for being a Helo. And if Persis chose to trust him now—as he hoped—it wasn't because he was a Helo, it was because he was trying, at last, to make up for the worst thing he'd ever done to the family name.

He almost laughed. Love from Persis Blake? He'd settle for forgiveness. Any hope of something more was pointless. Justen used to think that, although Persis was beautiful and kind and charming and funny and whatever else he'd most recently realized about his Albian hostess, she did not have the qualities he looked for in a woman. She wasn't smart enough. She wasn't serious enough. She wasn't dedicated to the betterment of mankind enough.

He'd been such an idiot.

"I think," he said slowly, "a girl like Persis Blake deserves someone much better than me."

Tero's grunt sounded remarkably skeptical, even over the sound of the water rushing beneath them. "Maybe you can revisit this topic once you've saved her life. I hear girls like it when a boy rescues them from his evil sister."

"She's not my sister."

Tero rolled his eyes. "Right. Sorry, I really need to stop trusting my own eyes, don't I? Vania's not your sister, Persis isn't your girlfriend, you're not wearing a bushy gray wig and trying to sneak into the Galatean royal labs to steal some expired medication on a shelf somewhere. Silly me."

"It might be expired," Justen muttered, "but it's better than nothing." And what was he supposed to do? Sit around in Albion and wait while Isla's royal guard went to Galatea and demanded the return of two Albian nationals? The relative arguments of Albian immunity from the revolution versus the crimes the Wild Poppy had committed on Galatean soil would take a significant amount of time to untangle; and until they were released, Andrine and Persis were in danger every moment of being Reduced. If it wasn't already too late.

The port of Halahou loomed large before them, but Tero moved east, beyond the city limits to the edge of Queen's Cove. The cove was silent now, the water still and peaceful but for the occasional dark hump of a mini-orca back breaking the surface to breathe.

"Did you see that?" whispered Tero. "You know, we studied them in school but I've never seen them in person."

Justen wondered if his companion would be less in awe of the creatures had he seen them eat the corpse of their last mistress. He wondered if Tero would be so calm about the almost-certain capture of both his sister and his friend if he knew what happened to regs who received the Reduction drug.

Justen had been thinking that if he wound up with

genetemps sickness, he'd drop Tero down a lava tube. But if the gengineer's sister was permanently damaged by the drug Justen created, what would Tero have the right to do to him? If Persis was damaged . . .

Justen shook his head. He just wouldn't let it happen. That was all.

# Thirty-two

IN A BEAUTIFUL ROOM in the royal palace in Galatea, Remy Helo sat alone, searching the news from Albion for any information about the Wild Poppy—about Persis Blake. The gossip was extremely light. There'd been a single item a few days ago about her hair, and nothing whatsoever about Justen— not since the night before Persis's trip to the prison.

Not since before Remy had confirmed for the spy that Justen was responsible for creating the Reduction drug.

And she hadn't heard from the Wild Poppy since then either. The mission had gone well—Vania had certainly gotten in a lot of trouble for it—but Remy was surprised that the Albians had never contacted her again. Things had been quiet in Halahou for two days, but she expected at least some recognition of the work she'd done for the Albians. Weren't they concerned that her part in the operation remained secret? Weren't they worried that she was staying safe and not ratting them out to her uncle?

Of course, she was a traitor now, so she had as much

to lose by telling the Aldreds the truth. And maybe, given Justen's behavior, the Wild Poppy and her League wanted nothing more to do with Remy Helo.

Ironic. She'd gotten herself into this mess by trying to keep Justen safe from the revolutionaries. Now she was worried he wouldn't be safe from those trying to fight the revolution.

Maybe she should have told the Poppy why she'd gone to the Lacan estate in the first place. Maybe she should have explained how Justen had been sabotaging the pinks, and how she'd tried to step in before anyone noticed and traced the problems back to him.

Then again, that might just give the Poppy more nanothread to hang both the Helos with. She'd wanted to message Justen and warn him, but couldn't figure out any way to do so without incriminating herself, should anyone else read it. And given her uncle's suspicions—and worse, Vania's suspicions ever since she'd gone to Albion the day the prison had been breached—Remy was certain messages to and from Justen Helo were being monitored.

Maybe that's why she hadn't heard from him. Remy refused to think of other reasons. Still, it was odd that the gossip waves, which had previously been so full of items about Persis and Justen, were suddenly silent on the subject. Tonight, Remy had grown frantic as rumors had leaked out about a giant party to be held at Princess Isla's royal palace. Justen would have to be at that, right? But so far, nothing had come through. Stupid Uncle Damos and his stupid news delay. She'd even tried hacking the system, to no avail. How ironic that she could borrow her uncle's oblet to give herself a secret soldier identity, but she couldn't find some simple gossip. Uncle Damos should really get his priorities straight.

And Justen had better be safe and sound and at that Albian princess's swanky luau, or the Wild Poppy was in serious trouble.

A false identity. No wonder she'd thought that she and the Wild Poppy were such similar souls. But what if she'd been wrong there, too? What if the Albian spy, the beautiful Persis Blake, had deceived her just as the revolution had?

For if the Poppy truly valued their alliance, wouldn't she have promised Remy that, no matter what, Justen would be safe from her wrath? After all, Remy had done her a great favor in helping the Fords escape. She'd even hurt poor Vania's military career in doing so. Not that Remy regretted helping the Fords. The Fords' hatred of the revolution was not mired in aristo bigotry. They had many reg allies. They just hated the path the revolution had chosen to pursue, one in which people were suffering. Remy was too much of a Helo to do anything other than agree. If the choice was between Vania's quick promotion up the ranks and people being tortured because they just wanted to be left in peace, Remy knew which side she came down on.

And the same held true for Justen. He was her only family. She would not let him be hurt, no matter what the Wild Poppy thought he deserved for his involvement in the drug. How was Justen supposed to have known how Uncle Damos might use it? But what if Persis was avoiding Remy now because her plans for Justen would destroy their alliance? After all, if Remy were the Poppy and she were about to hurt one of her spies' brothers, she wouldn't let the spy in question know.

On the desk, her oblet pinged, and she saw Justen's face glow in the area above her desk. At last! Remy rushed over to view the message, only to find there wasn't one at all. Instead, it was a notification that he'd accessed the keypad at the royal lab. Remy had activated the notification at the same time she'd arranged a military position for herself on the Lacan estate. At the time, she'd thought it vital to know exactly when Justen might sneak back into the lab to sabotage more pills. At the time, she thought she needed to save Justen from himself. Now, she figured she needed to save him from the Poppy.

Was he back in Galatea?

Remy sprang into action. She grabbed her military jacket and rushed from her room. The labs were only a few blocks from the palace. If she could catch him there, she could finally talk face-to-face, without fear of their messages being intercepted by the revolution. She could finally tell him what she'd discovered, what she'd been doing, and what kind of danger she believed him to be in. Together, they'd find a place to hide where they could be safe from both the revolution and the treacherous Wild Poppy.

No one stopped Remy at the gates of the palace. No one bothered her as she moved through the streets of the city. Was it her famous name? Her military jacket? There was a single guard minding the entrance to the royal lab, but she did little more than nod in Remy's direction as she approached.

"I'm Remy Helo," she said. "Did my brother come this way?"

"Thought your brother was whooping it up with some swanky aristo in Albion," the guard replied, rolling her eyes. "Kinda disgraceful, huh?"

Remy narrowed her eyes. "Thanks for your help," she said in a tone that was anything but grateful. The guard merely shrugged and buzzed her in.

Most of the corridors were dark, and a scary possibility came to Remy's mind. If the guard hadn't seen her brother, who was it in the lab? Maybe it wasn't Justen here at all. The Poppy had a lot of resources at her disposal: gengineering, nanotechnology. Maybe she'd found a way to steal Justen's lab access? Maybe . . .

*Get ahold of yourself, Remy. Maybe Justen is helping the Poppy. After all, last time you talked to him, he was a traitor to the revolution, just like you.*

But the deadly look on Persis Blake's face when she'd asked Remy about the pinks . . . Remy started running. She rushed down corridor after corridor, searching for any trace of human presence. At last she found lights on, far in a back storage room filled with old oblets and records of immunizations from the time of the Helo Cure.

But that wasn't all she found. In the middle of the floor, lying in a heap and twitching, lay a figure. She hurried over and knelt at the person's side, turning him over to see what was wrong. Steely hair, a lined face, and a pained expression met her eyes, and Remy gasped. This was impossible.

"Papa?" she whispered.

"Tero . . ." the man who looked like her father wheezed, "promised."

The voice was gravelly but familiar. Remy leaned in and her eyes widened as she took in all the details of the man's face. "*Justen?*"

He made no response, unless eyes rolling back in his head counted. He was wearing an unfamiliar set of clothes, but at least they looked Galatean. In his hands, Justen held a tin of lavender pills.

"Justen," she said, "what happened to you?"

"Persis . . ." he struggled to say, and then his whole body went slack.

Terrified, Remy pressed her ear to his chest. His heart was still beating, and now at least, it looked like he was breathing steadily.

*Persis*. Remy clenched her jaw. Persis had done this to her brother. She'd . . . given him something to hurt him, to avenge those who'd received the Reduction drug. Whatever these pills were must be meant to counteract the effects, but he hadn't gotten to them in time. She grabbed the tin and opened it, crushing one of the pills inside and dusting his tongue with the pulverized powder.

Nothing happened. Maybe they weren't meant to work immediately. Remy bit her lip. She refused to cry. She was to blame for this. She never should have run off that night he'd confessed his sabotage to her. If she'd stayed and they'd figured this out together, maybe they wouldn't be in this trouble. Maybe they would have found a way to apologize to Uncle Damos. To reconcile, to stay safe.

She never should have trusted an Albian aristo. She never should have let the Wild Poppy have free access to her brother. She'd made the wrong choice.

She had to find Vania.

BEHIND HER EYELIDS, THE light was cool and gray, but Persis's body was on fire. Pain coursed through every nerve and fiber of her being, hot and achy and electric. She dared not move, not that she *could* move much. Even through the agony, she could feel the bite of nanoropes on her wrists, elbows, and ankles. She lay on her side on soft, springy ground, with her hands bound at her back and the dampness of dawn soaking through her clothes.

"Awake?" came Vania's voice from above. "I know how you feel. I'm too excited to sleep myself."

Persis opened her eyes—painfully—to see the captain standing above her. She was lying on the lawn near what appeared to be military barracks. A few lights shone in the windows, but most were black. Palm trees waved softly around the perimeter and she could hear the sound of distant waves. The sky was still dark, but far away in the east, there was a hint of violet tingeing the horizon.

"I've been trying to figure out what to do," Vania said now, crouching beside Persis's head. Her tone was conversational. She gestured off to Persis's left, and as Persis craned her head—painfully—she could see a fuzzy outlined lump of cloth. Was it Andrine?

Vania's words confirmed it. "I think I'm going to Reduce your friend first, so you can see what happens to her before it's your turn, but there's no point in that until she wakes up, right?"

"Certainly," Persis muttered.

"Of course, she's been asleep so long . . ." Vania sucked air through her teeth. "Maybe if her head wound's bad enough, we won't have to use the drug to Reduce her at all, right?"

"One can hope," Persis ground out. Whatever she could do to delay Vania and her gleeful revenge would be best for Andrine's brain—and her own.

"The problem," Vania went on, standing up and brushing her hands free of imaginary dust, "is that I'm getting really impatient. I'm torn. On the one hand, how great would it be to Reduce you in Halahou prison for all the people of Galatea to see? On the other hand, the longer I delay, the more chance there is that your little princess is going to swoop in here and rescue you." She nudged Persis with her foot, but it felt more like a barrage of razors against her skin. "Am I right again?"

"You're very smart," Persis said through gritted teeth.

"Coming from a mastermind like the Wild Poppy, that's quite a compliment." She leaned over and looked at Persis. "I just . . . I'm having a really difficult time believing this is all real, you know? I thought I had you pegged. Such a great cover, Lady Blake. I have to give you that. I'm so impressed."

Persis remained silent.

"What, no thank you? Don't aristos learn any manners where you're from?" Vania nudged her again. Persis bit back a scream.

"Where I'm from," Persis managed to get out in a relatively calm voice, "we're taught it's bad manners to kick people when they're down."

"Ah." Vania resumed pacing for a moment, then hopped back to Persis's side. "I really am impressed by all you accomplished. Honestly. And even younger than me. I'd love to pick your brain—I mean, while you still have one."

The sound of lifter fans shifting gravel interrupted Vania's victory speech. "Reinforcements, perhaps?" she asked no one in particular. Persis could see nothing from her position, but it sounded like some sort of skimmer had pulled up to the barracks. With any luck, it would be some-one telling Vania that Albian nationals were off limits for Reduction, even if they were in the League of the Wild Poppy. With a huge amount of luck, it would be the Albian military itself, granted the full weight of Isla's blessing.

Vania went off to investigate and Persis tried to ignore the pain in her body and take in her surroundings. The outpost appeared to be located on the shore, and from the sound of the waves, they were near some sort of bluff, which probably meant they were still on Galatea's northern shore, possibly still close to Fisherman's Rest, where she and Andrine had been captured. Good. Should Isla wish to attack, she had easy access from the sea.

Persis sincerely hoped Isla wished to attack.

Though every movement was utter agony, she pushed

herself into a kneeling position and inched over to Andrine. The cut on her friend's head was bloody but not deep. And there was little bruising or swelling to indicate that she suffered a serious concussion. Perhaps their bloated disguises, faded now from what Persis could see of Andrine's face and figure, had actually helped protect them when the skimmer had crashed. Perhaps Vania had been lying, and Andrine wasn't actually injured that badly. Maybe she had been drugged unconscious, just as Persis had.

What was she thinking? Of course Vania was lying. Persis wondered if Vania even had the visitors at all. Maybe this had all been a trap for the Wild Poppy. Maybe Justen was in on the plan with Vania, and she'd stupidly, *stupidly* trusted him . . . and why?

Why did she so badly want to believe everything he said? Because he was a Helo? Because he was handsome? Because he took care of her mother and laughed at her sea mink and stole her breath whenever he kissed her—even though they were supposedly faking it all?

She might be the cleverest girl in Albion, but it turned out she had a huge blind spot when it came to good-looking revolutionary medics with famous names. And if he'd been lying to get the Poppy to trust his information back at the luau, maybe he was lying about his discovery regarding the Helo Cure as well. Even now, tied up and maybe only minutes away from being Reduced, Persis had been berating herself for not forcing Tero to track down a few doses of the cure before she and Andrine left. She'd been so concerned about getting the visitors back before anything happened to them. But maybe it was a waste of her energy, to regret rushing off before she protect herself with the cure.

Maybe his confession was a lie, too, like everything else Justen had ever done.

"You certainly look like you're feeling better, Lady Blake," came Vania's voice from behind her. She turned to see Vania returning with three others: two guards who carried a bundle between them and a third, shorter one. Persis blinked through the darkness, and her heart lit up. *Remy.*

But the younger girl wasn't looking at her at all. Her entire focus was on the bundle the guards were carrying, her face awash with fear.

"Look, I brought you something," Vania said as the guards placed the bundle nearby. "Your boyfriend."

Persis stared down at the unconscious body a meter away. Was it Justen? From this angle, she could hardly make out his features, and his sideburns seemed flaked with a lighter color. She looked down at his hands—the large, caring medic's hands that had held her so carefully in the star cove, that had held her when they danced near the fire at court, that had mopped her brow when she'd had genetemps sickness and helped her mother during her spell tonight. Yes, it was Justen.

What was he doing here? Unconscious?

"Careful!" she heard Remy cry to the guards, sounding more like a little girl than she ever had on the floor of Isla's throne room. "He's sick. Ask her what she did to him."

Vania looked questioningly at Persis. What new trick was this?

"I don't know what you're talking about," Persis replied truthfully. "I left Justen safe and sound in Albion." And he should still be there.

"Lies," Vania said, and wagged her finger at Persis. "All lies. I'll tell you what you did to him, you aristo scum. You turned him against his family, against his work, and against the revolution. The Justen that Remy and I know would never have gone anywhere with someone like you. He never would have left us here, abandoning everything he believed."

Persis narrowed her eyes, more confused than ever. What kind of information did Vania hope to get from her now? If she knew Justen was one of her spies, why was she accusing him of treason against the revolution? As the sky in the east grew ever lighter, she took another look at Justen's unconscious form. Galatean military uniform, slightly longer sideburns than she remembered him having, and that flaky light color in his hair. She recognized it now. It was the same temporary hair dye she used when she was in disguise.

Had Justen been sneaking around Galatea in disguise? Impossible notions began boiling up in her mind. She'd left him at the court, tending her mother. There was no way he'd come here, unless . . .

Unless he was telling her the truth back at the luau. Unless he'd come to help. If Justen hadn't been lying to her, it changed everything. Everything. Maybe Isla's forces were in Galatea, even now. Maybe that's what Remy had come to tell her.

But why like this? Why not simply overtake Vania

and her crew of guards? She looked to Remy, but the girl's expression was harsh and closed, as it had been the day they'd fought near the skimmer, as it had been the moment she'd woken up in Isla's court. Something had gone terribly wrong.

"The Justen I know," Persis said, directing her response to Remy, "wanted to help people. He knew that the revolution was never meant to torture anyone." There was not a glimmer of recognition in the girl's eyes. Whose side was she on? Had Vania won the girl back to the revolution? If so, it must have happened recently, since Vania seemed to have been sincerely surprised to discover the Wild Poppy's true identity.

"Helping people? Was that what he was doing partying with a princess in Albion?" Vania asked snidely. "How exactly does that help anyone?"

"Everything she says is a lie," Remy said now, her voice as cold as Vania's had ever been. "She sits here and lectures *us* on the true meaning of revolution, and she's as bad an aristo as any of them."

Vania put her hand on Remy's shoulder. "Don't worry," she said. "We know how to take care of aristos around here."

# Thirty-three

JUSTEN WAS NEVER, EVER, ever taking genetemps again. This was worse than three days sitting in the sun and drinking nothing but kiwine. He felt split at the seams somehow, as if the code breakdown had left his body in the wrong position and slightly out of place. How anyone found this fun was beyond his reckoning. How Persis could tolerate it regularly was inconceivable.

Slowly, the universe came back to him, and he blinked and groaned.

"Oh!" cried a voice that sounded something like his sister's. "He's waking up."

His eyes began to focus, but the second he tried to move, he was overcome by waves of nausea. He rolled onto his stomach and tried to swallow, but his tongue was dry and coated with some sort of powder. He spat into the grass, a pale mark against the dark ground.

Grass. Ground. He was outside? The last thing he remembered was entering the royal lab in Halahou. He blinked again and attempted sitting. This time, it worked.

He was, in fact, on the ground. The sky was lightening all around, the soft silver blue you saw right before dawn. In front of him stood Vania and Remy along with a few guards, and . . . to his right knelt Persis Blake, tied hand and foot with nanoropes. She was wearing a dark, voluminous robe, and her yellow and white hair was tangled all over her face and neck, but her keen, amber eyes were as bright as ever. She stared at him, her expression pointed, as if there were a million or two things she'd like to say.

He knew the feeling.

"Justen!" Remy threw herself to the ground next to him and hugged him. "You're all right. I was so scared when I saw you in the lab—I thought maybe she'd hurt you."

"What?" he croaked. "Vania?"

"Yes?" Vania answered sweetly.

"Vania's the only one who'd hurt me—"

"See what I mean?" Vania rolled her eyes. "Totally brainwashed. I mean, look at him, Remy. Would the Justen you know ever willingly take genetemps?"

Remy shook her head vehemently.

Justen closed his eyes in despair. "Remy, I know it looks odd, but I—"

"Enough of your lies!" Vania snapped. "I think we're both a little sick of hearing them at this point." From his place on the ground, Justen could see Vania's oblet ping in her pocket. "Oh, now what?" she said, annoyed, and pulled it out.

"You took *genetemps* for me?" Persis whispered at him, her voice filled with awe. "*You?*"

"Yes," he grumbled in reply. "And look at the good it did us, *Poppy.*"

"Still," she said as she shrugged her bound arms, "I'm impressed. It's the most romantic thing anyone has ever done for me."

Tied up and still making flirty jokes. Apparently the Wild Poppy was not entirely different from the Persis Blake he knew.

"If we get out of this alive," he said, "we're going to have a long conversation."

"Oh, yes. I look forward to hearing all about your first genetemping trip."

"That's not what I mean."

Persis turned his way, all amusement vanished from her features. Her gaze was dark and piercing, and her words were even more so. "Neither do I, Justen. And let's not assume that, even when we do get out of this alive, either of us will retain the power of speech."

Justen felt woozy again as his brain sought to reconcile the girl he knew with the spy tied up beside him. Was this what had been lurking beneath Persis's spoiled aristo persona all along?

He had no idea where he was anymore. Not Halahou. On a lawn outside some nondescript military installation somewhere. He could hear the sound of waves. They seemed to be coming from beyond the bluff that stood about twenty meters in front of them.

He looked at Vania reading her message on her oblet. Though he couldn't make it out from this angle, whatever the display said made her face contort with rage.

"Listen, Remy—" he began, but Vania began to shout at her oblet.

"I don't think so," she snapped. "Not after everything I've been through."

At his side, Persis craned her neck to see, but Justen doubted she got anything.

"All right, enough!" Vania cried. "*I* caught the Wild Poppy. I did it all by myself. And I don't care what General Gawnt or even my father has to say about it." She held her hand out toward the other two guards. "Pinks, please."

Everything grew cold. "Vania, no—" Justen began.

"Shut up!" she screamed without moving. "You, Justen Helo, are in no position to say *anything* right now. You'll be lucky if you get out of this without being Reduced yourself, at this rate."

"But he's right, Citizen Aldred," said Persis in a voice Justen wasn't sure he'd ever heard before. Or maybe he had. This was her voice in the baths at the sanitarium, her voice in the safe darkness of the star cove, her voice the night she tried to talk her mother out of madness. This was the real Persis Blake. The Wild Poppy. "You're making a terrible mistake. That ping you just got—from one of your superiors, I'm guessing. And I bet I can guess what it says, too. My princess has made a bargain with your father. We are to be released unharmed."

"Too late!" Vania shook her hand, though the guards seemed to hesitate. "It's too late. Message didn't get here in time. Oh well." She turned toward the guards. "Pinks! Now!" she roared.

Remy flinched, as did Vania's underlings. "Vania," said Remy, standing and backing up until she stood right near the guards, "let's not start a war. You'll still win. Now that she's been revealed, the Wild Poppy will never be able to come back to Galatea."

"Oh, I still win," Vania insisted. "I always win. But I will see the Wild Poppy Reduced anyway. I will watch her grovel in the muck before she goes back home. I promise you."

"Vania," said Justen, rising on unsteady feet. "Stop."

"No, you stop!" She pulled her gun out of her holster and pointed it at him. "Take another step and I'll hit you with more than a toxin pricker. You're just digging yourself in deeper." She glanced behind her. "And you, too, Remy. And," she said, raising her voice, "any soldier under my command who does not follow my direct orders. Now, a pink, please."

Remy sighed and turned toward a guard, who offered up his tin of pills. With a grim face, Remy took it then handed it off to Vania. "I still think you're making a mistake," she said. "We're going to get into trouble, and it's not like it'll even last long."

"No, Remy—" Justen cried. She didn't know about the effect the pills had on regs. "No, Vania. Don't. You have no idea what you're doing."

Persis wasn't an aristo. Not totally. Her brain might work like a reg's. Like her mother's. Just as she could develop DAR, she could be permanently damaged by the Reduction drug.

She could lose her beautiful, extraordinary mind. Forever.

Vania stalked over to Persis, eyes on the prize, shaking

a handful of pills into her hand as she went. "Oh yes I do, Justen. I saw your research. I know *exactly* what I'm doing."

And with that, she grabbed Persis's face and crammed the pills down her throat.

PERSIS SLAMMED TO THE ground and was still. Nothing moved in the gray dawn light—not the breeze, not the birds—even the waves seemed to go silent. Or maybe that was just the blood roaring in Justen's ears.

*Persis. No, no, no.*

Heedless of Vania and her gun, Justen rushed to Persis's side. He started to roll her over, then stopped as she began to twitch uncontrollably, shaking and shuddering as foam seeped from her mouth. He held her gently on her side so she didn't choke, tightened his arms around her until she grew quiet again.

*No, not Persis. Not Persis.*

Vania sighed, rolling her shoulders with relief. "There, that's done."

Remy stood silent, watching them. Tears rolled out of her eyes and over her cheeks, ignored. The guards behind her waited.

Justen wanted to attack Vania, to beat her senseless, but what was the point? She'd only prick him with one of her toxin stingers or shoot him or even Reduce him. And wasn't that what he deserved?

"You just started a war, Vania," he said instead. "Princess Isla will not stand for what you've done to her friend."

Vania snorted. "The princess doesn't scare me. She can't get anything done in her country—what makes you think she's going to be able to get something done in ours?"

"You were ordered to release her," Justen set Persis gently on the ground and stood, pointing an accusing finger at his former friend. "And you dosed her anyway. We're all witnesses. What do you plan to do to silence us?"

But she just shrugged. "I really don't care if anyone finds out when I dosed her or how or why. Talk all you want. True Galateans will be on my side. The Wild Poppy deserves what she gets, same as the queen did." She peered past Justen. "Ooh, look, she's waking up."

Justen turned and indeed, Persis had sat up. Her nanoropes lay slack now, and she wiped foam from her face with the back of her hand then stared at it, curiously. She licked it, then made a face and wiped the rest off on her dress.

"Aww," Vania said, "isn't it cute when they try to eat everything?"

Justen's stomach roiled. Persis's eyes were wide and blank as a baby's, and her gait was just as unsteady as she pushed herself to her feet and looked at him, her head cocked. He stared at her, barely able to breathe. What was this feeling? It was not sadness, was not even horror. He felt numb—the flare of anger at Vania vanishing to be replaced by a dull roar of nothing.

Nothing. That's what shone from Persis's gaze as she looked curiously from one person to the next. Was there anything at all left of her in there? How many doses did it take to do total damage? He knew he'd had it written down some-where in his notes, but he couldn't remember it. Couldn't remember anything in that moment except the look in her bright eyes the moment before she'd first kissed him.

Vania bounced on her feet. "Oh, I wish I could keep her. She'd make such a great handmaiden, don't you think? Can you imagine me being dressed and groomed and followed around by the great Wild Poppy?" She clapped her hands and Persis gave a little start, then turned toward Vania. "Come here, you. Come on, it's all right. I'm not going to hurt you . . ." Vania shook the tin of pills. "Don't you want more?"

Persis shuffled over, her expression one of stupid trust.

"Stop it, Vania," Justen said, catching Persis by the hand. It lay limp in his own, but she kept tugging toward Vania. "You've made your point."

"Not yet, I haven't." Vania beckoned Persis again.

Persis grunted and pulled free of his grip, continuing on toward Vania.

"You know," she said, when Persis reached her, "I think we've been doing it all wrong with these morons, keeping them as prisoners. We should retrain them to be pets." She smiled broadly. "All the cachet of a gengineered animal but potty trained, too." She leaned in. "You are potty trained, right, Lady Blake?"

Persis looked at her blankly.

Vania chuckled. "Let's see if she does any tricks."

Justen heard a soft moan at his left. Andrine, it seemed, was waking up. He silently willed her to stay down. If Vania saw that the other girl was awake, she'd no doubt want to dose her, too.

But Vania was no longer paying attention to anyone but Persis. "Let's see," she was saying. "We've seen her sit up and come. We could have her fetch, maybe, or roll over?"

Justen stole a glance at Andrine, whose eyes were wide open, though she hadn't moved. She looked at him, a question in her eyes, and he gave a nearly imperceptible shake of his head. What could Andrine do to help all tied up?

He turned to Remy, who was standing stock-still, an expression of horror painted across her features as she stared at Persis. "It'll be all right, Remy," he said. He lied.

"No," she whispered, her voice shuddering. "I don't think it will. I think I've made a terrible mistake."

He reached his hand out to her, keeping his voice soft and even. "You didn't know. You haven't seen what Reduction is really like."

She looked at him out of the corner of her eye then laughed mirthlessly. "You really do think I'm a child, don't you?" she said. "Well, you have no idea what you're talking about."

Vania was happily skipping in circles now, as the hapless Persis stumbled behind her. "Oh, I know!" Vania cried. "I'll make her beg." She held the tin of pills up in the air. "Come on, Persey-worsey. Beg. Beg!"

Persis stopped and lifted her face up to the tin. The pills inside made a pleasant clatter as Vania shook it. Persis lifted on her tiptoes, reaching out.

"Very *good*," Vania exclaimed. "Persey-worsey *likes* her pills, doesn't she? They're *good*."

Persis nodded. Justen could barely watch.

"Want another?" Vania fiddled with the tin.

Justen couldn't take it anymore. He stepped forward and grabbed Vania by the wrist. "That's enough."

She whirled to face him with a dangerous glare. "I think I'd watch it, if I were you," she said, shaking him off. "I have a whole bracelet full of prickers, you know." He stumbled backward as Vania resumed her triumphant grin.

A moment later, she went down as Persis slammed a rock against the side of her head.

"Help!" Vania screamed as Persis leaped on top of her and began pummeling her with her fists. She appeared to be standing on Vania's arms, keeping her from using her prickers.

Justen stood, baffled. He'd never seen a Reduced attack.

"Hey, brother," Remy called. "Lend me a hand?"

He looked right to see Remy standing, a gun drawn on the two guards. He blinked. *Remy, standing with a gun drawn on two guards.*

"Justen!" she said, annoyed, and cocked her head at Andrine. "Go untie her already. Persis can't hold off Vania unarmed forever."

And Reduced.

*And Reduced, right?*

Andrine was already sitting up. Shaking free of his shock, Justen hurried to do as his little sister said.

"Are you all right?" he asked Andrine as he started overwriting the code keeping her ropes tight.

"Better every minute," she replied tersely.

As he worked, he glanced up at Persis and Vania, who

were still locked together. Somehow, Persis had ripped off Vania's pricker bracelet, and Justen had no idea where the gun had gone.

This was no Reduction he'd ever seen. How was it possible?

Andrine's ropes came loose and she jumped up and started to sprint for Persis and Vania. Remy smiled, which was when one of the guards went for her, while the other ran toward the building for reinforcements.

"I'll get him. Help your sister!" Andrine shouted, and changed course to chase the runaway guard.

Justen rushed over to where Remy and the guard were wrestling for the gun, doing his best to stay out the line of fire. He grabbed the guard by his hair and yanked him off his little sister's body, and then, almost before he knew what he was doing, rammed his fist straight into the man's nose. The guard went down, flat.

Remy sat up and stared at him with her mouth open. "Justen! I didn't know you had it in you!" Then she very smoothly reached out and wound a nanorope around the guard's wrist and ankles and pulled it taut.

"Some other time," he said to her, eyes wide, "we're going to talk about what kind of secrets you've been keeping yourself."

She shrugged, then said, "Yeah. We should probably do that."

Justen took a deep breath. "Let's go help Persis. A Reduced is no match for Vania."

Remy laughed. "Justen, she's not Reduced."

"What?" Justen turned back to the fight, mouth agape.

Persis and Vania were still locked in a death grip. Somehow, Persis had tangled her long cloak around Vania's legs, preventing her from kicking out. Their hair was flying everywhere, and as they whirled, black and white and yellow strands whipping in the morning wind, Justen could just make out a flash of red blood. He thought it was coming from Vania, but he couldn't be sure. They were still grappling with each other, stumbling in a wide arc halfway across the lawn.

Justen and Remy started running toward them as Vania reached up and grabbed Persis by her hair, yanking back as hard as she could. The taller girl lost her balance and went careening backward, pulling Vania with her, all limbs and cloaks and hair against the dawn sky.

Then they plummeted off the side of the bluff and out of sight.

# Thirty-four

JUSTEN RACED FORWARD, SCREAMING Persis's name. Distantly, he noticed the evidence of the struggle on the lawn—Vania's lost bracelet, a lock of Persis's yellow and white hair, a smear of blood on a blade of grass. . . . How high was this bluff? How rocky the beach? How far had they fallen?

Time seemed to pass slowly; he seemed to be running through molasses. He couldn't see. He couldn't tell. Were they all right down there? What was happening?

As they neared, a hand came up over the edge. It was followed by an elbow and then, at last, a face. Smeared with black sand and blood, exhausted and sweaty and beautiful.

Justen had never seen anything so beautiful.

"Persis!" He reached out and grabbed her, pulling her to safety. She collapsed into his arms, and he thought he'd never felt anything so wonderful either. She was here. She was Persis. How was it possible?

"Guess what?" she gasped, pointing vaguely into the harbor below. "Someone brought me my yacht."

VANIA ALDRED WAS GOING to be fine. That was the diagnosis that floated up from the cabin of the *Daydream* as it sped back to Albion through the cool morning light.

Persis wasn't sure what to think. Of course, it would be far better politically to hold captive and hostage and *healthy* the daughter of Galatea's military dictator than otherwise, but Persis wouldn't mind terribly if Vania had sustained a few serious injuries in her tumble from the cliff. After all, the girl had tried to Reduce her. A minor head injury and a few scrapes from the rocks didn't seem like significant retribution.

She sat on the prow of the *Daydream*, Slipstream cuddled in her lap and a palmport supplement forgotten in her hand, and stared out at the sea as the dawn turned the surface to molten gold.

Andrine was below, helping Justen with his three charges. Persis's friend had found the visitors inside a cell in the outpost's building after neutralizing the guard. Andromeda had some bruises on her face but looked all right, and Tomorrow was frightened but otherwise unharmed. Persis was certain the guilt the foreign captain probably felt over her choice to go with Vania far surpassed any superficial injuries she might have received as soon as she realized what her host's true intent was. She'd put up a fight, though, if the bruises were anything to go by. They still didn't know if the Galateans had gotten their genetic sample from Tomorrow, though Persis imagined they must have. There was almost certainly something of the Reduced girl's left behind in that cell. Perhaps Justen would know what they intended to do with it and how they might be stopped.

But that wasn't her problem any longer.

Tero was at the helm, showing Remy how to work the controls. From time to time they waved at Persis and she waved back, forcing a smile. Remy was so proud of herself. She'd been quite eager to explain everything to Persis—so eager that Tero had a tough time holding the girl still long enough to bandage the small wounds she'd received in the fight with the guard. Persis, however, had been a captive audience while Tero administered medicines and wraps to all her various cuts and scrapes. She'd sat and listened as Remy told her exactly how she'd switched the guard's Reduction pills for whatever it was that Justen had been carrying when she'd found him passed out in the lab.

Which meant Remy hadn't known what she'd given Persis, other than that it wasn't a Reduction pill. Persis hadn't had the heart to point out the danger to her. Not when Remy was acting so apologetic about having ever doubted Persis, and about turning Justen over to Vania, and about . . . well, whatever else the girl had been chattering on about. Persis hadn't been paying quite close enough attention, because unlike Remy, Persis had instantly known exactly what Justen had gone to the Galatean royal lab to collect.

So now she'd taken the Helo Cure. Tero had confirmed that was what he and Justen had been after when they came to Galatea, though Tero, unlike Justen, didn't realize the danger regs were in from Reduction. Justen did, though. She'd never forget the look in his eyes when she rose from the ground, covered in foam and almost as confused as a real Reduced. He looked like he'd killed her, and in a way, he'd thought he had.

But Persis had felt fine. Felt like nothing at all had happened, which had momentarily scared her more than anything. When you lose your mind, do you even know that it's gone? One day, when she Darkened, would she even miss the person she'd been?

Very quickly, however, she realized that whatever had happened to her, it wasn't Reduction. And then she put on the performance of a lifetime. Persis Blake may have spent six months acting dumb, but it hardly prepared her for six minutes acting Reduced.

Remy had even admitted that for a moment, she was afraid her switch hadn't made any difference. "I thought you were Reduced," the girl had told her sheepishly. "I thought I'd messed up again."

But Persis had taken the cure. And now she would never be in danger of Reduction, just in time for the Wild Poppy to disappear forever.

There was no way Isla would ever allow Persis to go on a mission again. Isla or Persis's parents, actually. She was about to be grounded for life. And it didn't matter anyway. Her secret was blown sky-high. The guards knew who she was, and Vania would have to be returned to Galatea eventually. The Wild Poppy was dead.

And yet, did anyone really need the spy anymore? After all, once they spread the knowledge of the protection derived from the Helo Cure, the revolutionaries would no longer be able to use their weapon of Reduction. The people of Galatea would be safe. Without that threat, the refugees could return home, and the rumblings of resistance to Aldred's government would grow into a roar. And Isla could help with that, too, especially with the bargaining power derived from holding Citizen Aldred's daughter captive. The Galateans could form a republic now. A true republic, not a nation cowering under the rule of another cruel leader.

Perhaps it would serve as a model. Even for Albion. After all, with Councilman Shift soon to be a nonentity at court, perhaps Isla could finally rule alongside the Council, rather than in opposition to it.

No, the Wild Poppy was no longer needed in New Pacifica. And so, the only question that remained was, did Persis need him herself? He was her duty, yes, her service to her princess and to the people who were needlessly suffering. But he was also her love. As the Poppy, Persis could forget a future that included a marriage to a man who would control her life and her precious Scintillans, a court that expected girls like her to be ornamental and obedient, a mother she was losing a little more every day, and a future as misty as the steam rising off the sea. As the Poppy, Persis could be sure that, no matter what happened to her somewhere down the line, she had done something with her mind while she'd still had the chance.

Without the Wild Poppy, there was nothing to keep Persis from spending her days watching her mother slip into nothingness and her nights wondering if and when it would begin for her, too.

Slipstream chittered then slid off her lap, and Persis looked up to see she had company on deck. Justen.

There was another man whose place in her life had grown rather murky in the past few hours.

She watched the sea mink prance over to Justen, who reached down and scratched the animal behind the ear, then scooped him up and took a few steps forward.

"Do you want him back?" he said.

She stood, leaning against the rails for support. "No. Let him fish if he wants."

Justen nodded and let the animal down. Slippy darted between his legs and over the side to swim in the wake. "I think your rat is growing on me."

"Sea mink," she corrected.

He smiled. "Sea mink." He kept coming toward her and she scooted over to make room. Was she supposed to apologize for acting like an idiot . . . twice? Was he supposed to apologize for creating a torture device? What was going to happen now?

The sky was coral and pink and a brilliant, brilliant blue. It was going to be another gorgeous day in New Pacifica, but Persis wrapped her cloak more tightly around her body and shivered in the sea breeze. Justen was still wearing the black Galatean military uniform he'd used to sneak into the lab, though the gray flakes were almost completely gone from his hair.

"So . . ." he began quietly.

"So," she said. "Do you think that Tomorrow will help you with your DAR research? I'm sure her experiences have given her a real fright, but if we have a little patience, we'll be able to convince her that we mean her no harm. And your models show that her genetics might be promising, right?" She was babbling. Even flaky Persis never babbled.

"Maybe," he said. "But I . . . don't want to talk about work right now."

"Really?" she asked, skeptical. "That's a new one for you. For as long as I've known you, it's the only thing you wanted to talk about. Your precious research and your beautiful revolution, and how it's all so very, very important—"

"It is important," he broke in. "And it'll be there when we get to Albion. We're going to fix the refugees, and we're going to protect the Galateans and their revolution, and somewhere in the middle of all that, I'm going to get back to my research. And I'm not going to rest until I find a way to help your mother and everyone like her. I promise you, Persis."

She swallowed heavily, then turned from him and took a deep draft from her supplement to calm her nerves. It was very sugary, though, so it did nothing of the sort. Instead, her heart pounded so hard she thought she might bruise. *He promised.* He promised he would save her. And, like always, she wanted to believe him.

"That's what I'm going to do," he said softly, very near her ear. "What are *you* doing?"

She turned back. When had he gotten so close? They were face-to-face on the deck, inches from each other. "What do you mean?"

"Come on," he said, teasing. "We both know you're

not going to be the Wild Poppy anymore, and with my sister safely with me—"

"Your sister," she pointed out, "can take care of herself."

"So I see." He frowned. "That's something else we can talk about . . . later, the advisability of recruiting my little sister into your spy ring."

"Don't underestimate her."

"Don't change the subject," he replied. "Remy will be safe with me from now on, and Isla is going to be a huge hero after she reveals how we've saved the regs *and* the aristos of Galatea, so it's not like she needs our help with her public image."

"True." Part of her wanted to look away, but she couldn't. His eyes never left her face, and there was something in his gaze, something dark and unexpected that made her catch her breath. "I suppose I'll go back to school. I know it'll make my father happy."

"The Wild Poppy taking classes in history when she's used to making it?" Justen considered this, a small smile playing about his mouth. "It would be entertaining, at least."

"Don't act so superior," she said. "I think I know some medic who isn't quite *officially* finished with his studies, either. Without your uncle Damos getting all nepotistic, you're going to have to finish school, too."

"True," he echoed. "But what I'm asking is, since all the reasons for having a fake relationship have evaporated, does that mean we don't have to pretend to be in love anymore?"

"That's what it means," she said with a brusque nod.

"Good."

"Yes," she managed, though her throat was choking on the words. He was standing so close. She tried to back up a step, and he caught her by the hand. His thumb traced the outline of her wristlock, then slipped inside to rest against the golden disk.

She hadn't yet finished the supplement, but every nerve in her palm buzzed to life.

"What are you doing?" she whispered, though, smart as she was, she already knew.

"It's good," Justen added, as he cupped her face in his other hand and tangled his fingers in her hair, "because, Persis Blake, the next time I kiss you, I want you to know it's for real."

# Acknowledgments

I COULD PROBABLY POPULATE New Pacifica itself with all the people I owe thanks to over the course of putting this book in your hands. As always, seas of gratitude to Kristin Rens, who fought by my side for this book through all its iterations, and the entire team at Balzer + Bray (especially Sara Sargent, who actually did get a name-check this time around), with extra kudos to Ray Shappell and Colin and Sasha for actually capturing the hard-to-capture Persis. And, of course, my thanks to agent Deidre Knight, who among her myriad talents, helped me nail down the title.

My husband, my daughter, and my dog all sacrificed much (maybe too much) during the writing of this book—thank you for putting up with me. And yes: Batman. My long-suffering parents finally have fictional counterparts on the good side of the equation . . . though we all know that even the Blakes can't throw dinner parties like you.

A short and no doubt insufficient list of fellow writers who kept me sane during the composition of this caper, by giving advice, reading drafts, and just listening: Carrie Ryan (my rock), Julie Leto (my hard place), Lavinia Kent, Justine Larbalestier, Jo Treggiari, Jon Skovron, Jessica Spotswood, Sarah Brand, Erica Ridley, Marianne Mancusi, E. C. Meyers, Holly Black, Sarah Rees Brennan, Robin Wasserman, Michelle Hodkin, R. J. Anderson, Franny Billingsley, and Maureen McGowan. Special shout out to Vania Stoyanova, who is just as clever and cunning and talented—and, okay, a good bit less evil—than her namesake.

Gratitude (and a few regrets) to Baroness Orczy; her creations Sir Percy Blakeney, his lady Marguerite, and the villainous Chauvelin; and their legions of fans. I also owe a debt to anyone and everyone who ever tackled their own adaptation or reinterpretation of the sprawling stories Orczy spun about the Scarlet Pimpernel, especially the 1980s version featuring Anthony Andrews/Jane Seymour/ Ian McKellan (my personal first).

And as always, thank you to you, dear reader, who makes it all worthwhile.

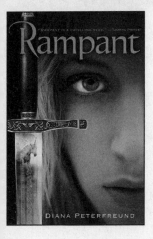